**REFUGEES AND EXILES,
BORNE ON CURRENTS OF PASSION,
BUFFETED BY DESIRES BEYOND THEIR
CONTROL. . . .**

KATIE O'MALLEY—A high-spirited American beauty rescued from the icy clutch of the sea and whisked to a country younger and wilder than the land of her birth. She had no choice but to accept the love of the man who had saved her—and to try to forget the man she loved.

RICK TEMPEST—He came to the new land in quest of a peaceful farming life. Instead, he found the promise of a wealth so vast it might destroy everything he'd fought for—and a love so consuming, it was only a razor's edge from heartbreak.

GEORGE DE LANCEY—His unshakable sense of justice set him irrevocably at odds with the men who ran the colony. His passion for Katie O'Malley set him against everything he thought was right.

**THE CHALLENGE OF THE UNKNOWN, THE
PROMISE OF LOVE, WEALTH, AND GLORY
MADE THEM . . .**

THE ADVENTURERS

**Other books in THE AUSTRALIANS series
by William Stuart Long**

THE ADVENTURERS

VOLUME V OF THE AUSTRALIANS

William Stuart Long

A DELL BOOK

 ™

Created by the producers of **Inheritors of the Storm, The Heiress,** and the **Wagons West** series.

Executive Producer: Lyle Kenyon Engel

Published by
Dell Publishing Co., Inc.
1 Dag Hammarskjold Plaza
New York, New York 10017

Produced by Book Creations, Inc.
Lyle Kenyon Engel, Executive Producer

Dell ® TM 681510, Dell Publishing Co., Inc.

ISBN: 0-440-10330-4

Printed in the United States of America
First printing—August 1983

To the people of Australia,
who made this series possible.

Acknowledgments and Notes

I acknowledge, most gratefully, the guidance received from Lyle Kenyon Engel in the writing of this book, as well as the help and cooperation of the staff at Book Creations, Inc., of Canaan, New York: Marla Ray Engel, Philip Rich, Glenn Novak, Marjorie Weber, Pamela Lappies, Carol Krach, Mary Ann McNally, Jean Sepanski, Charlene DeJarnette, and last but by no means least, George Engel. All have given me encouragement and a warm friendship that has made my work as an author so much happier and less lonely than it was before I teamed up with BCI.

I should also like to put on record my appreciation of the help given me by my British publisher, Aidan Ellis of Aidan Ellis Publishing, Ltd., in publicizing The Australians series in the United Kingdom, and my appreciation of the help always so patiently given in the domestic sphere by my spouse and Ada Broadley.

The main books consulted were:

Lachlan Macquarie: M. H. Ellis, Dymock, Sydney, 1974; *A Near Run Thing:* David Howarth, Darrold, 1971; *Waterloo:* David Chandler, Osprey, 1980; *Australian Explorers:* Kathleen Fitzpatrick, Oxford University Press, 1958; *The Life of Vice-Admiral William Bligh:* George Mackaness, Angus & Robertson, 1931; *The Macarthurs of Camden:* S. M. Onslow, reprinted by Rigby, 1973 (1914 edition); *Description of the Colony of New South Wales:* W. C. Wentworth, Whittaker, 1819; *The Convict Ships:* Charles Bateson, Brown Son & Ferguson, 1959; *History of Tasmania:* J. West, Dowling, Launceston, 1852; *A Picturesque Atlas of Australia:* A. Garran, Melbourne, 1886 (kindly lent by Anthony Morris); *Macquarie's World:* Marjorie Barnard, Melbourne University Press, 1947; *A History of Australia:* Marjorie

Barnard, Angus & Robertson, 1962 (copy kindly supplied by Bay Books); *Philip Gidley King:* Jonathan King and John King, Methuen, 1981; *James's Naval History:* William James, Bentley, 1837; *Australian Historical Monographs,* various titles, edited by George Mackaness, Ford, Sydney, 1956; *Francis Greenway:* M. H. Ellis, Angus & Robertson, 1949; *Let the Great Story Be Told:* H. W. Jarvis, Sampson Low, 1945.

These titles were obtained mainly from Conrad Bailey, Antiquarian Bookseller, Sandringham, Victoria. Others relating to the history of Newcastle and Hunter River, New South Wales, were most generously lent by Ian Cottam, and research in Sydney was undertaken by Vera Koenigswarter and May Scullion. Gifts of books for research were received from Kim Santow, members of the Sydney P.E.N., and Women Writers of Australia, and practical help and hospitality in Sydney were given by Neville Drury and Dana Lundmark of Doubleday Australia Pty. and George Molnar. Research material was also made available by John Chisholm Ward of Oskamull, Isle of Mull, a descendant of the Australian Chisholms.

Truth, it is said, is sometimes stranger than fiction. Because this book is written as a novel, a number of fictional characters have been created and superimposed on the narrative. Their adventures and misadventures are based on fact and, at times, will seem to the reader more credible than those of the real-life characters with whom their stories are interwoven. Nevertheless—however incredible the real-life characters may appear—I have not exaggerated or embroidered the actions of any of them.

Governor Macquarie—truly "the father of Australia" and arguably its best Governor—was treated as badly by the British Colonial Office as I have described. Samuel Marsden, John Macarthur, Jeffrey Hart Bent, Colonel Molle, and Commissioner Bigge were all allied against him, and their concerted enmity almost destroyed him. On his return to England, the "Old Viceroy" defended himself valiantly against his detractors, and in particular against the public calumny of Henry Grey Bennet, M.P., replying to the latter by means of a printed pamphlet. Macquarie sought an official inquiry but was denied it. He was never paid his pension, although after his death his widow was allowed three hundred pounds a year.

Macquarie died on July 1, 1824, having been kindly received by the Duke of York and Lord Bathurst on June 1, and by King George IV a few days later. He breathed his last in a thirty-four-shilling-a-week lodging in London's St. James's. His body was taken to the Isle of Mull, and he is buried there in a family tomb. In the colony he had ruled for twelve years, his passing was mourned as if he had been a king, and only the Macarthurs and their adherents were absent from the memorial service held for him in November 1824.

Elizabeth Macquarie died in 1830; young Lachlan died at the age of thirty-two.

In the taverns and workshops, and on the far-flung farms of the humble emancipist settlers, they sang on Foundation Day:

> Macquarie was the prince of men!
> Australia's pride and joy!
> We ne'er shall see his like again—
> Bring back the Old Viceroy!
>   (See *Lachlan Macquarie*, M. H. Ellis.)

Finally, I should like to mention that I spent eight years in Australia and returned there, for a very happy visit, in 1982.

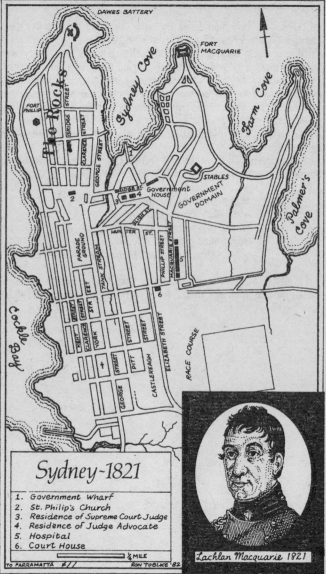

DAWES BATTERY

FORT MACQUARIE

Sydney Cove

Farm Cove

FORT PHILLIP

The Rocks

BRIDGE STREET

CLARENCE STREET

GEORGE STREET

Palmer's Cove

STABLES

Government House

GOVERNMENT DOMAIN

BRIDGE ST.

3 ▪▪▪ 4

2

HUNTER ST.

PHILLIP STREET

MACQUARIE STREET

5

Cockle Bay

PARADE GROUND

TANK STREAM

6

PITT STREET

PERCY STREET

CLARENCE STREET

YORK STREET

CASTLEREAGH STREET

ELIZABETH STREET

PHILLIP STREET

RACE COURSE

GEORGE STREET

Sydney - 1821

1. Government Wharf
2. St. Philip's Church
3. Residence of Supreme Court Judge
4. Residence of Judge Advocate
5. Hospital
6. Court House

¼ MILE

TO PARRAMATTA

RON TOGLKE '82

© BOOK CREATIONS INC. 1982.

Lachlan Macquarie 1821

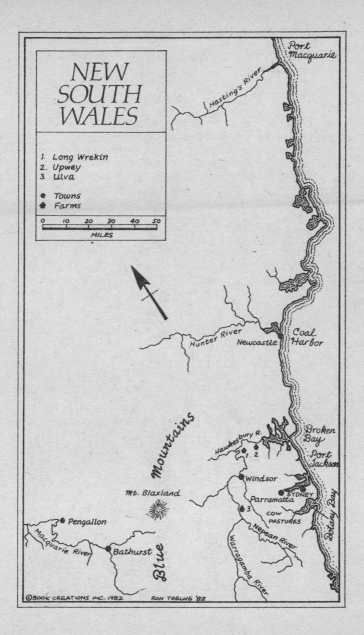

PROLOGUE

"Murdoch Henry Maclaine, in view of your youth and the jury's recommendation that you be treated mercifully," the old judge had said, emphasizing his words with an admonitory gesture of a bony forefinger, "I shall commute the death sentence pronounced on you. You will, instead, be transported to the penal colony of New South Wales for the term of your natural life. And," he had added, with derisive piety, "may God have mercy on you!"

Seated in the jolting covered wagon, one of a row of fettered prisoners from Winchester Prison, Murdo Maclaine recalled the scene in the courtroom with remembered bitterness.

True, he had been given his life. He had not been topped, like poor old Sep Todd and Dickie Farmer, his two companions in the ill-fated holdup of the London mail coach. But for all that . . . His dark brows met in a resentful pucker. To what manner of life had he been condemned? Botany Bay, some of the other inmates of the jail had told him, was hell on earth for all who were sent out there as convicted felons.

It would be different, of course, for his mother and Jessica and the two bairns. They had gone out with the 73rd Highlanders and Colonel Lachlan Macquarie, who had been appointed Governor of the colony, five years ago. To the best of his knowledge, all four of them were still in Sydney, forced to accompany his brutal swine of a stepfather—Sergeant Major Duncan Campbell of the 73rd—after he himself had run away.

He had it in mind to go out there and join them sooner or later, Murdo reflected, but not, God help him, as a lifer—a wretched convict, in chains! The disgrace would break his mother's heart, no doubt of that; she had always been a proud woman, and he and Jessica had been brought up in accordance with her strict code of

God-fearing honesty. She would be shocked and appalled if she knew that her only son had been tried and convicted of the crime of highway robbery.

Murdo shifted uneasily in his narrow wooden seat. His career on the High Toby with Nick Vincent's boys had been rewarding, and he could not, for his part, regret having embarked on it. Nick had befriended him, given him a home and work—initially as his groom and horse minder, at five shillings a week. Even that had been better than the miserably paid toil he had been forced to undertake when, as a boy of barely fifteen, he had fled from his stepfather's bullying into the icy cold of the Glasgow streets in midwinter.

He had begged in those streets, he had worked briefly in the cattle market and as a drover, and had finally been employed as roustabout by a foulmouthed old gypsy peddler, with whom he had come south to Guildford. And there the old skinflint had abandoned him, Murdo recalled bitterly, without settling their score, and making off with the only decent garment he possessed, his oilskin jacket. It had been when he was penniless and near to starvation that Nick Vincent, giving him his horse outside an inn where he had halted to refresh himself, had taken pity on him and offered him work.

"I can use a likely lad who knows how to handle horses," he had said, and had then added, with a tight-lipped smile, "so long as he don't ask too many questions and knows how to keep his mouth buttoned up. Think you'd fit the bill, eh?"

He had accepted without hesitation, Murdo reminded himself; he had asked no questions and had kept a careful guard on his tongue. Even when he had found out the true nature of his new master's profession, he had continued to work for him hard and willingly, and a year later—when he was seventeen—Nick had accepted him as a fully fledged member of the gang.

It was a large gang and a well-organized one, the holdups, as a rule, meticulously planned and efficiently carried out; but the night that he and Todd and Farmer had robbed the London mail coach outside Winchester, Sep Todd had been careless. In his cups that same night, he had talked too freely. An informer had heard his drunken boasting with the result that the law had, at last, caught up with them . . . and his two partners in crime had met their end at the hangman's hands.

While he . . . Murdo gave vent to an unhappy sigh. He was chained up like a wild animal, on his way to Portsmouth or Southampton, and a six-month voyage to the unknown was in imminent prospect. True, he had a useful nest egg, stashed away in Nick's safekeeping. It was to be delivered to him, Nick had promised, before the convict transport to which he was consigned had pulled up her hook—or, if he were sent first to one of the hulks, which sometimes happened, he would receive the money before boarding the transport. Murdo repeated his sigh.

He hoped, uneasy for the moment, that Nick would keep his promise, and then thrust his doubts from his mind. Nick Vincent was a man of his word, and he had always played fair with the men who worked for him, seeing that their widows and families were taken care of, should any of them get topped, and providing lawyers to plead their case, if they were brought to trial, or held on suspicion.

And on a couple of occasions he had staged a rescue—once from a broken-down country jail, which had been easy, and once, with considerable daring, from a magistrates' court, under the noses of quaking, terrified constables, who had put up no resistance.

Murdo grinned, his spirits lifting. He had taken part in the second rescue himself, and it had been easy, because Nick had planned and led it and no one had talked out of turn. The fat old sheriff's officer, a pistol to his head, had ordered the release of his prisoner, and they had taken the chairman of the bench hostage, to ensure that there was no pursuit.

So that maybe—he glanced through the small, barred window across the van's narrow aisle, straining against the leg-irons that held him in his seat.

Nick had hinted, on the brief visit he had paid to Winchester Prison before Todd and Farmer had gone to the gallows, that he might try his hand at holding up the convict wagon, if he were to find out for sure that Murdo was in it. The little runt of a turnkey had accepted a bribe in return for providing that information, but there was, alas, no way of finding out whether the fellow had kept his bargain or, as his kind often did, had simply pocketed the half-guinea and forgotten his obligation. But if he had kept it, then—

Murdo leaned forward, hearing the sound of galloping hooves in the distance, his hopes suddenly rekindled. The man beside him cursed ill-temperedly and bade him sit still, but as the hoofbeats came nearer, Murdo ignored his sullen complaints.

A pistol shot rang out and his heart leaped when he heard Nick's stentorian command.

"Stand and deliver! You've a cargo we want. Stop the wagon or we'll drill you as full o' holes as a colander!"

The wagon came to a jarring halt. The driver, with the two jailers accompanying him, was seated, exposed and vulnerable, on the box. His voice trembled on the edge of panic as he answered the unexpected summons.

"Whoa there!" he bade his jittery pair of workhorses, and added pleadingly, "For mercy's sake don't shoot, mister! We ain't armed an' we ain't about to give you no trouble!"

"Then get down off the box," Nick ordered. "All three of you—that's the way. Now hands above your heads and face about. Frisk 'em, Joss, just to make sure."

"They're tellin' the truth," a deeper voice asserted—the voice of Joss Gifford, Nick's right-hand man, Murdo recognized. He tried to rap on the window, but his chains held him back and the man beside him clapped a manacled hand over his mouth, preventing him from calling out.

"Quiet, you oaf," the man hissed. "Bide quiet, till we see what they're after!"

"You, there!" Nick's voice came nearer, evidently addressed to one of the jailers. "Inside with you and let 'em all out, fast as you know how! How many are you carrying?"

"Twenty-four, sir. But they'm—"

Nick cut him short. "Jump to it," he demanded. "I want every man jack out of that wagon and lined up in front of me, understand? But leave their irons on till I tell you."

The jailer offered no reply, but a moment later a key scraped in the lock and the rear door of the wagon opened. Murdo's companions, who until now had maintained a stunned silence, realized suddenly that they were about to be set free and started to cheer wildly.

Nick cursed them. "Keep quiet, you stupid rogues! *Quiet,* I say! You'll get your chance to run, if you do as I bid you. Out, as soon as your legs are unhitched, and let us look you over. Murdo, lad—" His tone changed. "Are you there?"

"Aye, that I am!" Murdo responded eagerly. The man beside

him was already on his feet, and Murdo, still resenting the fellow's attempt to silence him, thrust past him and hobbled to the door.

Big Joss Gifford was standing at the foot of the steps, he saw, holding two horses. Behind him, their pistols leveled at the wagon's crew, were three other mounted men, all masked. He recognized them, despite their masks, and grinned delightedly up at Nick.

"God bless you! I'll never forget this, Nick, as long as I live."

Nick nodded. "See you don't, boy." He jerked his head at the second jailer, who was standing scowling beside the driver. Pointing to Murdo, he said impatiently, "That's the one we want. Strike off his irons and look sharp about it."

Murdo held out his fettered wrists, and the jailer, his fingers clumsy in their haste, freed him from the heavy cuffs. The leg-irons, which had to be struck off with a hammer, took longer, but the man, urged on by Nick, completed the task with commendable speed. The chafing irons came off, and Big Joss, grinning from beneath his mask, took a folded cloak from the saddlebow of one of the horses he was holding and flung it deftly in Murdo's direction.

"Wrap that around you, lad," he invited. "And get yourself onto the roan mare. Nick's got a change o' clothes ready for you, but we don't want to hang about on this road for longer than we have to. You can rid yourself o' them prison duds after we've made our getaway."

Sensing that they were about to be abandoned, the other prisoners set up a concerted howl of protest.

Nick silenced them harshly. "Turn 'em all loose," he ordered the jailers. "Go on—jump to it, if you don't want your skulls stove in!" The younger of the two jailers hesitated, and Nick, implementing his threat, kneed his horse forward and brought the butt of his pistol down on the man's bare head. It was not a forceful blow; the jailer staggered and then, recovering, hastened to do his assailant's bidding.

Murdo, seated on the roan's back, watched the last of his erstwhile companions come tumbling out of the wagon, cowed into sullen acquiescence and flexing their cramped leg muscles as the irons were struck off and they were able at last to move freely.

"Cut the traces, Joss!" Nick directed, indicating the horses harnessed to the wagon. "And drive off those nags. You lot of scalawags"—he turned to the freed prisoners—"tie up the screws before you make a run for it, but don't harm 'em—if you do, they'll top you for sure if you're caught." He cut short an attempt by one of the men to thank him with a crisp "Good luck, boys. Don't hang about—this is the main Portsmouth road. I hope you make it." Then, seeing that Joss had done as he had asked and had remounted his own horse, he waved a hand in the direction from which they had come and dug in his spurs. With Murdo close on his heels, the small cavalcade formed up and galloped off.

A hundred yards down the road, Nick put his horse at a low post and rails and, clearing it effortlessly, led them in single file along the edge of a plowed field and into a stand of thickly growing beech and hazel. Screened from the road, they all drew rein and Nick said curtly, "Right, off with your lag's gear, Murdo, and get into these."

He dropped a rolled-up bundle at Murdo's feet and added, eyeing his cropped head critically, "I should have brought a wig for you, damme, to go with that gentlemanly accent of yours. Well, you'll have to make do with a hat. Cram it well down on your head . . . and hurry, boy, for the Lord's sake! I want to put a few miles between us and that infernal prison van before someone spots it and calls in the law. They'll have their work cut out, rounding up the others, which will give us a few hours' start on 'em, but . . ." He shrugged. "Bury those filthy garments, Liam—you don't need to dig a hole. Under the leaves'll do."

The young Irishman, Liam O'Driscoll, clapped Murdo on the shoulder and, as he divested himself of the coarsely woven gray jacket and trousers that were the mark of a felon, took them from him and hid them under a pile of rotting leaves. Their masks were off now, the men beaming their pleasure at the success of the rescue and calling out in ribald encouragement as Murdo donned the garments Nick had brought for him.

"How's it feel to be out o' lumber, Murdo old son?"

"Bet you're mighty glad we saved you from bein' boated, ain't you?"

"That'll do, lads." Nick was in no mood for premature celebration. "Time enough for crowing when we're home and dry," he cautioned them. "Bestir yourself, Murdo, and let's be on our way. We've a tidy ride ahead of us."

Murdo wasted no time. His jacket still unbuttoned but the ill-fitting tricorne crammed hard down to hide his shaven head, he was back in the roan mare's saddle before Liam had remounted.

"Where are we going, Nick?" he ventured, as they again set off across open country.

"To Buck's Oak," Nick answered shortly. "And the Alton Arms, where I've arranged for someone to take care of you for a while."

He lapsed into moody silence and rode on, making it plain that further questions would be unwelcome.

"Murdo!" Joss Gifford motioned to him to rein in. When they were riding side by side at the rear of the cavalcade, the older man said, lowering his voice, "We're heading for Hinton Marsh, son, and I fancy Nick means to ride through the night. He's a mite nervous these days, and small wonder—we've had a few close calls o' late."

"Close calls?" Murdo echoed, frowning.

"Aye, very close. 'Twasn't only your caper that went sour. We lost old Harry—Harry Lee—and Barney Deakin. They was nabbed ten days since, and they come up before the beak next Monday. The heat's on, Murdo, in this part o' the country. Nick's thinking o' going north. If they top Harry and Barney, I reckon he will."

Murdo was deeply shocked. This part of the country—the pleasant, rural area between Guildford and the coast—had always been Nick's stamping ground. He had been born in Farnham and had friends everywhere—innkeepers, cottagers, small farmers, and a host of others. Even a few of the local constables and excisemen were well-disposed toward him. He knew every nook and cranny, every road, and he had ostlers and postilions in his pay, who tipped him off concerning the coaches and post chaises, plying between London and the coast, that were worth robbing . . . and those that were not. Latterly, Murdo knew, Nick had formed a lucrative liaison with two gangs of brandy and 'baccy smugglers, who plied their trade in small fishing boats across the Channel. During the war with France it was a risky business, but now, with the two countries at peace, the trade was flourishing. Nick surely would not want to abandon its fat pickings by going north, unless he were compelled to do so.

As if reading his thoughts, Joss said, with a resigned shrug of his broad shoulders, "He'd have to be hard pressed to go, you understand. But he can't afford to run no risks with you, son. Right now you're pretty hot property . . . an escaper from one o' His Majesty's jails. There'll be a hue an' cry out for you."

"Aye, I know there will," Murdo conceded uneasily. "But Nick told me he's arranged for someone to take care of me—for a while, he said—at the Alton Arms."

Joss nodded in confirmation. "That's right enough. Nick's made plans for you, but I doubt if you'll like 'em much. The idea is to safeguard all o' us and to make certain sure you ain't picked up. And I reckon you owe it to him to do as he wants, Murdo. He sprung you, he saved you from Botany Bay, so you owe him, don't you?"

"Yes, I owe him," Murdo agreed. But his uneasiness was increasing, and he turned in his saddle to look at Joss. "Do you know what he wants me to do?"

"I know, lad. But it's not for me to tell you—Nick'll do that. I just thought I'd give you a friendly warning."

"Thanks," Murdo acknowledged. Clearly, he told himself, Nick wanted him to do more than simply lie low in a village inn. Perhaps he intended to cast him adrift or send *him* back to the north until the hue and cry died down. Whatever it was, he would do it, of course, and he would have his nest egg and his freedom. And if Nick should decide to come north with the gang, he could join up with them again.

There was nothing to be gained by idle speculation; Nick would tell him, as Joss had said, in his own good time. He had kept his word—he had taken a dangerous risk in holding up the jail van, in order to spring him. Murdo smiled at the anxious Joss.

"I'll do whatever Nick wants, Joss."

"Good lad," Joss approved. "I reckoned you would." He nodded affably and, kicking his horse into a canter, rode ahead to Nick's side.

As he had predicted, they rode through the night, halting only once, at an isolated inn, in order to rest and water their horses and break their fast. Nick led them on a roundabout route, avoiding towns and main roads, and it was noon when they finally drew rein outside the Alton Arms in Buck's Oak. Dispatched, with Liam O'Driscoll, to bed down their weary animals, Murdo awaited the expected summons from Nick without undue disquiet. It came, within less than an hour of their arrival, and he obeyed it with alacrity, only to halt, in stunned dismay, when he entered the taproom and saw that Nick was seated at a table with two uniformed strangers.

They were men in the King's scarlet, with gold chevrons on their sleeves—sergeants, *recruiting sergeants*, one in infantry uniform, the other a swaggering cavalryman in dragoon undress. Murdo guessed the reason for their presence before Nick rose to his feet and, a kindly arm about his shoulders, led him to the other side of the room.

"You are wanting me to *enlist*, Nick?" he blurted out, his voice shaking.

Nick nodded. "Aye, lad, that's about the size of it. Understand, you're a liability now, a risk to us all, with the whole countryside likely to be on the lookout for you in a matter of hours. They'll catch the lags that were with you, and the stupid sods will talk their heads off. We've got to plant you somewhere safe, Murdo son."

"But the army—" Murdo began bitterly.

Nick cut him short. "No one'll look for you in the army. As God's my witness, 'tis the one place they won't look!" His tone softened, became persuasive. "You know how highly I regard you—you're like a son to me, and it'll break my heart to let you go. But it won't be forever, and the war's over. Army of occupation, it is now—a real cushy lay. Let 'em take you across to the Continent and live a life of idleness in the Duke's garrison in Brussels."

"The army's not idle," Murdo protested. He had spent his youth in army camps and was all too well aware of the harsh discipline to which the rank and file were subjected. Had he not run away from his home and his family because Duncan Campbell had sought to treat him as the common soldiers were treated? He attempted to explain, but Nick impatiently gestured him to have done.

"It will be better than Botany Bay. And you'll not have to do any fighting."

"Maybe not. But for all that, I'd do anything rather than enlist. Nick, I—"

"Murdo, Murdo!" Nick reproached him. "Where's your loyalty, your gratitude? Do you want to put the rest o' us in danger of our lives? Joss and me, all of us . . . your friends, for God's sake? We took a big chance, springing you. Remember that, boy!"

"I do," Murdo conceded miserably. He glanced across at the

two sergeants, but they had their backs turned and were sipping their ale, seemingly indifferent to whatever he and Nick were saying to each other, the big cavalryman placidly puffing at a long-stemmed clay pipe, his long, booted legs extended to the warmth of the crackling log fire.

"It would not be for long," Nick said. His arm tightened about Murdo's thin shoulders. "Six months, maybe even less, and the heat'll be off. Then you can buy yourself out and come back to us. Look, I've your share of our loot on me, and it's a tidy sum. You'd be foolish to take it with you, but I'll stash it here with the innkeeper, Charley Finn, if you like. He'll keep it safe till you want it, or I'll go on keeping it for you, whatever you say. God's blood, boy, you trust me, don't you?"

"Aye, of course I do, Nick. All the same, I . . ." Murdo made a final plea. "Could I not go north and hide out there? In Glasgow, perhaps? I'd go on my own, I—"

"Without friends to help you, you'd be nabbed before you were within a hundred miles o' the border," Nick retorted, his tone one that brooked no further argument. Losing patience, he gestured to the brass-bound clock, ticking away on the wall above their heads. "We've wasted enough time. What's it to be, Murdo? Are you going to do as I ask? Because if you're not . . ." He left the implied threat unvoiced, but Murdo recognized defeat. Nick's threats were not to be taken lightly. He knew that he would never see the gold nest egg he had worked for, unless he fell in with the plans Nick had made for him. Old Joss had been right, he thought ruefully—he certainly did not like them overmuch. But the army was, undoubtedly, better than exile to the penal colony of New South Wales and better by far than being topped, as he would be if he were caught.

Besides, he thought, pride coming to his rescue, a soldier could hold his head high, for had not the Duke of Wellington's soldiers defeated Boney's Frenchies, driven them back from Portugal and Spain and Boney himself into ignominious exile on some island called Elba?

"Well?" Nick prompted. "Are you willing to enlist?"

"Aye," Murdo answered. He hesitated and then added firmly, "But I'll not enlist in an English regiment. I'm a Highlander, Nick."

Nick laughed and, grasping him by the arm, led him over to the recruiting sergeants' table. "Here's your lad, gentlemen," he announced. "He's free, willing and able to take the King's shilling. But he's from north o' the border, and he's wanting to join a Scotch regiment, so 'tis to be hoped you can indulge him. Provided, that's to say," he qualified hastily, "it is one under the Duke's command across the Channel."

"I reckon we can accede to his wishes, sir," the infantry sergeant assured him. "We're accepting recruits for all His Grace's regiments, kitting 'em out and licking 'em into shape at our depot and then drafting 'em to Brussels. That don't take above a few weeks. What's your name, lad?"

"It's Smith, Sergeant," Nick supplied. He flashed Murdo a warning glance. "Murdoch Smith."

The sergeant eyed Murdo thoughtfully and then, grinning, removed his ill-fitting tricorne. "An army haircut already," he observed, with amused tolerance. "Well, it takes all kinds, my lad, and a spell in the ranks'll be the making of you, I can guarantee. Which regiment do you fancy, eh? We've plenty for you to choose from. The Ninety-second are in Brussels, the Forty-second and the Seventy-first in billets outside, the Seventy-third at someplace called Grow-now or Grow-mouse . . . can't get me tongue round these plaguey frog names. Then there's the Camerons, the Seventy-ninth . . ."

He talked on but Murdo was scarcely conscious of what he was saying. The 73rd, he thought, feeling his throat tighten—his own father's regiment, the gallant 73rd. If he had to enlist, then surely this was the regiment he must choose. There would be small risk of his being recognized, since it was clearly the second battalion of the regiment that was now serving under the Duke of Wellington's command. Colonel Macquarie—Governor Macquarie—had taken the first battalion with him to New South Wales.

"Would ye be ony guid on a horse, Smith?" The cavalry sergeant took his pipe from his mouth and rose slowly from his chair to stand, a tall, imposing figure in his magnificent dragoon's uniform, dwarfing both Nick and his fellow sergeant.

His accent was Lowland Scots and the question clear enough, but unaccustomed to his new name, Murdo stared back at him blankly, and it was Nick who answered him. "He's the best, Sergeant, I give you my word. The lad's a fine horseman."

"Then ye could dae a lot worse than join my regiment. If you're a Scot, ye'll hae heard tell o' them." The big cavalryman spoke with pride. "The Royal North British Dragoons—the Greys, laddie, the famous Scots Greys! There is no finer regiment in the whole o' the British Army, ye may tak' my word for it. And if you're as guid a rider as this—ah, as this gentleman says ye are, why then ye'll be on your way in nae time at a'. Ye'll be aiding the Duke tae keep the bluidy frogs back where they belong, wi' their tails 'atween their legs!"

Murdo felt his heartbeat quicken. The cavalryman's words had been bombastic, but for no reason that he could have explained, they moved him deeply. The war was over and there could be no prospect of doing further battle with the French, but . . . He made his decision without any prompting from Nick, impulsively, yet with complete conviction.

"Aye, sir, 'tis the Greys I'll be joining, if you'll take me."

The tall dragoon donned his white-plumed fur cap and grinned derisively at his fellow recruiter.

"My turn wi' this yin, Billy!" To Murdo he said, still smiling, "We'll tak' ye and gladly. I'll attest ye right awa', just in case some ither body should try tae stake a claim on ye." He aimed a blow at Murdo's shaven head. "As they might, eh? Private Smith o' the Scots Greys, that's you now, laddie, and ye'll not regret your choice. 'Tis yon bluidy scoundrel Boney who'll live tae rue the day he cam' back tae tangle wi' us again!"

"What are you saying, Sergeant?" Nick demanded, his brows furrowed in bewilderment. "Has Boney escaped? Is the war not over?"

The sergeant's smile faded. He answered gravely, "Aye, have ye no' heard? The Emperor's back i' France. He landed a week ago, and they say he's making for Paris, wi' King Louis' troops deserting tae join him. There'll be a few ither battles tae be fought before the war's finally over, if I'm ony judge. 'Tis tae be hoped, sir, that your laddie has a bold hairt in him, for he's like tae be i' the thick o' it, before he's too much older!"

Both men turned to look at Murdo. There was pity in Nick's gray eyes, and he started to mumble an apology. "I did not know, Murdo. Believe me, I—"

Murdo affected not to hear him. He drew himself up. They had robbed him of his native pride in the jail, with their leg-irons and the hateful fetters, with their solemn courts and the harsh sentences they imposed. But he was a Highland soldier's son, he told himself, and his father had served in the 73rd and died with the regiment at the siege of Seringapatam. He was being offered an opportunity to regain his lost pride, and for all his earlier unwillingness to enlist, he was not going to let the recruiters accuse him of cowardice by backing out now.

The cavalry was fine in peacetime, but if there was fighting to be done, he would do it in his father's regiment.

"I'm ready to take the oath," he told the infantry sergeant quickly. "For the Seventy-third Highlanders, if you please. And my name is Maclaine."

Nick shrugged resignedly and let him go.

"Dearly beloved, we are gathered together here in the sight of God and in the face of this congregation, to join this man and this woman in holy matrimony, which is an honorable estate, instituted of God in the time of man's innocency . . ."

The minister's voice droned on, and standing stiffly at his brother's side, George De Lancey found his attention wandering, his hand relaxing its grip on his sword. A fugitive ray of sunlight, in seeming defiance of the April downpour that had soaked them as they entered the church, shone through the high stained-glass window behind the altar. It formed a bright, many-hued pattern on the ancient flagstones at the bride's feet and lit her small, veiled face to sudden radiance.

Not that she needed the sun's aid to enhance her loveliness. Magdalen Hall was a beautiful young woman, George De Lancey thought, and his brother was a singularly fortunate man to have won her affections. The thought was devoid of envy; his elder brother was still—as he had been in their youth—the object of his veneration, on whose inspiring example he had endeavored to fashion his own life during the past three and a half years.

He had never, even in his dreams, imagined himself capable of matching William's achievements, still less of surpassing them. They were there in plain view for the packed congregation to feast their eyes on—the gold and enamel insignia of a Knight Commander of the Bath and, pinned beneath this, a Peninsular Gold Medal with two bars.

The military prowess to which these decorations bore witness would have been remarkable for any British officer in his early thirties, but they were the more remarkable in view of the fact that his brother was, like himself, American by birth. Indeed they were third-generation Americans, both born in New York, descendants of a Huguenot family that had sought refuge there, after the revocation of the Edict of Nantes.

The De Lanceys had been considerable landowners . . . until the War of Independence had brought about a conflict of loyalties, and General Oliver De Lancey, their uncle, had elected to fight for his King. Following the colonists' victory, his lands had been confiscated and the general compelled to seek refuge in England, where he had died in genteel poverty in Yorkshire, his loyalty to the British Crown unmarked and unrewarded.

Their own father had fared better, George recalled. Lord Shelburne had appointed him Governor of Tobago, and William, at the age of sixteen, had been offered a commission without purchase in the British Army. Within five years—and before his twenty-first birthday—he had risen on merit to the rank of major in the 45th Regiment of Foot, and during the latter part of the Duke of Wellington's campaign in the Peninsula, he had served as deputy quartermaster general on the Duke's staff, ranking as a full colonel.

George De Lancey stifled a sigh. He himself—no doubt foolishly—had remained in America, starved of funds and lacking patronage, and at times living from hand to mouth. He had read law at Harvard, keeping body and soul together by clerking in his spare time, but with the obstinate intention of setting up as an attorney on the completion of his studies. He had even chosen the small town near Boston and the building in which he would hang up his shingle, but the war had forced him to change his plans.

With his country's adherence to the French cause, the old, traditional conflict of loyalties had returned to plague him, and reluctantly, but driven by his conscience, he had taken ship to England and thrown himself on his brother's mercy. Since William's influence was limited to the military establishment, he had become a soldier instead of a lawyer, and—George glanced over his shoulder, seeing the rows of brilliantly uniformed officers who had come to witness his brother's nuptials.

He was one of them now, he reminded himself, the ties that had bound him to the land of his birth forever broken, and little Katie O'Malley—whom he had hoped one day to marry—a memory, cherished still in his heart but fading with each passing year. Her image was obscured by other, harsher images of war and bloodshed, for these had become the pattern of his life.

He had fought in the final desperate battles that had seen Bonaparte's once invincible legions defeated and driven back into France. He had been at the sieges of Ciudad Rodrigo and Badajoz as a fledgling ensign in the 52nd Light Infantry and, with the storming party on both occasions, had witnessed heroism beyond belief, appalling slaughter, and, following the capture of Badajoz, the horrors of a sacked and looted town.

It had been then, George reflected, that Katie O'Malley's image had started to fade, for he had sought solace from the carnage in the arms of a frightened waif, who had come to him for protection and whose name he had never known. She had bound up the slight wound he had suffered and wept in his arms as he took her, blindly and without desire. . . .

"William Howe, wilt thou have this woman to thy wedded wife, to live together after God's ordinance in the holy estate of matrimony?"

The minister's deep, resonant voice interrupted his train of thought, and George forced his attention back to the wedding service.

"Wilt thou love her, comfort, honor, and keep her in sickness and in health and, forsaking all others, keep thee only unto her, so long as ye both shall live?"

William responded with a firm "I will," and Magdalen listened, with downcast eyes, when the same question was put to her, and then, turning to look up at her tall bridegroom, answered it with shy eagerness.

Her father, the gray-haired Sir James Hall of Dunglass, gave his assent with the brief formality the prayer book required of him and stepped back into the family pew as the couple, in turn, made their vows, repeating them solemnly and with evident feeling.

Strangely moved, George felt in the pocket of his tight-fitting full-dress overalls for the ring. His hand was trembling a little as he laid the small gold circlet on the minister's prayer book, imagining for a moment that it was Katie who stood there in the white satin bridal gown, she who had just vowed to take him as her wedded husband. But Katie's eyes were blue, her hair like spun gold, and Magdalen, who was now his brother's wife, had brown

eyes and shining dark hair . . . there was no resemblance, one to
the other. What he had seen had been a trick of the light.

He stepped back, as the bride's father had done, leaving William
and his bride to kneel alone together in front of the altar, and as the
old minister intoned the prayer, he let his thoughts once again drift
away.

After the storming of Badajoz, William had been appointed
acting quartermaster general. That had been in May 1812, when at
last the tide had started to turn in Lord Wellington's favor and the
forces under his command could begin the march to Madrid.
William had appointed him as one of his aides; he had been
promoted to a lieutenancy in the 16th Light Dragoons, and it had
been in that capacity, George recalled, that he had fought in the
battle for Salamanca. Two days before the battle—although, at the
time, he had not known of it—President James Madison had
declared that the United States of America were at war with Britain
and her allies.

He felt his throat muscles tighten, as the congregation rose and
the choir sang the opening lines of the psalm "Beati Omnes." That
day he had charged with Sir Stapleton Cotton's heavy cavalry,
breaking and putting to flight an entire French infantry division,
and his brigade commander, the valiant General Le Marchant, had
been killed beside him. Three weeks later he had ridden in
Wellington's train into Madrid, to the enthusiastic *vivas* of the
Spanish citizens.

Thereafter had come setbacks, but by that time, even if the
military tactics were beyond his comprehension, he had come to
understand some of the reasons for the long forced marches, the
fighting retreats that had followed even such victories, and the
appalling toll these took in dead and mutilated men.

During the next two years, he had learned his trade as an army
officer, George reflected. He had served for several months on the
staff of Lord Wellington—since created Duke of Wellington—and
had come to admire him unreservedly. His coolness and personal
courage under fire were legendary; the men he commanded, who
openly called him Nosey, had been ready to follow him anywhere.
As, indeed, George himself had been, for all his inbred lawyer's
caution and the awareness of his American birth.

The psalm ended; the congregation seated themselves in
preparation for the sermon, and George stepped into the bride-

groom's pew, the tension draining out of him. He sat down, closing his eyes, letting the memories flood back, as consciousness of the present drifted away.

In January 1813, news had come that the Emperor Napoleon's campaign in Russia had ended in a more disastrous retreat than any the Peninsula had seen. Hopes were rekindled; the Duke's staff saw their commander smile again, and the army was on the move. At Vitoria in July, Joseph Bonaparte, the so-called King of Spain, was driven from his kingdom and narrowly escaped capture when the town fell.

He was replaced as French commander in chief by Marshal Soult on orders from Napoleon, who, it was said, was so hard pressed by the Russians and their new Prussian allies that he had been compelled, by heavy losses at Bautzen, to agree to an armistice.

But the Duke wanted no armistice. He had pressed on, advancing instead of retreating, his British divisions substantially reinforced, those of the Portuguese fighting with skill and tenacity, and twenty-five thousand Spanish troops joining the victorious advance. San Sebastian had been taken, the Pyrenees crossed, and then, at last, the fighting had been on French soil and the end in sight.

The minister continued his sermon, and George glanced up and then closed his eyes again, endeavoring to remember. But the rivers he had forded, the mountain passes up which he had struggled, the fortresses and cities that had fallen to assault were simply names on a map, his memories of people and of individual actions the only ones that remained clear in his mind.

There had been women along the way—willing Spanish women, a French peasant girl, an Irish soldier's widow, who had dressed the slight wound he had suffered at the Nive and given him comfort, in the only way she could. Their faces were blurred, as Katie's had become blurred; he saw more clearly the faces of the fallen—some his friends, but many strangers to him—British, German, and Portuguese, quiet in death as were those of the French dead who lay beside them, and all seemingly at peace, despite the hideous injuries that had laid them low. Of the wounded who still clung to life he dared not permit himself to think. George drew in his breath sharply.

But it was over, he told himself . . . for God's sake, the war was over! For William and his lovely young bride, as well as for himself. Napoleon Bonaparte might have escaped from Elba, but Ney—once one of his marshals but now a Royalist general with an army of thirty thousand men under his command—had vowed to bring the former Emperor back to Paris in a cage and no doubt would succeed in making good the boast. There was nothing to fear with a French king restored to the throne and his people weary of war. As weary as he was, George thought.

His services had been rewarded with a captain's commission in the 2nd Dragoons—the Scots Greys, at present in Belgium—but he could, when he wished, return to civilian life. He could sell his commission, as William intended to now that he was married. There could be no return to America, of course, for either of them . . . but he could stay in England. Or seek his fortune in one of the colonies. During his leave he had taken steps to have himself called to the English Bar, and while dining at Lincoln's Inn, he was told by a chance acquaintance that the penal colony in New South Wales was in dire and urgent need of qualified attorneys.

Two brothers, both members of Lincoln's Inn, had gone out there as judges, at handsome salaries paid by the Crown, and according to his informant, the younger of the two had only quite recently been called.

"Jeffrey Bent was in my own chambers," the barrister had confided. "And deviling for me, to keep the wolf from the door. Then his elder brother lands an appointment as deputy judge advocate at twelve hundred a year and has young Jeffrey made a civil judge at eight hundred, if you please. Together with a palatial dwelling house and perquisites in fees for civil actions . . . damme, I know where I'd go, if I wanted to make money. Penal colony or not, I'd go to Botany Bay!"

There might be worse places, George reflected. The West Indies or . . . He stirred uneasily, opening his eyes to find that the rest of the congregation was standing, the bride and groom starting to make their way to the vestry for the signing of the register. He collected his scattered wits and, spurs jingling, hastened after them.

William eyed him reproachfully, but Magdalen, turning to embrace him after the customary kiss from her new husband, was radiant with happiness.

"Dear George," she whispered, as he held her gently in his arms, "it is so divine to have you as a brother!"

The short journey, in carriages, from the church to Dunglass Castle was followed by a magnificent wedding breakfast and seemingly endless speeches. Determined not to be found wanting in the performance of his duties, George slipped back into the role of aide-de-camp and later, when he was assisting his brother to change into civilian clothes, was gratified by his thanks.

"You stood up for me well, George my boy," William told him, beaming. "Keep up the good work, if you please. I shall confide my address during the next three weeks only to you—and I rely on you to see to it that I am not disturbed, unless it is a matter of the gravest urgency. You understand, do you not? It isn't every day that a man takes a wife, and God knows, I've waited a long time to wed my sweet Magdalen."

"I understand," George assured him. "You shall not be disturbed, I promise you."

He anticipated no difficulty in keeping his promise, but within less than two hours of the newlywed couple's departure, a footman summoned him from the ballroom of the castle, where the wedding guests had gathered to dance the night away.

"There's an officer asking for Sir William, sir," the servant explained. "I told him that Sir William and Miss Magdalen—Lady De Lancey, I mean—had left, and he asked to speak to you, sir. He said it was very important. And . . ." The man's tone was awed. "He said he had come from the Duke of Wellington, sir."

George felt the color drain from his cheeks. A message from the Duke could mean only one thing, he knew, and the messenger—Lieutenant Henry White, of the 32nd Regiment, with whom he had served on Major General Thomas Brisbane's staff at Vitoria—confirmed his worst fears.

"Ney has betrayed us, George—he's gone over to Boney with his entire army, God rot his soul! The King has fled. Boney entered Paris within hours of his departure and was received at the Tuileries by a mob shouting 'Vive l'Empereur!' And he's lost no time in raising troops—all those who deserted last year, after he abdicated, are falling over themselves to join him, and he's called up the reservists and mobilized the Garde Nationale. Or so our spies tell us. It's damned serious, I'm afraid." He went into detail, and George listened in stunned silence, scarcely able to believe what he was hearing.

He had been a fool to imagine that the war was over, he thought wretchedly. And a still greater fool to believe that the French people wanted peace. . . .

Henry White added soberly, "We're back where we started, George my friend. And the Duke wants your brother as QMG as soon as he can make his way to Brussels. Within a week, if possible. He sent me to tell him in person and to arrange transport for him."

"He was married today," George said, his voice flat.

"Yes, so your man said. But you can get in touch, surely—you can inform him?"

He could not refuse, George knew. He inclined his head reluctantly, and White clapped a friendly hand on his shoulder. "Do I hear dance music?" he asked. "Are the wedding celebrations still in progress?"

"They are, yes. But—"

"Then should we not join in? Clearly we cannot reach the colonel tonight; so come on, my dear fellow!" Henry White's smile was cynical. "Let us eat, drink, and be merry, for tomorrow"—he broke off, his eyes bright—"tomorrow we go, once again, in search of military glory—if you will permit me to twist the quotation. Perhaps, though, you would be so good as to give me the loan of a clean shirt and a pair of dancing shoes? I rode through a great deal of mud on my way from Edinburgh and am hardly in a fit state to present myself to the ladies of Dunglass."

"I shall be happy to supply you," George responded flatly.

Sir James Hall's piper was playing a lively reel when George returned, with his fellow aide-de-camp, to the ballroom.

"There are some beauties, I see," young White observed appreciatively. "Excuse me, George."

George watched him cross the room to where a bevy of demure young ladies sat fanning themselves, under the indulgent eyes of their matronly chaperones. They were pretty enough, he thought, although not one could hold a candle to little Katie O'Malley. But he was a guest and had his duty to do. He straightened his tight-fitting cravat and followed White's example.

CHAPTER I

After nine days of gale-force winds and mountainous seas, the Atlantic storm had abated and the wind veered to the west. Turning out to relieve the sailing master at the end of the morning watch, Richard Tempest, first lieutenant of His Majesty's brig-sloop-of-war *Kangaroo,* was conscious of a feeling of weary relief as he gained the deck and looked about him.

True, the morning sky was gray and heavily overcast, with a threat of snow, and there was a strong swell running. Under double-reefed topsails, the ship rolled sluggishly, but she had ridden out the storm well and had suffered only minor damage, most of which could be repaired.

She had been blown many miles off course—it had not been possible to take a sighting, as yet, in order to ascertain how many—but, judging by the extreme cold and the ice on the rigging and upper deck, two hundred might well be an accurate estimate.

Rick Tempest tightened the thick woolen muffler about his neck as the men of the morning watch stumbled thankfully past him, bound for the mess deck and comparative warmth below. His own duty watch lined up shivering to answer to their names, called out in a shrill treble by Cadet Harris.

"Glass is rising," Silas Crabbe observed, when the formalities of handing over the deck had been completed. "I'd have shaken out a reef in the tops'ls, but the captain wouldn't hear of it. Maybe you'll be able to get the forecourse on her in an hour or two, Mr. Tempest, so's to take advantage of this wind. We're a sight too far south for my liking, and that's a fact."

The old master's thin, bony face was blue with cold, his rheumy eyes bloodshot, the lids heavy. He looked ill, Rick thought with concern, although that was scarcely to be wondered at, after what they had both gone through during the past week or so. Nights with virtually no sleep, closed in by a howling, impenetrable blackness; long days when they had had to lash themselves to the mast or the standing rigging to avoid being swept overboard as the pounding, wind-racked seas had come crashing over the deck in a savage green tide.

He and Silas Crabbe had had to bear the brunt of it, standing watch and watch when they had deemed it safe to do so, but more often on deck together waist-deep in water and, at times, taking long tricks at the wheel when the brig's very survival had been at risk.

While the *Kangaroo*'s commander—Rick's mouth tightened in resentment—while Captain John Jeffrey had been below with his wife, issuing his orders from the stern cabin and only occasionally making his appearance on the quarterdeck to see them carried out. And invariably they had been overly cautious orders, such as those at which Silas Crabbe had just hinted. The master was a fine seaman, with many years of service to his credit—years when Jeffrey had been ashore on half pay.

"I think, Mr. Crabbe," he said, with mock gravity, "that we can shake out those reefs now without incurring the captain's displeasure. Young Harris can inform him when it's done."

Crabbe nodded. "There's brash ice about," he volunteered. "I heard it growling against her sides when I came on watch. We don't want to linger in these latitudes longer than we must."

"That we don't." Rick sang out an order to the boatswain's mate of the watch, who put his call to his lips. The topmen, in obedience to the pipe, started to make their way warily up the icy shrouds.

They were willing enough, Rick reflected, watching them lay out along the yards. A number of the petty officers were volunteers, who had served in the navy throughout the war and had been paid off, to face penury and near starvation in ports that had no employment to offer them, now that a parsimonious government had laid up so many of its ships of war. Some of the older men, he knew, had been attracted by the announcement that the *Kangaroo* was bound for New South Wales and service there as a colonial vessel. They dreamed, perhaps—as he did—of making a new life as settlers when their time was served. He had the advantage of having been in Sydney before—in Sydney and, for over a year, in Van Diemen's Land as a midshipman of His Majesty's ship *Porpoise,* under the command of the colony's onetime Governor, Commodore William Bligh.

No . . . He checked himself. Not Commodore—*Rear Admiral* Bligh. Bligh had attained flag rank when Colonel Johnston, commandant of the regiment that had mutinied and deposed him, had been tried by court-martial in London and cashiered.

"You have a sister in Sydney Town, have you not, Mr. Tempest?" Silas Crabbe said, as if, uncannily, he had read Rick's thoughts.

"Not one—two. They've been there . . . good Lord, it must be all of eight years! They both married, but—"

"Officers of the garrison, Mr. Tempest?"

Rick shook his head. "No, settlers, Mr. Crabbe. The elder, my sweet Abigail, was widowed, but she wrote to tell me that she had recently wed one of the wealthiest farmers in the colony—a Mr. Timothy Dawson. Poor little Lucy has been less fortunate. She had not been long married when her husband—a young emancipist named Luke Cahill—was murdered by a band of escaped convicts, who raided their farm on the Hawkesbury. Bushrangers, they dub themselves . . . rogues and villains, I'd call the swine! They set fire to the farmstead and, I understand, burnt it to the ground."

"So it is not the land of milk and honey to which we're headed, Mr. Tempest?" the old master suggested. "Contrary to the general expectation."

"It is a penal colony," Rick qualified. "One has always to remember that. All the same, I intend to make my home there and become a farmer." He clapped a friendly hand on the master's shoulder. "What has the Royal Navy to offer these days, now that even the Americans have made peace with us? With half the fleet laid up and the other half under threat, I don't fancy spending years ashore in England on a lieutenant's half pay. Damme, I was lucky to be appointed to this ship, after the old *Seahorse* paid off! Their Lordships only approved my appointment because I had served in the colony before. And also because I gave a written assurance that I would forfeit all pay and allowances as soon as we drop anchor in Sydney Cove."

The master digested this statement with unconcealed disapproval. "I was not aware of that, Mr. Tempest. You've never mentioned it before."

"I supposed the captain would have told you."

"He did not," Silas Crabbe asserted. "Who, if I may make so bold as to inquire, is to take your place whilst we're in the colony?"

Rick smiled at him. "Oh, a most excellent young officer, who has Governor Macquarie as his patron. He was one of the *Hindostan*'s mids on the voyage home five years ago, under Captain Pasco's command. Pasco thought so highly of him that he gave Their Lordships no peace till they granted him a commission. We're bringing it out with us, signed and sealed. My successor's name is Broome—Justin Broome. He served under Captain Flinders in the *Investigator* as a boy, and from what my sister Abigail tells me, he's made his mark as an explorer. But . . ."
The topmen came streaming back to the deck, their booted feet thudding on the deck planking, and Rick broke off to attend to the trimming of the upper yards. The wind was still strong, but the *Kangaroo*'s sharply raked bows lifted buoyantly as the helmsman spun his wheel in response to a shouted order and the topsails filled.

Silas Crabbe stamped his cold feet and made, belatedly, to go below. He said, before moving away, "I'll try to take a sighting in an hour or so, Mr. Tempest. Maybe we'll catch a glimpse of the sun if this wind doesn't drop. More likely to be snow, though. But if we keep heading nor'east, then—"

A hail from the mainmast lookout interrupted him. "Deck there! Small craft under sail—fine on the larb'd bow, sir. 'Bout a mile distant, maybe less. Looks like a ship's boat to me, sir."

A ship's boat at sea, adrift in these cruel, lonely waters, could mean only one thing, Rick thought, dismayed. He reached for his glass, wishing that the visibility were clearer. But at least it was not snowing as yet.

"There's men aboard her, sir," the lookout shouted hoarsely.

"Have they seen us?" Rick was scrambling up the weather mainmast shrouds, the telescope thrust into the front of his oilskin jacket, so as to leave both hands free to aid his ascent. His booted feet slithered on the ice-caked ratlines and the wind tore at him, threatening to break his hold. Breathlessly, he dragged himself upward.

"I can't see no one moving," the lookout told him, through chattering teeth. "Just . . . bodies, sir. Half a dozen of 'em, all huddled together. More, p'raps; it's hard to make 'em out. An' there's no sign o' a ship that I can see."

He was right, Rick's glass confirmed. From his vantage point in the mainmast shrouds, he swept the powerful glass in a semicircle and then focused it on the pitching boat. It was waterlogged, a whaleboat of the kind most merchant vessels carried for their ship-to-shore errands, its single, storm-tattered lugsail split and flapping uselessly from the canting mast. A pair of smashed oars hung suspended from the rowlocks, moving with the swell. The crew's bodies, as the lookout had reported, were huddled together on the bottom boards, black, motionless shapes for whom, it seemed evident, rescue had come too late.

Exposed to the full fury of the icy wind for God alone knew how long, they must have frozen to death, Rick decided regretfully. He was about to snap his glass shut when he saw a hand feebly raised. Something white fluttered for a moment and was gone before he could identify it, but it told him that not all the unfortunate people in the boat were dead. Elated by this discovery, he called out to the man at the wheel to alter course, and with a reckless disregard for his numb fingers and the slithering seaboots, he descended to the deck.

"One of them is alive," he told Silas Crabbe. "We'll run in as close as we can and I'll volunteer a crew for the quarter boat and pick them up. Relieve me of the deck, will you please? And Mr. Harris . . ." The boy was beside him, eager and alert.

"Sir?"

"My respects to the captain. Tell him we have sighted a boatload of shipwrecked seamen and that I'm preparing to lower the quarter boat to pick them up. And then go below and fetch as many blankets as you can lay your hands on. We'll take as many as we can with us, and have the rest ready on deck."

Cadet Harris sped off. He returned with commendable promptitude, accompanied by two stewards carrying blankets. On his own initiative he presented Rick with a flask of brandy bearing the captain's initials, which, he said innocently, one of the stewards had been filling. "I thought it might come in handy, sir."

The captain himself followed close on his heels, a boat cloak draped about his shoulders to ward off the cold, and an expression of ill-concealed annoyance on his round, florid face. He was a small man, inclining now to corpulence, who looked much older than the forty-odd years to which he laid claim.

His shortness of temper and abruptly arrogant manner had not endeared him to the *Kangaroo*'s officers and men, but he had made little effort to court popularity. He took all his meals with his wife and had not, as yet, invited any of his officers to dine with him— an omission that had not gone unremarked in the brig's gun room.

His wife was a handsome woman, the daughter, as she had been at pains to make known, of a vice admiral of the red. In a condescending fashion, Mrs. Jeffrey had been less aloof than her husband, but . . . Rick braced himself for the anticipated outburst from his commander. Mrs. Jeffrey had also made it known that she did not welcome any departure from the leisurely routine she had introduced, and a summons to the quarterdeck, before her husband had had time to shave and break his fast, was calculated to incur her extreme displeasure.

That it had already done so was soon apparent. "For the love of heaven, Mr. Tempest!" the captain exclaimed irritably. "What tomfoolery are you engaged in? A boatload of castaways and I'm dragged on deck in my nightclothes! You are the first lieutenant, are you not? Can you not do what is required?"

"I can, sir, of course," Rick assured him. "And I did not send for you. Mr. Harris was instructed to inform you that I propose to bring to and put off a boat to pick up the survivors. And I—"

"Survivors, for God's sake!" Jeffrey interrupted. "What survivors can you hope to find, in these conditions? A boatload of frozen corpses, damme, if they've spent even one night in an open boat! And you want to risk our men's lives and the loss of a boat to recover them!"

"I've volunteered a crew, sir." Rick kept a tight rein on his temper. "And the risk is small, in my view. There is at least one survivor, I can vouch for that." He started to go into details, but Captain Jeffrey impatiently cut him short.

"Very good, very good. In common humanity, I suppose we must do what we can. But we don't carry a surgeon, as you well know. I take leave to doubt that, even if any of the poor devils are still alive, they're likely to survive for long without skilled medical treatment."

"No, sir. But if there's even a slight chance," Rick began, "I—"

"For the Lord's sake, carry on, Mr. Tempest," the captain bade him coldly. "I take it you'll command the quarter boat? Right, then—I shall be below. Report to me when you get back to the ship. And have a care with that flask of mine—it's silver."

"Aye, aye, sir," Rick acknowledged, his voice carefully expressionless. He watched the small, cloaked figure leave the deck and then rejoined Silas Crabbe, who, taking Rick's nod for the answer to an unvoiced question, sent the watch scurrying to man the braces. The yards were hauled round, the topsails spilled their wind, and the *Kangaroo* lost way.

"Lower away, my lads," Rick ordered, and with the coxswain keeping the small craft clear of the lurching ship's side, the quarter boat splashed into the water. Taking his place in the sternsheets, Rick realized that the swell was stronger than he had anticipated. But with six men at the oars, pulling with a will, it took only a few minutes to bring them alongside the waterlogged whaleboat. The bowman hooked on deftly with his boat hook, and the rest of the crew, their oars shipped, held both boats as steady as the swell would permit.

"You want me to board her, sir?" the coxswain asked.

Rick shook his head. "No, I will, cox'un."

Choosing his moment, when both boats lifted in unison with the swell, he jumped into the whaleboat's stern, landing awkwardly on hands and knees. As he did so, his shoulder inadvertently struck the boat's tiller and he saw that there was a hand on it, the owner lying facedown on the bottom boards, as if still endeavoring to steer his battered craft to safety. Despite the force with which he had cannoned into it, the hand did not relinquish its hold. It was, he saw, shocked beyond words, frozen to the tiller, and when he turned the helmsman, with difficulty, onto his side, the open, sightless eyes of a boy of perhaps fifteen or sixteen gazed back at him.

The body was ice-cold to his touch, still and quite rigid in death. He moved on, crouched low and conscious of a sick sensation in the pit of his stomach. There were five more bodies lying beyond that of the young helmsman, and he needed little more than a glance to tell him that all were dead. Captain Jeffrey, he reflected bitterly, had been right . . . there was nothing to be done for any of these poor fellows, save to speak a few words of Christian prayer over their frozen corpses and let the sea have them once more.

He must try to identify them, of course, or at least try to ascertain the name and nationality of their lost ship. There were some sodden papers held in the ice that had formed on the bottom boards, and what looked like a log, wrapped in oilskin, on its surface. Using his boot heel, Rick broke the ice and, picking up the log, tossed it across to his coxswain without attempting to examine it.

There was still the upraised hand he had seen, he thought, reluctant to admit defeat. He *had* seen it; it had not been a figment of his imagination. And the hand had waved something, a kerchief, probably, less than half an hour before—proof, surely, that one of the castaways had been alive then. Alive and aware of the *Kangaroo*'s approach.

His gaze lit on what appeared to be a bundle of clothing in the whaleboat's bow, half covered by a tarpaulin, and with suddenly renewed hope he pulled the covering aside. Beneath it, swathed in several layers of seamen's coats and jerseys, was a body that, although cold, was undoubtedly living. And, as he bent over it, a small hand was lifted as if in greeting, the fingers clutching a white kerchief.

Rick dropped to his knees, fumbling for the captain's brandy flask in his hip pocket. Uncapping it, he put an arm round the muffled shoulders and gently raised the slight form into a sitting position. Two pale eyes peered up at him from out of a pinched white face . . . a young face, Rick thought. This boy was probably younger than the poor little devil who had stuck so courageously to the tiller.

He held the flask against the blue, trembling lips and managed to induce the boy to gulp down a mouthful of the warming liquid.

"There, lad," he offered reassuringly. "You're quite safe, and we'll soon have you out of here and into a warm bunk." He shouted a warning to his boat's crew and, bracing himself against the whaleboat's sluggish pitching, picked the youngster up bodily, still wrapped in several layers of stiffly sodden clothing.

Two of his crew relieved him of his burden, and pausing only to toss the end of the whaleboat's painter to his coxswain, Rick hauled himself back into his own boat.

"One living," he announced grimly, "and six dead. We'll tow

their boat back to the ship, so that they can be given proper burial." He gestured to the pile of blankets they had brought with them. "Get those coats off the lad, Simmonds, quick as you can, and wrap him in the dry blankets. I'm afraid he's pretty far gone, but perhaps we'll be able to save him. And Ellis"—he passed the flask to the bowman—"see if you can get him to take a swig or two of this."

The men hastened to obey him. The coxswain secured the whaleboat's painter and let it drift astern with its tragic cargo of dead. He said, with a wry twist of the lips, "I had a quick look at the log, sir. Their ship was the *Providence* brig, out of Boston. Two hundred and twenty-seven tons burden, Master Phineas O'Malley and a crew of seventy-five. She was bound for Port Jackson, sir, same as we are, with a cargo of spirits and trade goods."

"A Yankee!" Rick exclaimed. He recalled his last commission and the three weeks of hectic action, when every American was an enemy. His ship, the *Seahorse,* and her sister ship, the *Euryalus*— both forty-gun frigates—had sailed up the Potomac River, without the aid of pilots, to anchor within musket shot of the batteries at Alexandria, with which they had been heavily engaged. They had run aground a score of times; the *Seahorse* had lost her mizzenmast when a squall had struck the squadron off Maryland Point, but in company with three bomb ships and a rocket ship— *Devastation, Etna, Meteor,* and *Erebus*—they had reached their objective in ten days and battered Washington's defenses into submission. A shore party had burned the President's residence, the White House, with the result that, on the return journey, their small flotilla had met with spirited opposition.

They had had to fight their way downriver, with twenty-one sail of prizes, and had suffered over forty casualties before rejoining the flag of Admiral Cochrane in Chesapeake Bay. A few weeks later, after landing with the admiral to lead an attack on Baltimore, the British military commander, General Ross, had been mortally wounded by an American rifleman, firing from the woods on the bank of the Patapsco River. But . . . Rick smothered a sigh. That had been almost a year ago. Since December of the previous year, Britain and America had been at peace. And—he put out his hand for the *Providence*'s log—now, it seemed, American merchant vessels were seeking to resume their trade with New South

Wales. Perhaps the unfortunate *Providence* had been the first of
them.

"She foundered two nights ago, sir," the coxswain went on.
"The last entry states that they took to the boats at five bells o' the
middle watch. Three boats capsized an' sank after lowering. The
whaler was the master's boat. They lowered her an hour after the
first three, an' she had twenty-five on board her when she left the
ship."

The master, Phineas O'Malley, would have tried, up to the last,
to save his stricken vessel, Rick thought, his throat tight. He made
a swift mental calculation. "Then it'll be no use searching for any
more survivors," he began. "Because—" A startled cry from the
bowman cut him short.

"Sir! Lawk-a-mercy, Mr. Tempest, this ain't no ship's boy
we've picked up. She'm a woman—a young woman, sir!" He
sounded shaken, and Rick stared at him in shocked surprise.

"A . . . *woman*, Ellis?"

"Aye, sir, right enough. In 'er nightclothes, she were. We've
wrapped 'er in the blankets, like you said, but she ain't conscious.
An' I can't get 'er to take no brandy, sir. I doubt she'm barely
alive."

"Then we had best get her back to the ship," Rick decided.
"Out oars! Give way together! And put your backs into it, my
lads."

What, he asked himself a trifle anxiously, would be the captain's
reaction to their return, with a boatload of dead American seamen
and a young American woman, who was probably close to death?

Captain Jeffrey had also taken part in the recent transatlantic
hostilities, and he continued to profess a deep and abiding hatred
for their erstwhile American adversaries, with, conceivably, some
justification. His ship, the *Reindeer* of eighteen guns, had been
taken and sunk by the American ship-sloop *Wasp* of twenty, after a
desperate battle in which all the *Reindeer*'s officers and almost half
her crew had been killed or wounded—her commander, William
Manners, mortally.

The survivors, including Jeffrey, had been received on board the
Wasp and then handed over, as prisoners of war, to the French at
Lorient, where the American ship had gone to repair her damage.
Neither of his captors had, according to Captain Jeffrey, treated
him with humanity. He had been kept in what he described as "a

filthy French jail" for six months, and even the fact that the U.S.S. *Wasp* had gone down with all hands off Madeira, during his captivity, failed to mollify him. His pride, Rick reflected glumly, as well as his body had been deeply wounded. But perhaps . . . He glanced astern, to where the *Providence*'s storm-battered whaleboat rose and fell to the motion of the swell. There had to be a time for pity; and when wars come to an end, old enmities should rightly be forgotten.

Their own boat, well handled by the old coxswain, came along the *Kangaroo*'s lee side, and as the bowman hooked on to the chains, Rick answered Silas Crabbe's shouted inquiry with a despondent shake of the head.

"Only one still living—a woman. We'll hoist her up in the boat, Mr. Crabbe. There are six dead in the other boat. Inform the captain, will you, please?"

He offered no other explanation until he regained the deck. Then, as the quarter boat was being winched inboard, he said quietly, "She was an American trading brig, the *Providence* of Boston, bound for Sydney. She went down in a storm two nights ago. I have her log; it was in the boat."

The *Kangaroo*'s second lieutenant, John Meredith, and two midshipmen had turned out of their hammocks and come on deck in the hope of witnessing a successful rescue, and their faces fell as Rick described what he had found.

"And there's only one of them left alive?" Meredith exclaimed. "A woman!"

"Yes," Rick confirmed shortly. "A young woman. I don't know who she is." He glanced at Silas Crabbe. "Did you inform the captain?"

"Er—I did, sir," Cadet Harris piped up shrilly. "He said he would come and—" The boy broke off, to add unnecessarily, "He's here, sir!" He hurriedly effaced himself, as Captain Jeffrey strode across the deck from the after hatchway. The other officers bared their heads, but the captain ignored them.

"Well, Mr. Tempest?" he demanded ominously.

Rick stiffened. His voice deliberately flat and expressionless, he repeated what he had told Silas Crabbe.

Jeffrey swore. "God in heaven! An American, a damned Yankee brig, was she? And on her way to New South Wales—a British Crown colony—on a trading venture. Damme, that means liquor, does it not? Cheap, rotgut liquor for sale to the convicts at a handsome profit, no doubt!"

Resisting the impulse to point out that the *Providence*'s hopes of showing a profit had gone with her to the bottom of the Atlantic, Rick said nothing. Norfolk King—son of the late Governor of New South Wales and his mistress, Ann Inett—had, he recalled, suffered a fate similar to Jeffrey's, when his first command, the four-gun sloop *Ballahou*, had been captured by the American privateer *Perry*. Norfolk had told Rick, with considerable feeling, "John Jeffrey won't forget. He'll hold a grudge till the end of his days."

Norfolk, it seemed, had not exaggerated.

"And you've brought a woman back with you?" Jeffrey said. "D'you know who she is?"

The captain's tone was offensive, but Rick, refusing to be provoked, merely shook his head. The quarter boat, he saw, had been winched up, and the coxswain was looking to him for orders. Whatever grudge Captain Jeffrey might hold against the Americans was no reason for delay, since the unfortunate young woman's life might depend on the speed with which she could be cared for below.

He said, with restraint, "Excuse me, sir, but with your permission, I'd like to have her taken below. And perhaps, Mrs. Jeffrey might—" He got no further. The captain eyed him balefully.

"Certainly, have her taken below, Mr. Tempest . . . but to your cabin, not mine. My wife will, I am sure, do what she can to give comfort to a female in distress. But she has no experience of nursing the sick, and in any event . . ." He paused, looking down at the muffled form of the *Providence*'s only survivor, as Ellis and the coxswain lifted it gently from the boat. A corner of the enveloping blanket slipped, to reveal the white, shuttered face beneath it, and he bit back an exclamation of what sounded like genuine pity. "Good God, she's young! Scarcely more than a child."

"Yes, sir," Rick agreed. He turned to the coxswain. "Two of you take her below to my cabin, cox'un." The cook, he recalled, had some pretension to medical knowledge; he was an elderly man, with a long record of service, who had dealt very competently with the injuries sustained by several of the ship's company during the storm. "Ask old Bill Onslow to do what he can for her. I'll be down myself as soon as I'm able." The bowman, Ellis, offered him the silver brandy flask, and taking it from him, Rick gave it to his commander. "Your flask, sir. You asked me to restore it to you. And there's the log, if you—"

Jeffrey appeared not to have heard him. The bodies of the *Providence*'s dead were being hoisted up, and he watched, an oddly thoughtful expression on his face, as the idlers of the duty watch laid them out in a row on deck.

"They must be searched for means of identification," he said, frowning. "I will conduct a funeral service this afternoon. Arrange it for five bells, Mr. Tempest. . . ." He gave precise instructions and then, to Rick's relief, added in a more placatory tone, "Mr. Meredith can stand the remainder of your watch. You had better attend to that unhappy young woman, and—ah, I will ask Mrs. Jeffrey to assist in any way she can. She will, I am sure, give her the loan of clothing and a warming pan . . . if the poor child lives long enough to require them. You said you did not know who she is?"

"No, sir. The *Providence* was Boston registered; that's all I know."

"So she is likely to be American, like the rest of them." Captain Jeffrey's brooding gaze went again to the silent bodies. "You think my attitude to their race reprehensible, do you not, Mr. Tempest?"

Rick reddened. "I did not say so, sir."

"But you thought it," the captain accused. "Devil take it, Tempest, you don't know how the infernal Yankees treated me, do you? Like Their Lordships, you supposed that the *Reindeer* struck to them and her people deserved what they got!"

"No, sir, I—" As before, the captain ignored the attempted interruption. He went on vehemently, "The *Wasp* smashed us to pieces with her thirty-two-pounder carronades—ours were twenty-fours, and the breeching bolts were defective. We could barely make reply. Manners was in command, William Manners. He was shot through both thighs, but he still attempted to lead a boarding party, and he bled to death on the *Wasp*'s quarterdeck. Then they boarded us, and we had to strike—our steering was shot away, and the only officer left standing was the captain's clerk."

He paused and pulled up the left sleeve of his jacket, to disclose what had obviously been a hideous wound, and added, with stark bitterness, "I can match these scars on my left leg, Tempest, and I was fortunate in that I did not suffer the loss of both limbs. My wounds were gangrenous by the time we were put ashore at Lorient and handed over to the mercies of the French. Captain Johnston Blakely of the U.S.S. *Wasp*—the *late* Captain Blakely, it causes me no distress to say—confined us in his hold for a week, without medical attention. We lost twenty-five officers and men in the battle, and out of twenty-seven seriously wounded survivors, fourteen died in that week of hell. I almost died myself."

It was possible, Rick reflected, that like the *Kangaroo,* the American ship had not carried a surgeon. Small sloops of war seldom did, but . . . He maintained a guarded silence. Jeffrey pulled down his sleeve and shrugged resignedly.

"You can, perhaps, understand why I have no love for the Americans," he finished sourly. "Less, even, than for the French. But we are now, supposedly, at peace with them. So . . . damme, we must do what is in our power to help! That means a search for any other boats from the—what was her name?—the *Providence,* before we endeavor to get back on course, does it not, Mr. Tempest?"

"According to the master's log, three boats—which were lowered before the whaleboat—capsized, sir," Rick pointed out. "The master's boat was put into the water an hour later, with twenty-five on board. We found six and the young woman, sir."

"I see." The captain repeated his shrug. "Then she is almost certainly the sole survivor. Very well, Mr. Tempest. Turn over the watch to Mr. Meredith and instruct him to get under way." He glanced up at the lowering sky and sighed. "I trust it will not be too long before it's possible to take a sighting. What course have you been steering?"

"Nor'eastly, sir. Mr. Crabbe reported brash ice during the night. Have I your permission to make more sail before I go below, sir?"

Captain Jeffrey hesitated, looking as if he were about to reject the suggestion, but finally he nodded. "Yes—heads'ls and forecourse, if you think fit. Carry on, Mr. Tempest. I will speak to my wife concerning the American girl."

Evidently his words carried weight. Rick had been in his cabin with the cook for only a few minutes when Mrs. Jeffrey made her appearance, followed by the captain's steward, who was bearing an assortment of clothing and a brass warming pan. She took immediate and efficient charge, dispatching the cook to fill and heat the warming pan and prepare hot gruel, and the steward to fetch fresh bedding.

To Rick she said crisply, "I shall have to undress her, Mr. Tempest—her nightgown is soaked through—and I shall require your assistance to lift her. But please keep your gaze averted whilst I am changing her night clothing."

Rick obeyed her, in silence. Selina Jeffrey was a dark-haired, statuesque woman, of imposing presence. Normally she held aloof and had little to say to him, but the shipwrecked girl's condition caused her so much distress that she became quite voluble.

"Oh, poor, unhappy little soul!" she exclaimed, chafing the girl's small, bloodless hands in an effort to restore the circulation. "She is deeply unconscious, is she not? Is she dying, or is there perhaps a chance that she may recover?"

It was the old cook, Onslow, who answered her. He slid the warming pan, wrapped in a scrap of blanket, carefully beneath the cot covers and said gravely, "Don't depend on it, ma'am. I've sailed round the Horn a time or two, and I seen men—big, strong sailormen, ma'am—in this same state. Unless you can rouse them, they just give up the ghost and don't put up no fight. It's the cold, see—it numbs their brains, as well as their bodies. We must try to rouse her, ma'am, soon as we've got some warmth into her. Make her sup some o' my broth." He set the lidded pan down on the floor of the cramped cabin and looked inquiringly at Rick. "Will you slap her cheeks, sir, or will I?"

Rick suppressed an involuntary shiver and then, gritting his teeth, did as Onslow had advised. It went against the grain to strike a woman, and the more so, in this case, since the girl seemed so small and vulnerable. The slapping had no effect, save to elicit an indignant protest from Mrs. Jeffrey, who commanded him instantly to stop.

"It is sheer brutality, Mr. Tempest," she asserted. Thrusting him aside, she picked up the pan of broth and, raising the girl's head, attempted vainly to spoon some of the hot liquid between the tightly compressed lips. Most of it ran onto the bedding, and Onslow, meeting Rick's worried gaze, shook his grizzled head.

"We got to rouse her first, ma'am. No use trying to make her sup when she ain't conscious."

Mrs. Jeffrey took no notice. She continued her efforts, with increasing despair, until her husband entered the cabin. Then, with expressions of fulsome regret, she allowed herself to be persuaded to leave, lest she exhaust herself.

"I can do no more, alas. I fear that she is doomed, poor young thing, and that you will have to—what does the prayer book call it?—consign her body to the deep, when you conduct the funeral service for the others, John."

Captain Jeffrey spread his hands in a gesture of resignation. "Death comes to us all," he declared unctuously. "I pray you, do not distress yourself, my dear. Come . . . you should lie down for a while." He offered his arm, and as they were leaving, he added, lowering his voice, "We have identified two of the dead, Mr. Tempest. The ship's master, Phineas O'Malley, and an apprentice, whose name was Lister or Larson, I forget which. The others appear to have been deckhands. One of whom"—his voice took on a note of cold anger—"one of whom was a British deserter, a man with ten or twelve years' service in the Royal Navy. The carpenter recognized him but could not recall his name."

Which was perhaps as well, Rick thought, since not even death could relieve the poor devil of the stigma of guilt in Jeffrey's eyes, for all that the war was over and thousands of British seamen had been paid off and put ashore, when their ships were laid up. But he knew from experience that it was futile to argue with his commander, and he prudently offered no comment. The canvas curtain, which afforded some privacy to his small cabin, fell back into place over the doorway, and Onslow picked up his soup pan again and carefully replaced the lid.

"I've dinners to serve to the watch below, sir," he said apologetically, "if you can do without me for an hour."

"Yes, carry on, Billy lad," Rick agreed. He glanced at the still form that was occupying his cot, conscious of a pity too intense to be put into words, and let out his breath in a long sigh of frustration. "I doubt if there is anything either of us can do for that poor lass now. It's a damnable shame and it breaks my heart, but—devil take it, what can we do?"

"There is one thing," old Billy Onslow offered suddenly. "I seen it work with seamen when they was in the same state." His sallow cheeks reddened. "Well, with one young lad, it were, Mr. Tempest, an' maybe I won't go into the reasons for what happened, 'cause none o' us never talked about it. And you might think—"

Rick impatiently cut him short. "I'll not think anything out of turn. Just tell me what was done, for God's sake!"

The cook avoided his eye. "The lad was a mid, about ten years old, always up to pranks. The captain mastheaded him in these waters an' forgot what he'd done. When he remembered and they brought him down, the little fellow was frozen—just like yon poor lass there. None o' us reckoned he'd live. There was an old mid—one o' the oldsters that was passed over an' never got a commission. He climbed in the little lad's hammock an' held him all night in his arms. The boy was alive next day, an' he's commanding a ship of his own these days." The cook looked up expectantly. "The heat o' the human body, sir, see? It beats any bedwarmers an' blankets, take my word for it!"

"Good God!" Rick exploded. "Surely you're not suggesting that I . . . The captain would have *me* mastheaded, and you know it, Onslow!"

Old Billy Onslow moved hastily to the curtained doorway. "I got to serve them messmen their dinners, Mr. Tempest. The pipe'll be sounding any minute." He vanished, leaving Rick to stare after him, his thoughts in turmoil.

From the deck above he heard eight bells strike and the echoing thud of footsteps on the planking as the watch changed. Young Meredith, who had relieved him earlier, had the afternoon watch, and the captain had ordered the burial service muster for five bells—two-thirty. As first lieutenant, he would have to be present, of course, but he had just over two hours, during which, unless there was an emergency, he was unlikely to be disturbed. He had had a hammock slung in Meredith's cabin, in the hope of being able to make up some sleep he had lost, and any of the mids, if sent to summon him, would seek him there. Only a thin bulkhead separated the two cabins—he would hear the summons.

Rick hesitated, in an agony of indecision. For a moment he considered making a request for Mrs. Jeffrey's aid, but then dismissed the thought. She would undoubtedly refuse, heaping scorn on his head or claiming exhaustion and the state of her own health as reason for her refusal . . . and the girl might die.

Onslow's suggestion was outrageous; the man had implied some sort of improper relationship between the oldster midshipman and the ten-year-old boy. But he had insisted that it had worked, and he was not one to exaggerate or lie . . . and perhaps it would work now. If there were the slightest chance of its doing so, he had to try.

Rick took a deep breath and started to divest himself of his outer garments, which were damp with salt-encrusted spray. Stripped to the waist, he climbed into the swaying cot and took the small, chill body of the unconscious girl into his arms. She did not stir, and he lay for quite a long time, holding her close to him. After a while, his own body—unaccustomed to the bedwarmer and so many blankets—started to sweat, and overcome by heat and weariness, he lapsed into a deep sleep.

A shrill young voice, calling him by name, finally roused him.

"Midshipman of the watch, sir! Mr. Meredith's compliments, and he's about to muster the ship's company!"

Rick, momentarily stupefied, managed a halting acknowledgment, and then, recollecting where he was, he listened with relief to the midshipman's receding footsteps. He slid out of the cot, careful to replace the blankets his going had disturbed. Suddenly filled with a sense of urgency, he began hurriedly to dress.

It was not until he had donned and buttoned his watch coat that he glanced anxiously at the cot's occupant, and his heart leaped when he realized that the girl's eyes were wide open. They were blue eyes, looking unnaturally large and deep-set in the small, pinched face, and they held first fear and then bewilderment.

"The . . . ship went down." Her voice was a faint whisper of sound in the silence of the cabin. "The *Providence* . . . my father's ship. We had to . . . to take to the boats, but I . . ." The blue eyes were brimming with tears. "It was . . . so cold, and my father . . ."

"You are quite safe." Rick went to kneel beside the cot, seeking to reassure her. "The storm has blown itself out. Don't try to talk unless you want to—just rest where you are."

"I would like to talk, I . . . did your ship come to our rescue? I—I can't recall what happened. I thought that we . . . that we were all lost, that we must drown." Her voice was a little stronger, but it was still bewildered.

"We picked up your boat," Rick told her gently. He found himself wondering whether she had been aware that he had lain with her in his arms, but could not nerve himself to ask. He had

not held her as a woman—and scarcely thought of her as such—
and the stiff, cold little body had not roused any desire in him,
probably because he himself had been cold and too long without
sleep. But she might misunderstand or . . . He got to his feet.
"You were frozen with cold, and you've been unconscious for—
oh, for several hours."

The devil take old Billy Onslow, he thought; he should have
finished his culinary chores by now, should have come back.
Excusing himself, he went into the passageway and sent a passing
steward to fetch the cook. "Tell him to bring some hot soup, as
quickly as he can. Jump to it, man!"

Returning to his cabin, he buckled on his sword. The blue eyes
watched him anxiously, taking in the details of his uniform.

"You are . . . an *English* officer? Is this an English ship, a
warship?"

"Yes. His Majesty's sloop of war *Kangaroo*. I am her first
lieutenant, Richard Tempest."

"And I am an American, from Boston," the girl said. She
added, with conscious bitterness, "We have no love for the
English in Boston, Mr. Tempest."

"That is understandable," Rick conceded. He reached for his
hat. "I have to leave you. I'm on duty, but I've sent for the cook,
who is a trustworthy man. He will bring you some hot soup. And
the captain's wife, Mrs. Jeffrey, is on board. She will come if you
need her assistance—you can send Onslow to call her." He forced
a smile. "We're not enemies any longer, you know."

She looked up at him blankly, and Rick hesitated, not certain
whether she understood what he had told her. "Try to take the
soup. You've had nothing for a long while. You weren't conscious
until a few minutes ago, and you are still very weak."

"Yes, I see," the girl acknowledged. "I guess that must be why
I remember so little." But memory was returning, and she
endeavored to sit up.

"Our ship was the *Providence*. She was bound for Sydney, in
the colony of New South Wales. She . . . but perhaps you know
that?"

"Yes," Rick confirmed. "We found the log."

The girl's brow puckered for a moment, but then she went on.
"The boat you picked up—it was the only one left. The others
sank. They had been damaged in the storm, and the poor men in

them had no chance in that terrible sea, my father said. But they were afraid, and they would not wait for the wind to moderate or for him to . . . It was his boat I was in, the whaleboat. Is he . . . is my father also safe, Mr. Tempest?" When Rick did not at once reply, she added, with evident pride, "He is Captain Phineas O'Malley, master and owner of the *Providence*. In the war, he served in the United States Navy, in command of a brig called the *Liberty*. I . . . could I see my father, if you please? I'm Kate O'Malley."

"Miss O'Malley," Rick echoed. How, he wondered, could he find words to break it to her that her father was dead? Clearly, she had not envisaged such a possibility, and equally clearly, she was in no state to stand a shock. As he hesitated, the pipe sounded, followed by the boatswain's stentorian bellow.

"All hands! D'ye hear there? All hands muster aft to witness the burial service for the dead!"

Kate O'Malley heard and puzzled over the order. Then, as understanding dawned, she let a heartbroken sob escape her. "Is it . . . is the service for our men? Are they all dead?"

Rick nodded, sick with pity. "I fear they are, Miss O'Malley."

"My—my father, too?"

"Yes. I am truly sorry. He was dead when we picked up the whaleboat. There was nothing we could do for any of your people."

"But you tried?" she whispered. "Even though we are—we *were* Americans and your enemies?"

"The war is over," Rick reminded her. "I told you—we are not enemies any longer, Miss O'Malley."

To his relief, Billy Onslow made his appearance at that moment. Close on his heels came the midshipman of the watch.

"Sir, Mr. Meredith sent me," the boy said breathlessly. "The ship's company are mustered and the captain's coming on deck, sir."

"I'm coming," Rick assured him. He was about to leave the cabin when Kate O'Malley called on him to wait.

"Please, Mr. Tempest," she begged. "My father was an officer in the United States Navy. Ask your captain if his . . . his body may be covered by the United States flag."

"I will ask him, Miss O'Malley," Rick promised.

He made the request, despite the glare with which his belated appearance was greeted; and somewhat to his surprise, Captain Jeffrey, after a few moments of frowning indecision, summoned the yeoman of signals to his side.

"You have a United States ensign in the flag locker, I don't doubt, Yeoman. Bring it, if you please, and drape it over the first of the bodies."

"Aye, aye, sir," the yeoman acknowledged.

Rick waited until the order had been obeyed; then, as the captain opened his prayer book, he called the men to attention.

"Ship's company—off caps!"

The captain started to read. "They that go down to the sea in ships and occupy their business in great waters—these men see the works of the Lord and his wonders in the deep. For at His word the stormy wind ariseth, which lifteth up the waves thereof . . ." His voice, strong and resonant, rose above the buffeting of the wind and the incessant creaking of the ship's timbers. He concluded the psalm with the words, "Then are they glad, because they are at rest," offered a brief prayer, and then motioned to the two waiting petty officers, who stepped forward to grasp both sides of the planking trestle on which the flag-draped body of Captain Phineas O'Malley now rested.

"We therefore commit his body to the deep, to be turned into corruption, looking for the resurrection of the body, when the sea shall give up her dead, and the life of the world to come, through our Lord Jesus Christ . . ."

The two seamen lifted the trestle level with the bulwark, against which its far end had been propped, and then levered it higher. The body, wrapped in its weighted canvas shroud, slid down into the water. It floated for a moment or two and then vanished, as the sea closed over it.

Rick, standing bareheaded, watched it go, his throat tight as Captain Jeffrey repeated the solemn words of the committal and the body of the boy Larsen followed that of his commander, into the pitiless, icy sea that had robbed them of their lives.

CHAPTER II

Reaching the brow of the hill, Justin Broome reined in his horse and waited for his brother, William, to catch up with him.

"There," he said, pointing. "That is where I've taken my grant, Willie. Eight hundred acres of what I'll warrant is the finest pasture you've ever seen in your life. Well watered—you can see the river running through it. Plenty of good, serviceable timber, including stringy bark . . . buildings will present no problem. I've already set up a hut on this side of the river, as you'll see when we go down there."

William, a brown hand shading his eyes, studied the prospect before him for several minutes before making reply. At fifteen, he was already a man, Justin thought, with affection; an experienced sheep farmer, dedicated to the land and caring for little else. If he was flattered that his elder brother should seek his opinion, he gave no sign of it, rather taking it as his due, and considering what opinion he should offer with some degree of caution.

"It's fine pastureland, Justin," he conceded finally. "Both cattle and sheep should do well up here. But . . ." He hesitated.

"But what?" Justin prompted.

"It is isolated. How far have we traveled from Bathurst? Fifteen miles?"

"Nearer twelve, as the crow flies. Fifteen on account of this detour. But I wanted you to have a good view of the whole country." Justin waved to the lush green expanse of sparsely wooded plain below them, bounded by a distant range of low hills. "From here, George Evans reckoned one could see for over forty miles to the west, and it's all good grazing land. Even the hill slopes are grassy, easy of access for sheep; and there's game in abundance, as you'll have observed."

"True," William acknowledged. "And I realize that because you were with Mr. Blaxland's party, and later with Mr. Evans's, you are one of the privileged few to be granted land here. Eight hundred acres is almost as much as the Governor allocated to Mr. Lawson, is it not?"

There was no hint of envy in his voice, and Justin smiled. "Blaxland and Wentworth were offered a thousand apiece, but they took their grants on the Sydney side of the mountains . . . and you know what Gregory Blaxland holds on the Nepean. Mr. Lawson has taken his up here. He's been appointed commandant of the Bathurst garrison, and he's brought up several hundred head of cattle already. He says he'll bring more . . . and he's a pretty shrewd man, Willie. And a good farmer."

"You like him, don't you?" William suggested.

"Yes. And I owe him a lot." Justin's smile widened. Was it, he reflected, really only two years since he had crossed the Blue Mountains as one of the convict servants in Blaxland's train, assigned to William Lawson after the fiasco of a trial, in which the seamen from His Majesty's ship *Semarang* had perjured themselves in order to have him convicted? In view of the *Gazette*'s failure to print his name in the official account of the first successful crossing of the mountain barrier, he could count himself fortunate that he had been given an eight-hundred-acre grant. Governor Macquarie was not eager to open this area to any but carefully chosen settlers as yet, but—thanks to William Lawson's advocacy—Justin had, as his brother had put it, been one of the privileged few.

"Are you," William demanded, with unexpected bluntness, "are you intending to quit the sea and become a farmer, Justin?"

Justin's denial of any such intention was vehement. "God forbid! You know I'm no farmer. And besides, after all the time and money I've expended on repairs to the *Flinders*, I'll have to take every charter I'm offered to defray her cost. I'll have no time to come up here."

William nodded sagely. "That was what I supposed. And, if I may make so bold as to ask, have you brought me up here with the idea of putting me in to manage your land?"

Justin laughed aloud. "Yes, of course, Willie! Who better than you? I'd give you half title to the grant and pay for half the stock, and you would be your own master . . . I'd never interfere or offer advice. And Dick Lewis, who came on the Evans survey with me, is overseer at Bathurst now. He's a good friend, and he would, I know, assign two reliable men to the holding permanently, if I asked, and also let us have half a dozen to do the building work and fencing. Or most of it, anyway. So . . . what do you say? Will you take the place on?''

William hesitated, giving the offer his careful consideration, but finally he shook his head. "I'd like to, Justin, truly I would. But I'm more or less running Ulva these days—Andrew takes little interest. He misses Mam, and I reckon he'd like to get back to soldiering . . . there are a sight too many memories for him at Ulva.''

Justin's stepfather, Andrew Hawley, had made a successful career in the Royal Marines and had served in several of Admiral Nelson's great sea battles. Farming had never had any great appeal for him, and since their mother's death, it had had even less. . . . He glanced across at William and nodded his understanding.

"Would Andrew go back to Sydney, do you think, if you take charge of Ulva?''

"I'm pretty sure that is what he wants to do. And Rachel's all for it, of course—our little sister isn't so little anymore, and there's no social life at Ulva. She would go with him to keep house. The Governor has offered him employment on his staff, and . . .'' Again William hesitated. "It seems, from what Andrew told me after his last visit, that there is some trouble over the courts and that he would be of considerable service as a magistrate. I don't know what is going on exactly, but perhaps you do.''

Justin shrugged. "There has been trouble over the administration of the civil court ever since Ellis Bent's brother came out here. The two of them are in a pretty powerful position, with one of them judge advocate and the other our only colonial judge. If, as they insist, they won't sit with emancipist magistrates or permit emancipist lawyers to plead cases before them, then the courts cannot function. And the Reverend Marsden has decided to back them up, with all the power of church *and* state behind him! The Governor can't do much against such a combination.''

"You don't greatly care for the Bents, do you?'' William suggested.

"No, by heaven, I do not!'' Justin's headshake was emphatic. ''They are a pair of greedy, arrogant rogues, in my view. They draw government pay, yet they're both coining money in private legal fees. By refusing access to the courts to lawyers like George Crossley—who is infinitely more able—they leave litigants with no alternative but to employ one or the other of them. And it's all cloaked under the guise of sanctimony . . . no man who came out as a convict must be permitted to practice law in this colony. Contrary, of course, to His Excellency's publicly stated policy in that regard. And you know what that is."

" 'Those who have earned their freedom by servitude, pardon, or emancipation shall, in all respects, be considered on an equal footing with everyone else in the colony, according to their station in life,' " William quoted, his tone dry. "I'd have thought that Mr. Marsden, as a minister of God, would have given such a policy his full support. Yet you say he does not."

Justin tapped moodily on the toe of his boot with the light riding cane he carried. Samuel Marsden, he reflected, for all his own humble beginnings and the fiery sermons he preached, was no crusader for human rights when the humans who pleaded for them were men who had come out in chains. It had been his refusal to accept Sydney's wealthiest merchant and shipowner, Simeon Lord, as an equal that had sparked off the Bents' campaign.

"Mr. Marsden owns almost as much land now as John Macarthur," he observed cynically. "And he ships out more wool than anybody else in the colony."

"Small wonder, Justin, when he breeds from Spanish rams from the royal stud. And damme, by all accounts His Majesty gave them to him, asking no payment." William was frankly envious. "I'd give my right arm for one of them, I can tell you."

"You're not likely to be given the chance, Willie old son." Justin reined up his horse, which was cropping grass, and gestured to the slope below them. "Let's ride on, if you've seen enough. The Lachlan's teeming with fish, and I reckon young Winyara will have speared enough to make us a good meal. He'll have seen us coming an hour ago."

"Is that the blackfellow you took to crew for you?" William asked curiously.

"The same. I tried to make a seaman of him, and he did well enough. But like you he prefers the land, and I've left him in charge of my grant." Justin smiled. "Maybe I'll make a sheepherder of him yet!"

"They're damnably unreliable, the blackfellows," William complained. "Look at those two Mam set so much store by at Long Wrekin—Nanbaree and Kupali. We were like brothers when we were kids, but they still went off on walkabout whenever they felt inclined . . . and that was usually when we needed them. Mam had a way with them, I know, but you can't really depend on any of them, can you?"

"Winyara has never failed me yet."

"He will. Oh, all right, I know you mended his busted arm and took him to Hobart in the *Flinders*. But he'll grow up and become just like the rest of them. And if you don't watch out, his tribe will raid your stock and burn any crops they can't steal."

"You sound like the Reverend Samuel Marsden, Willie," Justin accused banteringly, "when the Governor invited him to contribute to the Native Institution. He is on record as saying that our blacks are scarcely above the beasts of the field in intellect, and that all attempts to improve either their minds or their conditions would be totally useless. He prefers to take Christianity to the Maoris in New Zealand."

"Does he?" William ran a hand through his straggling auburn locks. "Well, a plague on him, then! Does he imagine that the Maoris are any better?"

"Oh, indeed he does." Justin spoke gravely, the banter forgotten, as he recalled the meeting to which his friend and onetime employer, Robert Campbell, had taken him. Samuel Marsden had spoken at great length and with conviction of his voyage to New Zealand, at the end of the previous year, and of the reception he had been accorded by the warrior Maori chiefs. In the brig *Active*—purchased as a missionary vessel, as he had repeatedly asserted—he had landed in Whangaroa Bay and preached the first Christian sermon only half a mile from the scene of the *Boyd* massacre, where the bleached bones of a murdered ship's company were yet to be seen.

He sighed and went on flatly, "Ever since his return from New Zealand he's been extolling the Maoris' virtues. I suspect, though, that the trade goods he brought back with him in the *Active* helped to form that opinion."

"Trade goods?" William echoed, puzzled. "I had supposed, from the report in the *Gazette* Andrew showed me, that his purpose in buying the *Active* was to take missionaries to New Zealand. Was that not why he went?"

"He took the missionaries, all right," Justin confirmed. "The ones who came out with him, four years ago—King, Hall, and Kendall, with their families, and Lydiard Nicholas. He left them, with a horse and some other livestock, to establish their mission in Whangaroa Bay."

William frowned, his lips pursed in a whistle of astonishment. "You've been there, have you not, Justin—to Whangaroa Bay? And . . . was that not where the sealers were murdered? The crew of the *Boyd*?"

"It was, yes. All seventy of them."

"Murdered and . . . *eaten?* Are not the Maoris cannibals?"

"That," Justin admitted grimly, "appeared to be the case from the evidence we found. They denied it, but . . ." He shrugged, recalling what the colony's senior chaplain had claimed at the conclusion of his speech to the assembled merchants in Robert Campbell's yard.

"Commerce promotes industry—industry, civilization; and civilization opens up the way for the Gospel . . ." It was to be hoped, he thought, with a certain skepticism, that Samuel Marsden was right. Perhaps the cannibal Maoris would prove, when converted to the Christian faith, more useful than the unreliable, fish-eating blackfellows of New South Wales. Certainly they had more to trade, and Marsden had made no secret of the fact that he hoped to defray the cost of the *Active*—eighteen hundred pounds borrowed from friends and well-wishers in England—by means of his trading profits.

"Justin," William persisted, "are they not risking their lives, those poor devils of missionaries? If the Maoris are still cannibals, and—"

To evade William's youthfully ghoulish questions, Justin kicked his horse into a canter. When they pulled up their lathered animals half a mile from the river, he said, with finality, "We were talking about the possibility that Andrew might decide to return to military service, leaving you in sole charge at Ulva, Willie—not about the merits or otherwise of Samuel Marsden. I resent his supporting the Bents against the Governor, that's all; but I'll not presume to question his activities in other spheres. He established the mission at Whangaroa with the Governor's full knowledge and consent, after he brought two of their chiefs here, last year, to offer guarantees for the missionaries' safety. So—if I've let my tongue run away with me, forget it, please."

"Yes, of course," William agreed readily. "But . . . you're very strongly for the Governor, are you not?"

"I am, certainly. I've seen what he has achieved in a few short years. Governor Macquarie is a man of integrity and vision, and it angers me when self-seekers like the brothers Bent set themselves up to criticize and thwart him. And it distresses Jessica." Justin's expression softened at the mention of his wife's name. His sweet Jessie, he thought fondly, still enjoyed the confidence of the Governor's lady, to whom she had been personal maid for some five years. There was a bond of affection between them, and it had grown the stronger since Jessica had become pregnant with his child . . . Mrs. Macquarie's only son, Lachlan, now just over a year old and the pride of her life, owed much to Jessica's care of him, for he had been a sickly infant.

"How is Jessica faring?" William asked, with somewhat belated concern.

Justin smiled, taking no offense and aware that his younger brother lived in isolation on the Nepean River farm, seeing few people save his immediate neighbors. "She is well," he responded. "And we hope that she will make you an uncle very soon." He brushed off William's embarrassed congratulations, gesturing ahead of them to where smoke rose from the far side of a small bark hut at the river's edge. "Winyara's preparing our meal, and I confess I'm ready for it, aren't you?"

"More than ready," William admitted. Reaching the hut, he dismounted, a short, lithe figure in his faded work clothes. His rein looped over his arm, he studied the hut with a critical eye as he tethered his horse to the branch of a gnarled gum tree. "Did your paragon of a blackfellow build this hut for you?"

"He did. Why?"

"Well, he made a neat job of it," William conceded. "Does he live here by himself?"

"When I come up here he seems to." Justin slid from the saddle, dwarfing his stockier brother by almost a foot. "I don't ask whom he entertains when I'm not about. His tribe are not unfriendly—just cautious and a mite afraid; so far they've given me no trouble. I shoot the odd kangaroo for them or a few duck, and they bring me fish and 'possums. And they've never tried to steal any of Mr. Lawson's cattle or molest George Evans, when he comes on a surveying trip. They've a better record than the Maoris, I promise you!''

He grinned and, cupping his hands about his mouth, called out to Winyara. The boy came at once, his skin cloak dangling from his shoulders and his startlingly white teeth bared in a welcoming smile. His injured arm had healed, leaving only a few puckered scars visible against the dark skin but in no way impeding his movements or his dexterity. His manner, even William was compelled to admit, was warm and friendly, and his preparations for their evening meal could not be faulted. Cooked native fashion, encased in damp clay and buried in the hot ashes of a fire, the half-dozen plump river fish he offered tasted delicious, despite the fact that they had been neither skinned nor gutted.

Winyara consumed all the entrails with evident enjoyment, making no attempt to share them, and, replete, he slapped his thin stomach and ran off, to return with a pannikin, blackened from much use, filled with strong, scalding hot tea, of the kind the early settlers had called Botany Bay, or sweet, tea, made from sarsaparilla leaves.

"Good!" he announced proudly. "You drink it down!"

His understanding, if not his command, of English was better than that of many of the natives living around Sydney and the Hawkesbury townships, and he had, as Justin demonstrated, a quick intelligence that enabled him to comprehend almost everything said to him. William, for all his earlier doubts, was impressed.

The sun sank in a blaze of glory, tingeing the distant mountaintops with molten gold; and after Justin and William had watered and hobbled the horses, they stretched out beside the stillsmoldering fire, sipping from a second pannikin of tea in relaxed and sleepy content.

"You must allow, Willie," Justin observed, leaning forward to take a brand from the fire and applying it to light his pipe, "that this is a pleasant, peaceful place."

William flashed him a rueful smile. "It is, indeed," he answered. "And I'm already wishing that I could take you up on your offer. But on Andrew's account, I don't see how I can."

"Don't concern yourself. I'll find a good man to manage the

stock for me. There's plenty of time . . . I've yet to raise the money to buy stock." His pipe going to his satisfaction, Justin leaned back, savoring the taste of the tobacco smoke as he drew on it. He went on pensively, "You know, if Andrew does decide to resume his military career, it's possible he might be offered command of the Hobart garrison—or even the lieutenant governorship. Major Davey is letting the settlements go to rack and ruin, and I know the Governor would like to see him replaced."

"Will the home government agree to replace him?" William asked.

"The Lord knows," Justin said. "I only know that the last time I was there—just five weeks ago, in fact—I saw a big difference. The free settlers, who were forced to take land there when Norfolk Island was abandoned, were in a state of near revolt. Their grants are far out and isolated, and between bushrangers and the natives, they lose stock and crops almost daily. Convicts escape and either take to the bush or pirate small craft on the river, and Davey apparently carouses with his cronies and does nothing to halt their depredations. Hey"—he broke off, sensing that William's attention had lapsed—"you're not listening!"

"Because I've just thought of something." William sat up, his eyes suddenly bright. "I believe I have it, Justin."

"What have you, little brother?" Justin demanded indulgently. "A means of furthering Andrew's career?"

"No, not that. A suggestion concerning the good man you want—the partner to manage this holding. Why do you not make Rick Tempest the offer you made me?"

"Rick Tempest—Abigail's brother? But he's making a career in the navy. A good career—he was commissioned two or three years ago, and Abigail told me he had distinguished himself in the American War." Justin shook his head. "He's not likely to come back here, is he?"

"Oh, but he is," William assured him. "He wrote to Andrew and said that he had applied for appointment to one of the sloops the Admiralty is sending out . . . the *Kangaroo,* I fancy it was. He said he had decided to quit the navy and settle here."

"Did he, by George?" Justin felt a warm glow of pleasure. Rick Tempest was a good fellow and one very much after his own heart. Rick's sisters owned the Yarramundie property, on the Hawkesbury, two thousand acres of prime land, well stocked and cultivated. Neither Abigail nor Lucy lived there; since a raid by a party of escapers, in which the house and most of the buildings had been burned to the ground, they had left the property and put it up for sale. Rick might have made plans to take it over, as a going concern; if that were the case, the idea of joining a pioneering enterprise would be of little appeal to him.

Justin started to voice his doubts, but William cut him short. "Rick doesn't intend to settle at Yarramundie," he stated with conviction, "because the reason he wrote to Andrew was to ask if Long Wrekin was for sale. He said he'd amassed some prize money and could afford to buy land of his own. Andrew showed me the letter, and from what I recall of it, Rick seemed to regard Yarramundie as his sisters' property."

"Well, probably it is," Justin conceded. He knocked out his pipe and added thoughtfully, "You know, Willie, you may have solved my problem for me. Certainly there's no one I'd sooner go into partnership with than Rick . . . excepting yourself, of course. I wonder when his ship will get here? I did hear that the Governor had requested two ships of war to be on station here. One was the *Emu,* a brig-sloop of sixteen guns, but she was taken prize by a Yankee privateer on her way out, and there's been no word of her since. Presumably, now that the war with America is over, she'll be exchanged and arrive here eventually. Or perhaps Rick's *Kangaroo* has been ordered here in her place."

"The letter was written in January," William supplied. "Nearly six months ago—she could make port any day."

"Aye, that she could," Justin agreed. He lay back again, his head resting on his clasped hands. "That's a good suggestion of yours, Willie, the more I think about it. And there's no hurry . . . I'll hang fire until the *Kangaroo* makes port. That will give me time to get the building work started. Dick Lewis would oversee it for me, I'm sure . . . he's on the spot, and he has the men. And I can get back to sea to earn the price of my stock."

"When the time comes," William promised, "I will help you to drive your stock up the road. You may count on me for that, Justin."

"Thanks, Willie," Justin acknowledged. "I'll hold you to that."

They lapsed into companionable silence as darkness fell and the shadows lengthened. Justin, thinking of it afterward, was never sure for how long he slept, but he woke, chilled to the bone and shivering, despite the heat of the fire.

Winyara was beside him, on his knees, and in the moonlight his dark face was twisted in an expression of intense distress.

"Dream time come," he whispered unhappily in his own tongue. He grasped Justin's arm, shaking it urgently. "I see *ghereek . . . cambewarra!*" The words Justin translated as "blood" and a "mountain on fire," and he struggled to his feet, still shivering, to look about him anxiously. But all in their immediate vicinity was quiet and still, the river flowing placidly on its way, bathed in the silvery glow of moonlight, the distant hilltops deep in shadow.

William, roused by the native boy's high-pitched voice, sat up, rubbing his eyes and still bemused by sleep.

"What is it?" he questioned dully. "Is there something wrong?"

"I don't know," Justin admitted. "But someone must have walked over my grave—I can't stop shaking. And Winyara's mighty alarmed about some dream he had." He turned to the aborigine, holding him gently by the shoulders. "What ails you, Winyara? Tell me in English, boy! There's no mountain on fire here that I can see."

"Not here—*munong!* Far away. Many men die." The boy was in a trance, Justin realized, his eyes raised to the sky and only their whites visible. "Dream come *wilparina . . .* winds bring *wonda.* Men fighting, killing! *Cambewarra . . .* I see fire, hear thunder. . . ." He shuddered violently and would have fallen but for Justin's supporting arms. Then, quite clearly in English, he said, "Two great warriors lead them."

His eyes closed, another convulsion seized his slender, dark body, and he slithered free of Justin's grasp, to lie quietly on the ground, seemingly asleep.

"What in the name of all that's wonderful was he talking about?" William demanded irritably. "It sounded like gibberish to me."

"Perhaps it was," Justin allowed. "But you can't be sure . . . these people possess strange powers." He bent and covered Winyara's slight body with his blanket. "He said, as nearly as I can make out, that a great battle is being waged on a mountain a long way away. That many men are dying, and that two great warriors are leading them." He paused, struck by a sudden thought. "What date is it, Willie?"

"It's Sunday," William answered. "Sunday the . . . eighteenth of June, eighteen hundred and fifteen." He laughed a trifle uncertainly. "I thought the war was over. But you believe what Winyara just told you, don't you, Justin?"

Slowly, Justin inclined his head. "Yes," he said, and shivered again. "I do."

CHAPTER III

Outside in the Brussels street, as darkness fell, all was bustle and confusion. Soldiers mingled with civilians; a procession of carriages trundled past, laden with brilliantly uniformed officers and their ladies on their way to the Duchess of Richmond's ball; and with ever-increasing frequency, military couriers on lathered horses, slowed to walking pace by the press of people, thrust their way through the crowds.

Watching from the window of their lodging, Magdalen De Lancey awaited her husband's return with an impatience engendered by anxiety. It was over an hour ago that William had been summoned to the Duke of Wellington's headquarters, and it had been evident, both from his expression and the low-voiced message the Duke's aide-de-camp had delivered, that the situation was one of extreme gravity.

All day there had been rumors of an impending French attack. Bonaparte was known to have crossed the frontier, and the latest rumor Magdalen had heard was that part of his army was about to engage the Prussians at a place called Fleurus, whence they had retreated after making a stand at Marchienne. Still more alarming was the as yet unsubstantiated news that a very large French force was advancing on a strategically situated point on the road to Brussels, marked on the map as Quatre Bras.

William's maps were spread out on the desk he had been using, and Magdalen had glanced at them before he had been called away. Quatre Bras, she had ascertained, was perilously close to Brussels; and as she had assisted him to don his uniform coat and pin on his medals, he had told her that the place was only lightly held, and by Dutch and Belgian troops under the Prince of Orange's command . . . not, alas, by the British.

"I expect I shall be up all night, my love," he had warned her regretfully as he kissed her on parting. "There will be fresh orders to send out—the Peer seems, for once, to have been at fault in his belief that Napoleon would endeavor to cut our lines of communication with the Channel ports. From what reliable reports we have received, he's aiming to drive a wedge between us and Blücher's Prussians . . . with Quatre Bras as his first objective."

She could not pretend to an understanding of military strategy, of course, but the maps had gone some way to enlightening her, and . . . Magdalen stifled a sigh as she turned back from the window, and seating herself once more at her husband's desk, she sought to trace on the map the names the Duke's aide had mentioned.

There was Gosselies, where the Prussians had initially come under attack, and . . . yes, there was Sombreffe, where Field Marshal Blücher was supposed to be, with a place marked as Ligny—a village, between Fleurus and Sombreffe. Quatre Bras was to the west—no, to the northwest—and still further to the west were the main Allied forces, spread out in what William had described as a triangle, to defend the ports of Ostend and Antwerp.

Magdalen traced them with a finger that, for all her efforts to control it, trembled visibly. The Prince of Orange's headquarters lay nearest to Quatre Bras, at Braine-le-Comte, with Lord Uxbridge's cavalry division at Ninove more than twenty miles away, and Lord Hill's infantry at Ath twice that distance . . . William had marked them in as square symbols, in his neat, precise hand. There was the reserve, of course, in the immediate vicinity of Brussels, under the Duke's own command. Magdalen frowned over the symbols, trying to understand them. She made out two Anglo-Hanoverian divisions, commanded by Generals Picton and Cole, and a Brunswick detachment under their own Duke—and then tears blurred her vision. If only William would come back, so that she might see and talk to him, reassure herself that he had not been sent to Quatre Bras and into heaven knew what danger.

But of course he would not be sent there, unless the Duke himself—the Peer, as his officers called him—decided to go. William's place, as quartermaster general and chief of staff, was at headquarters, at the Duke's side . . . she was being foolish, imagining dangers that did not exist. In an almost childish gesture,

Magdalen brushed the tears from her eyes with the back of her hand—it would never do to let William see that she had been weeping. Although perhaps there was some excuse . . . she loved him so deeply and passionately, and in their all-too-brief marriage, she had found more happiness than, this side of heaven, she had believed possible, even in her dreams.

Their interrupted honeymoon had left her distraught and heartbroken; but then George had come, with the news that she might go to Brussels—her husband needed and wanted her, and had sent him to escort her across the Channel. She had packed in an hour and made the long journey with joy in her heart, eager for the sight of him, laughing at the discomfort and her own weariness. And here, in these cramped, sparsely furnished lodgings, they had been reunited and, for a week, had slept in each other's arms, seeing only those whom it was William's duty to see, and refusing the invitations to dinners, routs, and balls with which they had been inundated.

William wanted no other company than hers, and she . . . Magdalen drew in her breath sharply, as the memories of that past week came flooding back. Memories of their lovemaking, of their two bodies so perfectly attuned as to seem as one, of his sleeping face on the pillow beside her, and of the smile with which, on waking, he had greeted her. She had gloried in her husband's tender affection, knowing herself so deeply loved, so precious to him, so essential to his well-being and comfort, as well as to his happiness, that he could not bear to spend even an hour away from her.

But now, this evening, he had been away for more than an hour. Magdalen had got up and started restlessly to pace the room, pausing occasionally by the window in the hope of seeing his tall figure in the street below. First he had had to leave her in order to call on the Spanish ambassador, and then, even as she had knelt at his feet to help him divest himself of his riding boots, the summons had come—the Duke wanted him urgently, and she knew that, very soon, they would again have to be parted.

The war had caught up with them; what had previously been only rumor and speculation had become hideous reality. The monster Bonaparte was on the march and—

There was a soft knock on the door, and she turned, her heart

beating like a wild thing in her breast, only to sink when she saw
that it was her maid.

"Yes," she said impatiently, praying that the girl had not come
to tell her that William had been delayed. "What is it, Emma?"

"I was thinking that perhaps your ladyship would like some
tea." Emma's voice was concerned. "You've taken nothing since
luncheon."

"I'm not hungry. I—you can make tea when Sir William comes
back. He'll be glad of it, I'm sure."

"Very good, m'lady." The girl was about to go, but Magdalen
called her back. "All the traffic in the street . . . are they still
going to the ball, do you know? It has not been canceled?"

"They are all dressed in their finery," Emma answered. "The
ladies in ball gowns. I do not think it has been canceled. Just now I
saw the Prince of Orange go past and two of our generals. . . ."
She started to describe the Prince's uniform, but Magdalen was not
listening. If the Prince and two British generals were going to the
Duchess of Richmond's, then perhaps there was, after all, no
imminent danger of a French attack.

Relieved by this thought, she dismissed the maid and returned to
her vantage point at the window. There were no troops marching
out of the city; all the foot traffic, the carriages, and the mounted
officers were, as Emma had confirmed, proceeding in the direction
of the Richmonds' ducal establishment. The ball was due to begin
at nine o'clock, and it was almost nine now; she and William had
been invited to attend, but . . . Magdalen felt the warm color
flood her cheeks.

William had refused, as he had refused all their other invitations. "George can represent the De Lanceys," he had said. "I
want to spend every minute I have left with you, my darling, not
share you with a host of others, who will lay siege to you and seek
to take you from me!"

The clatter of hooves on the pavé below interrupted her
thoughts, and Magdalen thrust open the window and leaned out,
overjoyed when she recognized her husband. As an orderly hurried
forward to take his horse, William slipped from the saddle, a tall
figure in his resplendent full-dress uniform, and he looked up in
response to her welcoming wave, a smile curving his lips as he
doffed his hat to her. A shaft of wayward moonlight fell on his bare
head, and to Magdalen's consternation, it seemed for a moment to

have turned his dark hair to silver. It did not age him but appeared momentarily to transform him into . . . oh, merciful heaven!— into a ghost, and she became aware, once again, of the premonition that had haunted her ever since word of the French advance had reached Brussels; and she found herself shaking as if with ague.

But she had herself under stern control by the time William joined her in the quiet, lamp-lit room, and her smile echoed his as she lifted her face for his kiss.

"You have not to go? Are we to have a little more time together . . . this night, at least?" Her question was almost a plea, and William De Lancey answered it ruefully.

"I shall leave with the Duke, soon after dawn, my love. But in the meantime"—he gestured to the desk, with its piled maps and papers—"there are orders to be written and sent out, all of them urgent. This room will be teeming with messengers—every aide-de-camp on Wellington's staff and mine will be coming here." William held her to him, looking down at her gravely. His face was lined and tired, Magdalen saw, but his eyes were bright with anticipation. Could it be, she wondered wretchedly, that despite the love he bore her, he was eager to go into battle? He was a soldier, she knew, but . . . She clung to him wordlessly, reluctant to leave his embrace.

It was he who released and put her from him. "Magdalen, my dearest, go to bed, will you not? There is no need for both of us to lose our sleep. I will come to you as soon as I can."

"Oh, please . . ." The thought of entering the great, curtained bed in the next room without him appalled her. "Will you not permit me to stay with you? I will be quiet—I will sit in a corner, out of your way, I promise."

"Without uttering a word?" he admonished gently. "I have work to do, my love, and it will require all my concentration."

"Whilst the Duke himself and most of his commanders dance at the Richmonds' ball?" Magdalen flung back at him, suddenly rebellious. "But you must work?"

"The troops will start moving out within the next two hours, Magdalen," William told her. "They would be hopelessly impeded if the citizens of Brussels jammed the streets in panic flight. Panic must be discouraged at all costs, and in order to do so, Her Grace of Richmond has been requested to continue to hold her reception, as if nothing untoward were about to happen. The Peer will attend in person, with his senior commanders, solely for that purpose. He has issued his orders for the defense of Brussels and entrusted their implementation to me. Some are contrary to orders issued earlier, before we knew from which direction the French attack would come."

"But you know now?" Magdalen whispered sadly. "And it will come?"

"It has already begun, darling, and it ceased only at nightfall. We have to deploy our troops to meet it when it is resumed, and there is not much time." William was already moving toward his desk, setting down his bulging dispatch case and impatiently thrusting the maps aside to make room for the fresh papers he had brought back with him. He turned, his expression relaxing as he looked at her. "Go to bed, my little love. Order me some tea, if you will, before you go, and tell them below to admit my clerks when they arrive."

"May I not stay?" Magdalen begged. "I'll not interrupt you, dearest, truly I won't. I want to be with you, I . . . there will be time enough to sleep when you are gone. Too much time."

He relented then. "Very well. But not a word, you understand? Whatever you may hear—not a word!"

Magdalen gave him her promise. Throughout what became a seemingly endless night, she contrived to keep it. The clerks arrived and were admitted; she served William the tea he had requested, but before he had had time to drink it, a procession of men in a variety of different uniforms came to throng about him, talking in a variety of different tongues. Much of what she overheard passed over her head—the guttural German, Dutch, and Flemish voices were unintelligible to her—but the faces of the officers revealed more than enough to fill her with alarm. Almost all were grave and grimly set, and she guessed that the crisis was a great deal worse than, initially, she had supposed.

A handful of young officers, fresh from the Duchess of Richmond's ball and in exuberant spirits, lightened the atmosphere briefly, but then they were gone, their laughter abruptly silenced when the import of the orders they were given started to sink in. One, a slim boy in Highland uniform, wearing the Gordon tartan, paused shyly by her side to bid her good-night, but it was not until he reminded her, that Magdalen recalled how they had crossed from Dover in the same ship.

In a whisper, lest William accuse her of breaking her promise, she wished him well, and he gave her a warm smile and said proudly, "This will be the first time that I have gone into battle, Lady De Lancey. But I have no fear—the Ninety-second will acquit themselves well, and I shall try to be worthy of them."

His was a simple philosophy, she reflected, but she was inexplicably saddened as she watched him go.

A little while later, George made his appearance, so bespattered with mud that, for a moment, she did not recognize him. She offered him tea, but he shook his head and, with no more than a cursory greeting, crossed to his brother's side and started to speak to him urgently. It was a low-voiced exchange, but Magdalen, anxiously straining her ears, was able to hear most of what they said.

"Saxe-Weimar's brigade of Nassauers is holding its ground half a mile south of Quatre Bras—four thousand men and eight guns," George stated grimly. "But Bylandt's moving forward to support them. They ignored the order to fall back on Nivelles, on the grounds that they were in possession of information not available to the commander in chief."

"Thanks be to God that they did!" William exclaimed. "My dispatch will not have reached Perponcher yet. Were you able to ascertain the enemy's strength between Frasnes and Quatre Bras?"

George nodded wearily. "Prince Bernard's skirmishers took a prisoner—an officer of the Fourth Lancers and a Belgian, by a stroke of good fortune. He said that two corps were advancing on Quatre Bras—d'Erlon's and Reille's. And, if he's to be believed, Ney—the Prince of the Moskowa himself—is in command. But they appear in no hurry. I could see the glow of their bivouac fires when I was there at eight o'clock. I take it the Peer's ordered up reinforcements?"

"The entire reserve is under orders to move into position at Mont St. Jean at first light," William answered. "That's where he plans to hold them." He reached for a map, jabbing his finger on the place he had indicated and, head bent over it, went on talking. Magdalen missed the next few words, and then she heard him say, "Picton and Van Merlen are on their way to Quatre Bras now—or they will be, as soon as my gallopers reach them, and Daddy Hill's been alerted. But it's going to take time, devil take it, George!"

"Fifty thousand Frenchmen," George observed, with bitterness. "And only four thousand Dutchmen ranged against them. Is the Peer losing his touch?"

"God, no!" William retorted. But he expelled his breath in a long-drawn sigh. "I waited on him, when he was dressing for the ball. Müffling had just appeared—having taken thirty hours to ride thirty miles! He brought news of the attack on the Prussians and said that Blücher was deploying three corps in the Sombreffe area, with his left at Ligny." Again he lowered his voice, and Magdalen missed what were evidently details of the Prussian position.

She heard George observe, with barely contained indignation, "And you still say the Peer has not lost his touch? For the Lord's sweet sake, Will, he's concentrated our best divisions and most of the cavalry miles to the west of where they're needed!"

"He admitted that Napoleon had humbugged him," William conceded. "But he has his plans well laid, and at most we've lost only twenty-four hours. Picton's brigades will make a forced march, the Ninety-second are already preparing to move out from here, and Uxbridge won't need more than five or six hours to bring his cavalry into the reckoning. Talking of which . . ." He put out a hand to pick up one of the papers on his desk. "I'm sorry you had to miss Her Grace's ball, but since you have, you can oblige me by taking this to Ponsonby. Take a fresh horse, and leave yours in my stable. You'd best join your regiment, George, because there'll be hot work to come very soon . . . and doubtless we shall meet at Quatre Bras. God go with you, brother!"

"And with you, Will." They embraced and George bent to kiss Magdalen's hand. He said nothing, and his smile was tight; then he was gone, the sound of his heavy, booted feet on the stone staircase gradually receding, leaving Magdalen with the same sense of helpless sadness that the departure of the young Highland officer had earlier engendered. Their going would, she was bitterly aware, hasten that of her husband, for already the first gray light of dawn was seeping through the window.

At long last, William stretched his cramped limbs, dismissed his clerks, and, with one of his aides, left the house in order to report to the Duke of Wellington that his task had been completed. The revised instructions to the Allied divisions had been written and dispatched, the supply trains set in motion, and the ordance and commissariat staffs alerted.

To Magdalen's heartfelt relief—for she had feared that the Duke might detain him—he returned to take his leave of her. She served him with more tea and a light breakfast, and then they stood together, William with his arm about her, and watched from the window of their room as the troops marched out of the city. The kilted 92nd led them, to the stirring music of their pipes and drums, and Magden held back the tears that threatened to overwhelm her, the soldiers' marching feet sounded like a knell on her heart.

"The Duke was asleep when I arrived," William said. "Sleeping like a baby, as if he had not a care in the world! I must leave at six to join him . . . we have just two hours to be together, my darling, and I want to spend them in your bed."

Gladly, she let him lead her to the great four-poster, with its sagging brocade curtains—the bed that she had been so reluctant to climb into by herself. They made love with the desperate intensity of despair, the imminence of their parting rousing both to an emotional pitch where even ecstasy was overshadowed by pain. Tears ached in Magdalen's throat, burned in her eyes, and echoed in her heart as she clung to him, giving herself to him almost wantonly, yet numb and unable to reach the glad climax in which, hitherto, their coupling had always ended. She feigned it, fighting back her tears, and hoped that he had been deceived. Then afterward, lying beside him as he slept, she wept silently, not daring to sleep herself lest the short time left to her should pass too quickly or that she might awake to find him gone.

But the last hour did pass in, it seemed to her, the space of only minutes. The servant's knock on the door brought it to its dreaded end.

As always, William wakened to instant alertness; he had been a soldier since the tender age of fourteen, Magdalen reminded herself. Before he had joined the Duke's staff, he had campaigned in the East Indies, in Holland and the Peninsula, and had survived the retreat to Corunna under Sir John Moore. Surely now, for all her haunting premonitions, he would, by the grace of God, survive the battle that was to come?

She watched as he shaved with the swift skill of long practice;

and then, dismissing the servant, she assisted him to dress, herself buckling on his sword.

"I've made arrangements for you to go to Antwerp," William said unexpectedly. "There will be a hired carriage waiting at noon and a room booked for you at the Inn of the Grand Laboureur in the Rue des Palmes. I want to be sure that, whatever happens, you will be safe, my dearest love."

"Is Brussels not safe?" Magdalen questioned, staring at him wide-eyed, for he had previously expressed no such fear.

"Antwerp is safer, sweetheart—from there you can take passage back to England if need be." William was emptying the contents of his purse onto the desk, she saw, his tone one that brooked no argument. "This should take care of whatever financial needs you may have. Use it, I beg you—for God alone knows whether we can prevent Boney from taking Brussels. We shall try, it goes without saying; but where your safety is concerned, I want to take no chances. And there will be wild panic here, should the battle go against us. Promise me that you will go, so that I may rest easy on your account. Please, Magdalen . . ." He came to take her into his arms. "You are more precious to me, my darling, than life itself."

She wanted to refuse and looked up at him miserably. It was he who was going into danger, not she, he who must take part in the coming battle. And if he should be wounded . . . She braced herself, reluctant to reject the request he had made of her, yet unwilling to put an added distance between them.

"I shall be waiting for your return, dearest husband," she said softly. "May God have you always in His care!"

"I want your promise," William said sternly.

"Then you have it," Magdalen managed.

He kissed her gratefully. The knock came again and suddenly she was alone, the sound of his footsteps echoing on the stairs as George's had echoed, a few short hours before.

From the window, her heart near to breaking, Magdalen De Lancey watched her husband ride away.

The Allied forces were retreating from Quatre Bras. It was not a rout; they had not been defeated—indeed, they had more than held their own; yet in spite of this, the orders had come for withdrawal.

In the kilted ranks of the 92nd Regiment, which had fought with stubborn courage from two o'clock till dusk and suffered heavy casualties, there was anger as well as disappointment in the men's weary, smoke-grimed faces as they headed northward, abandoning the crossroads for which so many of their number had died.

Murdo Maclaine marched with them, as disconsolate as any. Some error in his enlistment papers had sent him to the 92nd instead of the 73rd—his father's regiment—but he had no regrets on that score now. The few weeks he had spent with them in billets in Brussels had been, to his own surprise, the happiest and proudest time of his life. The men were Highlanders, drawn from the crofts and mountains of his homeland, and he had been instantly accepted as one of them, finding a comradeship such as he had never before experienced, even in Nick Vincent's gang. And in any event, the second battalion of the 73rd was, a sergeant had told him, no longer kilted, and recruited mainly in the Lowlands.

As he plodded stolidly along, the events of the past twenty-four hours passed, like a series of pictures, through his mind. He was, Murdo dimly recognized, in a state of shock, for so much that had happened had been agonizingly painful; indeed, had he not been powerless to do so, he would gladly have erased every vestige of it from his memory.

It had all begun auspiciously enough; and when, at daybreak on the morning of June sixteenth, the 92nd, with their comrades of the 42nd, had marched through the Place Royale to Brussels' Namur Gate with their pipes playing "Cock o' the North," Murdo recalled, he had been pleasantly intoxicated. Deaf to the warnings of the veterans who had served in the Peninsular campaign, he and his fellow recruits had been eager to go into battle; and the Belgian family with whom he had been billeted had seen to it that he was well primed with liquor before he took leave of them.

And there had been more, at the grand ball given by Her Grace of Richmond, at which his skill as a dancer had ensured his appearance as a member of the regimental display team, detailed to entertain the guests during supper. He had seen the great Wellington there—the revered commander whom his troops irreverently called Nosey—moving composedly among the distinguished throng, with a beautiful young woman on his arm and apparently without a care in the world.

He himself, Murdo remembered ruefully, had found time to take

one of the serving wenches into a lechcrous embrace; and fueled
by the whiskey he had consumed, he no doubt could have cajoled
her to permit him other liberties, had not his sergeant ordered him
to obey the bugle call to muster. Her body had been warm and
enticing, but now he could not recall her face or the color of her
hair, and—

"Company!" The sergeant's bellow broke into his thoughts;
from the habit of discipline, he stiffened, awaiting the command,
and it was with sick relief that he heard it. "Halt and fall out!"

He slumped exhaustedly to the ground, aware for the first time
that it was raining and that the road verge on which he lay was
damp and muddy. A troop of horse artillery galloped through the
space their halt had cleared, heading for the battlefield they had
left behind them, the wheels of the guns and limbers spattering the
resting Highlanders with churned-up mud. But no voice was raised
in protest; the gunners were riding back to protect their rear from
the pursuing French cavalry, and in grim silence the men watched
them go.

"Have ye ony water in your canteen, Murdo?" his front rank
man asked, and Murdo shook his head, not bothering to verify his
denial. The canteen had been empty since dawn, when he had
gulped down its contents in a vain attempt to slake his raging thirst
and rid himself of the stench of death.

He had seen many men die, the previous afternoon—men who
had been his friends, others who were strangers and his enemies.
The regiment's colonel, John Cameron of Fassifern, had died from
a sniper's bullet—fired from the upper story of a farmhouse—
which had brought him down as he led them in a charge across the
Charleroi road, quite early in the battle. Murdo's eyes stung as he
recalled the grief of Ewen MacMillian, the colonel's foster brother,
and the vengeance the regiment had taken on the occupants of the
farmhouse.

He shivered, as the memories returned. He had feared for his
own life many times that day, his bowels turned to water and bile
rising in his throat, and he had been tempted to run from the
carnage, to fling down his musket and take blindly to his heels.
But pride had held him where his orders had ordained that he
should be. He had stood in square and repulsed repeated assaults
by the French heavy cavalry, fearsome figures in their gleaming

cuirasses, trampling down the high-growing corn that had, initially, hidden them from view.

Once the Duke himself with members of his staff had had to take refuge in the 92nd's square, narrowly escaping capture, and the French gunners had lowered their sights and fired round after round, in the hope of breaking the square and leaving him defenseless. But, with the sergeants bawling "Close up! Close ranks!" they had held, and as the cavalry came again, they had loaded, rammed, primed, and fired their deadly volleys, the front rank kneeling and the gaps swiftly filled.

Murdo closed his eyes, seeking to blind himself to the remembered scene, but the vision was still there, the ceaseless thunder of the guns still echoing in his ears. His company commander, Captain Little, had been killed beside him, his skull split in two by a Frenchman's saber and . . . He shuddered. He had struck out with his bayonet and brought the cuirassier's splendid chestnut horse crashing down, and the men on either side of him had dealt savagely with its rider. Looking back, it was—oddly—the horse's death that now moved him to pity and for which he felt the greater regret.

"On your feet, lads! On your feet!" The sergeants were shouting, the bugles shrilling. Like a man in a dream, Murdo scrambled up; and in driving rain, the regiment moved on, still northward, still in retreat, still unaware of the reason why they had been robbed of the fruits of their victory.

At nightfall, with the rain continuing to pour down, turning fields and roads into glutinous quagmires, the order to halt and bivouac came at last. There was no shelter, and it was too wet to light fires; but the sodden, footsore Highlanders were thankful simply to end their march and find oblivion in sleep.

Murdo slept, after a fashion, his sleep haunted by dreams, in the most vivid of which he was running, breathless and bare of foot and with enemy cavalry close on his heels, toward Brussels, where the serving wench he had embraced so passionately was waiting, beckoning him on.

He wakened to watery sunshine, the desire to take flight uppermost in his mind. But after the regiment had been ordered to ascend the low hill on which they had bivouacked and take position in the shelter of its crest, the supply wagons came up and the men of his company started to boil a big iron kettle on a smoky but cheerful fire, and he decided to wait and break his fast.

" 'Twas the Prussians' fault that we'd to retire," the adjutant's clerk told the waiting group as they squatted round the fire attempting to dry their wet clothing. "Boney beat them fair and square at some place called Ligny. Old Blücher was wounded, Captain Alexander said, and the plaguey frogs overran half o' his divisions and massacred them. But they're rallying an' regrouping, seemingly, an' Nosey's sent tae tell yon Blücher that we'll hold here, sae lang as he joins up wi' us before nightfall." The clerk was one of the regiment's few Lowlanders, and he grinned mockingly at the dismay reflected in the dirty, unshaven faces surrounding him. "Och, now, ye gallant Hie'land warriors, we're in bonnie company . . . look around ye! The Camerons, the Forty-second, ourselves an' the Royal Scots, wi' the Union Cavalry Brigade and oor ain Scots Greys no' far behind us."

"But the bluidy Walloons on our right," one of the veterans observed sourly. "Were ye not seeing them hightail it from Quatre Bras, after our colonel was killed? Frenchies and Boney-lovers, that is what they are!"

No one answered him. The men washed down the commissariat biscuit with scalding black tea, fired off their muskets to clear them of damp powder, and had barely time to replenish their ammunition boxes and pouches when the bugle sounded for roll call.

Fewer than half of those who had marched out of the Namur Gate were there to answer to their names. The battalion was only two hundred and fifty strong now, and it had lost twenty-five of its thirty-six officers, including Colonel Cameron and his second-in-command. Murdo's spirits plummeted as this fact sank in, but he knew that he must leave it to the foreigners to run, for he could not, whatever his dream had urged on him. After the battle, perhaps; but not now, with so few men left to uphold the regiment's honor . . . aye, and Scotland's, too, if the rogue of a clerk had spoken truly. And it seemed he had, for the tartan was there as the drums sounded the call to arms and the line began to form, two deep, behind the crest of the ridge to await the French attack.

It came just before noon, heralded by a furious cannonade aimed at the Château of Hougoumont, to the front of the Allied right wing, and held by some two thousand British Guardsmen.

Murdo could see nothing—the hedge running along the crest of the hill obscured his view—but within an hour, the French had positioned within seven hundred yards of the Allied line a formidable number of guns, and they soon opened up with a thunderous barrage.

This did comparatively little damage. Because of the heavy rain of the previous night, the round shot did not ricochet and plunge over the crest to land among the men sheltering behind it; but instead, landing on the forward slope, the bulk of the cannonballs were swallowed up in the mud. The men of the 92nd lay still, obediently waiting the order to rise up, aware that the barrage was the prelude to an enemy advance.

The Duke of Wellington, accompanied by his staff and escort, was everywhere, seemingly indifferent and immune to the furious assault of the French guns. Murdo glimpsed him more than once, a few yards to the rear of the 92nd's line, giving his orders with so studied a calm that Murdo wondered whether the great man was really without fear. Certainly he appeared to bear a charmed life; members of his staff, exposed as they were to the fire, fell, killed or wounded—but he did not flinch. A tall, impressive figure, in dark blue coat and cape, and his hat, with its four small cockades, clamped down over his ears, he sat his great chestnut charger impassively, a spyglass to his eye, occasionally gesturing one of his aides to his side when an order had not been carried out to his satisfaction.

The men did not cheer him—he was known to dislike any acclamation—but his mere presence put fresh heart into them, and Murdo, like the others, felt elated by the sight of such arrogant and confident leadership. The Duke had moved on when, with startling suddenness, the guns fell silent.

The silence lasted for only a few minutes, and it was broken by the reverberating roll of drums, beating the *pas de charge,* and thousands of men's voices could be heard cheering and crying out *"Vive l'Empereur!"*

They came through the eddying cannon smoke, rank upon rank of them, led by officers on horseback brandishing their swords, flanked by cavalry, and with a line of skirmishers spread out in front. And there were many thousands of them, advancing in massed columns, not deployed in line, their trumpets blaring and their drums continuing to beat out the rhythm that had sent them on their way.

The Walloons, to the right, who had taken cruel punishment from the prolonged gun barrage, wavered and broke, flying in terror through the Scottish-held line, in which their flight had left a yawning gap. The divisional commander, Sir Thomas Picton—an incongruous figure, in civilian frock coat and top hat, for his uniform had been lost in transit—waved the Scots to their feet, to fill the gap and advance to meet the enemy. He shouted "Fire!" at the pitch of his lungs, and, at forty paces, three thousand muskets opened on the advancing French, who, supposing the line broken and endeavoring to deploy, were taken by surprise when the Highlanders rose from their concealment to meet the advance.

"Charge, my lads! Charge! Give 'em the bayonet! Hurrah!" General Picton ordered. It was the last order he ever gave, for as the Scots moved forward, a musket ball hit him in the head and he died instantly, slumped over the neck of his frightened horse.

The charge completed the havoc that first volley of musketry had begun. The French, hampered by their own formation and not yet deployed into line, started to break. Murdo, carried forward down the slope by the press of the line behind him, lunged and slashed with his bayonet, urged on by the regiment's pipers and all fear gone.

From somewhere behind him, he heard the thud of horses' hooves and his own sergeant yelling to the men to let the cavalry through. And then they came on, at the gallop, leaping the hedge at the road border and thundering down the hill on their great gray horses—the North British Dragoons, the famous Greys, the sunlight glinting on their drawn sabers as they tore after the Royals and the Inniskillings, who had been ordered to charge before them.

Murdo heard some of the men about him cheering them on. "Go at them, the Greys!" they yelled. "Scotland forever!"

He saw several of his comrades seize the cavalrymen's leathers and run with them at the French column, and without a second thought he followed their example. They cut through the column and spurred on, across the valley bottom, scattering the French infantry and sabering them as they ran.

"Charge the guns!" an officer cried.

Murdo, breathless, looked up at the rider whose stirrup leather he was holding, and the man, an officer, flashed him a brief smile and thrust his hand away.

"You've come far enough, lad!" he shouted above the din and spurred on, leaving him where he was. Murdo started to yell out in protest, and then something struck him on the side of the head and he fell helplessly into the churned-up mud, as a squadron of French lancers galloped over him, trampling him into the ground.

He felt himself falling into a dark and seemingly bottomless pit; and as the darkness closed about him, he saw again the face of the Belgian serving girl who had come to him in his dream. This time her face was quite clear and distinct, and she was holding out her hand to take his.

CHAPTER IV

Darkness had fallen when George De Lancey struggled back to painful consciousness. The guns, he realized, were silent. No drums beat the French *pas de charge*, no Highland pipes skirled in defiant answer; there was no tramp of marching feet; there were no echoing cheers nor, in his immediate vicinity, any movement that he could discern. Only the cries and groans of wounded and dying men told him that he was not alone.

The battle, it seemed, was over; but whether it had ended in victory or defeat for the Duke of Wellington's hard-pressed command he had no means of knowing. His last memory had been of his regiment's death-defying charge. With a thudding heart he recalled how they had thundered down the slope, crashing through the advancing French columns, meeting the cuirassiers and sabering them aside, carrying off two of Bonaparte's eagle standards as they went and then plunging among the enemy gunners and driving them from their guns.

It had been wildly exhilarating, a moment of supreme courage and triumph, led recklessly by the colonel, Sir William Ponsonby, who, his arms hanging uselessly by his sides, had galloped at their head with his reins in his teeth. But . . . George drew in his breath sharply. They had charged too far and too fast; the men, on blown horses, had failed to rally, and a counterattack by fresh cuirassiers and a regiment of lancers had scattered them in sad disarray. He had fought back against half a dozen of them, expecting to die at their hands, he remembered, but . . . that was all he did remember.

He had no recollection of the blow that had felled him, only of finding himself on the ground, the breath choked from his lungs and the agonizing sensation of a great weight pressing down on him, which made all movement impossible. His horse, the gallant animal that had carried him so well . . . With a smothered exclamation, he attempted to sit up. The weight was still there, holding his legs as if in a vise, but he contrived, with infinite effort, to raise himself on his elbows.

The dim shape of his dead horse met his shocked gaze, and he saw that the poor creature had fallen across the lower part of his body and bled to death where it lay, crushing both his legs beneath it. His legs were numb, quite devoid of feeling, and try as he might, he found that he could not free them.

The struggle to do so exhausted him, and recognizing its futility, George let himself fall back. There were glowing bivouac fires below and to his right, he saw for the first time, but they were too far out of earshot for anyone to hear him, if he were to shout for help. In any event, those who sat round them—the survivors of the battle—were seemingly too exhausted to heed the cries even of those wounded who were close at hand. There would be no help for any of them until daylight came and wagons could be brought up, to convey the ones who still lived to field hospitals and the surgeons' care.

The women would come then, also—the devoted women, classed as camp followers, who accompanied their men to war— but in darkness, few of them would dare to venture onto the battlefield. Experience in the Peninsular campaign had taught him that, but—

George tensed, hearing a cry from somewhere, uncomfortably close behind him. The cry was muffled, cut abruptly short, but it froze him into immobility; he was all too well aware of what it portended. Looters were abroad, those evil, unprincipled men, of whom every army had its share, even his own. They searched the bodies of the dead for anything of value—and did not always confine their predatory searching to the dead. The man who had cried out had clearly been alive—but he was silent now, and . . . Twisting with difficulty onto his side, George saw three shadowy figures moving toward him.

They came slowly, pausing frequently to bend over the heaped corpses in the hope of plunder, then moving on with knapsacks bulging, not speaking to one another or working in concert, each keeping his distance and warily conscious of the presence of the others. They were Prussians, in dark uniforms, and all three were armed, the moonlight glinting on their unsheathed bayonets.

George felt bile rise in his throat. Was he to lie there helplessly and let them rob him, strip him of his uniform and, perhaps, if he resisted, plunge a bayonet into him to silence him? There had been a pistol in his saddle holster, if only he could find it. It was loaded but not primed; still, if he could find it, the threat of the weapon might serve to hold them off. He dragged himself into a half-sitting position and, ignoring the stabbing pain in his chest, groped blindly in search of the pistol holster. His fingers closed about it, but before he could withdraw the pistol, one of the Prussians reached him and a big hand grasped him by the shoulder and flung him back.

A guttural voice, speaking in German, warned him to lie still, and then, roughly, the man started to go through his pockets, exclaiming with satisfaction when he found George's fob watch and the handful of coins he had on him. Not content with his find, the Prussian used his bayonet to hack off first one and then the other of his victim's epaulets, and, adding insult to injury, he leaned across with the intention of purloining the holstered pistol.

Humiliated and sick with frustration, George struck out at him with a clenched fist, heedless of the consequences. The man stumbled and then, recovering his balance, raised his bayonet, swearing angrily. He would have used it without compunction; but providentially, before he could do so, two British soldiers appeared on the scene—kilted Highlanders, George saw, with heartfelt relief. He called out to them urgently, careless of whether or not they, too, were looters, and the Prussian threw himself on the muddy ground beside him, feigning death, his sack of booty abandoned.

"For God's sake!" George gritted. "Help me! I'm a Greys officer and that swine's not dead. He's just robbed me."

The two Highlanders responded swiftly. One of them buried his bayonet in the Prussian's back; the other picked up the discarded sack and tipped its contents onto the ground.

"If you'll show me which are your belongings, sir," he offered politely, "I'll restore them to you."

"You may keep them," George returned, "if you will lift my horse off me."

The soldier grinned at him. He was young and passably good-looking, with a bloodstained bandage about his head and another, equally stained, wrapped around his left arm. "We'll do what we can," he promised. "But as you may see, sir, I'm somewhat weakened from loss of blood." He turned to his companion, a black-browed, heavily built man who was engaged in wiping the Prussian's blood from his bayonet. "Hey, Jamie—this officer's one of ours; he's a Scots Grey, and he's wanting us to lift the horse off him. Will you lend a hand?"

"Aye, that I will," the black-browed Highlander agreed readily. He thrust the butt of his musket beneath the dead horse's quarters and heaved. "Grab the officer's shoulders, Murdo, an' pull him free."

Between them they dragged him free, and George gasped out his thanks. His legs were completely numb and he could not attempt to stand up, but his relief was overwhelming. The soldier addressed as Murdo assisted him to sit up and, with persistent honesty, again asked him to identify his own possessions, an oddly mocking smile curving his lips.

"I'd not want you to think ill of us, sir."

"I do not," George answered him. "You saved my life." He took back the watch and his pistol, leaving the coins. "Keep these and the rest as your reward. The swine who stole them has no use for them now."

The two soldiers exchanged glances, and the older, without argument, stuffed the Prussian's plunder back into the haversack.

"We'll need tae get back tae our company bivouac," he said, avoiding George's gaze and, it was evident, anxious to forestall any request he might make for further help. "There'll be roll call at first light, and we'll be in trouble if we're no' there tae answer our names. Are ye coming, Murdo?"

"I'll be after you," the younger man answered. "But I'll just see this officer on his feet and find a horse for him. Don't wait on me."

He was as good as his word. The horse he found was a French cavalry charger, apparently unwounded; and as he helped George to clamber stiffly onto its back, he answered his anxious question as to the outcome of the battle.

Victory, it seemed, was theirs. Bonaparte had sent his famous Old Guard against them, in a last, despairing attempt to stem the tide, but even that had failed. Blücher's Prussians had joined in the battle at the eleventh hour—a fact he should have deduced from the presence of the looters, George reflected wryly, had his mind been capable of reasoned thought.

"The scurvy frogs are in full retreat," his informant added. "And the cavalry after them, with Boney running for his life! We won, sir, have no doubt on that score." He glanced uncertainly up at George's face, as if to assess his ability to sit a horse, and asked with concern, "Are you in much pain, sir? Will you be able to find your way to a dressing station on your own? They've been sending the walking wounded back up the hill to the village they call Mont St. Jean, and it's not far, sir."

Both his legs were still without feeling, and it was taking all his dwindling strength to hold himself upright in the saddle, but . . . the young Gordon had done enough and was clearly anxious to return to his regiment's bivouac before his absence was noted. George managed a wan smile.

The boy had an educated voice, he realized, with little trace of accent, and his manners were unusual for a mere private soldier. But for all that, it seemed probable that he and his black-browed comrade had been in quest of plunder when they had appeared, so fortunately, in time to save him from the murderous Prussian. They would run the risk of severe punishment, should their conduct become known to their officers; and to permit that to happen would, George decided, be a very poor return for the help they had given him.

He gathered up his borrowed charger's reins and said quietly, "I shall manage well enough if I take it slowly. Cut along back to your bivouac, my lad, before your sergeant finds you gone. I'm grateful to you, and I shall not forget your timely aid. Perhaps you would care to tell me your name?"

The young soldier hesitated and then shook his bandaged head. "I'd as soon not, sir, if you'll not take it amiss. As to gratitude"— he smiled with a sudden, unexpected warmth—"I fancy 'tis I who am in your debt, if the truth were known. Godspeed, sir!"

George did not dispute his statement, although its meaning was far from clear. He set off across the littered battlefield, trying vainly to shut his eyes to the hideous scenes of carnage all about him, which the swiftly lightening sky was now beginning to reveal. Wrecked guns and overturned limbers were everywhere, mutilated horses and the piled bodies of the dead, and already the stink of corruption was rising with the morning mist, causing him to retch violently and attempt to quicken his pace.

He would go first to the Duke's headquarters, he told himself, to ask for news of his brother, and after that—provided William had come through unscathed—he would seek a surgeon's aid. His legs were bruised and badly twisted, but he did not think any bones were broken. He would let them bandage and probably bleed him, and then report back to his regiment.

Or to what, after that disastrous charge on the French guns, was left of it . . .

Murdo watched the Greys officer until he was lost to sight. He had made up his mind, long before the encounter with him, that he would desert at the first opportunity that presented itself. Indeed, he had slipped away from the bivouac some hours before, supposing his stealthy departure to be unobserved; but to his dismay, his front rank man, Jamie Duncan, had seen and followed him.

Jamie had misunderstood the reason and, taking it for granted that he was out to plunder French corpses, had stuck to him like a leech.

"We'll not be touching oor ain men," his companion had stipulated. "Only the frogs . . . and maybe some o' those bluidy Walloons who did not run fast enough when the frogs came at us the first time."

They had kept to that resolve, Murdo recalled, and—conscious that he would need money, if he were to get himself safely back to England—he had not flinched from plundering the enemy dead. And he had amassed a fair sum, mostly in gold. . . . He jingled the sporran girt about his waist. Jamie could keep what they had taken from the Prussian; he, Murdo, had sufficient without that, and by giving Jamie the laden knapsack, he had freed himself of his front man's leechlike presence at last. Jamie Duncan was a Peninsular veteran; it would never enter his head to desert the regiment, and for all his predatory instincts, he would have no sympathy for any man who thought of doing so.

But *he* was going to; and no one, least of all Jamie, was going to be given the chance to stop him. He had had enough and, God knew, had done enough today—aye, and at Quatre Bras, too—to uphold the regiment's honor and its fighting reputation, as well as his own pride.

Murdo expelled his breath in a long-drawn sigh. He would have to plan carefully. The last thing he wanted was to run the risk of being recognized and arrested as a deserter; and in order to avoid that risk, he would have to rid himself of his conspicuous uniform. Or—his dark brows contracted in deep thought—he would have to exchange it for one in which he would not be recognized . . . and there were plenty to choose from, lying all around him. Civilian clothes would be better, undoubtedly; and he could probably obtain those in Brussels . . . old Père Lachasse, with whom he had been billeted, would supply him with what he needed for two or three of the French gold coins in his sporran.

He had only to get to Brussels and his wounds would provide him with justification for his return . . . for the Lord's sake—he could probably contrive to make the journey in one of the wagons that, quite soon, would be picking up the wounded.

With this thought, some of the tension drained out of him and he moved on, looking about him cautiously and keeping well away from the other shadowy figures that, in increasing numbers, were also moving about the battlefield. The new arrivals were peasants from nearby villages, and, Murdo saw with disgust, not content with robbing the dead of their valuables, they were stripping them of their clothing and carrying off great bundles of jackets, breeches, underwear, and boots, leaving the bodies naked.

It was one thing for soldiers who had taken part in the battle to loot their fallen foes, he thought indignantly, but quite another for these rapacious civilians to enrich themselves in ghoulish desecration of the dead. Filled with unreasoning anger, he drove one group away at the point of his bayonet, heedless of the curses they hurled back at him as they fled, dropping their spoils. The bodies they had been stripping were British; and like Jamie Duncan, he drew the line at robbing British dead.

Swearing under his breath, Murdo was about to move away when a faint voice called out to him to wait.

"Please . . . you are a British soldier, a Highlander. In God's name, help me!"

The voice, coming from one of the stripped bodies, was an English voice, tremulous with despair. Its owner lay shivering on the muddy, blood-soaked ground, surrounded by a veritable mound of corpses, a few of whom were still clad in British scarlet. Moved to pity, Murdo responded to the tremulous appeal, his own quest momentarily forgotten. He dropped to his knees in the mud and, as gently as he could, slipped an arm behind the naked shoulders and raised the man's head to a level with his own.

"Water," the wounded man pleaded. "I am parched, I . . . have you any water?"

He had filled his canteen the previous evening from a flooded ditch, after he and most of his company had slaked their thirst and washed their smoke-grimed faces in its slimy depths, Murdo recalled. But, foul though it was, he had nothing else to offer, and he uncapped the canteen and, in silence, held it to the man's lips.

"Oh, God bless you!" the weak voice exclaimed. "I've lain all night thinking of little else but my need for water. And when those peasants came, I hoped that they would take pity on me. Instead, they stripped me of my uniform and handled me so sorely that the bleeding has started again."

He gestured to his legs, and Murdo saw, with horror, that only the stump of the right one remained. The left, twisted beneath him, was reduced to bloody pulp, the foot crushed and adhering by no more than a few sinews to the shattered ankle bone. Someone—probably the wounded man himself—had fashioned a rough tourniquet with a kerchief about the left thigh, but it was now dislodged, and as the poor fellow had said, the bleeding had restarted.

Mardo put out a hand, with the intention of tightening the scrap of silk, but the wounded man shook his head.

"It will be of no use, my friend. I was struck by a roundshot when we formed square to repulse the last attack the French cavalry made on us. That was many hours ago, and I have lain here ever since. I have not much longer to live."

"Oh, come," Murdo began, seeking to cheer him. "The wagons will be here soon, and the women of your regiment. I will carry you to them; I—"

"No!" The interruption was whispered, but it brooked no dissent. "I have no legs. There is no hope for me, and I have made my peace with God. But if you would be of service to me, good fellow that you are, there is one thing you can do. Recover my uniform . . . those heartless fiends let their plunder fall, did they not, when you drove them off?"

"Aye," Murdo confirmed, his throat tight. Time was passing, he knew, and with daylight his chance of escape would be lessened. But he could not leave this poor, mutilated young soldier to die alone, and . . . He glanced over to where the marauding peasants had let their booty slip from their hands. It would be easy enough to accede to the poor devil's request; and among the jumbled red coats there might be one to fit himself, one that he could exchange for his own. He rose slowly to his feet. "What regiment are you serving in?" he asked.

"The Fifty-second. My name is Dean, Michael Dean, commissioned as an ensign." There was pride in the halting voice. "I joined only two days ago from England, but they entrusted me with the regimental color, until I was wounded and Ensign Leeke relieved me of it. I . . . please"—the young officer attempted vainly to sit up—"will you . . . will you make sure that it is *my* tunic you bring? There are letters in the pocket—the breast pocket—and my commission. Even if they stole my money, they will have left those, perhaps. Our . . . our facings are buff."

"I'll find it," Murdo promised.

"*Buff* facings," the ensign repeated. He was shivering so violently that Murdo, before leaving him, divested himself of his knapsack and spread the sodden blanket it contained across the chilled white body. Dean, he thought pityingly, was about his own age, and he was dying, after—what had he said?—after only two days with his regiment. He had probably joined straight from some exclusive public school, his commission purchased for him by an indulgent father.

"There," Murdo urged. "Bide quiet. I'll not be long." He added "sir," and then smiled grimly to himself. Much good his rank had done the unfortunate lad; even if, by some miracle, he were to survive, what would life hold for him, without his legs? Murdo placed his knapsack carefully under the boy's lolling head and went in search of the tunic.

"There is a letter," Ensign Dean called after him. "In my . . . breast pocket. It is addressed to Miss Amelia Archer. She is . . . on the London stage. The Haymarket Theater, I . . . I should be greatly beholden if you . . . would arrange for its delivery. I . . ." He choked and his voice trailed off into ominous silence. Murdo hesitated, worried, and then walked on.

The tunic was easily found, for it was the only scarlet garment among a pile of French blue. In the breast pocket was, as the wounded officer had claimed, a bundle of papers, including a folded square of heavy vellum—obviously his commission, which, for some reason known only to himself, he had chosen to bring with him to war.

Murdo picked up the tunic and with it a pair of dark blue overalls, so heavily stained with blood that their ownership could be in no doubt. A black rain cape, which seemed most likely to meet his own needs, he also added to the tunic and trousers, rolling all three garments into a bundle and tucking this under his arm.

More and more people were moving about amid the carnage, he saw. Two Prussian officers on horseback passed uncomfortably close, but they paid him scant heed; and the peasant looters, although their number had increased, seemed to be congregating down the slope. Some sudden pistol shots startled him momentarily, but on looking round he realized that a pair of British farriers were putting a merciful end to injured horses, the two men's tall, plumed bearskin headgear identifying them as members of the Scots Greys.

The horses, he thought wryly, were in this respect more fortunate than many of the human battle casualties, for whom, as yet, no succor had come. He stumbled back through the churned-up mud, compelled to ignore several pitiful cries for water from some of the French wounded, and, breathing hard, laid the bundle of recovered clothing beside its owner.

"I have your tunic, Mr. Dean," he announced. "And your papers are still in the pocket. Your money, too, I believe, and . . ." There was no reply, and bending closer, he found himself staring into the blank and sightless eyes of the man he had sought to help. Ensign Michael Dean had, like the mutilated horses, found merciful release from his pain. He no longer had need of his tunic or his commission, and the letter to Miss Amelia Archer would have to be delivered to her at the Haymarket Theater by a stranger, as he had requested.

But if he no longer had need of his tunic or his commission . . . Murdo swallowed hard, feeling his throat tighten. *He* could put both to good use—they would serve to get him to Brussels without fear of being recognized or risking arrest as a deserter. Officers went wherever they wanted to go, without question, and . . . He fumbled in the pocket of the scarlet tunic, finding the thick sheet of precious vellum. In the dim light he could not read it, but he was in no doubt as to its authenticity. Commissions could be sold; an ensign's commission in the 52nd Regiment would be worth several hundred pounds, and . . . Scarcely aware of what he was doing, he thrust the document back into the pocket and started to unbutton his own tunic.

Michael Dean's fitted him well enough; he donned it, and looking round to make sure there was no one near enough to observe him, he unbuckled his kilt. The overalls, caked with mud and blood, made a poor substitute, but, retching, he dragged them on. His own boots would have to do; he could not bring himself to hunt for Dean's beneath the blanket with which he had covered him. And . . . suddenly sick with pity, he knew he could not leave the dead man naked, as he had found him, without dignity and without any identity, perhaps to be mistaken for a Frenchman.

Kneeling, he wrapped his Gordon kilt about the limp body, with its hideously shattered legs, and—after removing the gold coins from it—he strapped on the sporran. His discarded tunic came next.

"It's maybe not a fair exchange, laddie," he said aloud. "And the facings are yellow. But if they bury you with the Ninety-second's dead, it will be with honor, have no fear of that. And I'll deliver your letter, as you asked."

The sightless eyes held no reproach, but Murdo, meeting their gaze, expelled his breath in a lengthy sigh. The carts were coming at last, he saw, and the women. And day was breaking. . . .

He got heavily to his feet and went unsteadily to meet them. One of the women, recognizing his insignia, took him gently by the arm and led him to a waiting carriage.

"This is for officers," she told him. "My lady has sent it for that purpose. And you are in need of a surgeon's care, I think."

The carriage, laden with wounded Guards officers, survivors of their regiment's heroic defense of the farm at Hougoumont, set off at a brisk pace for Brussels. Fearing their questions, Murdo feigned sleep; but his companions appeared to be utterly spent, and they showed little disposition to converse with him or even with each other. All he could glean from their few laconic remarks was the fact that the château at Hougoumont, in which their wounded had been placed, had been set ablaze by the sustained fire of the enemy howitzers, and that most of the wounded had burned alive. In the face of their bitter anguish, he felt ashamed.

Long lines of wagons and unsprung country carts, crammed with the injured of both sides, slowed the carriage to a walk, and it was over three hours before they reached the outskirts of the city and, leaving the mainstream of traffic, finally drew up in front of a tall, imposing private residence, set in an extensive garden.

Servants helped them to alight, and Murdo was conducted to an improvised hospital ward. There, after he had been assisted into a bed made up with sweet-smelling linen sheets and given tea, a Belgian surgeon inserted a dozen stitches into his lacerated scalp, dressed his arm, and bled him.

"Ze tyrant Napoleon is fleeing toward Paris," the surgeon told him, with unashamed relief. "And ze noble Duc de Vellington leads our army in pursuit . . . already he is at Nivelles. *Bruxelles est sauvé*—eet has been for us a great victory, *n'est-ce pas?*"

Murdo could find no words to answer him, and the white-haired Belgian smiled at him reassuringly. "Do not concern yourself, my brave young friend. For you, ze battle is over. Zat arm, eet is badly infected, but I shall try to save eet for you." He waved to an orderly carrying a jar of leeches and added kindly, "*Restez tranquil, mon cher!* Soon you vill be on your way back to England."

For Magdalen De Lancey, also, the battle was over. And with it, she thought with infinite sadness, her life, for without her beloved husband to share it with her, she no longer wanted to exist.

She looked down at his pale, dead face, seeing it through a mist of tears. Ever since the battle had ended, she had endured an agonizing nightmare of suspense, alternating between hope and despair. At first, when the casualty lists had reached Antwerp and her husband's name had been on none of them, she had dared to believe that her premonition of disaster had been false. But then the wife of a senior staff officer had sent for her to tell her that she had copied out the list and had deliberately omitted Sir William De Lancey's name, in the hope of being able to break the news to her in private that, although alive, he was desperately wounded.

In a fever of anxiety, Magdalen had set off for Brussels in the carriage, only to be caught up in the throng of wagons, mounted and walking wounded, civilian refugees, and deserters, coming from and going to the battlefield. When she was scarcely halfway, an officer had recognized her and stopped the carriage.

"Alas, Lady De Lancey, I have bad news for you," he had said; and she had listened, in numb silence, to what he had to tell her of the manner in which her husband had been struck down.

"He was with the Duke throughout the whole day and both of them seeming to bear a charmed life, for they were always under fire. Almost at the end, a roundshot bounded up off the ground, ma'am, and struck him in the back. I saw him flung from his horse. He lay for a moment, then jumped up and fell again. All of us dismounted, and the Duke went to him and held his hand. Your husband begged us not to move him, but at that time we feared that we might be compelled to retreat, and the Duke would not have him left in our rear. He was given into the care of some soldiers, who were ordered to carry him in a blanket to the dressing station at Mont St. Jean. His cousin, Colonel Barclay, went with him and—"

"Then," Magdalen had burst out, unable to contain herself, "he is alive and I must go to him!"

But the officer had shaken his head sadly. "When the battle was over and our victory assured, the Duke sent me to Mont St. Jean to inquire for him. He was not there and must, I am deeply distressed to say, be presumed dead. You had best return to Antwerp, ma'am. If there should be any more news of Sir William, it will be brought to you."

She had done as he had advised, Magdalen recalled, but with a heavy heart, still uncertain of the truth, for the staff officer had admitted that his body had not been found. In her small room at the back of the Grand Laboureur Inn, she had shut herself in, refusing to see callers or receive condolences, yielding at last to her bitter grief.

But then George had come—William's staunch, devoted brother, who had been best man at their wedding. He had limped in, clearly in pain and supporting himself with the aid of a walking stick, to give her the news for which she had scarcely dared to pray.

"He is alive, Magdalen—alive and asking for you—in a peasant's cottage near Waterloo. Pack what you need and I will take you to him at once."

Hope had been born again. With her heart too full for any words, Magdalen had ordered the carriage once more and, with George's comforting presence to sustain her, had resumed her interrupted journey to Brussels and the battlefield. Meeting the same mournful traffic, she had fretted at the delay and then been sickened by the stench of corruption, which grew stronger as they neared the once green slopes on which so many thousands of men—British, Dutch, German, and French—had fought and died.

In a cramped hovel not far from the village of Waterloo, Magdalen's search came to an end. Her husband was there, conscious and overjoyed to see her, and for a little while she had believed that his life might be saved. The surgeons who called each day to bleed him and dress his wound encouraged this hope, and she had carried out their instructions with meticulous care. She had applied the leeches they prescribed, gladly sacrificed her petticoats to make bandages for him, bargained with the owners of the hovel for eggs and poultry and milk, and patiently fed him with a spoon when he admitted to being too weak to help himself.

They had talked, as she sat beside him, her hand clasped in his, making eager plans for their future together—a future which, they had both fervently agreed, should see the end of his military career. He would sell his commission, William had promised her, and they would settle in Scotland and farm, or even—and he had smiled as he had said it, Magdalen remembered with a pang—seek a new life, as George intended to do, in the colony of New South Wales, by all accounts now a land of peace and plenty under General Macquarie's governorship.

"They have crossed the mountain barrier that hemmed them in for so many years, General Grosse was telling me," he had said. "And found vast acres of splendid pastureland, which is to be had virtually for the asking. That's where we'll go, my darling; that's where we'll live, turning our swords into plowshares and counting this wound of mine as a blessing because it will have brought us there."

But instead his wound had brought him death, Magdalen thought, with despairing bitterness. She dropped on her knees beside the rough wooden bed on which he lay so still and cold, and let the tears overwhelm her.

They had had just six days together since she had gone to him, and she had known, even before the surgeons had warned her, that the seeming improvement in his condition could not last. Day by day she had watched him grow weaker, had seen the light in his eyes slowly fade, his sleep become deeper and longer, until finally she had known that it was her duty to tell him that the surgeons could hold out no hope of his recovery.

William had taken the disclosure with his usual calm courage. "I had begun to suspect it," he had confessed. "My only regret is that it means I must leave you, my sweet love. But you mustn't grieve—I beg you not to grieve for me, Magdalen. We had so much in so short a time, but it was worth everything in the world to me . . . remember that, darling. You made me so very happy, and I can go proudly, because you have loved me and because you have been my wife."

For one more day he had clung obstinately to life, but he was in constant pain and sank frequently into unconsciousness. Magdalen had not left him; she had crouched beside his bed, holding his hand in hers and not relinquishing it even when one of the army chaplains came wearily from Mont St. Jean to join them both in prayer.

That night, he had roused himself to ask her to lie in the narrow bed beside him, and—she bit back a sob. She had lain with him, clasping his pain-wracked body to her, pillowing his head on her breast, and had fallen into an exhausted sleep.

On waking, she had found him dead, and had been reproaching herself ever since because she had slept. . . .

George touched her arm. "Magdalen," he said gently. "Let me take you back to Brussels. You can do no more here, my dear. And after the funeral I will escort you to Scotland."

"Or to New South Wales?" Magdalen challenged sadly. "That was where my poor darling wanted to take me—did you know that?"

"I heard him speak of it," George confirmed. "Our swords were to be turned into plowshares, were they not?" He raised her to her feet. "Well, mine shall be, that I swear. I have seen enough of war!"

CHAPTER V

Mrs. Jeffrey emerged onto the *Kangaroo*'s quarterdeck and, her shawl wrapped closely about her, motioned Kate O'Malley to her side. Outwardly submissive but inwardly rebellious, Kate obeyed the gesture and fell into step beside her for their accustomed evening promenade.

The captain's wife acknowledged the master's raised hat with a stiff little bow. Standing orders ordained that, save in extreme emergency, the duty watch must not intrude at this time, and Kate found herself smiling at the efforts the men made to efface themselves. The young cadet, Nigel Harris, was halfway up the mainmast shrouds, a telescope to his eye; taken by surprise at Mrs. Jeffrey's sudden appearance, he froze, mindful of his captain's command and afraid to descend to the deck while she was there.

Mrs. Jeffrey, however, was disposed to be gracious. The long voyage was almost over, they were in sight of the New South Wales coastline, and, with an imperiously raised hand, she beckoned the boy to her, as she had previously summoned Kate.

"And what can you see with your glass, Mr. Harris?" she inquired.

Cadet Harris reddened under her scrutiny. "Not a great deal, ma'am," he confessed. "Tall cliffs, with trees growing right to their summits and surf breaking beneath. Sandy coves here and there, and some fine long beaches, but that's about all, ma'am."

"No human beings?" Mrs. Jeffrey persisted. "No aborigines or signs of habitation?"

The boy shook his head. "Not that I could see, ma'am."

"Then your eyesight cannot be good," Mrs. Jeffrey reproached him. "Because even without a telescope, *I* can see smoke rising over there . . . look to your right, boy! That surely suggests the presence of native inhabitants, does it not?"

Harris's color deepened and spread, as he followed the direction of her pointing finger.

"I . . . I suppose it does, ma'am."

"Unless you are more observant," the captain's wife said severely, "you cannot expect Captain Jeffrey to recommend that you should be rated as a midshipman, can you? I feel sure," she added repressively, giving the boy his official rating, "that your dear parents will be most disappointed in you if you remain a captain's servant on the ship's books for another six months, Mr. Harris."

"Yes, ma'am," the youngster acknowledged miserably. His humiliation complete, he scarcely noticed Kate's quick smile of sympathy, though it was not lost on Mrs. Jeffrey. She dismissed him and, giving Kate a withering look, gestured to her to resume their brisk pacing of the deck.

"That boy is a lazy little rapscallion," she observed. "Possibly his kind may be tolerated in the American Navy, but not in ships of the Royal Navy, I can assure you."

Kate preserved a tight-lipped silence. She ought by now to have become accustomed to Mrs. Jeffrey's taunts, she told herself. She had been the recipient of so many of them since leaving Capetown, when Captain Jeffrey's avowed intention had been to put her ashore there. It had been thwarted by Rick Tempest's obstinacy and her own frail state of health, she was aware. The authorities at the Cape had not been eager to receive her; a penniless young woman, victim of a shipwreck, who was still barely able to walk, had evidently seemed to them liable to become a public charge, and the medical officer sent to examine her had reported unfavorably on her condition.

But it had been Rick's assurance that his sisters in Sydney would accept responsibility for her care that had, in the end, caused the *Kangaroo*'s commander to change his mind and permit her to continue the voyage. He had two sisters, Rick had told her—Abigail, who was married to one of the colony's most substantial landowners, and Lucy, who was widowed. There was also a lady he referred to, with deep affection, as Frances Spence, whose hospitality was boundless and who, it appeared, was related to him by marriage.

"You will be inundated with invitations, I give you my word,"
Rick had promised, and . . . Conscious of a tightening of her
throat, Kate quickened her pace. Rick, she saw, had come on deck;
he was not due on watch for another hour or more, but he had
formed the habit of appearing during the daily promenades that,
morning and evening, Mrs. Jeffrey insisted that they should take
together. Because of her oppressive chaperonage, however, the
officers could do little more than doff their hats and give her good
day; since her recovery, Kate reflected with bitterness, Mrs.
Jeffrey had seen to it that she was kept a virtual prisoner, confined
to her cabin for long hours at a time and—apart from the few
occasions when she was invited to the captain's spacious quarters
to dine—having her meals served to her there by the old cook,
Billy Onslow, or by little Jackie Ross, the loblolly boy, who was
not quite eleven years old.

"You must understand, Miss O'Malley," Mrs. Jeffrey had
warned her, more than once, "that passengers of the female sex are
carried in British ships of war only on sufferance. On long
voyages, their presence—unless it is carefully restricted—is liable
to prove unsettling to the seamen and perhaps also to some of the
junior officers, thus impairing their efficiency."

"And," she had added, a wagging finger emphasizing her
words, "even the commander's wife is in duty bound to adhere
strictly to his orders in this respect. As you will no doubt have
observed, I am no exception, Miss O'Malley. You are young and
unmarried, and so, whatever may have been the custom on board
your late father's ship, it will behoove you to follow my example
whilst you are a passenger on board *this* ship."

But Mrs. Jeffrey had, it seemed, forgotten—or she had chosen
to forget—the days immediately following her rescue from the icy
waters of the South Atlantic, Kate thought, still smarting under the
implied insult to her father. Because the captain's wife had
considered it beneath her dignity to play the role of sick nurse,
Rick Tempest and the old cook had been left to care for her as best
they might. True, none of them had expected her to live, yet
Rick . . . She caught her breath, meeting his gaze with a
spontaneously warm smile. Then, as Mrs. Jeffrey's hand closed
about her arm, her smile swiftly faded and she responded to his
salute with a decorously bowed head, and moved on obediently.

It was absurd, in the circumstances, when she owed him her life and when she now knew to what lengths he had gone to bring her back from the frozen limbo in which he had found her. Old Billy Onslow had let his tongue run away with him; he had hinted, he had told her a rambling story about how some poor young midshipman, in a condition similar to her own, had been brought back to life; and then, when she had demanded to know the truth, the old man had told her.

She had made no mention of it to Rick, of course, sensing that it would embarrass him beyond bearing. But all the same, she was glad that she knew, although how she would ever repay the debt she owed him was at present impossible to decide. The more so, in the face of Mrs. Jeffrey's determination to confine their meetings to a twice-daily promenade on deck, in her own forbidding company.

Kate sighed. Perhaps, she reflected, even if she were unable to repay Rick himself, she could lessen her indebtedness to him by serving his sisters in some way. Perhaps as a governess to their children—she had received a good classical education, and her mother, until her untimely death two years ago, had seen to it that she acquired a full range of domestic skills. And there were children, she knew. Rick had made mention several times of his sister Abigail's stepdaughters and of her small son, Dickon, who was apparently deaf and dumb, poor little soul. He . . .

"You will have had no experience of a penal colony, of course, Miss O'Malley. . . ."

Mrs. Jeffrey was talking—expounding what, of late, had become her favorite theme—and Kate made an effort to listen, out of courtesy, rather than interest.

"No, Mrs. Jeffrey," she acknowledged. "I have not."

"It is said that the Governor, General Macquarie, is greatly biased in favor of what are termed emancipists. That is to say, in favor of persons who came out as convicted felons and have since been pardoned for their crimes or who have served their sentences," the captain's wife went on, her tone openly critical. "Naturally, his officers and civil officials do not mix with such riffraff, although I have been led to believe that, on occasion, their kind do attend certain Government House functions, at Governor Macquarie's invitation."

Kate said nothing. This topic was one that Captain and Mrs. Jeffrey frequently discussed during dinner. She had heard their

views when she had dined with them and was aware that both
intended to restrict their acquaintance to those inhabitants of
Sydney whom they considered their social equals, whether or not,
by so doing, they incurred the Governor's displeasure.

"No lady of breeding," Mrs. Jeffrey said, with firm conviction,
"should be expected to sit at table with former thieves and
robbers. And still less with women of easy virtue, no matter if they
have since reformed. I could not bring myself to countenance such
a state of affairs, and I cannot imagine how the Governor's wife
can do so, however charitably inclined she may be."

Kate maintained a wary silence. Mrs. Jeffrey wanted only a
passive audience; she had said all this before, in different words, if
seldom with more indignation, and any attempt to argue only
provoked her to icy disapproval. Yet the picture Rick Tempest had
drawn of the colony had been one of a different hue. Not that he
had told her much—and, of late, there had been no opportunity to
question him on the subject—but what she had heard had been
sufficient to persuade her to keep an open mind.

It would be time enough, she told herself, to wait until the
Kangaroo reached Sydney Town and she was in a position to judge
for herself and to choose, on their own merits, those with whom
she could mix on mutually friendly terms, be they emancipist or
free. It was so in America; a man was accepted for what he was
and what he had achieved in American society, and the only
enemies were those who, calling themselves loyalists, had chosen
to oppose the republican cause.

Men such as George De Lancey, whose conscience had
compelled him to leave the land of his birth and fight for a king and
a country he had never seen, because that was where his family
loyalty lay.

Kate was conscious of an aching in her throat as she recalled
what had passed between them, when George had broken it to her
that he was taking ship to England. They had known each other
since childhood, had fallen in love when she had been in her early
teens, and it had never occurred to her that anything would stand in
the way of their marriage, when she was old enough to be wed.
Her parents had approved of the match. Despite the fact that the
De Lancey family estates had been taken from them following the
Declaration of Independence, George had had every prospect of
making a successful career as an attorney, and the match, even in

her father's eyes, had been a suitable one, to which exception could not be taken.

But then he had gone, with no promise that he would ever come back to Boston, only the hope that, in the dim and distant future, his return might be possible. There had been one letter, telling her that he had been commissioned into the British Army and that his regiment was in Portugal; and then war had been declared between their two countries, and all communication between them had ceased. Kate breathed an unhappy little sigh. She did not know if George was alive or dead, and he had not written again. So that . . .

Mrs. Jeffrey's voice intruded once more into her thoughts.

"It is hoped," the older woman observed disparagingly, "that you will not find, when you accept their hospitality, that Mr. Tempest's sisters are married to emancipists, Miss O'Malley. He has kept very quiet on that score, has he not? All he has ever admitted to me is that neither is at present married to an officer of the garrison. Although one, I believe, is recently widowed."

Kate could no longer contain her resentment. "It would not concern me in the least if both ladies were emancipists, Mrs. Jeffrey!" she exclaimed indignantly. "Or even if Mr. Tempest himself chanced to be one. The British courts sentence many poor souls to deportation for what we would consider minor crimes—I know because my father told me so. One of his best officers was the descendant of a whole family whom your government shipped to Virginia as convicts, and he said—"

Mrs. Jeffrey cut her short, and her tone was withering as she proceeded to dismiss Kate's argument with the contempt she obviously deemed it had invited.

"The United States Navy was ever eager to enlist our British deserters. You are an American, Miss O'Malley, and your standards are overly liberal, I fear. That is the fault of your upbringing, which is why I have been endeavoring to warn you of the situation you will find when you disembark." Kate again tried to speak, but she was waved imperiously to silence. "Disregard my advice if you will, but I do assure you, it will be to your cost if you expect to find acceptance in the *respectable* society of Sydney. However, I will say no more on the subject, since clearly you do not understand and I should only be wasting my breath were I to do so. Let us go below."

She turned majestically in the direction of the stern hatchway, and Kate, still seething with resentment, followed reluctantly at her heels. Rick Tempest moved, without haste, to intercept them. Smiling, he put one foot on the hatch coaming, effectively barring Mrs. Jeffrey's way. Whether he had heard her earlier outburst Kate had no means of telling, but he met her swift, questioning glance with a broadening of his smile.

To the captain's wife he said courteously, "Are you going below already, Mrs. Jeffrey? It is a fine evening, and if this wind holds, we shall be in sight of the entrance to Port Jackson within the hour. The harbor is a sight not to be missed, ma'am."

"In my eyes, it is unlikely to match an English harbor," Mrs. Jeffrey returned without enthusiasm. "Or bear comparison with Portsmouth or Spithead. In any event, are we not to come to an anchor outside, to await the pilot cutter and the hours of daylight?"

Rick shook his head. "Not if this wind holds . . . the captain can take her straight in if he wishes. Sydney Cove is barely six miles from the Heads—we can make the anchorage before dark, ma'am."

"I had not supposed that to be the captain's intention," his wife demurred. "He is feeling a trifle unwell, Mr. Tempest, and I do not expect that he will wish to be troubled by port officials and the like until tomorrow morning at the earliest. But I will tell him what you say, in case he is desirous of changing his mind."

Mrs. Jeffrey put a plump white hand on Rick's extended arm, and he helped her over the hatch coaming. She descended to the lower deck, and Kate, from force of habit, made to follow her—but Rick's whispered "Wait just for a moment, if you please," brought her to a halt.

"What is it, Mr. Tempest?" she asked, puzzled.

He eyed her gravely. "I am already in receipt of the captain's orders, Miss O'Malley. We shall anchor off the Heads overnight, fair wind or foul . . . and possibly for longer, since in his present state of health, Captain Jeffrey does not feel inclined to put himself about."

"Oh, I see. But . . ." Kate was still puzzled. "Why did you tell Mrs. Jeffrey quite the opposite?"

Rick's gravity evaporated, and he gave her a boyishly impish grin. "I hoped it might afford me an opportunity to speak with you alone. Of late there have been few opportunities, have there?"

"Not many," Kate conceded. "I've been told that passengers of the female sex are carried only on sufferance in British warships, because their presence may prove unsettling to the ship's company. And," she added, echoing his smile, "that it might impair the efficiency of the junior officers."

Rick laughed with genuine amusement and offered her his arm. "I am a senior officer, and it is my watch below, so my state of efficiency is of no consequence. Shall we walk a little? I have something to say to you that . . . oh, damme, Kate O'Malley! Something I've had to keep bottled up for the deuce of a long time. But I must say it before you go ashore."

Kate accepted the proffered arm and fell into step beside him. The old master, Silas Crabbe, who had the watch, tactfully moved out of earshot, taking young Harris with him and vacating the weather side of the quarterdeck, which normally he was required to do only when the captain came on deck. Rick raised two fingers to his hat in acknowledgment of the compliment and led the way to the larboard rail. From there the New South Wales shore could be seen very clearly, and he pointed out landmarks. Despite his insistence on talking to her alone, he seemed oddly reluctant to voice whatever it was that he had intended to say.

Kate waited, without impatience. Had he, she wondered, overheard Mrs. Jeffrey's lecture on the subject of Sydney society and her suggestion that his sisters might have married emancipists? Certainly he must have heard what his captain's wife had said to poor young Nigel Harris, for, indicating the billowing clouds of smoke now rising above the treetops, he said flatly, "Those are not campfires, you know."

"Aren't they, Mr. Tempest?"

"No. That is a bush fire—probably started by the blackfellows to drive out game. It doesn't matter much in that particular area; but where there are farms and settlements, with growing crops, a bush fire can spell ruin. The trees are eucalypts—gum trees—and tinder-dry, and the fires get out of hand very rapidly. It's quite a hazardous life, farming in the colony. The settlers face drought, as well as fires. The best wheat-growing area is in the Hawkesbury River valley, and the danger there is from flooding."

"But you are going to leave the navy and become a farmer, are you not?" Kate questioned, recalling what he had once told her.

"Yes," Rick confirmed. "That's my intention. I made application to the Colonial Office for a grant of land before we sailed. It's five years since I was here, and much has changed, I've been told . . . changed for the better, I mean. There is now a road over the Blue Mountains, with rich grazing land—thousands of acres of it—about to be opened up for settlement. I want to take my grant there and stock it with sheep, and I've my prize money to put toward the purchase of stock. It will have disadvantages, of course—distance from Sydney and isolation, no buildings or fences, and probably others I haven't thought of, but . . . it will be a challenge."

"Yes," Kate agreed, "it will; it is bound to be. But—" An inkling of what he was leading up to caused her to draw in her breath sharply. "Mr. Tempest, I should go below. I—"

"Hear me out, will you, please?" Rick pleaded. He turned to look down at her, his blue eyes very bright and expectant. "There is an alternative. I could buy an existing farm near Windsor or Richmond or on the Nepean River, nearer to civilization, which was my original intention. In fact, I tried to buy one from friends before I came back from America. I wrote to them, but—"

"But you would rather accept the challenge of the new land beyond the mountains, would you not?" Kate hazarded. The look in his eyes alarmed her and set her heart beating wildly. It was too soon, she thought, too soon to make any decision as to the future before they had even set foot in Sydney Town.

"I'd only want to accept it if you will face it with me," Rick said. His hands reached out for hers, and grasping them firmly, he drew her closer to him, careless of who might be watching them. "Miss O'Malley . . . Kate, will you do me the honor of becoming my wife? Not at once," he qualified, as if she had spoken her thoughts aloud. "You will want time, and so shall I. At present I have no home to offer you. But if I may take you ashore and introduce you as my affianced wife, it will free you from the—oh, the devil take it!—from the irksome guardianship of my commander's lady, which has kept me from even talking to you since we left the Cape. My sister Abigail will, I promise you, be a much more understanding chaperone."

Kate glanced down at their linked hands, and then, flushed and uncertain, she looked up into his eyes. She owed Rick Tempest so much, she reminded herself—so much that, only a short while ago, she had been wondering how she could repay him. But for him, she would have died, frozen to death, as her father and all his ship's company had been, in their open boat. It was thanks to Rick's concern, his compassion, that she was standing here now, on the *Kangaroo*'s quarterdeck, at the end of a long and perilous voyage, almost in sight of their destination.

True, she was not in love with him; despite all that had happened, he was still virtually a stranger to her in so many respects, but . . . there could be no doubting his good qualities or his charm. And George De Lancey had gone out of her life, the possibility that she would ever see or hear from him again was remote. For all she knew, George might now be married and making a new life for himself in England . . . or he could have been killed in action in Spain.

Rick's strong brown fingers tightened about hers. "I'd give you time, Kate," he promised gently. "All the time you need, my sweet girl. But I want the right to care for you—that is all I am asking of you now, all I can say. Except that . . . dearest Kate, except that I've fallen in love with you! Throughout my waking hours I think of you and pine just for the sight of you, even if it is only walking the deck with Mrs. Jeffrey, which God knows is frustration enough! But in my dreams, Kate . . . ah, that is very different. In my dreams you belong to me."

His hands were trembling, Kate realized, and once again her heart quickened its beat.

"I should be proud to belong to you, Rick," she answered, meaning it. "And proud to be your wife when—when the time comes."

There on the open deck, he could do no more than raise each of her hands, in turn, to his lips, but it was enough, and Kate felt a swift upsurge of happiness as her eyes rested on his bent fair head. Then he resumed his headgear, and from the open hatchway, Mrs. Jeffrey called out to her in scandalized tones.

"Miss O'Malley, you should be below! You are aware of the captain's orders—come with me at once, if you please, and permit Mr. Tempest to attend to his duties."

The color leaped to Kate's cheeks, but Rick offered his arm and, when she took it, led her unhurriedly across to confront the captain's wife.

He said, smiling, "Miss O'Malley has just consented to become my wife, Mrs. Jeffrey. So with your permission, I will escort her to her cabin. Mr. Crabbe has the deck, and I am not due to relieve him for half an hour, lest this concern you. And I feel sure," he added, still in the same pleasant, unhurried voice, "that neither you nor Captain Jeffrey will take it amiss if I invite Miss O'Malley to dine in the gun room, so that we may announce our betrothal formally to my brother officers."

Bereft of words, Mrs. Jeffrey stared from one to the other of them in disbelief. Finally, with what dignity she could muster, she inclined her head and, gathering up her skirts, descended the hatchway ladder with almost indecent haste. At its foot, she recovered her composure and offered her congratulations coldly.

When she had gone, leaving the narrow passageway deserted, Rick's simulated casualness swiftly vanished.

"The others will be happy for us," he said gravely. "And, oh, my darling Kate, I love you!"

His kiss was gentle, making no demands, and he held her briefly and let her go. "We'll dine at eight-thirty, when I come off watch. After dinner I'll show you Port Jackson and the Heads, Kate, and you'll be able to see the lights of Sydney Town in the distance."

Kate watched his tall figure ascend the companion ladder and, to her own surprise, felt her eyes fill with tears.

To everything else he had given her, Rick Tempest had added his love, she told herself. She had not expected such a gift; until a few short minutes ago, she had had no inkling of his feelings. But . . . gaining the sanctuary of her own cabin, she let the canvas curtain fall behind her and dropped to her knees.

"Please God," she whispered, "let me not fail him . . . let me love him and be worthy of him."

Unbidden and, on that account, unwelcome, a sudden vision of George De Lancey's handsome face swam before her eyes. Kate closed her eyes, seeking to shut it out.

It was over, she chided herself; her first love had been a child's love, and she was no longer a child. She was a woman—a penniless young woman in a strange country, and likely to meet with hostility from those with whom her country had lately been at war. Had not the Jeffreys' attitude been proof of that? There would be others, probably, holding similar views—perhaps even the Governor himself, since he had been a soldier and, as Captain Jeffrey had told her, had fought as a young officer on American soil, and suffered defeat at American hands.

Kate thrust her knuckles into her tear-filled eyes. It was a petulant, childish gesture, and she felt ashamed. But George's face vanished, and she repeated her prayer.

CHAPTER VI

More than a little to his surprise, Rick was ordered to go ashore as soon as the *Kangaroo* dropped anchor in Sydney Cove.

He was not ill pleased by the order, since it would enable him to call on his sister Abigail sooner than he had anticipated, and he was eager to see her, after their long separation. She would, he was confident, be only too happy to offer warm hospitality to his affianced wife; and should she be absent from Sydney, there were Frances and Jasper Spence and probably his younger sister, Lucy, to fill the breach.

He dealt briskly with the few formalities required by the port naval officer's clerk and the harbor master and walked the short distance from the government wharf to Government House, to make the official report of his ship's arrival.

The secretary, John Campbell, received him, shaking his hand in friendly recognition.

"Welcome back to Sydney, Mr. Tempest. His Excellency, I am sure, will be delighted to see you and to meet your captain in due course. He's unwell, you say?"

"Yes, sir. A trifle under the weather," Rick confirmed. "Captain Jeffrey has his wife with him, and I am instructed to say that they will call on Their Excellencies as soon as the captain's health permits."

"There is no undue hurry," the Governor's secretary assured him. "Their Excellencies are both away at present, attending the musters at Parramatta and Windsor, and I don't expect them back until the end of the week." He gave a rueful shrug, his thin, austere face set in grave lines. "The poor Governor is being given a pretty rough passage these days, Tempest, and it distresses me to see how it worries him. He revived the Sunday musters, you know, for all convicts, including those given tickets-of-leave to work for settlers in the districts. But Marsden and Hannibal Macarthur, who are the chief magistrates in Parramatta, opposed the order strongly and at one time refused to enforce it in their district. Nicholas Bayly, Dr. Townson, and even Sir John Jamison backed them up."

"Good heavens!" Rick exclaimed. "For what reason? Musters were held in Governor King's day and Governor Bligh's."

Campbell sighed. "The reason the Reverend Samuel Marsden gives is ludicrous in the extreme. The musters, as I expect you know, are always followed by compulsory attendance at divine service. According to our senior chaplain, the vast majority attend in a state of intoxication, and they rob houses and gardens on their march to and from his church! And according to Bayly, anything that brings convicts together in large numbers and in one place is open to serious objection. So they object, although mainly, I am forced to conclude, because Dr. D'Arcy Wentworth—who has recently been appointed to superintend our police force—insists that musters are essential, if escapers are to be apprehended."

"Do many attempt to escape?" Rick asked.

"Far too many," the secretary answered glumly. "The self-styled bushrangers constitute a major problem these days. Our convict population has risen steeply. The government road and building gangs employ fewer than two thousand male convicts at the present time, whilst approaching three times that number are assigned to the service of landowners and small settlers. Those with small agricultural grants, the emancipists, lose very few; it is the large landowners, like Jamison and Bayly . . . aye, and Marsden, too, whose lax supervision leads to the escape of the laborers they employ. Without up-to-date registers, compiled at muster, it is virtually impossible to keep track of them."

John Campbell repeated his sigh. Then, as if suddenly aware that he had been lacking in hospitality, he crossed to a sideboard set with decanters and invited Rick to take a glass of Cape brandy with him.

The secretary was a tall, thin man in his early forties, who gave the impression of being considerably older. He was an accountant by profession and an expert in banking practices, and the Governor had enlisted his services at Capetown, on the way out, with a view to founding a bank in the colony. Even in the early days he had been known as one of Macquarie's staunchest supporters . . .

but, Rick reflected, as he accepted the proffered glass, it was evident that the cares of his office were beginning to weigh heavily upon John Campbell.

"Your very good health, sir," he offered, raising his glass.

Campbell thanked him. "I presume you are returning here to settle on the land, as your sister, Mrs. Dawson, mentioned the other day. . . ." He talked on, making an effort to display an interest in his caller, although clearly his thoughts were elsewhere . . . in Parramatta, probably, with his patron.

Rick nodded. He replied politely to a few general questions concerning his intentions and the *Kangaroo*'s passage out, and then, draining his glass, he prepared to take his leave.

"Do you happen to know whether my sister is in town, sir?" he inquired. "If she is, I'd like to take this opportunity to call on her."

Secretary Campbell frowned abstractedly.

"I fancy she is still here, Mr. Tempest . . . yes, I'm almost sure she is. At Mr. Jasper Spence's residence in Pitt Street. Do you know where that is, or shall I give you directions?"

"I know, thank you, sir."

"Of course, I'm forgetting—it's not so long since you left, is it?"

"Over five years," Rick pointed out. "I sailed from here on the twelfth of May, eighteen hundred and ten, on board the *Porpoise* in Admiral Bligh's convoy."

"The *Porpoise*?" Campbell's interest quickened. "You were with Commodore—that is, Admiral Bligh in the Derwent, then? That must have been an experience."

"Not one I look back on with great pleasure," Rick admitted. Indeed, he thought, that year had been the worst experience of his service career, when the leaking old *Porpoise* had skulked in the river off Hobart Town, with the deposed Governor Bligh on board with his daughter, and, on shore, a hostile Lieutenant Governor who had turned every man's hand against the ship and her passengers. He added, a trifle stiffly, "My duty was to the late Governor—and at that time, Mr. Campbell, Admiral Bligh *was* the lawful Governor. My sympathies were with him, too, and I admired him greatly."

"He was not a gentleman I took to myself," Campbell confessed. "But I applaud your loyalty, Mr. Tempest, believe me I do."

Rick bowed in acknowledgment. He tucked his cocked hat under his arm and again moved toward the door, impatient to make his call on Abigail and acquaint himself with her news in the short time he had left before returning to his ship. He wanted to take Kate ashore with as little delay as possible and free both himself and his betrothed of Mrs. Jeffrey's irksome chaperonage.

"I thank you, sir, for receiving me—" he began, but the Governor's secretary seemed not to hear him. He refilled their empty glasses and thrust Rick's into his hand.

"I've long listened to the claims of Governor Bligh's enemies," he went on, as if there had been no interruption. "They abound still in the colony, you know, and almost all of them have made their fortunes here. They accuse Bligh of everything from tyranny to peculation, and until a short while ago, I believed them. But now, God rot them, they have turned their venom on *my* Governor, and I know their accusations to be untrue! His Excellency is such a fine character, the soul of integrity, and with a keen sense of justice. He has done so much to restore the colony to order and prosperity . . . and to improve the lot of its less fortunate inhabitants, Mr. Tempest—those who have served their sentences and been pardoned. So they claim that he is autocratic and biased in favor of the emancipists!"

Campbell gulped down his brandy, his bony face flushed with indignation. "Sydney was a veritable den of iniquity when His Excellency took office, and he has changed it beyond recognition. You will observe the change, after five years, Mr. Tempest. The streets are clean and well kept, the people go about their business soberly, and everywhere fine new buildings are springing up. We have a qualified architect now—a young man named Francis Greenway, who came out here as a convict, but with Admiral Phillip's highest recommendation. He has been working under Major Gill on plans for a number of new public buildings—offices for the naval officer, a more commodious barracks for the troops, and a new jail. These have been accorded priority, but the breadth and scope of Greenway's ideas are positively inspiring. Given a few more years, I am confident that Sydney will become a truly beautiful city."

If the British Colonial Office did not scotch such grandiose plans on account of their expense, Rick thought wryly—but he made no attempt to interrupt, and the Governor's secretary talked on. A bank was envisaged, he learned, additions and repairs to Government House, a fort from which Port Jackson Harbor could be defended, new churches, a covered marketplace on the west side of Sydney Cove, and a second, for farm produce from the Hawkesbury, at Cockle Bay. Even a stone-built lighthouse on South Head . . . He managed to take his leave at last, his curiosity aroused by Secretary Campbell's enthusiasm so that, as he walked toward Pitt Street, he found himself looking about him for evidence of the changes that had already taken place.

They were there, on all sides, in the neat, white-painted houses—most now built of brick—the fenced-in gardens, and the wide, firmly surfaced streets, devoid of the livestock that, in the old days, had wandered through them at will. Flowers and colorful flowering shrubs grew in the gardens, fronting the streets, with vegetable patches relegated to the rear, and each house was numbered, each street named prominently on a wooden board.

There were larger houses, also—many of them two-story and built of local brick or stone, Rick observed—increasing in number as he approached the Tank Stream on Bridge Street. Turning left toward the more affluent residential quarter of the town, he recognized Simeon Lord's imposing dwelling, although it no longer stood out from among its neighbors, as it had once done, for many now matched it in size.

The people he encountered were sober and orderly, as Secretary Campbell had claimed they were, and apart from those in the jail gangs, it was impossible to tell, from their dress, which were convicts and which free men and women, going about their lawful business.

Skirting the Tank Stream, he could see, on the other side, the lumberyard and the government workshops, as always a hive of activity. He crossed Hunter Street and, quickening his pace, turned into Pitt Street. Here very little had changed; he recognized the pleasant, red-brick house where William Bligh had been accommodated during his brief return to the colony, and saw, outside the bungalow next door to it, a red-coated sentry on guard, denoting it an official residence—probably that of the Lieutenant Governor.

And then, turning into a flower-bordered driveway, he was on familiar ground, approaching the large, rambling house that had been a second home to him as a young midshipman. The house had been built some eight or nine years previously by Mr. Jasper

Spence, a wealthy merchant, who had come to the colony from India; Rick fondly recalled the warm welcome that had always been accorded to him by the owner and his second wife, the Irish emancipist, Frances O'Riordan.

He remembered tea on the spacious lawn, whence a view of the harbor could be obtained, and the children's voices, echoing throughout the house, for Frances Spence—herself childless—had mothered the children of countless others, had indeed helped raise his own two sisters, Abigail and Lucy.

Today, however, the house was wrapped in a brooding silence, and no excited cries reached him from the lawn. Rick halted, looking about him; seeing no one, he strode toward the door. A veranda had been built around it—a new addition—with chairs and tables set along its length and bamboo curtains, reminiscent of India, shading it from the sun. He was about to ring the doorbell when, from the shadows at the far end of the veranda, a small figure emerged to eye him uncertainly for a moment and then, with a strange, inarticulate cry, run to meet him.

"Why, Dickon!" he exclaimed in astonishment, holding out his arms. "You've grown so big I hardly knew you!"

Abigail's son—his namesake and his nephew—had been not even three years old, Rick reminded himself, when he had last seen him. The boy was deaf and dumb and, as a child, had been shy and self-effacing, imprisoned by his handicap in a world of his own where few people could reach him and fewer still were able to communicate with him. But now, the Lord be praised, he was the picture of healthy boyhood, slim and straight as a young tree and, with his dark hair and vivid blue eyes, already giving promise of exceptional good looks.

"Your mother . . ." Remembering that Dickon could lip-read, Rick held him at arm's length, articulating his words slowly. "Is she at home?"

The boy nodded vigorously and, freeing himself, ran to open the door of the house. His cry, although seemingly unintelligible, brought Abigail flying down the stairs from the upper floor.

"Oh, Rick! Dearest Rick, how wonderful to see you! We watched your ship come in but had no idea you'd be able to get ashore so soon. I wasn't even certain that it *was* your ship . . . someone told me she was the *Emu*. You must think me very remiss, but I . . . oh, truly, I am so pleased and thankful that you're here!" She hugged him, her words falling over each other in her eagerness, and Rick held her close.

"My commander is unwell, so it fell to me to pay the official call at Government House to report our arrival. And . . . I've come to request a favor of you, Abby my dear."

"Anything," she promised readily. "Anything at all. You have only to ask. But . . . we'll talk of it over tea. Dickon, tell Kate to serve tea, would you, please?" The boy nodded his understanding and sped off, and taking Rick's hand, Abigail led him into the familiar, somewhat untidy drawing room, with its wide windows looking out across the distant harbor.

She looked pale and tense, Rick noticed, and she seemed oddly distrait, brushing his request aside as if it were of no consequence. He had been looking forward with keen anticipation to telling her about Kate and his marriage plans, but . . . making an effort to hide his disappointment, he seated himself in the chair she indicated.

Abby was as beautiful as ever, he thought—perhaps even more beautiful than she had been as a young girl. Maturity had added to her fair loveliness, lent dignity to her graceful carriage, and womanly curves to her once overthin body . . . yet, despite this, she did not look well, and there was no mistaking her tension.

"Is there anything troubling you, Abby?" he asked anxiously.

"Did they not tell you at Government House?" Abigail exclaimed. "Rick, the *Kelso* is almost a month overdue!"

The *Kelso*, Rick recalled, was Jasper Spence's fine Indiaman, a vessel of over four hundred tons burden in which he and his wife sailed on trading missions to Calcutta and the Dutch islands, usually once a year.

He shook his head, and Abigail went on unhappily, "We have had reports from a Dutch ship, which arrived about two weeks ago, of a typhoon in the Java Sea. Her master said it was very severe and that he himself suffered damage, although he was only on the edge of the storm. Mr. Lord—Simeon Lord—told Tim that the *Kelso* must be presumed lost if there's no news of her during the next week. And"—she caught her breath on a sob—"Frances was on board, with Grandpa Spence, and Lucy, too . . . she had gone with them to—to recoup her health, Rick."

Rick stared at her in shocked dismay.

"Lucy, too? Oh, dear heaven, that is appalling news!"

"Yes," Abigail said bleakly. "That's why I am here, in this house, and not at Upwey with Tim. The girls are here—my stepdaughters, Julia and Dorothea—to attend school. Frances always had them in term time, and I . . . I'm standing in for her, until she returns. That is, *if* she returns . . . Oh, Rick, I'm heartbroken. Frances is—was such a special person, to me and to the girls, and Dickon simply adored her. I can't bear to think that she may be dead, drowned in that typhoon, and that we'll never see her again. And poor little Lucy, too. She was just beginning to recover from her terrible experience when that gang of escapers raided Yarramundie. I believed she was over the worst, but now this! I—" She broke off, hearing the sound of voices, and held a warning finger to her lips. "The girls are back. They don't know; I haven't told them yet. I hadn't the heart to tell them, until I was certain that the *Kelso* is lost. Don't speak of it in their presence, will you?"

"No," Rick assured her. "Of course not, Abby." Little Dickon came in, followed by the faithful Kate Lamerton, who had been his nursemaid during his babyhood. Both set to work to arrange the contents of Kate's tray on a long, low table by the window, and they provided a welcome distraction, Dickon's oddly high-pitched laughter and Kate's subdued chuckles testifying to the continued warmth of their relationship.

"Kate received her pardon from Governor Bligh before Dickon was born," Abigail whispered, behind her hand. "And she could have married long ago; she had scores of willing suitors. But"— she smiled, as the cheerful, buxom woman left the room, with Dickon clinging to her hand—"she has stayed for all these years for Dickon's sake, and truly, Rick, I thank God that she has, for I shouldn't know what to do without her. Yet they sent her out here as a convicted felon, sentenced to seven years; and when she first came out, they obliged her to work in that terrible female factory at Parramatta, carding wool!"

"Dickon does you both credit," Rick said, with sincerity. "He's grown into a splendid-looking lad, Abby, and he seems to be as happy as the day is long."

"He is," Abigail confirmed. Tears started to her eyes, and she turned her head away, adding softly, "I think his father would have loved him as much as I do."

He had never known his sister's first husband, Rick thought, searching his memory, and Abigail, to the best of his recollection, had never spoken of him, but . . .

The appearance of the two Dawson girls saved him from the necessity of a reply. They came in, chattering excitedly, and then fell silent at the sight of him; Kate Lamerton, it seemed, had not informed them that their stepmother was entertaining a visitor.

"You remember my brother, Richard Tempest?" Abigail prompted, smiling. "He has just arrived on board His Majesty's ship *Kangaroo*. This is Julia, Rick, who is sixteen and in her last year at school. And Dorothea, whom we all call Dodie, is three years younger."

They were pretty girls, Rick realized, as he shook hands with each in turn. Julia, slim and dark, recovered swiftly from her surprise at his unexpected presence, and started to make polite conversation with him, fluttering her long, dark lashes with a coquettishness that secretly amused him. Dorothea, shorter and plumper than her elder sister and with an impish smile, brought the cup of tea her stepmother had poured for him, plied him with cake, and spoke hardly at all.

Watching and listening, Rick found himself wondering what his Kate would make of them, and then recalled that he had not yet broached the subject of Kate's accommodation or, indeed, told Abigail of his betrothal.

"Abby, my dear," he began, when Julia came at last to the end of a glowing account of Sydney's most recent race meeting. "I mentioned that I—"

"That you wanted to ask a favor of me," Abigail put in contritely. "Dearest Rick, in all the excitement of our reunion, I completely forgot to ask you what it was. But I fancy I can guess. . . . You are leaving the navy and your ship and you want somewhere to live. That is what you plan to do, is it not? You will stay here now and take a land grant?"

"Yes, that is my intention," Rick confirmed. "But I also intend to marry, and—"

"Marry?" Abigail exclaimed. "Oh, but I'm delighted! Who is she, Rick? A girl you knew here? Someone *we* know?"

The two Dawson girls were regarding him wide-eyed, and Rick smiled at them. "No, not anyone you know. Her name is Kate O'Malley, and she's at present languishing on board the *Kangaroo*. She is an American, the sole survivor of the wreck of her father's ship in the South Atlantic. We picked her up from an open boat, well nigh frozen to death. . . ." He went into brief details, and saw Abigail's eyes again fill with tears. She was thinking of Lucy, he knew, and of Frances and Jasper Spence, and he put out his hand to take hers. "You will love her, I am sure, Abby, and think me the luckiest man in the world."

"I am sure I shall, Rick. And . . . we will make her welcome, of course, won't we?" Abigail turned to appeal to the two girls. Dorothea nodded vigorously, and Julia, after a momentary hesitation, said with a certain look of warmth, "Of course we will . . . even if she's American."

"When will you bring her here?" Abigail asked. "Tonight or tomorrow?"

"Tomorrow," Rick decided. "If that is convenient for you."

"This is a big house, Rick. There is plenty of room for us to put both of you up."

"I cannot leave the ship until my relief takes over my duties. And"—Rick was smiling broadly—"since my relief is not yet aware that Their Lordships have granted him a commission, that may take some time. The poor fellow has waited long enough for his commission, heaven knows."

Abigail drew in her breath sharply. "You don't mean Justin Broome? Has the Admiralty granted *him* a commission?"

"Yes—and most deservedly. He—"

Julia interrupted, with asperity, "But Justin Broome is a currency kid—his parents were convicts!"

"Emancipists, Julia," Abigail corrected. "And most highly regarded, both of them. His father served with distinction in the war with France, you know, and with Captain Flinders."

"And Justin married Mrs. Macquarie's maid," Julia retorted scornfully. "No doubt the Governor will appoint him a magistrate now, and you will tell us that we must acknowledge him, when we pass him in the street!" She held out her hand to Dorothea. "Come, Dodie, let us go into the garden before our stepmother takes me to task for being an exclusionist!"

Dorothea started to object, but Abigail waved them both away. When the door closed behind them, she said wryly, "I fear I made a grave error in sending them to Mrs. Jones's Academy, which opened recently in Castlereagh Street. They are being *taught* to be illiberal there, and Julia is becoming typical of what we now call the exclusionist clique. And I took them away from the Forty-sixth's school for officers' children because I feared precisely that! It is not easy, playing the stepmother to girls of their age, Rick, and I'm not making a good hand of it, I'm afraid. Alex is turning out better, but then, he attends Mr. Fulton's school in Windsor, and as I expect you remember, the Reverend Fulton is a most excellent teacher and a very good man. And he says he will take Dickon later on, if I can teach him to read."

Abigail poured him a second cup of tea and sipped thoughtfully at her own.

"You've made up your mind to become a farmer, Rick?"

"Yes," Rick asserted. "So long as Kate is agreeable. If she's not, then I might take a leaf out of Justin's book and buy a small trading brig and ply for hire. He made a living at it, so there's no reason why I should not, is there?"

"Does your Kate realize the sort of life she will be leading, if you settle on the land?" Abigail pursued. "This year we've had a severe drought, and Tim has gone nearly out of his mind with worry. His horse breeding has prospered, thank heaven, but he's lost sheep and cattle at Upwey; and at Jenny Hawley's old place, Long Wrekin, the wheat crop was a dismal failure and lambing a disaster. Poor Tim, he works so hard! The one bright spot in a terrible season has been the success of the vineyard he started, at Grandpa Spence's property at Portland."

Rick's brows rose. "Has he gone in for making wine?"

Abigail smiled. "Yes, indeed he has. Hannibal Macarthur bought the Schaffer vineyard at Subiaco Creek on the Parramatta River, after he married Governor King's daughter, and he expanded it, with excellent results. That was what gave Tim the idea. Grandpa Spence was willing to invest money in the venture, and now it's paying dividends. Tim is very proud of the results . . . he employs forty men and has built a pressing house, cellars, and a large workshop, so that it is virtually self-supporting. You might do worse than follow his example yourself, Rick."

Rick shrugged. "I can't see myself as a—what is it called?—a vigneron, Abby. I want land in the new country, beyond Bathurst. I fancy trying my hand as a grazier."

"The Governor has not opened the new land up for settlement yet," Abigail pointed out. "Oh, he says he will, but . . . it will be very isolated, if you're planning to take a young wife there. And you would have to build on it before you could take her with you."

"Yes, I know. But Kate will be equal to it. She is . . . oh, Abby, she is a most courageous girl! Full of Yankee spunk, quite apart from being lovely to look at. I'm sure you will approve of my choice when you get to know her."

Abigail's expression softened. "You are very much in love with her, are you not?"

"Yes," Rick answered simply. "I worship the ground she treads on." He was conscious of a warm glow as he said it. God in heaven, he thought, recalling the clumsiness of his proposal and the time it had taken him to nerve himself to make it, he was indeed the luckiest man on earth because Kate O'Malley had consented to wed him!

"We shall have to address her as Katie," Abigail said, "to distinguish her from our other Kate. You don't think she will mind, do you?"

"Her father called her Katie, she told me, so I'm sure she won't." Rick glanced at the window, now suffused with the warm red glow of the sunset. "I must get back to the ship, Abby. But I'll bring Kate—Katie—ashore at about noon, if that will suit you. She has no baggage—everything she possessed went down with her father's ship. Mrs. Jeffrey lent her a few garments, but she will want to return those, so perhaps you could help her to replenish her wardrobe when you have time?"

Abigail set down her cup and rose. "Gladly, Rick. Julia can help, too—she has impeccable taste—and there is a profusion of dress material in the traders' stores. Silks from India and China, muslins from England, and quite good woolen cloth from the female factory, though the colors are somewhat drab. And—" Her expression changed. "Oh, dear, I was just going to say that darling Frances would make them up for her, and then I remembered. . . . Oh, Rick, I pray that the *Kelso* will return safely!"

"Amen to that," Rick said gravely. He took his sister's arm, and she walked with him into the hall, lifting her cheek for his kiss when they reached the door.

"There's so much I have omitted to tell you," she said apologetically. "Things I ought to have warned you about—all the feuds, the differences, the unseemly squabbles that seem to be an inescapable part of life in the colony now. The Governor's policy to aid the emancipists to reestablish themselves is at the root of it, I'm afraid."

Rick's mouth tightened. "So I have gathered, in the few short hours I've spent on shore," he said flatly. "But you are a supporter of the Governor, are you not?"

"Governor Macquarie is a Christian gentleman," Abigail answered, without hesitation. "And the best Governor this colony has ever had. Tim and I both support him wholeheartedly. I admit that I used to have doubts concerning the manner in which he and Mrs. Macquarie permitted certain emancipists the freedom of Government House, but then I began to realize that those he entertained there were as good—and socially quite as acceptable— as the so-called exclusionists. And then there was Frances . . . *she* was an emancipist, after all, was she not? I love her, Rick! And poor Jenny Hawley, too—Justin's mother. Tim was inconsolable when he heard of her death."

"Jenny Hawley's dead?" Rick was stunned.

"Yes, she died early this year. At Bathurst, when she was on her way to see the new land. Justin has a grant there, and—"

"Has he, by Jove! I thought you said it was not yet opened for settlement?"

"Justin was with the party that found a way over the Blue Mountains," Abigail supplied. "And he helped with the road building and surveying. The Governor granted him eight hundred acres on the Lachlan River, and it is exceptionally good grazing land, according to Tim."

Rick pursed his lips in a silent whistle. "Don't tell me that Justin's become a farmer?"

Abigail smilingly denied it. "No, he still has that small sailing vessel he built . . . the *Flinders;* and if you are worrying about your relief, Rick, he should be back here fairly soon—he took Tim to Upwey ten days ago. And as to his land, I think he is looking for a manager or a partner to run it for him." She stood on tiptoe to kiss Rick again. "I'm delaying you with my chatter, and there will be time to talk now, will there not? All the time in the world! *Au revoir,* Rick dear, and I shall look forward to making Miss O'Malley's acquaintance tomorrow morning."

Rick thanked her and took his leave.

In the garden, little Dickon was playing quietly by himself, seemingly absorbed in whatever it was that he was doing. He did not look up; but the two girls, who had been engaged in the leisurely pursuit of a white-feathered shuttlecock, abandoned their game and came running across the well-kept grass of the front lawn to join him.

"Are you going back to your ship?" Julia wanted to know.

"For the time being I am, yes," Rick confirmed. "But I shall be bringing Miss O'Malley here tomorrow."

Dorothea clasped her small, plump hands in delight, but Julia said, with deliberate offensiveness, "How awkward that her name is Kate. Suppose I call out to Kate Lamerton to serve me with tea or to brush my hair—will *your* Kate imagine I'm calling her? How shall I address her, Rick, so as to avoid confusion?"

"As Miss O'Malley," Rick answered icily. "And I'll thank you to mind your manners in her presence, Julia. And for good measure," he added, "you should address me as Uncle Richard until I give you permission to do otherwise."

He waved to Dickon and Dorothea and, leaving Julia visibly deflated, set off for the wharf and his waiting boat.

CHAPTER VII

George De Lancey stood on the deck of the transport *Conway*, moodily watching as the first boatload of convicts came alongside. All were from Cork Jail, all were heavily fettered, and all wore the same expression of sullen defiance as, prompted none too gently by the warders who had accompanied them, they clambered awkwardly up the accommodation ladder and vanished into the bowels of the ship.

Halting beside him, the *Conway*'s master, red-faced and grossly corpulent, observed contemptuously, "Your fellow passengers, Mr. De Lancey . . . scurvy Irish traitors and rebels, the lot of 'em! A turbulent, desperate, and dangerous set o' men, the head jailer warned me last night, to be handled with extreme care."

"Is that so, Captain Barlow?" George returned, his tone cold. He had taken an intense dislike to the master since boarding the *Conway* at Portsmouth and wished that, in his eagerness to leave England, he had not taken passage in the first available ship but had waited, to make his choice with more care.

The *Conway* was large enough, her passenger accommodation spacious, but she was filthy and ill found, her officers, from the master down, loudmouthed and uncouth, her crew sullen and lacking in discipline—clearly, George had decided, the sweepings of the docks, discarded and set ashore by other ships.

He frowned, hoping to discourage the master's confidences, but Barlow ignored the warning signs.

"One 'undred an' seventy-two male convicts," he went on. "Dangerous as they come, an' how many bloody sojers am I given to guard the scum? Just twenty-five, an' some 'arf-baked young ensign, who's kept my gig waiting for over an hour 'cause he ain't ready to come aboard! I ask you, Mr. De Lancey, is that any way to treat a ship's master?"

"Presumably you've experienced similar treatment on your other voyages?" George suggested, his tone still cold. He made to move away, but the master followed him.

"I never made no voyage to Botany Bay with convicts before," he admitted glumly. "Nearest I come to this kind o' thing was when I was first mate o' the *Mercury*, ten years since. Ivory Coast to the West Indies was her run, but 'twas black ivory she carried. Slaves, Mr. De Lancey," he added, with a leer, when George said nothing. "But they didn't give us no trouble. Any that tried to got put over the side, see? An' no questions asked—we was paid for the ones we delivered in healthy condition." He broke off to growl an order to the third mate, a weedy youth, with long, straggling hair, on which his faded peaked cap sat oddly askew.

The young man stared at him openmouthed, and then, with a subdued "Aye, aye, sir," he shambled off to the forward accommodation ladder, displaying no haste.

"Get a move on, mister!" the master shouted after him. "I want them chain cables rigged on the prison deck right away! An' the leg-irons passed through 'em, understand?"

George had not heard the initial order, but there was no mistaking the implications of the second. He rounded on Barlow in angry disgust.

"For God's sake, man, you're not in a slaver now! These are white men . . . surely you don't intend to keep them in chains below deck?"

"They're bloody Irish rebels, like I told you," the *Conway*'s master defended. "An' what I *don't* intend is to give 'em a chance to organize a mutiny. They'll be let out if they behave themselves, never you worry, Mr. De Lancey. Huh!" He gestured to an oared boat, making its way out to them from the quay. "His High an' Mightiness Ensign Dean's decided to join us at last!"

A lone, scarlet-jacketed figure was seated in the sternsheets, George saw. The boat—the master's gig—was low in the water, evidently heavily laden, and under the sluggish efforts of the men at the oars, it moved slowly.

"Irish whiskey," Barlow said, with a smirk. "Or what they call poteen. I reckon to make a small profit on the stuff when it's unloaded in Botany Bay. They say the inhabitants o' the colony are cryin' out for liquor an' that they'll sell their benighted souls for it." He added, flushing under George's disdainful glance, "Hell an' set fire, Mr. De Lancey, we ain't all lawyers an' judges an' heroes o' Waterloo like yourself, with government appointments an' grants o' land waitin' on us! I have to show a profit on this voyage, or my owners'll want to know the reason why I ain't done so. Carryin' government stores at five quid a ton don't allow no profit, an' how far d'you suppose eighteen quid a head for each convict goes, when the scum'll eat their heads off, given half a chance?"

He shrugged his portly shoulders and, to George's relief, moved ponderously over to the rail, whence he could observe the approaching boat and, speaking trumpet to his lips, bawl instructions to the coxswain.

To avoid further contact with him, George limped across to the taffrail and, standing with his back turned to the activity below the entryport, stared out across the cold, gray expanse of the Cove of Cork to the huddled rooftops of the city beyond.

It was all good and fine, he reflected wryly, for Captain Barlow to speak with evident envy of his future prospects in the colony of New South Wales. On paper, no doubt, they appeared bright enough. The Colonial Office had welcomed his application, had agreed to defray the cost of his passage, and had granted him a license to practice law throughout the territory now officially to be designated Australia.

He was to be appointed, at the Governor's discretion, a judge of the colony's supreme court, should his services in this capacity be required. Alternatively he might set up in private legal practice as a barrister—this alternative having been agreed to at his own request—and, in either case, was to be allocated up to one thousand acres of land free of quitrent, its situation to be subject to arrangement with the government surveyor and the approval of the Governor.

Much, George thought, was likely to depend on the Governor's discretion, and General Lachlan Macquarie was, to him, an unknown quantity. He was, George had heard, highly regarded by those who did know him, but because he had served for so long in India and on the staff, only one officer whom George had encountered had claimed to know him well. And he had said, "Lachlan Macquarie is an upright, high-principled Scotsman, possessed of great administrative skill and deeply religious. But . . . he is a Highland Scot. He'll use his power paternally, as a Highland chieftain does, and he'll tolerate no opposition. Those who do not understand this will regard him as an autocrat . . . so woe betide you if you cross him, George!"

George's dark brows lowered in a frown. There had been other warnings, from barristers of Lincoln's Inn and the chancery bar, concerning the two Bent brothers. Ellis Bent had gone out with the Governor, five years before, and was judge advocate to the colony. His younger brother, Jeffrey Hart Bent—also of Lincoln's Inn— had followed him out, on appointment as Australia's first civil judge, and from both had come numerous letters of complaint against General Macquarie.

Jeffrey Bent, an elderly bencher had revealed, had been expected to sit in court with onetime convicts—men who had been pardoned by previous governors—and on his refusal to do so, he had incurred the full force of the autocratic Macquarie's wrath.

"The residence the Colonial Office promised the poor fellow has not been allocated to him, and he told me, in a recent letter, that he had been compelled to move into the house occupied by Ellis and his family. And his courtroom—officially designated the Supreme Court of New South Wales—is to be within Sydney Hospital, when the building of that is completed! I fear you may regret your decision to go out there, Mr. De Lancey . . . I fear very much that you may."

He was beginning to experience a similar fear, George reflected, but it was too late to turn back now. Yet how different it might all have been if William had lived and they had gone together, he and William and lovely Magdalen. As a distinguished soldier, William would have been a man after Governor Macquarie's heart, and Magdalen . . . who could fail to love and respect Magdalen De Lancey, William's adored wife and now, sadly, his grieving widow?

After the funeral, the Duke himself had given permission for him to escort the heartbroken girl back to Scotland, George recalled. His wounds had barely healed and, in fact, still caused him considerable discomfort, and Magdalen, despite her over-whelming loss, had insisted that he remain at Dunglass, in her father's opulent castle, to recoup his strength. And she had nursed him, as devotedly as, in the mud-floored peasant's hovel at

Waterloo, she had nursed poor William, refusing to let her father's servants relieve her of even the most menial tasks.

The Allied army, led by the Duke of Wellington, had marched on, pursuing the defeated Bonaparte to Paris and the final humiliation of surrender and his second abdication and exile. For that army and for his own regiment there was now only the chore of occupation and garrison duty, and, George reminded himself, he had not regretted selling his commission and becoming once again a civilian.

It had been Magdalen who had urged him to approach the Colonial Office, to seek an interview with the Undersecretary, Henry Goulburn, in order to discuss the prospects of employment in Australia in his professional capacity.

"I can never forget, George," she had said a dozen times, "how eager my darling William was to go out there. Even when he was dying, he talked of how you would both turn your swords into plowshares and find peace and plenty in the new land beyond the mountain barrier . . . those were almost his last words to me. For his sake, you must go, even though neither he nor I can come with you. . . ."

And so . . . George sighed resignedly. He was on board this foul, ill-manned convict transport with its cargo of fettered Irish rebels, with them facing a four to five months' voyage to the other side of the world, and leaving behind him all that he had held dear during his boyhood and his adult life. Even Katie O'Malley was lost to him now, he told himself bitterly. He had written to her twice since the battle of Waterloo, but there had been no reply. Not that he had expected one, for he had, he knew, left her with no promises, save the hope that he might return to Boston when the war was over . . . and he had not attempted to go back. Worse, during the campaign in the Peninsula, he had deliberately not written to her—he had been caught up in the war, fearing, much of the time, that he would not survive it. And Katie was a charming, attractive girl; she would have had suitors galore and had almost certainly married one of them a long time ago.

In any event, it would have been difficult, if not impossible, for him to return to the United States, since his defection and the fact that he had fought on the British side in the war would have rendered him more of a traitor, in American eyes, than were the wretched Irishmen in the eyes of the British magistrates who had condemned them to exile in the penal colony of New South Wales.

Restlessly, George crossed the deck, in time to see the last of the shackled convicts being herded below. The boat that had delivered them pulled away, taking the jailers back to the shore, and the *Conway*'s gig, with its solitary passenger and the wooden casks of poteen, came alongside, the crew thankfully shipping their oars.

Captain Barlow's bellow summoned the duty watch to bestir themselves and warned them to have a care when hoisting the gig inboard. The gig's bowman hooked on to the midships chains, and the scarlet-clad commander of the military guard stepped awkwardly onto the bottom rung of the accommodation ladder. He was still only halfway up to the entryport when Barlow loosed a string of oaths in his direction, intended as a reprimand for his late arrival. The ensign lifted his head to make a low-voiced reply—which George did not catch—and then he, too, vanished from sight through the entryport.

A little over an hour later, the *Conway*'s anchor was hove up and catted, her dingy head and topsails set, and, pitching heavily under a stiff southeasterly breeze, she wallowed out of the Cove of Cork to head for the open sea.

From the dark confines of her orlop deck, above the sound of her ancient timbers' creaking, rose the heartrending cries of close to two hundred Irishmen, mourning their enforced departure from the homeland few, if any, of them would ever see again.

Murdo was frustrated and angry when he gained the sanctuary of his cabin, and unbuckling the sword that had hampered his ascent of the accommodation ladder, he flung himself full length on his bunk.

The master's unseemly reprimand, delivered at the pitch of a strong pair of lungs, had been intended to humiliate him in front of his men and, from the insolent smirk with which Sergeant Holmes had greeted him, had succeeded in doing so. Holmes was the type of old soldier he detested; a harsh disciplinarian to those who ranked beneath him but ready, given the slightest opportunity, to put his superiors at a disadvantage.

And heaven knew, Murdo thought grimly, he was finding his impersonation of Ensign Dean hard enough to carry through successfully without Holmes's provocation, which bordered on, but always fell just short of, insubordination.

Luck had been with him at first, no denying that; his sojourn at the Belgian civilian's house, after the battle of Waterloo, had been providential. He had been accepted for what he appeared to be, no awkward questions had been asked of him, and after three weeks of being cosseted and treated as a hero by the old Belgian surgeon and his staff, he had gained confidence in the playing of his new role. Even the eventual return to England had presented no problem; the old surgeon's skill had saved his arm but left him officially classed as an invalid, and he had traveled with other survivors of the battle, officers and men of a dozen different regiments, virtually all granted sick leave, since their regiments were still in France with the Allied forces.

His first move had been to purchase civilian clothes and, on a horse hired from a livery stable, make the comparatively short journey to Buck's Oak. And Nick had kept his word; the landlord of the Alton Arms had made no demur when asked for the gold nest egg held for Murdo Maclaine. He had handed over eighty-five sovereigns, having deducted ten for his services, and all Murdo had been required to do was sign a receipt for the money. On the strength of his having fought at the glorious battle that had seen the defeat of the hated Boney, the landlord had bought him drinks and given him the best room in the house, together with the news that Nick was still in the North, but expected to return very soon to his old haunts.

Almost, Murdo reflected, he had been tempted to stay and join up with Nick again, but . . . there had been some doubt as to when he would return, and there was also the fear that to remain in the country Nick had made his own might lead to recognition. A prowling constable, a turnkey from Winchester Prison, or even one of the gang's many victims might become suspicious; and besides, there had been Ensign Dean's commission. That could be sold for three or four times the amount of the nest egg; and added to the money he had taken on the battlefield of Waterloo, it would make him a rich man, free to do whatever came to mind . . . perhaps even to go out to New South Wales as a settler, instead of remaining in England, with the ever-present fear of recognition.

That idea had persisted, and he had gone to London with a view of putting it into effect and, because his conscience was troubling him on poor dead Michael Dean's account, with the intention of keeping the promise he had made and delivering the letter to Miss Amelia Archer at the Haymarket Theater.

The letter was innocuous; he had taken the precaution of reading it while he was still convalescing in Brussels. Poor young Dean had not expected to die; he had written only of his love for the delectable Amelia and of the hope that she would wait for and remain true to him, until he could come back to claim her as his own. He had mentioned the probability that his uncle might raise objections to their marriage, but the letter had ended with a defiant promise that nothing, "not even Uncle John Maitland," should stand in their way.

There had been no other clue to the uncle's identity or address, and Murdo had worried a little on that account, uncertain whether word of the sale of Dean's commission might somehow reach his ears. But he had delivered the letter, finding Amelia Archer as beautiful as he had imagined from the fervor of her lover's protestations, and had then suffered disillusionment. Far from remaining true to him, the young actress had taken another lover, and . . . Murdo smiled grimly to himself. Dean's supplanter had been present, in Amelia's dressing room, and she had denied all knowledge of Michael Dean's existence, assuring him that the letter must be intended for someone else and refusing to accept it.

Her new paramour, a powerfully built young prizefighter, had proved even more unwelcoming, and, Murdo recalled, still smiling, it had taken a number of the tricks he had learned from Nick to leave him, flat on his back, in an alleyway at the rear of the theater.

Only then had Amelia Archer accepted the letter and unwillingly divulged the information that Michael Dean's parents were in India—his father a serving officer in the East India Company's cavalry—and that the uncle, Sir John Maitland, was governor of some obscure West Indian sugar island. An aged aunt, who lived in Norfolk, was apparently his only relative in England.

Feeling at last that it was safe to do so, Murdo had nerved himself to report to his regimental depot in Banbury, at the end of his allotted sick leave. The depot adjutant had proved unexpectedly helpful when, uncertain of the exact procedure, Murdo had sought his advice regarding the sale of his commission. Learning that he wanted to go out to New South Wales, the kindly fellow had suggested that, instead of selling his commission, he should seek an exchange into the 46th Regiment—currently stationed there—and had arranged the matter for him with commendable speed.

And so . . . . Murdo lay back, his head resting on his linked hands. He had been ordered to take command of a draft for the 46th Regiment of Foot and proceed to Sydney on board the transport *Conway,* his draft acting as guards over the convicts to be shipped out from Cork. His men had been transferred from other regiments doing duty in Ireland; he and Sergeant Holmes had picked them up in Waterford, marched them to Cork, and boarded the transport the previous day, and . . . Murdo smothered a weary yawn. He had dumped his baggage in his cabin and gone ashore to spend his last hours of freedom in a Cork brothel, making the excuse that he wished to bid farewell to relatives in the city.

The master's reprimand had, perhaps, been deserved, he thought, since the heady charms of a young woman named Mollie O'Brien had kept him longer than he had intended to stay, but . . . devil take the foulmouthed bastard! Barlow had no right to bawl him out in front of the draft and Sergeant Holmes, no damned right at all. As a King's commissioned officer, Murdo told himself—no longer doubting his claim to the rank—he would make it abundantly clear that he would take no insolence from anyone, least of all from the master of an old tub like the *Conway.*

He was a cabin-class passenger, along with some others on whom, as yet, he had not set eyes. But they would be civilians—settlers, in all probability, and doubtless not even gentlemen. He had nothing to fear from them. . . . He yawned mightily and, yielding to his weariness, let his heavy lids fall.

A steward roused him, what seemed only a few minutes later, with the information that the evening meal was being served in the cuddy.

"If you're wanting any liquor with your meals, sir," the man said, "I've a fair stock—whiskey, brandy, madeira, an' a few French wines. It's usual for passengers to order at the start o' the voyage—paying in advance, sir, if you please—an' I keep the stock, labeled with your name, Mr. Dean, sir."

Murdo grunted and sat up, rubbing the sleep from his eyes. He struck a bargain with the steward, noticing with disapproval the fellow's stained white jacket and slovenly appearance. But he was helpful enough, finding a fresh shirt in his valise and, as Murdo stripped off his creased jacket in order to don it, taking the jacket away to press it, and bringing shaving water and towels to enable him to make himself presentable.

He said, when he returned with the jacket, "There's only one other gentleman in the cuddy, apart from yourself, sir. A Mr. De Lancey . . . a lawyer, seemingly, though from the cut o' his jib, I'd say he's been in the army. Cavalry officer, if I'm any judge, an' a very pleasant gentleman."

Who had doubtless paid more than he himself had done for his stock of liquor, Murdo thought cynically, to earn such approbation.

He inquired, buttoning his jacket, "Who else messes in the cuddy? The master?"

The steward shook his grizzled head. "Oh, no, sir. Cap'n Barlow has his meals in his own cabin. The mate, Mr. Fry, and the second, Mr. Lawrence—they do, an' the surgeon, Dr. Shea. But you'll not be seein' much o' him."

"Oh, why not?"

"You'll find out, sir," the steward answered with a thin smile. "Er . . . my name's Lewis. If you're wanting anything, you've only to tell me. And now, sir, if you're ready . . . the cuddy's on this deck aft. I've kept your dinner hot for you."

He led the way, and Murdo entered the stern cabin at his heels. It was filled with a smoky haze, and the dinner table was deserted—the four occupants all seated round the bar at its far end, with pipes going and glasses beside them. A slight, bald man in a faded blue uniform looked up indifferently. His face wore a hectic flush, and he returned Murdo's greeting in a slurred voice and without warmth, before picking up his glass and draining it thirstily. He pushed the empty glass across the bar counter to be refilled and observed, more to himself than by way of introduction, "Barnabas Luther Shea, Surgeon."

The two seated on his far side, evidently the ship's officers Lewis had mentioned, Fry and Lawrence, rose almost in unison. "You are a mite late, Mr. Dean," the older of the two said, smiling. "Sleeping off your turn ashore, were you?" He winked at his companion, a bearded giant, and then excused himself. "I'm due on watch, and Charlie here has to inspect your convicts. But don't worry—your meal's been kept for you, and you can do your own inspecting tomorrow. Ah . . . permit me to introduce you to our other passenger. Mr. De Lancey, sir—Mr. Dean, who commands our military escort."

"Good evening, Dean," De Lancey said courteously. "Allow me to offer you a drink. Will a glass of Cape brandy suit you?"

Murdo stared at him; jaw dropping and momentarily bereft of words, he fought down a sick sensation in the pit of his stomach. He recognized the voice instantly; the thin, high-boned face and dark eyes registered seconds later. A cavalry officer, the steward had suggested, and, of course, he was—the Greys officer, whose horse had fallen on him after his regiment had made its magnificent charge on the French guns at Waterloo. God in heaven, what diabolical ill luck to meet this man, of all men, just when he had thought himself safe!

De Lancey was regarding him with a puzzled air, and Murdo made a despairing effort to recover his lost composure before the tall Greys officer could question him.

"Thank you, sir," he managed hoarsely. "A g-glass of brandy will suit very well."

The question came nonetheless.

"Have we met before? There's something about you . . . but you're an ensign in the Forty-sixth, are you not?"

"Yes, sir," Murdo confirmed, licking at lips that had suddenly gone dry. The bartender put a bulbous glass into his hand, and he gulped gratefully at its contents. Hoping to forestall further questions, he added, "I transferred lately from the Fifty-second."

"Ah! Then you were at Waterloo with your regiment?" De Lancey pursued. Receiving Murdo's nervous nod of assent, he went on, "So was I, with the Union Brigade Cavalry. It was a savage battle, was it not? And, as the Duke himself admitted, the nearest-run thing he ever saw in his life. I must confess I did not expect it to end in our victory."

He talked on about aspects of the battle and the awful carnage that had followed it, and Murdo listened, numb with shock, not daring to make any contribution of his own, lest he unwittingly betray himself.

"I was left for dead, pinned down by my unfortunate charger," the deep, resonant voice continued. "And I owe my life to a young Highland soldier—a man of the Ninety-second, I think, although I cannot be sure, and he would not give me his name. There were two of them, both Highlanders, and his companion addressed him as Murdo. . . ." The story unfolded, every detail of it all too familiar to the listening Murdo. "He caught a French cuirassier's horse for me," De Lancey concluded, "and set me on my way to the field hospital. I tried to trace him, but"——he spread his hands in a resigned gesture—"without success."

Murdo swallowed the last of his brandy. Emboldened by this and by his companion's concluding words, he said diffidently, "I was wounded in the last attack the French cavalry made on us." He hesitated, searching his memory, and then, as if it had come from beside him, he heard again Ensign Dean's halting, pain-racked voice. "I had joined only two days before from England, but they entrusted me with the regimental color, until I was wounded, and Ensign Leeke relieved me of it. . . ."

He did not realize that he had said the words aloud until, looking up, he saw pity in De Lancey's dark eyes.

"There must have been many like you, my poor young friend," the Greys officer said quietly. "To receive your baptism of fire in such a battle . . . God Almighty, what an experience! But you carried the Fifty-second's color—you can be proud of that."

"Yes, sir," Murdo stammered. "I—I am, I . . ." To his relief, the steward, Lewis, touched his arm.

"Your meal, Mr. Dean, sir. I can't keep it hot much longer. An' it's fresh mutton, sir, an' Irish potatoes an' greens . . . be a pity if you missed it."

Thankfully, Murdo went to seat himself at the long mess table, and although the sight of the greasy food sickened him, he took up knife and fork and forced himself to eat.

From his chair by the bar, the surgeon roused himself from what had appeared to be sleep. He hiccuped, raised his glass, and said, with mock solemnity, "Sweet Mother of God, so we have two heroes of Waterloo on board! Gentlemen, I drink to you, for 'tis all I can do. Damnation to the King's enemies, including those scurvy Irish rebels below!"

Very pointedly but in silence, George De Lancey turned his back on the slumped figure and, ignoring the toast, limped out of the cuddy, letting the heavy teak door—a relic of the old ship's days as an Indiaman—slam shut behind him.

Surgeon Shea lapsed into his former stupor, and Murdo pushed his plate away, fighting down nausea. He shook his head to the steward's offer of a plate of cold plum duff, and having allowed sufficient time for De Lancey to gain his own cabin, he followed him out.

The strains of what, at first, he took to be a hymn reached him from the prisoners' deck. Then the words came clearly, and he knew them for what they were.

> They are hanging men and women
> For the wearing of the green,
> The wearing of the green!
> But we've hearts—oh, we've hearts, boys,
> Full true enough, I ween,
> To rescue and to raise again
> Our own immortal green!

When he reached his cabin, Murdo found Sergeant Holmes waiting in the passageway, lounging easily against the bulkhead. He straightened up at Murdo's approach but did not come properly to attention.

"They're a bad lot, them convicts, sir," he said self-righteously. "But I've posted two sentries at each of the hatchways, and the Irishmen are to remain in chains and fetters overnight." He added, before Murdo could speak, "On Captain Barlow's orders, that is."

"They're not supposed to be kept in chains below deck," Murdo objected. How easily, he thought, conscious of a sense of heartfelt relief, might he himself have been making this voyage in fetters, like the unhappy Irishmen!

"That's for the master and the ship's surgeon to say, Mr. Dean," Holmes pointed out woodenly. "It's their responsibility—ours, sir, is just to stand guard over 'em and make sure none o' the swine make trouble or try to escape. And this lot'll make trouble, if we let 'em. There's a plaguey papist priest down there, and it's him leading them to sing that sodding rebel hymn. I'd like to give him a piece o' my mind . . . the wearing o' the green be damned! They should've hanged 'em, I say."

Murdo eyed him with a dislike he made no attempt to conceal, and the sergeant belatedly drew himself to attention and snapped a salute.

"You'll see for yourself, sir, when you're able to find time to make an inspection," he said, with heavy sarcasm. "I give you good night, sir."

He strode off, his very back a reproach. Murdo stared after him resentfully. Poor devils, he thought; between Barlow and Holmes, and with a drunken ship's surgeon, this voyage augured ill for the Irish rebels.

He went into his cabin and, this time, undressed before climbing into his bunk. But sleep eluded him; and faint, yet defiantly persistent, the singing from the orlop went on, and it was a long while before he was able to shut his ears to it.

CHAPTER VIII

Justin brought the *Flinders* sloop expertly in to her usual anchorage off Robert Campbell's wharf on the west side of Sydney Cove. He had a cargo of grain from the Hawkesbury and mail from Newcastle and the Hunter River settlements to deliver, but his crewman, Cookie Barnes, could take the mail sack to Sydney's new post office, and the grain could wait, he decided, until someone from the government store signified a willingness to receive it.

The new addition to his crew, a young emancipist named Elder, went forward to assist Cookie to lower the headsails, and Justin smiled approvingly. The lad had never served at sea before, but he was shaping well . . . better, by a long chalk, than Winyara, who preferred the land.

"Cookie," he called, cupping his hands about his mouth, "that canvas had better dry—show young Elder, will you?"

He was anxious to go ashore himself, as soon as he could, to make sure that Jessica was still well and in good heart. His wife was now over eight months pregnant, and he had worried about leaving her at such a time. But he had seen her cheerful wave from the garden of their small cottage on the waterfront, and the kindly Kate Lamerton—whose services as midwife had been engaged—would, he knew, keep a close eye on her.

Cookie Barnes came to stand beside him, pointing with a gnarled forefinger in the direction of a naval sloop of war on the opposite side of the anchorage.

"She's new here. Must be the *Emu*. An' the *Kelso* ain't shown up yet."

"No," Justin confirmed regretfully, thinking of Frances Spence, whom he had known and loved since his childhood. "She has not.

I'll ask Mr. Campbell if there's been any word of her." He trained his glass on the warship and let out a whoop of delight. "That's not the *Emu*, Cookie old son—she's the *Kangaroo*, Rick Tempest's ship, praise be! You remember Lieutenant Tempest, Mrs. Abigail Dawson's brother, surely?"

"Aye, 'course I remember 'im, Mr. Broome. He was out here with the old *Porpoise*. Went home with her, too, didn't he, along wi' Gov'nor Bligh." Cookie gave him a gap-toothed grin. "Didn't you tell me, a while back, as he was comin' out to settle?"

"He may have changed his mind," Justin answered, lowering his glass. "But I hope not. It will be good to have him here, in any capacity. Well—let's get the gig alongside, Cookie. You can take the mail to Isaac Nicholls, and I'll call on Mr. Campbell and then go home, in case Jessica has need of me." He started to issue instructions concerning the wheat, but Cookie interrupted him.

"I don't reckon you'll be goin' ashore yet awhile, Mr. Broome. There's a boat puttin' off from the *Kangaroo*, and looks like it's heading this way, with an officer on board." For all his years, Cookie Barnes had sharp eyes, and focusing his glass on the approaching boat, Justin saw that he was right—there was an officer in the sternsheets who looked very much like Rick Tempest.

"Could you—?" he began, but Cookie, grinning, forestalled his request.

"Sure, I can call an' tell Mrs. Broome you've bin delayed. I'll pop in on me way to Mr. Nicholls."

He was already on his way to the wharf when the *Kangaroo*'s boat came alongside, the naval crew tossing their oars smartly, and Rick—taller and broader than Justin remembered—waving a greeting from the stern.

He came on board the *Flinders* and, to Justin's astonishment, saluted him, his cocked hat raised high above his head.

"My felicitations, Lieutenant Broome! And may I say how delighted I am to see you."

"And I to see you! But . . . " Justin stared at the new arrival uncomprehendingly. "What's all this about felicitations and Lieutenant Broome, Rick? Their Lordships refused me a commission, you know that. Even poor Matt Flinders could not persuade them to reconsider my application."

"You have other friends in high places," Rick assured him, beaming. "Admiral Bligh, for one, and Captain Pasco for another . . . and Their Lordships *did* reconsider. Your commission, duly signed and sealed and dated six months ago, is reposing in my commander's safe aboard the *Kangaroo*. And furthermore, you are appointed, in my place, as her first lieutenant. My second holds only acting rank."

"Good heavens above!" Justin exclaimed, scarcely able to believe it. "I don't know what to say, Rick, truly I don't."

"Let's drink to it, anyway," Rick suggested. He held up a bottle he had brought with him, and Justin, reminded of his duty as host, led the way to his cabin. As he hunted for glasses, his guest moved about the cabin, admiring its teak bulkheads and the shining brass fittings.

"This is a snug little vessel," Rick said, with genuine appreciation. "Did you design and build her yourself?"

"I designed her, but I had some help from the crew of His Majesty's ship *Semarang* for the building. Then she was accidentally set on fire, and I had virtually to rebuild her."

"You made a fine job of her," Rick said. The two glasses found, he poured their drinks. "What shall we drink to?"

"How about the future?" Justin suggested. "Yours and mine, God willing." They drank solemnly, and he asked, "Do you really intend to quit the navy and become a settler, Rick?"

"Yes, indeed," Rick asserted, without hesitation. "As soon as you can relieve me." He grinned. "I also intend to get married, Justin—to a charming young lady we plucked from the South Atlantic on our way out. She's American, her name is Kate O'Malley, and she's at present staying with my sister Abigail at the Spences' residence. I want you to make her acquaintance at the first opportunity."

"I shall be delighted to," Justin assured him. He listened, with growing astonishment, to Rick's account of the sinking of the American ship and, with a seaman's awareness of all it had entailed, to his description of the finding of the sole survivor of the ill-fated *Providence*.

"We buried Kate's father, who was the master, and five of his ship's company at sea, under the American flag," Rick ended. "And brought Kate—whose survival was a God-given miracle— on with us, although not entirely to my captain's pleasure. He would have abandoned her in Capetown if he had had his way."

"What is he like, your captain?" Justin asked. "Between ourselves, I mean."

"Well, he is not the commander I would have chosen, had Their Lordships consulted me," Rick answered dryly. "And, between ourselves, I fear that you will not find serving under him greatly to your taste, Justin my friend. He has his wife on board, and she . . ." He spread his hands in a rueful gesture. "Mrs. Jeffrey is the daughter of a distinguished admiral—a vice admiral of the red, no less—and Captain Jeffrey commands from his cabin."

"D'you mean that he—?"

"You must draw your own conclusions. I can say no more, save that I shall be very glad to sling my hook. Indeed, I look forward with the keenest pleasure to taking Kate O'Malley to wife and settling down to farm my own land . . . and the sooner the better."

"Have you applied for a grant?" Justin questioned.

Rick nodded as he refilled their glasses. "Yes—although I haven't yet registered my claim with the government surveyor. Yarramundie was sold, of course, after my poor sister Lucy . . . You've heard that she is missing, with Jasper and Frances Spence?"

"I know that the *Kelso* is overdue. But God grant she may yet make port."

"Amen to that," Rick responded gravely. His brows furrowed thoughtfully. "Abigail tells me that you've taken an eight-hundred-acre grant beyond Bathurst and that you are looking for a partner. Would you consider me in that capacity, Justin?"

"Would I . . . oh, my word, of course I would, and most gladly!" Justin's response was enthusiastic. "Oddly enough, my young brother, Willie, suggested I should approach you. I offered him a partnership initially, but he has his hands full at Ulva, our mother's farm on the Nepean River."

"I'm no farmer, Justin," Rick reminded him. "Like you, I've been at sea all my life. But with a good foreman, I'd be willing to try. And I have six hundred pounds in prize money to contribute to the cost of stock and buildings and the like. I take it you haven't yet moved any stock up there?"

"No, none," Justin confessed. "I've been hampered by lack of capital. There's a small bark hut on the land—I have a native boy keeping an eye on things there—and the promise of some reliable

convict labor from the Bathurst settlement. It would not take long
to build a house—wooden, of course, like most of the dwellings in
Bathurst—provided you could supervise the work. But it's isolated
at present, Rick, and will continue to be, until the Governor opens
the land in that area for settlement. He says he intends to,
but . . . I think you should go up there and see it for yourself
before you decide to come into partnership with me. With the
capital you have available, you'd be entitled to a thousand acres of
your own."

"Which I could take up there, in the new area, could I not?"
Rick raised his glass, smiling. "Justin, you're a good friend and
one I trust completely. So let's drink to our future partnership, shall
we?"

"To the possibility of it," Justin amended cautiously. "You may
change your mind when you see the land, Rick. And with a new
young wife—as I mentioned, it is isolated, and—"

"But not for long," Rick argued. He drained his glass, still
smiling. "We can have a partnership agreement drawn up by a
lawyer, surely, for your protection and mine, and—"

"There is a dearth of qualified lawyers in the colony at
present," Justin put in. "And the very devil of a rumpus going on
amongst the legal fraternity. Mr. Ellis Bent, as you may recall,
came out with the Governor and serves as judge advocate. His
brother, Jeffrey, came out after him, on being appointed as a civil
judge. They've both refused to sit with emancipist magistrates or
to permit any emancipist lawyers to plead in their courts—and that
includes George Crossley."

"But Crossley was legal adviser to Governor Bligh, was he
not?" Rick said, puzzled.

Justin nodded. "Indeed he was—and to Governor King. He
practiced for twelve years out here and has the reputation of being
the best and most experienced lawyer in the colony. I don't pretend
to understand all the legal wrangling, but I can tell you that Jeffrey
Bent closed the civil court months ago and hasn't sat since, on
account of it. The only government solicitors are William Moore,
who is something of a rogue, I believe, and a man named Garling,
who's only just arrived—the Yanks captured his ship, the *Francis
and Elizabeth*, off Rio just before the war ended. So . . ." He
shrugged. "There are just two civil lawyers without a convict

record in the whole colony, and they cannot cope with the work of three courts and the Lord alone knows how many litigants."

"How many are there *with* convict records?" Rick asked curiously.

"Well, there are the two who applied for licenses to practice and who were refused by the Bents. Edward Eager, who was convicted for forgery and is still on ticket-of-leave, and a jovial fellow named Chartres, who keeps a tavern in his wife's name and has a somewhat unsavory record." Justin shook his head to the offer of a third glass of wine. "No, thanks, Rick. The sun's not yet over the yardarm, and I have to go home to my wife, who is expecting our firstborn in a week or two."

Rick offered congratulations. "How will your wife fancy your serving in the Royal Navy, Justin?"

Justin sighed. "I truly do not know. At least when plying for hire with the *Flinders* I'm a free agent—I can come and go as I please, and Sydney's my home port."

"It will be for His Majesty's sloop of war *Kangaroo*, if Captain Jeffrey has any say," Rick suggested cynically. "You'll probably see more of your wife and family as her first lieutenant than you would as master of the *Flinders*. The Jeffreys will relish the social life, and they'll be in no hurry to leave port." He consulted his fob watch. "I'll have to go, Justin. My revered captain is lunching with the Governor, and he'll expect me to see him over the side with due ceremony. He'll also expect *you* to report to him. When do you suppose you'll do so?"

"I can report to him today or tomorrow. But"—Justin frowned—"I'll need a week or so before I can report for duty, Rick, and relieve you. I shall have to make arrangements for this sloop and equip myself with a King's uniform; and there's Jessica, there's my wife. As I told you, she's due to be brought to bed very soon, and I'd promised to stay with her until the birth."

"I'm sure that can be arranged. With the ship in port and due for an overhaul, Captain Jeffrey will not be unreasonable. And as to uniforms—I shan't be needing mine when I become a settler, and we're much of a size, are we not?" Rick rose and clapped an affectionate hand on Justin's shoulder. "But I'd like to have our partnership agreement drawn up without delay . . . if we can find a lawyer to do it for us. Whom do you suggest?"

Justin smiled. "George Crossley, of course. I'll try to see him in the next few days. But I want you to go up to Bathurst to inspect my grant before we sign any agreement, Rick.''

"I don't need to, for God's sake! Your word is good enough for me, and Crossley can sort out the financial ramifications.''

"Yes, but—''

"Justin, I'm in a hurry to make a start. I want to marry and I can't, until I've a house to take Kate to, and my future settled. Listen,'' Rick pleaded. "Let us meet at Crossley's office as soon as possible and agree to the terms of our partnership, have it signed and sealed, and then I'll go up there. I can start things moving, can I not? Perhaps I could begin building a house.''

Justin smiled at his impatience. "I understand how you feel, Rick old man. But these matters can't be hurried, and believe me, it will take the two of us—or you and my brother, William, perhaps—to start things moving, as you put it. There's plenty of local building material, provided you are prepared to start with a small wooden cabin, but we'll have to gather reliable labor. And, in addition to your cabin, feed stores, pens, shelters for stock, and fences will have to be constructed.''

"You make it sound complicated,'' Rick complained.

"I'm not trying to. I'm only being cautious,'' Justin countered. "Look, we'll make that appointment with Lawyer Crossley this week. When the agreement is prepared and signed, you go up and look over the land with young Willie or, better still, with Tim Dawson as well. They will tell you what needs to be done and help you to buy stock and engage the right sort of convict labor. Skilled labor is as hard to come by here these days as legal advice, but as I mentioned, I have a good friend in Bathurst—Dick Lewis, the overseer—who promised he would let me have the best men available. Willie knows him, too.''

"Where *is* Willie?'' Rick asked, making an effort to curb his impatience. "How can I get in touch with him?''

"He's at Ulva, on the Nepean River . . . on your way to the new Bathurst road. You could spend the night there, before you tackle the road,'' Justin told him.

"Could I?''

"Of course—I'll send word to him to expect you. And, Rick—''

"Yes?''

Justin said quietly, "Willie is still only a lad, but he's a first-rate farmer, and what he doesn't know about sheep isn't worth knowing. You can do worse than take his advice. And he's been up with me to inspect my holding—he can tell you more about its potential than I can."

"Then I shall seek his advice," Rick promised. "Well . . ." He held out his hand. "I'll get back to my ship. And we'll meet tomorrow when you come out to the *Kangaroo* to make yourself known to Captain Jeffrey. I'm truly delighted about everything, Justin."

"That goes for me, also, Rick." Justin wrung the extended hand. Cookie Barnes, he saw, when they regained the *Flinders*'s narrow quarterdeck, was rowing across from Campbell's wharf but making no haste, since the *Kangaroo*'s gig was still tied up to his sloop's starboard chains. Rick lowered himself into his waiting boat with the skill of long practice and, a hand raised briefly in farewell, ordered his bowman to cast off.

Cookie, when he returned, asked no questions, and Justin decided to tell him nothing concerning his new status until this should be confirmed. There was, he thought wryly, many a slip 'twixt cup and lip, and it would be a very long time before he forgot the humiliation of his visit to the Admiralty with Captain Pasco, when his application for a commission had been refused. True, Rick had asserted that Their Lordships had relented and that the coveted commission was in the hands of the *Kangaroo*'s commander, but . . . He smothered a sigh. From the guarded references Rick had made to him, there seemed a fairly strong probability that Captain Jeffrey would not receive him with open arms.

"Mrs. Broome's fine," Cookie volunteered. "Had visitors when I called on 'er—that Mrs. Lamerton and a real pretty young lady wi' an Irish name I didn't rightly catch."

"O'Malley?" Justin guessed, remembering what Rick had told him. "Miss Kate O'Malley?"

"Aye," Cookie confirmed. "I didn't stop, seein' as your missus was busy with them, talkin' an' drinkin' tea. But she's fine, an' I told her you'd be along, soon as you could. An' Mr. Nicholls gave me a receipt for the mail—" He produced it from his pocket. "You goin' ashore now, Mr. Broome?"

Justin nodded. "Elder can come with me to row the gig back. I'll see Mr. Campbell and then go home. You're in charge, Cookie.

If the commissariat want the grain taken to Cockle Bay, send me word, will you, please?"

Only the younger Robert Campbell was in the warehouse office when Justin entered it, and he said, forestalling the expected question, "No word of the *Kelso*, I'm afraid, Justin. My uncle fears that she must be officially declared lost, and Captain Piper is to inform the Governor." He shrugged despondently. "But at least the *Kangaroo* made it to port, as you'll know, and the *Emu* should arrive from Hobart in a week or so." He talked on, and Justin listened in silence, his thoughts, once again, sadly of the *Kelso* and Jasper and Frances Spence. Lucy Cahill, too, of course . . . He said abruptly, interrupting the flow of shipping gossip, "Rob, would you tell your uncle, please, that I may be in a position to offer him my *Flinders* for hire, if he wants her? Two crew—old Barnes and the lad Elder—go with her, but he'd have to take on a skipper."

Robert Campbell stared at him in surprise.

"*You're* quitting the *Flinders*? For God's sake, Justin, are you out of your mind? Don't tell me you're going to become a damned grazier on that land of yours?"

"No," Justin assured him. "But something else is in the offing. I'll confirm it, one way or another, in a couple of days. All I want to do now is ascertain whether or not your uncle could use the *Flinders*. I'd rather he had her than Mr. Lord or Mr. Reiby, but—"

"I'm sure he'll jump at the chance," Campbell said, with conviction. "In fact, he'd almost certainly buy her, if you decide to sell."

Justin answered unhesitatingly and with equally firm conviction, "No, I shan't be selling her, Rob. It would just be a year or maybe an eighteen months' hire, if your uncle's willing." He reflected, as he left the office and walked through the shipyard toward his own house, that a career in the Royal Navy was not without its perils. He might lose a ship, displease a commander, or be killed or wounded in an affray, and he had to leave Jessica and their coming child sufficient on which to live.

The *Flinders* was worth several hundred pounds, twelve hundred or a thousand, perhaps, if he put her up for auction, but . . . Justin glanced back, over his shoulder, at the anchorage, his heart gladdened, as it always was, by the sight of her, riding the slight swell like some graceful seabird momentarily at rest, the canvas that gave her wings spread out to dry in the warm sunshine. However long—or however short—his naval career might prove, he knew he could not sell the *Flinders*. But she would provide for Jessica should he die in the King's service, and that, at least, was a comforting thought.

The visitors had taken their leave by the time he reached his own cottage, a single-story brick building, white-painted and shingle-roofed, standing in a row of similar dwellings at the foot of the slope leading to Dawes Point.

Jessica came to meet him at the garden gate. She looked as radiant and lovely as ever, despite the advanced stage of her pregnancy, and after embracing her, Justin took her hand and they walked together through the small garden, gay with native flowering shrubs and English roses, which she tended with infinite care.

"Did Cookie tell you who came to call with Kate Lamerton this morning?" she asked, and went on eagerly, without waiting for Justin's reply, "The young American lady Rick Tempest is to wed, Miss Kate O'Malley . . . only they all call her Katie, so as to avoid confusion with dear Kate Lamerton. Rick Tempest saved her life in the South Atlantic. . . ." Justin listened again to the account of the rescue, told somewhat differently from Rick's brief and modest version.

"Did you like Miss O'Malley?" he asked, and received the expected answer.

"Indeed, yes," Jessica assured him. "And I am sure my lady will also." She always referred thus to the Governor's wife. "They are to lunch at Government House today, Miss O'Malley and Mrs. Dawson, and I believe that the captain of Rick Tempest's ship, Captain Jeffrey, and his wife are invited, too." She eyed her husband thoughtfully before adding, "I had the impression that Miss O'Malley would have preferred an invitation for another day."

"Did you, now?" Rick had not said much about the Jeffreys, Justin reminded himself. In fact, he had been very guarded and had invited him to draw his own conclusions concerning them. He maintained a studied silence as Jessica busied herself with preparations for their meal, talking away happily the while. He would, he was fully aware, have to tell her of Their Lordships' unexpected decision to grant him a lieutenant's commission and to appoint him, in Rick's place, to the *Kangaroo*, since there was the strong likelihood that this would bring a drastic change to the hitherto settled pattern of their lives.

But it could wait until tomorrow, he decided. In any case, he had yet to present himself to Captain Jeffrey, and . . . watching his wife, seeing the heaviness of her slight body and the enforced slowness of her movements, he hoped that her time was very near. Their calculations might have been amiss; the birth might well come later than either of them had anticipated, and the fear—whether or not it was well founded—that he might have to break his promise to stay with her until she was brought to bed might hurt and upset her.

Jessica set a sizzling platter in front of him and announced proudly that it was pork fillet, made according to a recipe passed on to her by Mrs. Ovens, the Governor's cook.

"I was at Government House the day before yesterday," she told him, "visiting little Lachlan. He's sixteen months old, the brightest little fellow you ever saw for his age, Justin, and both Their Excellencies dote on him. Mrs. Ovens says he's in danger of becoming spoilt, but I saw no sign of it. Of course, he's an only child, which makes it a temptation to spoil him, and he's got his mother's looks into the bargain. I was hard put to it not to burst out laughing when I saw the Governor, crawling round the nursery, with a rug over his head, growling and pretending to be a Himalayan bear!"

Hungrily plying knife and fork, Justin grinned at the picture her words evoked. In public, Governor Macquarie was the epitome of dignity, and the idea of his relaxing in so droll a manner for the benefit of his sixteen-month-old son struck Justin as both touching and amusing.

"I shall probably behave just as absurdly, when our son is of an age to appreciate his father's clowning," he warned. "This is an uncommonly good meal, Jessica India. Mrs. Ovens could not have made it any better than you have, I swear!"

Jessica beamed with pleasure at the compliment. "It was expensive," she confessed. "Pork is ninepence the pound, fillet tenpence, but I wanted to welcome you home. I . . ." She hesitated, the warm color rushing to her cheeks. "Justin, have you set your heart on our firstborn being a son?"

"Good heavens, no!" Justin pushed his plate away and reached across the well-scrubbed table to capture her hands in his. "My sweet wife, if it's a daughter I shall be equally happy . . . surely you know that? And there'll be others, will there not? You said yourself that an only child can become spoilt."

"Yes," she agreed gravely.

"Well, then, don't worry, my love. All I want is for you to suffer no harm and for our child to be strong and healthy."

"Yes," Jessica agreed again, still grave. "Are you thinking of little Dickon, Mrs. Dawson's boy?"

"Perhaps," he conceded. "Being deaf and dumb is a grievous affliction."

"But Dickon is happy," Jessica told him. "And everyone loves him. Kate Lamerton said that his uncle Rick spends every spare minute playing with him. She said there was a strange sort of affinity between them, as if they'd known each other for years."

"All the same, my dearest, I'd sooner that our child is not so afflicted," Justin said soberly. "But . . . we shall soon know, shall we not?"

"Sooner, perhaps, than you suppose." Jessica freed her hands from his grasp and, rising a trifle clumsily, came round the table to his side. "Feel him," she invited. "He is very lively and, I think, impatient to be born. But . . . you will be here now, until he is, won't you? Please, Justin dear . . . you won't take the *Flinders* out again until after I'm delivered?"

His fingers resting lightly on her distended belly, Justin felt the strong movements of his unborn child, and his resolution hardened. Captain Jeffrey would just have to wait until he was free to enter the King's service once again. . . . Their Lordships had taken long enough, in all conscience, to decide that he was worthy of a commission, and their decision had come as something of a shock to him.

"I'll be here, my little love," he promised. "For as long as you need me, I'll be here."

Jessica bent to kiss him, and he held her close.

CHAPTER IX

Governor Macquarie sat at his desk, a quill pen in his hand and an unhappy frown creasing his brow. It was early; as was his custom, he had been astir at first light, taking a frugal breakfast before spending a blissful half hour with his little son, Lachlan, and then, punctually at nine o'clock, he had received those of his civil and military officers who had official business to discuss, or matters of policy to settle.

This morning, to his relief, there had been few, and he was free of interruption until twelve-thirty, when his wife had arranged a luncheon for new arrivals in the colony, including the commander of His Majesty's ship *Kangaroo,* with his wife and a female passenger. Elizabeth, in whom respect for protocol was inbred, had also invited Colonel and Mrs. Molle to meet them, which was a pity, for Molle—while affecting outward friendship toward him—had, he was well aware, joined the ranks of his enemies and those detractors who sought to question and undermine his authority.

Not that George Molle was, by any stretch of the imagination, a foe to be feared. He was a military officer and a gentleman, who knew how to behave, and the opposition he offered was at once honorable and consistent . . . unlike the insolent, rapacious, and arrogant Bents, who, sent out to administer justice, had between them deprived the colony of its courts of law.

The Governor's hand clenched about his pen. The elder Bent, Ellis, had been reasonable enough when he had first taken up his appointment as judge advocate—and the poor devil was said to be seriously ill now, with a dropsy of the chest, so that he could not be judged too harshly. Nevertheless, since the arrival of his younger brother, Jeffrey Hart Bent, he had changed beyond recognition, gone back on arrangements to which he had agreed, broken promises he had solemnly made, and demanded, on his brother's behalf, privileges to which he was not and had never been entitled. . . . Lachlan Macquarie gave vent to a sigh of mingled rage and frustration.

The courthouse was a perfect example. The Governor searched among his papers and brought to light a copy of the *Gazette*. In this, Sydney's new hospital had been described in glowing terms. . . . He glanced through it, his frown deepening: ". . . massive pillars, wide verandas, and windows placed at a proper distance . . . in proportion so well adapted as at once to gratify the eye of taste and science. . . ." The editor had even gone on to profess an inability to convey "an adequate idea of the beauties of the place or of the solemn impression which the mind received on entering this stately building."

Yet Jeffrey Bent had refused to hold court there, despite having initially agreed to do so, complaining that the courtroom was a common hospital ward, in a most disgraceful state from dirt and vermin—a palpable untruth, since the part of the building earmarked for his court was separate from the hospital wards and had its own, dignified entrance. He had insisted that he must have not only a courthouse, built for the purpose, but also a residence for himself, in keeping with his position as supreme court judge.

His brother, Macquarie reflected sourly, had already cost government funds close on three thousand pounds, in cash and kind, for the erection of *his* residence, which had been supposed to include a courtroom . . . for which purpose he had provided a room a mere twenty feet square. The rest of the money had gone to build a palatial residence for his wife and four children, together with numerous servants.

The real bone of contention, however, had come with Jeffrey Bent's obstinate claim that he could not and would not sit as judge in any court where transported felons were admitted to practice as advocates. As a result, the supreme court had been closed for the past ten months, and the Governor's court, over which the judge advocate normally presided, had also ceased to function, following a disagreement between Ellis Bent and one of the civil magistrates.

The Governor sighed as, with his free hand, he sifted through the now bulging file of correspondence pertaining to these closures. There was a letter from the magistrate, William Broughton, which expressed precisely his own view of the matter:

> Those individuals granted a royal pardon have the undisputed title to be restored to all the rights and privileges of free British subjects within this colony; to deprive them of the benefit of their professions would be to destroy the effect of the pardon. . . .

But his attempts to order the reopening of the courts had achieved nothing, save a stream of disrespectful and discourteous letters, addressed by the two brothers to himself, and—Macquarie repeated his sigh—and other letters, he did not doubt, defending their stand and harshly critical of himself, addressed to Lord Bathurst at the Colonial Office.

He picked up a letter at random, frowning as he read it. Jeffrey Bent had written:

> Feeling it inconsistent with my dignity and independence as a judge, to submit to any interference or investigation into my judicial conduct on the part of the executive government of this colony, I shall decline entering into any further discussion with Your Excellency on this subject, except we are understood to meet on terms of equality and independence of each other.

In an earlier note, Bent had complained bitterly that the Governor had not had the courtesy to address him by the title of "Honorable." The Governor's frown deepened. His own reply had been brief and unequivocal, and he had written to Lord Bathurst, describing the situation in careful detail and requesting that both the Bents be recalled and others appointed in their stead. It would be nine months or even a year before he could hope for his request to be acted upon, but in order that it should be, he had offered his own resignation should the Colonial Office fail to remove both men from the colony.

He did not want to resign his governorship, and Bathurst would surely know that he did not, when there was so much to be done to ensure the future of the colony. There were the new lands to open up for settlement; churches, barracks, and schools to be built; and here, in Sydney   Impatiently, he thrust the file of letters from him and reached for another. This, too, was bulging, but it was infinitely more pleasing, for it contained the plans that the convict architect, Francis Greenway, had drawn up, at his instigation, for the improvements he had long wanted to make to the growing town.

Many of the public buildings were falling into decay because of the use of inferior materials and lack of skill in their construction; Government House itself was crumbling, despite numerous attempts at repair and renovation. There was no water supply or sewerage system, and still no fort by means of which the harbor could be defended.

Greenway had taken note of these deficiencies, and while giving first priority to the sewerage system, he had also submitted plans for a barracks for the garrison, for a new citadel—enclosing the old Fort Phillip behind substantial ramparts—and for a castellated building, modeled on Thornbury Castle in Gloucestershire, to serve as the Governor's residence. This would contain a grand hall, a vestibule, a magnificent staircase, and adequate domestic apartments, with a facade a hundred and eighty feet long. Situated on the high shoulder of the Government Domain, it would face north and command a breathtaking view of the harbor, and also front a quadrangle, on the west side of which would be a library, a museum, and a viceregal chapel, with staff and domestic apartments sited on two minor quadrangles beyond.

There were also plans for convict barracks to house a thousand felons, a courthouse with a portico forty feet high, a cathedral, and a quay and docks along the present government wharf, with three hundred feet of building ground between Dawes Point and the present Government House gate where offices, warehouses, and other public buildings would be situated.

With conscious pride and pleasure, the Governor studied Greenway's drawings, attempting to visualize what each would look like, when translated into brick and stone, interspersed by pleasant, tree-shaded squares and streets a hundred and fifty feet wide. The fact that the money for building would have, somehow, to be raised from within the colony gave him pause, for the Colonial Office had made it abundantly clear to him that he could expect no financial aid from the British government.

Even the now increasingly urgent repairs to his own official residence would have to be paid for by taxes or any other means he might devise, and . . . Macquarie scowled, as dust from the cracked ceiling of his office descended, in a choking cascade, onto his desk and the papers and drawings spread out in front of him.

He was governor of a penal colony, Lord Bathurst had reminded him in a recent dispatch. Well, be that as it may, he thought obstinately, he could not abandon his governorship until he had seen some of these visions realized and the convict stigma removed from those of the penal colony's inhabitants who had earned the right to pardon—Francis Greenway among them. God—the God he worshiped devoutly—had sent him, in the person of that strange little man, with his talent and his dreams, one who could transform Sydney Town into a place of beauty . . . aye, and other settlement villages, too—Parramatta, Windsor, Liverpool, Newcastle . . .

The arrogant Bents, the elitist Molle, even that arch-hypocrite Samuel Marsden, the colony's chaplain, would not drive him away before his God-given purpose was accomplished, his task completed.

Lachlan Macquarie picked up his quill once more and read through the letter he had started to write to his brother Charles, on leave from the Peninsula the last time he had heard, and staying at his estate in Mull.

He had written:

These two illiberal men, Ellis and Jeffrey Hart Bent, wish to exclude the emancipated attorneys from practicing in their courts, and I wish them to be admitted. On this point therefore we are at issue, and the business is referred home to the decision of His Majesty's ministers.

In the meantime, the Courts of Civil Judicature are suspended and no law proceedings can go on, owing to the pride, arrogance, and illiberality of these two brothers, who have made a most ungrateful return to me for all the kindness and favors I have heaped upon them.

I should not so much mind the mere objection to allowing men who have been convicts officiating in the courts as attorneys, but these two upstart fellows of judges wish to exclude all persons of this description from all places of trust and consequence, as well as from society altogether.

As I have however been all along the patron and champion of all meritorious persons who have been convicts, I cannot now desert them, and I am resolved to support their cause both at home and abroad.

The Governor pursed his lips. These, he reflected, were his sentiments, his firmly held beliefs. He dipped his pen in the inkwell and added a few final lines:

The subject will probably be laid before Parliament by the Ministry, and if so I am sure of a complete victory. Perhaps, however, this question may be given against me, and if so, you will see us in Mull eighteen months sooner than we intended being there.

He signed his name and was affixing seals to the letter when, heralded by a soft tap on the door, his wife came in. Elizabeth was now thirty-seven, and they had been married for exactly eight years—their wedding anniversary having been celebrated just a week ago—but, Macquarie thought fondly, the years had treated her kindly. A great deal more kindly than, alas, they had treated himself, at fifty-four almost twenty years her senior. He looked up to meet her smiling blue-eyed gaze, conscious, as always, of the deep affection he felt for her.

"What is it, my dear?" he questioned. "Have our guests arrived already?"

"Colonel Molle has," Elizabeth told him, a faint but undisguised note of disapproval in her soft Highland voice. "Mrs. Molle, he says, is to follow. He came early to bring you some most distressing news. Lachlan my dearest, it *is* distressing, I fear."

Macquarie jumped to his feet, suppressing an angry exclamation. The last thing he wanted at the moment was bad news, but . . . controlling an impulse to snap at her, he asked with well-simulated calm, "Well, break it to me, wife, if you please."

"Ellis Bent is dead," Elizabeth responded sadly. "It seems he took to his bed two or three days ago, and poor Eliza found him . . . that is, she found that he had passed away in his sleep, when she took a tray into his sickroom. And he was only thirty-four! I am so sorry, Lachlan. Sorry for Eliza and the children, of course, but . . . this has come at a very bad time for you, has it not?"

"Yes, it has indeed," her husband conceded, recollecting the ultimatum he had sent to Lord Bathurst and his demand that both the Bents should be relieved of office and recalled.

But Ellis had not been the one who had most troubled him. Certainly it had not been he who had thrown down the gauntlet in arrogant challenge to his viceregal authority . . . it was Jeffrey who was the troublemaker. It had been the younger Bent's malign influence that had caused his brother to renounce his earlier loyalty and go back on all the promises he had made, so eagerly, when he had first come out to take up his appointment as judge advocate to the colony of New South Wales.

They had traveled from England together in the same ship, the Governor reminded himself, and they had been on the most harmonious terms—their wives equally so—until Jeffrey Bent had arrived, aflame with ruffled dignity and with an exaggerated notion of his own importance, just over a year ago. Sixteen months, to be precise, as a passenger aboard the *Broxbornebury* transport, in July of the previous year.

In sixteen short months, Jeffrey Hart Bent had contrived to disorganize the colony's judicial system and then virtually to destroy it. He had personally flouted its laws, antagonized its civil magistrates—even putting the unfortunate Broughton under arrest and charging him with contempt—and earned the distrust, as well as the intense dislike, of most of the colony's emancipists. But God, in His wisdom, had ordained that it was Ellis who had died. . . .

"Colonel Molle is waiting," Elizabeth prompted sympathetically. "And he is insisting that he must see you at once, Lachlan."

"Very well, my dear," the Governor said, recovering himself. "Be so good as to send him in. But . . . have luncheon served, will you, please, as soon as our other guests arrive?"

Elizabeth kissed him fondly on the cheek.

"Of course," she promised. "The instant they arrive."

It was an oddly ill-assorted luncheon party, Katie O'Malley thought, as she took her seat at the long dining table, with the tall, somewhat uncommunicative secretary to the Governor on one side, and on the other a corpulent, florid-faced gentleman in military uniform, whose name she had been told but could not now remember.

Captain and Mrs. Jeffrey were on either side of the Governor, at the head of the table; Abigail Dawson on the captain's right, and her husband, Timothy—lately returned to Sydney from his farm on the Hawkesbury—next to Mrs. Jeffrey, who confined her conversational essays strictly to the Governor. Probably, Katie decided, with a newfound cynicism, because she was not yet certain whether Timothy was one of the colony's respectable inhabitants or one of its emancipist untouchables.

The Governor, also in military uniform, was older than she had expected, a thin, slightly bowed figure, with a bony, sallow-complexioned face and dark, lackluster eyes. His hair—for he wore no wig—was graying and cut short, and apart from a pair of sparse side-whiskers, he was clean-shaven, his cheeks sunken and deeply lined. But he was courteous and kindly, and his smile as he had greeted her had been genuinely warm, his brief words of welcome seemingly sincere. And his wife . . . Katie glanced shyly down the length of the table, to where Mrs. Macquarie was sitting, her neighbors as yet unidentified. Considerably younger than her husband, she was a smiling, delightfully friendly woman, with curling, red-bronze hair and wide-set blue eyes, which twinkled with good humor. The twinkle faded abruptly, however, when her own corpulent neighbor cleared his throat and, addressing the table at large, observed pointedly that he was too grief-stricken to bring himself to eat.

"This colony has suffered a truly tragic loss," he went on. "Some of you will, perhaps, not have heard the sad news that it was my painful duty to bring to His Excellency, half an hour ago. Our judge advocate, Ellis Bent, a young man in the prime of his life, has today passed over to the other side, leaving a sorrowing widow and four poor children, not one of whom has yet attained his tenth year."

In the sudden, embarrassed silence that followed his announcement, Katie caught her breath, sensing a subtle change in the atmosphere, which at once puzzled and frightened her.

Mrs. Jeffrey, never usually at a loss for words, looked across at her husband and then said unctuously, "Those whom the gods love . . . Of what, if I may make so bold as to inquire, did your poor friend die, Colonel Molle?"

The colonel absentmindedly helped himself from a dish offered by one of the servants. He answered in a voice fraught with emotion, "Ellis Bent was not only my friend, madam—he was a friend to all the respectable members of this community. As to the cause of his most untimely death, the poor, unhappy fellow had for some time been afflicted with a dropsy of the chest. Despite this, he went on working, and in my view, it was that which killed him, for he was never one to spare himself. Don't you agree, Ted?"

The officer he addressed—one of those seated at Mrs. Macquarie's end of the table—was, Katie observed, a slimmer, slightly less choleric version of himself. As she had anticipated from their resemblance to each other, the colonel's plea for confirmation was answered vehemently, and she saw Mrs. Macquarie recoil, her cheeks drained of color.

The Governor opened his mouth as if to speak, and then, meeting his wife's eye, he closed it again as she said, with quiet firmness, "I grieve most deeply for Eliza Bent. I am sure we all do, Captain Sanderson. Both became our valued friends on the voyage out here, and I shall, of course, take the first opportunity to call and offer my condolences."

Her composure fully recovered, Mrs. Macquarie turned to Captain Jeffrey and adroitly introduced a change of subject. "I understand, from what Mrs. Dawson has told me, that your ship was engaged in a most courageous rescue, Captain . . . to which, indeed, we are indebted for the presence of one of our guests at this luncheon. In arctic waters, was it not?" She smiled across the long table at Katie and added warmly, "You are doubly welcome on that account, Miss O'Malley."

Nothing loath, Captain Jeffrey launched into an account of the rescue. He told a dramatic story, and Katie, listening in silence and with shyly downcast eyes, found herself wondering why this should differ so significantly from Rick's modest and matter-of-fact description of what had occurred.

But she offered no comment; it was not her place to do so, she decided, since, with Colonel Molle and Captain Sanderson also silent, Mrs. Macquarie's conversational ploy had obviously succeeded. Even the Governor appeared enthralled, only occasionally interposing a shrewd question, when Captain Jeffrey's narrative faltered. Thus encouraged, he talked on, painting a chilling picture of the perils his own ship had faced, at the mercy of pack ice and towering bergs and shrieking, gale-force winds.

"We searched until dark for survivors," the *Kangaroo*'s commander asserted. "But, alas, there were none . . . save for the young lady who is with us now. And even she would not have been here had it not been for my dear wife's skilled and devoted nursing."

The other ladies emitted gasps of mingled astonishment and congratulation, and one—a small, stout matron in an elaborate dress of blue taffeta, whom Katie took to be Mrs. Molle—leaned across to exclaim, "My poor child . . . what a terrible experience for you!"

"I don't remember very much about it, ma'am," Katie evaded, quite truthfully. A servant removed her empty plate and set a clean one in front of her; Colonel Molle, she noticed, despite his insistence that grief at the loss of his friend had left him without appetite, seemed to have made a reasonably good meal, and the Governor was beaming, his good humor quite restored.

"You acquitted yourself most creditably, Captain Jeffrey," he said. "You and your ship's company lived up to the highest traditions of His Majesty's Navy, indeed you did. Ah . . . you mentioned that the vessel that was lost, the *Providence*, was on her way to this colony with trade goods. She was, I take it, British?"

"No, sir," Captain Jeffrey denied. "She was American, owned and commanded by Miss O'Malley's father. He had held commissioned rank in the United States Navy, and we"—he glanced swiftly at Katie and then away—"we consigned his body to the deep under the United States flag, deeming that to be right and proper in the circumstances."

"*American!* An American trading vessel on her way to this port, sir!" The interruption, indignantly voiced, came from Colonel Molle. "Carrying trade goods to offer for sale here, if I understand you aright?"

"Yes, that is so, sir," Captain Jeffrey confirmed.

"By God, that is not to be countenanced!" Molle swore, without apology. "The war scarcely over and thousands of our seamen and soldiers dead, and the damned Yankees send ships to trade with us! They are hard-necked rogues, devil take them! One minute they stab us in the back, betray us by giving armed support to the French, and the next they want to trade with us."

"I think, sir, that you have said enough," the Governor warned him coldly. "You have, I fear, forgotten that Miss O'Malley is our guest. She has endured enough, without having to submit to such offensive and insulting remarks as you have just uttered concerning her countrymen. You will oblige me by offering her an apology."

Molle's red face was suffused with a fresh wave of hectic color. He stared at Katie, his expression the reverse of contrite, but he had the grace to claim that he had forgotten her presence and offer a stiff apology, which she accepted, close to tears.

Timothy Dawson said crisply, "No doubt, sir, you've also forgotten that, over the years, when this colony has been close to starvation, American trading vessels have brought sorely needed supplies to us. His Excellency's predecessors welcomed each and every one of them, for they came when British ships brought only more mouths for us to feed . . . if they came at all. I'd have you know, sir, that we owe a great deal to those whom you are pleased to call the damned Yankees."

Colonel Molle threw down his napkin and rose to his feet, motioning to his wife to follow his example.

"Permit me, sir, to take my leave," he requested the Governor. "And to thank you for your hospitality. I shall not accept it in the future, since, when I do, I am expected to sit at table with persons who came here as convicted felons, on terms, sir, of social equality—a privilege you may see fit to grant them, but I shall not." He glared at Timothy Dawson and then bowed stiffly to Captain and Mrs. Jeffrey and finally to the Governor's wife. "And if I may say so, sir, without giving further offense to your American guest, I cannot, in all conscience, sit down with my country's enemies, even when they are female."

He took his wife's arm and stumped arrogantly from the room. Captain Sanderson hesitated, and then, with a murmured apology, followed his commanding officer to the door. Reaching it, he turned, pink with embarrassment.

"The colonel is not himself, sir," he told the Governor. "Mr. Bent's sudden death has upset him greatly. I beg Your Excellency's indulgence."

"Certainly, Captain Sanderson," Governor Macquarie responded, with faultless courtesy. "I shall endeavor to forget this unfortunate episode, if that is possible. I give you good day, sir."

The door closed behind him, and there was a brief, uneasy pause. Then Mrs. Macquarie rose, and the other ladies rose with her.

"We will take tea in the withdrawing room," she told the majordomo, and slipping swiftly round the table, she took Katie's hand and tucked it under her arm. "You must think us very uncivilized, my dear," she said apologetically. "And perhaps we are at times. There are feuds and rivalries simmering beneath the surface, which occasionally erupt and shatter the peace we try our hardest to maintain, in a deeply divided community. My husband is a good man, and he endeavors to be impartial, however bitterly he is provoked." Reaching the withdrawing room, she invited her guests to be seated and motioned Katie to a seat beside her, on a wide, chintz-covered sofa. With a change of tone, she said softly, "You will always be welcome here, in this house, Miss O'Malley, believe me."

"Thank you," Katie managed awkwardly, wishing that, like Colonel Molle, she might make her escape, even from the kindly and well-intentioned Mrs. Macquarie. The colonel's outburst had been so unexpected and unpleasant that she was still more than a little shaken and, under the simulated submissiveness, coldly angry. But good manners demanded that she remain where she was, at her hostess's side, and she sat very straight, with her head held high, while the Governor's lady dispensed tea from the fine silver service that the majordomo set down in front of them.

Abigail smiled at her, in mute sympathy and approval; Mrs. Jeffrey was at pains to avoid meeting her gaze; and the elderly, white-haired lady who had been on the opposite side of the dining table from her came up and introduced herself as Mrs. Robert Campbell.

"I told Abigail that I hoped she would bring you to dine with us, my dear," she said warmly and added, lowering her voice, "The war is over and should be forgotten . . . and it will be, by most of us, I promise you."

She returned to her seat at Mrs. Jeffrey's side, and Mrs. Macquarie, cup in hand, sank gracefully back onto the sofa. "Abigail has just informed me that you are to wed her brother, Lieutenant Richard Tempest, Miss O'Malley," she remarked. "And that he is to quit the navy and become a settler. That is splendid news, and I am delighted to hear it. When do you plan to wed—or is the date for your wedding not yet settled?"

"It's not yet settled, Mrs. Macquarie. Rick—Richard has to wait until he is relieved. His relief is here, but—"

"Here?" the Governor's wife echoed. "In Sydney, do you mean? One of the *Emu*'s officers?"

Katie shook her head. "No, ma'am." Rick had told her the name of the officer who was to replace him as the *Kangaroo*'s first lieutenant, but it was all she knew, and she repeated the name in all innocence. "By a young man named Justin Broome, I believe."

She was conscious of Mrs. Jeffrey's eyes on her, and sensed the older woman had broken off her conversation with Abigail in order to strain her ears in the hope of overhearing what Mrs. Macquarie's reaction might be.

The Governor's wife appeared unaware of her guest's sudden interest, and her delight was evident and unconcealed. "So Their Lordships of the Admiralty have relented at last!" she exclaimed. "Oh, I am so very pleased, for no one in the whole wide world deserves it more. Justin Broome is a truly fine young man, and my husband recommended him for a commission in the navy when we first arrived here. Indeed, his act of bravery was the first thing we witnessed, whilst our ship was still at anchor outside the Heads. Justin risked his life to save a seaman who had fallen from the *Dromedary*'s rigging."

She described the incident with a wealth of remembered detail, but Katie took in little of what she was saying, her whole attention being caught and held by the look of shocked dismay on Mrs. Jeffrey's normally composed and pink-cheeked face.

"Mrs. Macquarie," she interrupted almost rudely, "is this—this young man an *emancipist*? Did he come out here as a convict?"

"Oh, no!" Mrs. Macquarie turned the warmth of her smile on the questioner, seeking to put her fears at rest. "Justin was born here. His parents were emancipists, and he is living proof of what fine stock this colony can produce. His father had a most distinguished career in the navy, and his mother was one of the early settlers in the Hawkesbury Valley. After Mr. Broome's death, she married one of my husband's aides, Captain Hawley, who now commands the veteran company, and—"

"But for Their Lordships to commission him," Mrs. Jeffrey put in, "when he's . . . oh, when he cannot be considered officer material, is to me quite—quite incomprehensible. I'd no idea, I—" She broke off, her face suffused with indignant color.

"Captain Jeffrey must surely have known," Mrs. Macquarie suggested gently. "The Admiralty would have told him, I feel certain."

"No!" Mrs. Jeffrey's denial was emphatic. "Their Lordships did *not* tell him! And Mr. Tempest did not see fit to mention it to the captain, either." She turned resentfully on Katie. "Did he tell *you*?"

"Not—not that I can recall," Katie was compelled to admit. "But I . . ." To her relief, Abigail intervened.

"Neither you nor Captain Jeffrey need have any qualms on Justin Broome's account," she asserted, her tone quietly authoritative. "I have known him and all his family since I first came to the colony, over eight years ago, and my husband has enjoyed their friendship for much longer. He will tell you that Justin's mother was not only one of the first settlers in the Hawkesbury Valley— she was one of the most successful farming pioneers, who won the admiration and respect of the whole community. As to Justin himself . . . Mrs. Jeffrey, he holds a master's certificate, and he served under Captain Flinders in the *Investigator,* of which, on her last voyage, his father was sailing master. And my brother told me that Captain Pasco accepted him as a midshipman in His Majesty's ship *Hindostan,* and thought so highly of him that he subsequently became his patron. It was on his recommendation, as well as His Excellency's, I believe, that he was commissioned."

Mrs. Jeffrey had the grace to look ashamed, yet, for all Abigail's forceful defense of him, Katie sensed uneasily, there would be scant welcome for Justin Broome when he reported for duty on board His Majesty's ship *Kangaroo.* Despite his considerable achievements, he was still what the colony's exclusionist faction called a currency kid—unacceptable in their social circles. Selfishly, as Mrs. Macquarie again tactfully introduced a change of subject, she found herself hoping that nothing would happen to delay Rick's departure from the ship and their marriage.

Ten minutes later, when the gentlemen followed the Governor from the dining room, Abigail touched her arm to signify that the time had come for their departure. Government House was only a short distance from the Spences' residence in Pitt Street, and they walked back, Timothy Dawson's face as dark as thunder. Seemingly forgetful of her presence, he spoke in wrathful tones to his wife, and Katie listened, understanding only a little of what he was saying. But he was, she gathered, incensed by Colonel Molle's behavior, both on her own account and that of the Governor.

"The infernal fellow is arrogant beyond belief, Abby," he said as they reached the garden gate and he relinquished his grasp of Abigail's arm. "And you can take it from me that he's not done with his mischief-making yet." He smiled apologetically at Katie. "You must wonder into what caldron of dissent fate has pre-cipitated you! But never mind, my dear child . . . whilst Rick is making his arrangements with Justin Broome, Abigail shall bring you and the children to Upwey for a week or two. You'll see the real aspect of this colony there and meet the settlers on whom its future prosperity is being built. The majority of them are emancipists or currency kids, but they are fine people, Katie, believe me. Not all convicts make good here, but those who win pardons deserve them, and the proof is plain enough to see, on the farms and small holdings that have arisen in what was once just a wilderness. Abigail shall take you to Justin's mother's old farm, Long Wrekin, which I now own." He turned back to his wife. "Will you do that, my love?"

Abigail smiled. "Yes, of course I will, Tim—and most gladly. There are times, I confess, when the—the atmosphere of Sydney quite sickens me. Our luncheon party today was one of those times, and—oh, my heart bled for the poor Governor and for Mrs. Macquarie! That they should have to submit to gross discourtesy at their own table is unpardonable." Her smile had swiftly faded, Katie saw, and there were tears in her shining blue eyes as she asked, "But, Tim—can we both leave Sydney yet? With no word of the *Kelso*? I thought—"

Timothy Dawson's mouth tightened.

"It's no use waiting any longer, Abby my dear. Simeon Lord told me this morning that one of his traders reported sighting wreckage on a beach east of Coupang. From the man's description, Lord told me that the wreck was almost certainly the *Kelso*. It's not proof positive, but . . ." He shook his head in a gesture of resignation. "I've arranged to speak with the master this evening and hear his description for myself. I hadn't intended to tell you until I had spoken to him, only . . ."

"Only?" Abigail echoed, and now, Katie saw, the tears were

coursing unashamedly down her cheeks. "Tim, does that mean—?"

Timothy Dawson put his arm about her. "It means that the *Kelso* will be listed officially as lost," he said regretfully. "So why not come back with me to Upwey—you and the girls and Katie? Breathe some clean air for a change and escape from the damned feuding here."

"Yes," Abigail responded. "Yes, we will." She dabbed at her eyes with a handkerchief, and then, in a quiet, controlled voice, asked him if there were no chance of survivors having reached Coupang.

Timothy shook his head. "The beach is two hundred miles from Coupang, Abby. It's unlikely, I fear."

"I see," Abigail managed. "Then they're gone . . . Lucy, poor little soul, and Frances and Jasper. It is . . . oh, it is heartbreaking, Tim. And I . . ." She hid her face against his shoulder, and Katie, anxious not to intrude on her grief, started toward the house.

Little Dickon emerged from the front door, making the odd, high-pitched sounds that indicated pleasure at his mother's return. He had a ball with him and was bouncing it, clearly in the hope that Abigail would join him in a game.

Katie held out her hands to him.

"Dickon," she said, careful to speak distinctly, "I'll play ball with you. Your mama is . . . she's tired, honey. Will you play with me instead?"

Dickon hesitated, eyeing her uncertainly, and then he bounced his ball to her and, when she caught it, took her hand trustingly and led her out to the lawn

CHAPTER X

Justin rowed from the *Flinders* to the *Kangaroo* at noon the following day. He was feeling elated; Jessica's pride and delight in the news that he had been commissioned into the Royal Navy had rekindled his own, and the interview he had had with the emancipist lawyer, George Crossley, had been eminently satisfactory.

Rick's agreement—and his signature on the document the lawyer would draw up—was now all that was required to launch their partnership and, God willing, lead to a mutually happy and profitable association between them, when the new land grant was developed.

Justin whistled cheerfully to himself as he pulled unhurriedly across the cove and brought the *Flinders*'s small gig alongside the King's ship. A hail from the deck demanded his business, but before he could reply, it was followed by the warning that traders from the shore would not be permitted to board, on the captain's orders.

Annoyed by this churlish reception, Justin secured the gig's painter to the *Kangaroo*'s chains and, offering no explanation of his presence, ascended to the quarterdeck, which he saluted as naval custom decreed. A youthful lieutenant, whom he took to be Rick's acting second, came striding officiously over, to plant himself in such a way as to challenge his further progress across the deck.

"Are you deaf, man?" he inquired sarcastically. "Or merely stupid? Did you not hear me say that traders and bumboats from the shore are not wanted?"

Justin was not in uniform. Rick had not yet supplied him, and he had long since outgrown the midshipman's white-patched monkey jacket that, five years before, he had worn on board the *Hindostan*. But he was respectably clad, in white duck trousers, blue watch-coat, and the peaked cap of a ship's master, and the young lieutenant's assumption that he was a hawker from the shore increased his irritation. He controlled it and said coldly, "Be so good as to pass the word for your first lieutenant, if you please."

"He's ashore," the *Kangaroo*'s duty officer answered, sounding less assured as he took in Justin's height and his air of authority. "Do you have business with him . . . sir?" The "sir" was added hastily, and the boy reddened under the newcomer's uncompromising gaze. "Forgive me if I—that is, if I assumed that yours was a bumboat. We've had trouble with them in Madeira and at the Cape, and the captain's standing orders are to fend them off. So I—"

"They are not permitted at this anchorage," Justin put in curtly. "Is your captain on board?"

"Yes, sir, he is. Captain Jeffrey, sir. Shall I inform him that you are here?"

"If you please. My name is Broome."

"Aye, aye, sir. I'll tell him, if you'd be good enough to wait."

He sped off on his errand, and Justin waited, eyed curiously by the men of the duty watch, engaged in routine harbor chores under the eye of a petty officer. Captain Jeffrey, he thought, must be one of the navy's less wealthy commanders, judging by the thinned-down white paint one party was applying to the rails and hatch covers. The ship's figurehead, a carved wooden effigy of a kangaroo, was badly in need of a lick of gold leaf, which it did not appear to be getting—he had noticed it particularly, on his way across the anchorage, with the idea of rectifying the omission as soon as he took over the duties of first lieutenant.

"Sir . . ." The officer of the watch was beside him. "The captain will receive you now, if you'll follow me."

Justin thanked him. The captain's day cabin was, he saw when he entered, furnished luxuriously and without regard for cost. A desk, placed in front of the stern windows, was of inlaid walnut; a dining table of highly polished mahogany was set with gleaming silver, which was reflected by the table's surface in mirrored perfection; and, although the cabin was comparatively small, a sofa and two chintz-covered armchairs occupied the space usually taken up by the ship's stern-chasers.

A handsome, dark-haired woman was seated on the sofa—the captain's wife, Justin presumed, surprised that she should be present at what was, after all, a formal interview. The captain himself, a stout, red-faced man of stocky build, did not rise from his chair in front of the beautiful walnut desk. He nodded, in response to Justin's bow, but kept him standing, regarding him in frowning silence for an appreciable time before saying, in a flat, unenthusiastic voice, "Ah, Mr. Broome, you will have heard, no doubt, from Mr. Tempest that Their Lordships of the Admiralty have seen fit to grant you a lieutenant's commission, and that I am entrusted to deliver it to you."

"Yes, sir," Justin acknowledged. "Mr. Tempest did inform me."

Jeffrey offered no congratulations. He opened a locked drawer in his desk, extracted the commission from it, and held it out. His hand, Justin noticed as he accepted the sheet of vellum, was plump and white, the nails inordinately long. A puckered line of scar tissue ran unevenly across the palm, and—realizing that Justin had observed this, the *Kangaroo*'s commander exclaimed bitterly, "A relic of our war with the damned Yankee colonials! And I shall bear it until the day I die. But you'll know nothing of war, I imagine."

"No, sir. I have not seen action," Justin admitted. He waited, still not invited to seat himself and conscious that both the captain and his wife were subjecting him to a searching scrutiny. He had not been introduced to Mrs. Jeffrey, but she asked, her tone calculated to make it clear to him that she was addressing an inferior, "And where have you spent the war years, Mr. Broome? Out here?"

"For the most part, ma'am, yes." Justin's tone was even. She was, he knew, seeking to denigrate him, but he refused to be put out.

The table was laid with cutlery for luncheon; there were wine carafes set out at one end, and both the captain and his wife had half-filled glasses beside them. Mrs. Jeffrey took a sip from hers but made no attempt to offer Justin hospitality or an apology for her failure to do so.

"Of course," Mrs. Jeffrey added smoothly. "You were born here, I believe." She did not say "of emancipist parents," but the implication was there, and despite his self-imposed restraint, Justin reddened.

Captain Jeffrey took up the interrogation.

"I'm told that your father was one of a party of—er—of convicts who escaped from this colony in a stolen government cutter," he said. "In a name other than his own, was it not? And they were apprehended in Timor by Captain Edwards of the *Pandora*, who brought them back to England for trial?"

Justin kept his temper. Clearly, the *Kangaroo*'s commander had been making inquiries concerning him, and his delving into the past had proved rewarding. There were people here who knew the story of that incredible escape—people who had been in Sydney at the time, and the details were not hard to come by. Abigail Dawson knew it, and had even met the courageous Mary Bryant in Cornwall, where she had settled after her ordeal, in which she had lost her husband and her two little children. Like his father, Mrs. Bryant had been granted a King's pardon. . . . Drawing himself up, he looked down at the stout Jeffrey and managed a tight-lipped smile.

"That is so, sir," he agreed. "In his own name, my father received a pardon and volunteered for the Royal Navy. He served in the *Nymphe* action in ninety-three and was promoted to the rank of master's mate by Sir Edward Pellew. Before returning here with Governor Hunter on board the *Reliance*, he was in the fleet action of the First of June, under Lord Howe. His rank in the Royal Navy at the time of his death was that of sailing master, sir. I have no reason, I assure you, Captain Jeffrey, to feel ashamed of my parentage. My mother—"

Jeffrey cut him short. "I have been told about your mother by no less a person than the Governor's wife, Mr. Broome . . . and of your own—er—exploits by His Excellency. You are the owner and master of a small trading vessel called the *Flinders*, I understand?"

"Yes, sir, I am. She's in the anchorage now—a two-masted sloop."

"I have observed her," the captain conceded grudgingly. "A handy craft, certainly, for these waters and, no doubt, the rivers. You ply for hire in her, do you not?" Receiving Justin's nod of assent, he went on pensively, "I've no wish to—er—to compel you to abandon a profitable occupation, to which you are evidently well suited, in order to employ you on board this ship, Mr. Broome."

Justin drew in his breath sharply. "I had understood that I was appointed in Lieutenant Tempest's place, sir, and that he is to quit the King's service."

"Oh, yes, he is." Captain Jeffrey sipped from his glass, eyeing Justin over its rim with narrowed, speculative eyes. "I have given Mr. Tempest permission to terminate his service as soon as it is convenient for him to do so. But"—he paused, leaning forward to refill his glass—"I have a competent second-in-command in Lieutenant Meredith, and I have informed him that whilst my ship is on this station, he will act as first lieutenant. You—er—Mr. Broome, you must surely recognize that, while the *Kangaroo* is here, it will not be possible for you to take up your appointment. It would be a—well, to put it plainly, a social embarrassment to Colonel Molle and his officers, for instance."

He paused again, exchanging a pleading glance with his wife, who came swiftly to his support. "Mr. Broome," she said sweetly, "what Captain Jeffrey is endeavoring to explain to you is that you are well known here as the offspring of convicted felons. As such, however praiseworthy your personal achievements may be, you cannot be accepted as one of this ship's serving officers. In appointing you to replace Lieutenant Tempest, Their Lordships can hardly have been aware of the circumstances or, indeed, of the bad feeling such an appointment would undoubtedly engender in a penal colony."

Justin was momentarily shocked into silence. He had not expected to be received with any great pleasure by the *Kangaroo*'s commander, but this . . . Bile rose in his throat, and a futile anger tore at the remnants of his composure.

"And besides," Mrs. Jeffrey went on, still employing the honeyed tones in which she had just addressed him, "the fact that your wife was a Government House servant and the daughter of a noncommissioned officer would . . . oh, goodness, you must see how great an embarrassment that would prove!"

Justin managed somehow to control himself. "What, then, do you propose, Captain Jeffrey," he asked, with dignity, "in view of this"—he held up his commission—"and of the Admiralty's instructions? Am I to be kept on shore on half pay?"

Captain Jeffrey was ready for the question. "I have given the matter some thought," he said curtly, "and I propose to enter your name on the ship's books and grant you extended leave of absence, to enable you to continue your—what can I call them?—your commercial activities in regard to the sloop in which you ply for hire. I shall, it goes, I trust, without saying, make a full report to Their Lordships, and I anticipate that they will understand my predicament and give official approval to the decision I have reached. As to your pay, Mr. Broome, I imagine that Their Lordships would regard a request for half pay as reasonable, as you yourself suggested . . . in fact, I'm sure of it."

"Then I am not to be permitted to join this ship?" Justin said. He thrust the commission into his pocket, conscious that his hand was shaking visibly. Unless and until the Admiralty commissioners overruled Captain Jeffrey's decision, there was nothing he could do to alter it, he thought bitterly . . . and it would be close on a year before any reply from Whitehall could be expected.

"Not whilst we remain on this station," Jeffrey returned. "You will be recalled, should this be necessary, when I am ordered elsewhere." He rose, and since Justin offered no argument, his manner became more cordial. "I regret this, Mr. Broome, believe me. Clearly, you are an experienced and, I am confident, a most proficient sea officer. Had the—er—the circumstances been other than they are, I should have been more than happy to avail myself of your services."

"Thank you, Captain," Justin acknowledged without warmth. He avoided the tentative handshake, affecting not to see the movement of Jeffrey's plump hand, and bowed stiffly in Mrs. Jeffrey's direction. "Then I'll take my leave."

"Mr. Meredith will see you to your boat," Jeffrey said, "if you will pardon my absence. My wife and I are bidden to attend the funeral service for the late judge advocate, Mr. Ellis Bent, and since it is at two-thirty, we must take our luncheon at once, or we shall be late." He summoned his steward by ringing a handbell before Justin had reached the door of the cabin, and when he gained the deck, only a small midshipman was there to do the honors.

He did them, with commendable courtesy, a fresh-faced boy of about eleven or twelve who, a trifle to Justin's surprise, addressed him by name and sent a seaman scurrying down the accommodation ladder ahead of him, to untie the gig's painter and hold it steady while he embarked.

On board the *Flinders*, Cookie Barnes gave him a note, grinning widely as he unsealed it.

"From His Holiness," he announced, using the irreverent nickname by which the Reverend Samuel Marsden was known to some of the less devout of his flock. "An' I can guess what he wants."

"Well?" Justin read the note, which simply asked him to wait on the colony's senior chaplain in the vestry of St. Philip's Church at his earliest convenience. "What do you reckon he wants?"

Cookie's smile faded. He gestured to the trading schooner that had come to anchor off Simeon Lord's wharf the previous evening.

"She didn't only bring word about the wreck o' the *Kelso*, Mr. Broome—she brought two o' them cannibal savages from Whangaroa Bay. Maoris," he added, when Justin eyed him blankly, "from the New Zealand mission station where the *Boyd* was wrecked."

"Well?" Justin prompted again. Over the years, he had learned to respect old Cookie's ability to ferret out news and glean fact from gossip and rumor. "What does that signify?"

"Trouble, Mr. Broome," Cookie answered with conviction. "It seems that the Maori chief the missionaries was friendly with 'as gorn an' died, an' there's liable to be a war 'atween 'is tribe an' another, with the Bible thumpers caught in the middle of it. I seen Mr. Campbell this mornin', an' he told me about it."

"I don't see the connection, Cookie," Justin objected. "What does Mr. Marsden want of me, for heaven's sake?"

"He wants the *Flinders*. Mr. Campbell must've let slip as you're joinin' the *Kangaroo*, now that they've made you a King's orficer, an' that the *Flinders* is for hire." Cookie shrugged. "I reckon he's plannin' on going off ter Whangaroa ter try an' stop the war."

"But he has his own brig—the *Active*, Cookie. And besides—"

"Mr. Broome, the *Active* sailed for Otaheite a week since. Have you forgotten? She won't be calling at Whangaroa on 'er way out."

He was right, Justin realized. The Reverend Samuel Marsden's *Active* did a substantial trade in the islands and with the missionaries in Otaheite in particular, and if she had sailed only a week ago, it would be eight or nine weeks—or even longer—

before she put in to Whangaroa. And by that time the warlike Maoris would probably have treated Samuel Marsden's embryo mission colony as they had treated the unfortunate *Boyd*'s crew, whose blackened bones had been strewn across the beach.

"I'd better go and see Mr. Marsden, Cookie," he said. "And . . ." He clapped a hand on the old seaman's thin shoulder. "I'm *not* joining the *Kangaroo* whilst she remains on this station. Her commander has given me leave on half pay . . . indefinite leave, so the *Flinders* won't be leased to the Campbells. Where's the boy?"

"Young Elder? I sent him to the government store, Mr. Broome. We've that grain to unload." Cookie eyed him reproachfully. "Can't go harin' off whiles that's fillin' our hold, can we? I'll get it into the government boat whiles you're chin-waggin' with Holy Joe."

"Thanks, Cookie," Justin acknowledged. "I don't know where my wits are today." In the *Kangaroo*'s luxuriously fitted stern cabin, probably, he thought wryly. The shock of his reception by Captain Jeffrey had left him numb and consumed by an anger for which there was no release.

A fresh shock, albeit a much pleasanter one, awaited him when he called at his own house on his way to the church. Kate Lamerton was there, and she came briefly to the door of the bedroom to tell him that Jessica was in labor.

"It'll be a few hours yet, Mr. Broome," she warned. "And there'll be nothing for you to do, 'cept eat the meal your little lass left ready for you in the kitchen. But you could warn Dr. Redfern, after you've eaten, if you will. Tell him he'll be wanted here 'afore dark, if you please." She shook her head firmly to Justin's diffident request that he be allowed to see his wife. "Best you leave her to me. One o' the maids from Mrs. Dawson's will be along in a little to give me a helping hand. I can send her to fetch the doctor, if he should be needed any sooner."

She retreated, closing the door behind her, and Justin caught only a glimpse of Jessica's small, pale face lying motionless on the pillows of the big, old-fashioned bed he had so often and so happily shared with her.

He had no appetite for the meal she had prepared for him, but he made a pretense of eating—listening, heart in mouth, for some sound that would tell him that Kate was wrong in her estimate of the time the birth would take. But, apart from a few faint moans, he could hear nothing, and finally he pushed his plate away and set off in search of Dr. Redfern.

The doctor was not at his residence, and after a wasted call at the hospital, Justin ran him to earth at the house of a patient in Clarence Street and was able to leave his message. It was only a few hundred yards from there to the church, and reassured by the doctor's injunction that he was not to worry but permit nature to take its course, he decided to answer Samuel Marsden's summons. Since his services as a King's officer were not required, he mused resentfully, he would be as well to consider any offer to charter the *Flinders*—even one from the chaplain, who was not renowned for generosity.

In any event, if the unfortunate missionaries who had been left unprotected at Whangaroa were in the danger that Cookie had suggested, then in common humanity he could not refuse to join in an attempt to bring them succor . . . or, if the need arose, to evacuate them—although the task would seem to be one more suited to His Majesty's ship *Kangaroo*. . . . Justin expelled his breath in a frustrated sigh and strode on.

A small crowd of well-dressed people—the respectable inhabitants of Sydney—had gathered about the door of the church, he saw, when he came in sight of it. He recognized Colonel and Mrs. Molle, alighting from a carriage; and then a smart curricle, with two well-matched gray horses between the shafts, came trotting past him, Captain Sanderson on the box and Captain and Mrs. Jeffrey seated in the rear. Jeffrey was in full-dress uniform, his wife in somber black, and Justin realized, with a start, that they must be gathering for the late judge advocate's funeral . . . fool that he was, to have forgotten that, as well as the Hawkesbury grain in his ship's hold!

He would have turned away, conscious that he had no place in the growing throng of notables, when he heard his name called and found Rick Tempest hurrying to catch up with him.

"Justin—hold hard! I've been looking for you. But when I went to your house I found the redoubtable Mrs. Lamerton in charge and your child evidently preparing to enter this wicked world . . . not for some time, though, she assured me. And she said I might find you at the church." He broke off, to eye Justin in some bewilderment. "I'd no idea that you were likely to be among the late Mr. Bent's mourners, however."

"I'm not," Justin denied. He explained the reason for his presence and then added, with restrained bitterness, "Have you seen your captain this morning?"

Rick nodded. "I have seen and spoken with him . . . and I know what he has done. For God's sake, Justin, I was never so angry in my life! But I fear he's within his rights, you know."

"Is he? When the Admiralty appointed me to the *Kangaroo*?"

"He can claim he is waiting for Their Lordships' ruling—and you know how long *that* means he can wait."

"Yes, I do know." Justin again made to turn away, but Rick grasped his arm.

"I'm ordered to attend the funeral, although I never set eyes on the late Mr. Bent. Come with me, Justin. Let Jeffrey see us together; that might give him pause. And you can find out what Marsden wants when the service is over."

Justin hesitated, and Rick's grip on his arm tightened. "Come on, my dear fellow—look, the Governor's on his way! We must be in our places before he enters the church, or be guilty of grave discourtesy to His Majesty's representative."

"Very well," Justin agreed reluctantly.

They entered the church and found seats at the end of the aisle. A clatter of hooves heralded the Governor's arrival, with his escort, and the congregation rose as he made his dignified entrance, Mrs. Macquarie at his side and his staff bringing up the rear.

There was a brief pause, and then the coffin was carried in, followed by the judge advocate's widow, heavily veiled and leaning on the arm of her late husband's brother. She dropped to her knees in the pew allotted to her, and the Reverend Samuel Marsden's harsh voice started slowly to read the burial service.

He did not depart from it or give any undue emphasis to any part of the prescribed words, and it was not until he ascended the pulpit, and picked up the notes placed there, that the listening congregation sensed that anything untoward was likely to occur. It was the custom, Justin was aware, for a eulogy to be delivered if the deceased was a person of substance in the colony, but usually such oratory was brief.

Marsden, however, released from the confines of the Church of

England Prayer Book, gave his eloquence full rein. In ringing tones, he declaimed the virtues of the dead man, his selfless toil in the office he had lately held, his dedication and devotion, his Christian forebearance in the face of great adversity.

It became evident, as he thundered on, his voice echoing from end to end of the small, crowded church, that it was at the Governor his barbed utterances were aimed, since praise of Ellis Bent must, in the circumstances, imply condemnation of the colony's ruler. A shocked hush settled over the packed pews; the judge advocate's widow crouched weeping, her head in her hands, but beside her his brother, the judge—whose court had been closed to litigants and transgressors alike for almost a year—sat bolt upright, a triumphant smile curving his lips, and his eyes bright with the light of battle.

The Governor, Justin saw, shifted uneasily in his seat, his gaze fixed on the roof of the church and a wave of color suffusing his thin, lined cheeks, as Samuel Marsden, abandoning the subject of his eulogy, launched into an extraordinary tirade against the inhabitants of the colony itself.

"What lamentable depravity pervades every part of our society! There is no sin, however serious, that is not practiced without remorse amongst us. Lying and perjury and theft, and whoredom and blasphemy and drunkenness are daily committed amongst us. The effect of the Divine displeasure is felt by almost every individual in this colony! Some are pining and languishing and wasting away. . . ." He paused to draw breath, and gestured dramatically to the coffin. "So it was with our dear departed brother, Ellis Bent, who sought by every means in his power to bring these sinners back to God. His was the supreme sacrifice, and I ask your compassion for his sorrowing widow and his five young children—one as yet unborn. May his soul rest in peace and his noble and blameless spirit be received by God Almighty in heaven, wherein will lie his just reward!"

He descended from the pulpit, a rotund but muscular figure, and signing to the funeral cortege to precede him, followed the coffin out toward the burial ground. Most of the mourners moved silently out in his wake, but the Governor and his staff halted at the door of the church. The viceregal carriage was summoned by Major Antill; he handed Mrs. Macquarie into its cushioned interior as the mounted escort hastily formed about it, and the Governor, pale now with the effort required to keep his temper, got in beside her and bade the coachman drive on.

At the door of the church, waiting with a small knot of people who had decided not to watch the interment, Rick looked at Justin, an expression of ludicrous amazement on his face.

"Lord, it was bad enough when Bligh was Governor!" he exclaimed heatedly. "But that performance beats everything I ever witnessed in his day . . . even from Colonel Collins in Van Diemen's Land!"

"Yes," Justin managed tensely. He started to move away, and Rick, falling into step with him, said quietly, "I take it you're not waiting to see Marsden? What if he does offer to charter your sloop?"

"I'm not going to him. He can charter the *Flinders,* if that's what he wants, but"—Justin's mouth tightened—"I'll not give him passage, if he offers me a thousand pounds! I'll take his Maoris back to Whangaroa and bring his missionaries back here, if they decide to leave. But that is all I'll do."

"It is a task for His Majesty's ship *Kangaroo,* I should have said," Rick demurred.

"That would require the Governor's sanction, Rick . . . and Jeffrey's willingness."

"Quite," Rick agreed dryly. He halted, looking up at the sun-bright sky. "The day's yet young . . . I will go and wait on Lawyer Crossley and attend to my part of our partnership agreement. I'm out of the Royal Navy as of today, my captain informed me, and young Meredith is overjoyed at the prospect of becoming acting first lieutenant." He halted and turned to face Justin, his smile warm. "I'd have invited you to take a drink with me, Justin my friend, but you've more important matters on your mind, I know. We'll celebrate the arrival of your firstborn in due course, eh? The Dawsons are planning to take my Katie to Upwey, in order to give her an insight into the settlers' way of life, but I'll be at the Pitt Street house if you want me."

They parted and Justin returned to his own home, to learn that Dr. Redfern had been summoned. It was, however, not until three anxious hours had passed that the onetime naval surgeon came to tell him that he was the father of a son.

"A lusty little fellow," Redfern assured him and grinned, as the baby's shrill crying reached their ears from the adjoining room, in proof of his assertion. "Kate Lamerton's preparing him for your inspection."

"And Jessica?" Justin asked, his throat tight. "How is Jessica, sir?"

"She's tired, Justin—it was a difficult labor—but she'll soon be herself again, don't worry. You shall see her and the boy in a little while. In the meantime, let's follow naval tradition and splice the main brace, shall we?"

"Of course, sir. I'm forgetting my manners." They drank the new baby's health, and then Redfern raised his glass again. "Damnation to the King's enemies, Lieutenant Broome! And, I think, to the Governor's, don't you? Because they seem to be in full cry at the moment." He added grimly, as he set down his glass, "I heard what happened at the funeral service today; D'Arcy Wentworth told me, before I came here. It's a bad business, Justin."

"Yes, sir, it is," Justin answered. "I was there."

Kate Lamerton's appearance, with a small, blanket-wrapped morsel in her arms, interrupted his account of the chaplain's eulogy.

"Here," she announced proudly. "Here's your son, Mr. Broome. And his mother's waiting for you." She placed the tiny, squirming bundle in Justin's arms and stood back, beaming. "Take him to her, will you not?"

Justin, his heart full, obeyed her.

Jessica lay, with her eyes closed, propped up on her pillows, but she roused herself instantly when Justin went in, holding out her arms for the burden he carried. "He's lovely, is he not?" she whispered, settling the child into the crook of her arm and smiling happily up at him. "Could we christen him Murdoch, do you think, after my brother?"

"Of course we could." In that moment, he would have given her anything, Justin knew. He bent to kiss her small, flushed face. "It's a fine name, and he's a fine boy. Jessica India, you are beautiful and I love you! Thank God that all went well with you— with both of you."

Her eyelids fluttered. Drowsily she echoed his thanks to their Maker, and then, opening her eyes again, she caught at his hand.

"Justin, you will be able to stay ashore for a little while, won't you? Captain Jeffrey will give you leave?"

"He's given me leave, my dearest," Justin answered. He hesitated, uncertain of what more to tell her, and then, to his relief, he saw that she had drifted into sleep.

Marsden, he thought savagely, could go to the devil. He should not have the *Flinders* . . . if he needed a ship to evacuate his missionaries from Whangaroa, let him go, cap in hand, to the Governor he had so grossly maligned and plead for the King's ship *Kangaroo*. If the Maori tribes were bent on war and British lives were in danger, the Governor, being the man he was, would be unlikely to refuse.

He looked down at his sleeping wife and at the tiny, red-faced scrap of humanity that was his newborn son and murmured softly, "I'll not leave you unless I'm dragged from you by the scruff of my neck, I promise you! So rest easy, both of you."

The order for him to report for duty on board the *Kangaroo* came, in writing, at noon the next day, and Justin swore angrily as he read it. Signed by Captain Jeffrey and delivered by a midshipman, the note informed him that his leave of absence was canceled due to the fact that, on instructions from His Excellency the Governor, the ship was to proceed at once to New Zealand.

"On His Excellency's instructions," the tersely worded note concluded, "and on his assurance that you are familiar with these waters, your services are required to assist with navigation and perform the duties of first lieutenant."

CHAPTER XI

Lucy Cahill stirred uneasily and opened her eyes, only to be compelled to close them again by the fierce glare of the sun. Her brief glance and the slight motion she could feel sufficed to tell her that she was lying on the deck of a ship . . . but what ship and whither it might be bound she had no means of knowing.

But it was not the *Kelso*—of that she was certain. She had vivid memories of the *Kelso*'s end and of the violent tropical storm that, after untold hours of battling against it, had finally driven the listing Indiaman onto a jagged coral reef, where wind and sea had pounded her to destruction. The shouts and cries of the doomed crew were still etched in her memory, along with the crash of falling masts and spars and a terrible grinding sound as the ship's hull was hurled, again and again, against the sharp, unseen teeth of the coral, and the sea came pouring in through great rents in her planking.

Almost out of her mind with terror, she had lain in her bunk until the cabin floor had been filled with surging water, and Frances Spence had half carried, half dragged her onto the open deck and bade her lash herself to the stump of a mast with a length of rope she had provided.

And that, Lucy recalled, grief-stricken, had been the last she had seen of Frances . . . the merest glimpse, through the relentlessly driving rain, of her slim figure, fighting its way across the dangerously canting deck—in search, presumably, of her husband. Jasper Spence had been struck down by a fever, soon after leaving Batavia, and he, too, had been in his cabin below. Neither of them had, to her knowledge, reappeared. . . . Lucy caught her breath on a sob.

She owed her life to Frances and to the mate, Jonas Burdock, who, when daylight came, had forced her, screaming and fighting, to jump overboard and swim with him to the shore. Eight or nine of the crew had reached the shore, three of them injured. Those who could walk had gone with Jonas in search of human habitation and help, but they had not returned, and she had waited, hoping and praying and then losing hope as, one after the other, the injured men had died.

She had expected to die also, Lucy thought, and, once again, opened her eyes, seeking proof that the impression that she was on board a ship had not been a false one . . . or a figment of her fevered imagination. But it was not. Clear against the backdrop of a blue, cloudless sky, a sail hung, taut as the wind filled it . . . a dingy lateen sail, though, suggesting a fishing boat or a small coastal trader, rather than a ship like the *Kelso*.

And the deck was stained, smelling of fish. . . . She endeavored to sit up, and as the rough blanket with which she had been covered slipped aside, she realized that, beneath it, she was virtually naked, clad only in a torn shift. Hastily, fearing who might be watching her, she pulled up the blanket and once more lay down.

Someone must have seen the slight movement she had made, for bare feet pattered across the deck and a dark-faced man came to kneel beside her. He said something in a language she could not comprehend, but he spoke gently and, reassured, Lucy raised herself on one elbow, keeping the blanket wrapped tightly about her shoulder.

"Who are you?" she asked faintly.

The man smiled and shook his head. After studying her face for a moment, he jumped up and pattered away, to return shortly afterward with a hollowed-out coconut shell, which he held to her lips.

Lucy drank gratefully, her lips dry and cracked, so that the touch of the shell's edge was very painful against them. But the liquid was cool and soothing to her parched throat, and when she had gulped it down, she was able to smile wanly at her rescuer in token of thanks.

He beamed back, clearly pleased, patted her blanket-shrouded shoulder with a slim brown hand, then turned and called out something in his own language, which, as before, was quite incomprehensible to her. His call brought two other brown-skinned

men to his side, and all three stood looking down at her in friendly
solicitude.

Then, from below, the craggy features of Jonas Burdock
emerged, and, gaining the deck, he came shuffling slowly toward
her. He looked desperately ill, Lucy saw, his skin blistered and
burned almost black by the sun, his eyes sunken and lackluster,
and his cheeks hectically flushed.

"Fever," he told her, and dropped into a squatting position on
the deck beside her, as if unable to hold himself upright. "The
others are worse'n I am. They're below." He gestured to the
hatchway from which he had emerged. "Not much space down
there—that's why you're here. Skipper said it'd be best for you.
Glad to see you're recovering, Mrs. Cahill."

"Thank you, Jonas," Lucy acknowledged. She had never
particularly liked the big, rawboned mate or, indeed, until the night
of the wreck, spoken to him as an equal. He was the son of an old
river-trading master who carried mail and supplies to the Hawkesbury settlements in an ancient ketch, the *Fanny*, and although he
was not of convict stock, his social standing made him little better
than those who were. But clearly, she thought, she was deeply in
his debt now, and it would behoove her to treat him carefully. "Tell
me," she managed weakly. "Did you induce these fishermen to
help us?"

"Aye," Jonas confirmed. "It took us three days to walk to their
village and another two to persuade Hassim Ong to bring us back
to where the *Kelso* foundered. I didn't know if you'd be alive or
dead, Mrs. Cahill, but I reckoned I owed it to you to make sure."

"The men I was with—the ones who were injured, they . . .
they were dead, weren't they?"

He nodded, black brows furrowed. "Aye, all three of them,
dead as doornails. And there were some bodies washed up on the
beach. Ong and his fellows helped me to bury them."

"Whose bodies?" Lucy asked, dreading the answer.

The mate avoided her gaze. "The sea had taken its will of them,
and the sun, too, so it weren't possible to be certain sure,
but . . . Mrs. Spence and Cap'n Oliver. I buried them myself.
The others . . . well, you wouldn't know their names, Mrs.
Cahill."

"No," Lucy conceded. Her head was throbbing unmercifully,
and, for all the calm of the sun-bright water, a sick queasiness

threatened to overcome her. Sensing her distress, Jonas Burdock spoke to the dark-skinned man who had brought her the coconut milk, and he picked up the empty shell and went to replenish it.

"You speak their language?" Lucy said, surprised.

"Oh, aye. We mostly called at Batavia and Coupang, on the homeward voyage, see, and I picked up a smattering of Dutch. The natives don't speak it, but you can make 'em understand what you want." The native skipper returned with the coconut shell brimming, and Jonas took it from him. He put his arm round Lucy's shoulders and, raising her head, held the shell very gently to her lips. "Not too much at a time," he warned, "or it will make you sick."

His arm felt hot against her bare shoulders, and she remembered that he had said that he, as well as the men below, had fever. "You finish it," she invited, pushing the shell away. "I've had enough for the time being." She asked, as he drank thirstily, "Jonas, where are they taking us? Do you know?"

"To Coupang, Mrs. Cahill. We should be there tomorrow sometime . . . evening, maybe. And"—he hesitated, looking down at her uncertainly—"I don't want to worry you when you're weak and only just conscious, but we'll have to pay them. I had to promise Hassim Ong that we'd reward him. He'll have lost over a week's fishing."

Lucy peered up at him in dismay. She had salvaged nothing from the wreck; she had nothing, save the torn shift she wore. Even her feet were bare.

"Did not Mr. Spence have . . . what are they called? Letters of credit, trading credits?"

"Maybe he had, but they'll have gone down with the ship." Again the young mate hesitated, and then, as if reaching a decision, he went on, "I swam out to the wreck to see if there was anything I could salvage, but there was precious little. Except this . . ." From the pocket of his ragged trousers he brought to light a small, velvet-covered box and held it out for her inspection. It had been severely battered, and the lock was broken, but Lucy recognized it at once. She had seen it in Frances Spence's cabin, although she had no idea what it contained and had supposed it to be a jewel box of more than usual elegance. Frances had seldom worn jewelry, it was true, but . . . She put out her hand to take it.

"Careful when you open it," Jonas warned. "Don't let any of Hassim's men see." He moved so that his body screened the box from view, and motioned Lucy to open it. "One of the stones will settle our debt to all of them, and they'll count themselves lucky."

"Stones?" Lucy echoed, not taking in what he had said, and he warned her again.

"Careful, Mrs. Cahill. They're loose stones, and the box is worn."

Lucy opened it, her hands trembling, and when she saw the contents, she emitted a gasp of mingled pleasure and astonishment. The stones were rubies, emeralds, and amethysts, of a size and glowing beauty that took her breath away. Immersion in seawater had not dimmed their brilliance, and she could only guess at their value. With the exception of a ruby necklace and two ornately crafted silver rings, the stones were not set, but all had been skillfully cut and prepared for setting, and . . . she could not recall that Frances had ever worn the necklace or the rings. She had owned all these magnificent precious stones, yet had never had them made into jewelry for her own adornment!

She said, recovering her breath, "These must be worth a—a king's ransom!"

"Aye—or a queen's. An Indian queen's, Mrs. Cahill." Jonas's tone was dry. "To put it more precisely, a rani's." With a blunt forefinger he traced some faded gold embossed lettering on the inside of the box lid. "I picked up a bit of the Hindu language, as well as Dutch, on my travels, and as nearly as I can make out, this box once belonged to the Rani of Anraj. That letter's 'alif,' see, then 'neem,' a blank, 'alif' again, and the last one is their letter *j* . . . I forget what they call it. It's the way Moslems write, and Anraj is a Moslem state on the Bengal border." He mopped his sweat-streaked brow with the back of his hand and added pointedly, "I know because Mr. Jasper Spence told me that he was the honorable company's resident there, before he quit the service and came out to Sydney."

"But why, if he gave her these—these beautiful stones, did Mrs. Spence keep them hidden like this?" Lucy questioned. "She could have had them made up. . . . Calcutta has hundreds of skilled silversmiths and jewelers. And she went there regularly."

"I can hazard a guess, Mrs. Cahill. Can you not?"

"No," Lucy retorted. "No, I cannot."

She felt oddly light-headed, incapable of reasoned thought, but . . . there *had* been some scandal attached to Jasper Spence's name, and she recalled hearing that he had left the East India Company's service under a cloud. Which might explain why Frances had kept the stones hidden in their box and had neither used nor sold them—nor, for that matter, ever talked of them. Frances had had a strict code of honor, and—

Jonas put out his hand for the box. "You'd best let me look after the stones."

Lucy flared up angrily, clutching it to her. "They're not yours! You've no claim on them, Jonas."

"Have I not?" His smile was tight. "I found 'em, Mrs Cahill . . . and I didn't have to show 'em to you, did I? I could've kept my big mouth shut, and you'd never have known I had 'em."

He was right, Lucy was compelled to concede. Her anger faded and she relinquished the box to him.

"Where *did* you find them?" she asked.

Jonas eyed her gravely. "On Mrs. Spence's body, if you want the truth. I didn't go looking for 'em, if that's what you're thinking." He thrust the precious box into his trouser pocket but did not, as Lucy had hoped he would, attempt to leave her. "I reckon we've some serious talking to do, Mrs. Cahill."

"Talking?" Suddenly, for no reason she could have explained, Lucy was afraid of him. During the voyage, she had seen him often enough, it was true, but she knew very little about him, save that he was old Jed Burdock's son and that he had been in Jasper Spence's employ for five or six years.

He was, she supposed, studying him covertly, attractive in a rough, male way, but his manners were uncouth, his speech uneducated, and there was a strange, almost menacing air about him now that she found disconcerting. Certainly she owed him a great deal—her life, perhaps twice over, for she would have died had she been abandoned on the deserted beach for very much longer, without food or water, and only the dead for company.

Jonas had come back for her, but . . . "What," she asked faintly, wishing that her head would cease its painful throbbing, "what have we to talk about?"

"I'd have said plenty. You an' me, for a start."

"You and me?"

"Aye. We'll have to hang together when we get to Coupang. It'll be easier all round, I reckon, if we told the Dutch authorities that you're my wife."

"The other men will know I'm not," Lucy objected. "The ones below."

"They'll keep their mouths shut, if I tell 'em to." Jonas brushed her objection aside. He was looking at her with the unmistakable light of desire in his fever-bright eyes, and she shrank from him, repulsed by his coarseness and lack of finesse when he added softly, "I always fancied you, from the minute you stepped aboard the *Kelso*. And you knew it, did you not, for all your high an' mighty ways?"

Lucy gave him no answer, and he changed his tone, becoming practical. "With the stones in that box o' Mrs. Spence's, we'll not lack money. Coupang is just a fever-ridden outpost, with a small garrison, but I'll go to Batavia, sell some o' those rubies, and buy a seagoing vessel. We'll sail her to China, pick up a cargo of tea and silks, and hightail it back to Sydney, with our fortunes made."

"Questions will be asked," Lucy said. She tried to sit up, dismayed by her own weakness and the effort it took.

Jonas put out an arm to support her. "Aye," he conceded. "But we'll have answers to 'em." On the pretense of draping the blanket about her shoulders, he slid his free hand beneath it and cupped one of her breasts, his fingers caressing the nipple as he held her against him, his stubbled cheek laid on hers. "I could give you one or two answers right now," he boasted softly. "Only I've no more strength than a kitten, and old Ong's watching us. But just you wait till we get ashore and I shake off this plaguey fever!"

Before she could voice a protest, he released her and sat back on his heels, regarding her with a complacent smile. Lucy controlled an impulse to strike him and, instead, said icily, "Be good enough to leave me. I am too tired to talk any more now."

Jonas rose reluctantly. "All right, Mrs. Cahill . . . Lucy. But you'll remember what I've said? We'll be in Coupang by this time tomorrow, and the Dutch are a greedy lot. They'll expect to be paid for whatever hospitality they offer us, and—" He tapped his trouser pocket significantly. "I hold the purse strings, and I'm not letting go of 'em."

Lucy slept fitfully, her sleep disturbed by hideous dreams, in which she was back at Yarramundie, suffering once again the nightmare raid by the bushrangers, which had so nearly cost her her sanity. But now the face she saw, as the face of her tormentor, was not that of Ben Croaker, but Jonas Burdock's.

She awoke with the coming of daylight, and the remembered terror was still with her. Hassim Ong brought her more coconut milk, but she was unable to stomach even this, still less the greasy mixture of fish and rice he offered to her a little later. Wisely, the old fisherman indicated by signs that she should try to sleep, and though—fearing a return of her nightmare—Lucy fought against it, eventually she lapsed into a deep and dreamless repose, to awake this time feeling rested and refreshed.

The fishing boat was in sight of land, and even as she sat up to watch its progress, she realized that they were nearing Coupang. A small forest of masts and red-roofed buildings indicated the location of the town, and as Hassim Ong hauled on his tiller, she glimpsed what could only be a military fort, standing on a promontory toward which they were heading. But the breeze was fitful and the boat sluggish; it was dusk before they were level with the Dutch fort, and when the short-lived tropical twilight faded, all that was to be seen of the town were a few flickering lights, gleaming from behind banks of screening trees like so many fireflies in the gathering darkness.

As soon as he tied up to the quay, Hassim Ong sent one of his crew ashore to inform the Dutch authorities of the number and nationality of his passengers, and Jonas came staggering up on deck looking, in the dim light of Ong's lantern, a pale shadow of his normal self.

"The fever," he gasped, squatting down at Lucy's side. "It's burning me up, devil take it!" She moved away from him instinctively, and he scowled at her resentfully but did not attempt to follow her. Across the space that divided them he flung a crumpled, salt-encrusted garment that Lucy recognized as a dress that had once belonged to Frances. "Better look respectable," he said, "else the Dutch will start wondering if we're escaped convicts. And don't forget—when they start asking questions . . . you're my wife. You're Mrs. Jonas Burdock."

But the Dutch, when they came, asked them no questions. After a lengthy discussion with Hassim Ong, one of the men explained, in halting English, that he was a clerk, in the government service. The Governor, it appeared, was in Batavia; his deputy was the military commandant, who would call on the shipwrecked party next day. In the meantime, the clerk added, they would be taken to the hospital and kept in isolation until the port medical authorities were able to clear them. Arrangements to convey them were in hand.

The arrangements took a considerable time to put into effect. Jonas took no part in the discussion; he seemed utterly spent and he slept noisily, the breath rasping in his lungs and his powerful body lying limp and motionless on the dirty, unswept deck. He made no protest when a native stretcher party picked him up and carried him to a bullock cart waiting on the quay, into which the other sick men were also unceremoniously dumped.

For Lucy, however—to her intense relief—a covered chair was provided, and, borne on the shoulders of two native porters, she was carried swiftly and in reasonable comfort to a long, low building standing on top of a hill, about a quarter of a mile from the harbor. An airy room was put at her disposal; servants brought her water with which to wash and a light meal and left her to her own devices, pointing to a brass handbell and indicating that she should ring it if there was anything she required.

Again she slept, and by the following morning she had lost the light-headedness and nausea that had plagued her on the fishing boat, and was even able to enjoy the ample food provided for her to break her fast. The stained gown she had worn was brought back to her washed and neatly pressed; a woman servant assisted her to bathe, then to comb and braid her hair—at last free of the sticky residue of salt; and, to Lucy's infinite relief, a swift inspection in a mirror showed her that she looked, once more, a lady.

A lady, Lucy told herself, and by no possible stretch of the imagination could anyone—even a wooden-headed Dutch commandant—suppose her to be the wife of Jonas Burdock. Nor, for that matter, would they believe that Jonas was the rightful owner of a box of precious stones, worth a king's—or an Indian rani's—ransom, whatever he might claim.

She waited, with growing impatience, for the commandant's arrival, but her first visitor was a doctor, a thin, bearded little man whose English was little better than the clerk's had been the previous evening. He was helpful and conscientious, courtly in manner, and his examination, conducted with delicacy, was quite cursory.

"You are almost well now," he told her. "Soon you be ver' well, madame, as if . . . how you say in Engleesh? As if no bad thing ever happen you. Very fortunate. Not like the poor sailors wid you. Two of zem ver' sick. One I t'ink will die."

Lucy's heart missed a beat. Which of them, she wondered, was likely to die? If it was Jonas, then she had nothing more to fear, provided she could recover the box of precious stones from him.

She endeavored to question the doctor but could not make him understand, and her plea to be permitted to visit the sick men was met with a horrified refusal. They were in quarantine and must be isolated; their ward was not a suitable place for a lady of quality to visit.

"Ze commandant—Major Jos Van Buren—will come soon. To him, madame, you make appeal, yes?" The little doctor bowed to her politely and, after leaving her a concoction to drink and some pills to swallow, took his leave.

Major Van Buren made his belated appearance that evening, when Lucy had begun to despair of ever seeing him. She was conducted into his presence by one of the hospital servants and found herself confronting one of the handsomest men she had ever seen in her life. Far from the wooden-headed officer she had expected, he was tall and fair-haired, his age perhaps thirty-three or four, and both his manners and his English were impeccable.

He greeted her by kissing her hand, and as he pulled out a cane chair for her and assisted her to seat herself in it, she saw admiration in his intelligent blue eyes and instantly warmed to it.

"So old Dr. Reisner was right!" he exclaimed. "You are—you are truly beautiful, madame! I am delighted and honored to make your acquaintance."

A trifle taken aback by his outspoken tribute, Lucy flushed and responded shyly to the compliment. He questioned her about the shipwreck, listening intently to her description of the *Kelso*'s last hours, and when she spoke of her rescue, he expressed his pleasure in the miracle that had spared her life.

"The good God was watching over you, dear young lady, and it is our good fortune that He sent you here unscathed. We see few beautiful white women in Coupang—or, indeed, in these fever-infested islands, where, for my sins, I am compelled to serve. But we shall do all in our power to make your stay here comfortable and pleasant. My house is at your disposal until such time as you are able to continue your journey to Port Jackson. Your husband also, of course, when he recovers and our doctors declare him free of infection."

Lucy's cheeks drained of color. So Jonas had carried out his threat, she thought bitterly. However sick he was, he had claimed to be her husband. . . . She drew in her breath sharply.

"I have no husband, Major Van Buren. My name is Lucy Cahill, and I am a widow. I—"

"Ah!" The interruption was forceful, his frown at first puzzled and then angry. "I had wondered at what appeared to me a mésalliance. You were related to the owner of the *Kelso,* you said, and the fellow who told me that you were his wife is . . . a common seaman, is he not? Scarcely a gentleman, at all events. But . . ." The major did not wait for Lucy's reply. Rising, he strode to the door and barked an order to someone outside. When he returned to his own seat behind the desk, he was smiling, all trace of anger gone from his tanned, good-looking face. "Why should this fellow—his name is Burdock, is it not?—why should Burdock try to lie to me and to the good doctor also? Is he a convict, an escaper? Does he suppose that you will protect him?" His expression softened, and he put out a hand to take Lucy's across the desk. "Perhaps, dear Mrs. Cahill, you feel in his debt for the service he rendered you?"

"I . . . yes, yes, I do, sir." It was the truth, and Lucy admitted it in a whisper, avoiding his intent and searching blue gaze. His fingers tightened about hers, and she was conscious of a small thrill at the contact. She wished Jonas no ill, she thought—how could she wish him ill, after all he had done for her? But she would not connive at his lies. "He saved my life," she stated, nerving herself to look up. "And he brought the fishing boat back to—to where I was, Major Van Buren. I am greatly in his debt, but I . . ." She could not go on, tears choking her.

"Do not distress yourself, I pray you." He was on his feet, coming to stand beside her, still retaining his grasp of her hand. "We will settle the matter justly. *Is* he an escaped convict? You may tell me in confidence."

Lucy shook her head, biting back the tears. "No. He was first mate of the *Kelso*. He—"

A knock on the door interrupted her. Two soldiers brought Jonas in, half carrying him, and Major Van Buren motioned them to keep him at a distance.

The fever, Lucy saw, had taken a severe toll of him. His cheeks were flushed and sunken beneath their thick growth of stubble, his eyes were bloodshot, and he was shivering violently. She felt a twinge of pity for him when the Dutch commandant challenged harshly, "This lady is not your wife, is she, Burdock? You lied to me, did you not?"

Had she withdrawn the outrageous claim, she might have done no more, but, defiantly, Jonas repeated it, and Lucy turned on him in fury.

"Tell the truth, Jonas—for your own sake, if not for mine! I cannot protect you if you don't. I—"

"Protect me?" Jonas countered, with bitterness. "Protect me from what? In the name of God, what crime have I committed?"

His words and his continued obstinacy offered at once the excuse and the means by which he could be discredited. And discredit him she must, for Major Van Buren's interest in her would fade, Lucy was aware, if she permitted any suspicion to remain of a relationship with—what had he called Jonas?—a common seaman.

In a tearful display of emotion, she let her head fall onto her outstretched hands and, her voice muffled by sobs, whispered the damning accusation.

"This man is a thief, Major Van Buren. He stole my—my jewels from me. They are on his person, in a—a velvet-covered box. You will find them if you—if your soldiers search him."

The commandant rapped an order. The box was swiftly discovered, and one of the soldiers laid it on the desk. Van Buren's eyes widened when he opened it.

"All is explained," he said. "You need worry no more, Mrs. Cahill." Carefully he closed the box and put it into Lucy's hands. "I will make arrangements for you to be moved from here to more comfortable quarters." He jerked his head at the soldiers; grasping their prisoner roughly, they started to bundle him from the room.

At the door, Jonas contrived to halt them. He turned, his ravaged face filled with contempt, and spat on the floor at Lucy's feet.

"I hope," he croaked scornfully, "that you can live with your conscience, Mrs. Cahill. If you were the last woman left alive on earth, I'd not wed you . . . by heaven, I would not!''

The soldiers took him away, and as the door of the doctor's office closed behind them, the silence was broken only by Lucy's sobs.

Major Van Buren came to lift her gently to her feet. "Come," he invited. "I will take you to my house, Mrs. Cahill. You have nothing more to fear from that rogue."

"What will happen to him?" Lucy asked tremulously. "Please—he saved my life. I don't want him to be—to be punished."

"The good Lord will punish him," Van Buren told her. He smiled. "Dr. Reisner says that he and the others will be dead in twenty-four hours."

He offered her his arm, and—after a momentary hesitation—Lucy took it, and felt his strong fingers close, once more, about hers.

CHAPTER XII

The Reverend Samuel Marsden, Justin had long ago decided, was a hypocrite, prone to judge his fellow men—and in particular those of his fellows who came out to Sydney in chains—by standards he neither applied nor considered applicable to himself.

The talk among shipping men was that his lucrative trade with New Zealand and the Pacific Islands included gunrunning . . . yet, in the past, the reverend gentleman had been loud in his condemnation of the rum traffickers, whose profits were no match for his. As a magistrate, his sentences were harsh, the floggings he ordered excessively severe; but within a few hours of imposing them, he would stand up in his pulpit and exhort his congregation to display brotherly love, one to another. And then, although himself possessed of a devoted wife and numerous offspring, he was prone, almost in the same breath, to condemn what he insisted on calling "the evils of concubinage" and to extol the benefits to be derived from chastity.

All this to men who might search the length and breadth of the colony and fail to find a virtuous woman they might take to wife, or who, sentenced to years of exile, had been compelled, when their chains had been hammered on, to leave wives and children behind them.

Yet, for all that . . . Justin could not help but smile as his gaze rested on the bent heads of three hundred Maori warriors, squatting in peace together while they listened to Samuel Marsden's Christian message, delivered in a language that few, if any, of them understood.

Their respect for the fiery evangelist amounted almost to veneration. When the *Kangaroo* had dropped anchor in Whangaroa Bay twenty-four hours earlier, the tribes of Hinaki, Hongi, and Korokoro—successor to the deceased Ruatara—had been facing each other under arms, ready to do battle, with the site of the mission station as their battleground and the missionaries and their families destined to become the first victims . . . and spoil for the victors, when the battle ended and the ovens were lit.

But Marsden had not hesitated. He had gone ashore, carrying his Bible, and refusing Captain Jeffrey's offer of an armed guard of seamen.

"They know me, Captain," he had asserted. "Chief Hongi is to go to England soon, at my instigation. Korokoro came with poor Ruatara to Sydney, and my wife and I nursed that unhappy young man when he was taken ill during his visit to the colony. They *trust* me—and I trust them. Believe me, they are the finest and noblest race of heathens known to the civilized world. I have no need of your guard."

With faith in that mutual trust, the portly chaplain had approached the warriors, and Justin, standing by the boat that had set him ashore, had been compelled to revise his opinion of the man. Hypocrite he might be, but there was no doubt that the Reverend Samuel Marsden had courage—as well as a strange, almost mystic power over his warlike flock.

The Whangaroans had greeted him with joy, their cries of *"Te Matenga!"* echoing from end to end of the beach. Hinaki's warriors, grouped menacingly nearby on a low hill, each with his spear stuck in the ground before him, had, after a brief hesitation, taken up the cry and run down to join the milling crowd.

Marsden had slept there, in one of the missionaries' huts, despite the fact that they had told him that, for the past two months, they had kept watch, night and day, with their boat always afloat, oars and sails in readiness for instant flight should the expected attack on them take place. And he had slept soundly, on his own admission.

Now he was conducting a Christian service for all three tribes and any others who showed an inclination to attend. A missionary named Kendall interpreted for him in a low voice, which contrasted oddly with Marsden's impassioned and, at times, thunderous utterances. His congregation stood or sat at the appropriate passages in the service of Morning Prayer, their movements orchestrated by the chief Korokoro, using a switch as a baton. All three chiefs were arrayed in old military uniforms—

presented as gifts to them on one of the *Active*'s earlier visits—with plumed hats on their heads and British swords gripped proudly in their hands.

It was an extraordinary sight, and Captain Jeffrey, whom sheer curiosity had lured ashore, was standing with dropping jaw and a ludicrous expression of bewilderment on his round, perspiring face.

"It is unbelievable, Mr. Broome," he muttered to Justin. "And I would not have believed it, if I had not seen it for myself." He glanced about him, shaking his head. "And this is the very beach, you said, did you not, on which the *Boyd*'s people were massacred and . . . cannibalized?"

"That is so, sir," Justin confirmed, secretly enjoying his commander's mystification. "Their bones were scattered all over the sand, until Mr. King and Captain Hansen—master of the *Active,* sir—gave them Christian burial."

"Mr. Marsden is a truly remarkable man," Jeffrey said. "Truly remarkable! I confess that I'd expected to be taking his missionaries and their wives and children on board the *Kangaroo* within hours of our dropping anchor in the bay. And by force, too, by God! But now this . . . Damme, they're singing the Old Hundredth, are they not? And standing up to do it!"

"I fancy they are, sir, yes."

"Perhaps I should have made an—er—an official appearance at the service," the captain added, sounding doubtful. "But you did not suggest it, and it's too late now."

"It might not have been wise, sir," Justin demurred. "Mr. Marsden was anxious to offer no show of force, and he's been proved right, I think. The Maoris will have observed that our guns were trained on the shore, and—"

"A necessary precaution," Jeffrey interrupted irritably, "in the circumstances, Mr. Broome. However, since there appears no further need for such a precaution, take my boat back to the ship and have the guns run in and secured. I shall go and make the acquaintance of the Maori chiefs as soon as the service is concluded."

"Aye, aye, sir," Justin acknowledged. "Will you go alone, sir?"

Captain Jeffrey hesitated, frowning, but as the words of the familiar hymn faded into momentary silence, he glanced across at his waiting boat. The young volunteer, Harris, was seated in the sternsheets, watching alertly for any sign that he might be wanted, and the captain's expression relaxed.

"I'll take young Harris. He can make himself useful, I don't doubt. Tell him to bring my pistol from the boat, and . . . report back here to take me off in a couple of hours, Mr. Broome."

Justin did as he had been ordered. On his way out to the anchored ship, he heard a loud commotion from the shore and, looking back, saw that the Maori warriors, released from the religious service and the decorum it had imposed, were engaged in a savage war dance, performed with much shouting and clashing of spears.

It was to be hoped that Captain Jeffrey would display the same tolerance toward the converts' sudden change of mood as Marsden and his missionaries accorded them, he thought cynically, as he watched a huge black figure, clad in the King's scarlet, go leaping among them, brandishing his sword. The cries of *"Te Matenga!"* were fainter now, drowned by the heavy thud of the dancers' feet and the deep-throated sound of their accompanying chant.

"It seems pretty lively ashore," Lieutenant Meredith observed when Justin joined him on the *Kangaroo*'s quarterdeck. "What are they up to now, for the Lord's sake?"

"They've praised the Lord in the Christian manner," Justin told him, smiling. "Now they're doing it in their own. No cause for alarm, though—the captain's remaining on shore, and he wants the guns secured and the guns' crews stood down. Attend to it, will you, please?"

"Aye, aye," Meredith acknowledged, omitting, as he invariably did, the customary "sir." But he gave the order and then asked, a trifle anxiously, how long the captain intended to remain on shore.

"I'm to pick him up in two hours' time—unless you would like me to delegate the honor?" Justin's smile widened when Meredith shook his head vigorously.

"No, thanks, Mr. Broome. This is near enough for me. In any case, I'm off watch in an hour, and I'd like to get my head down."

"Which is what I intend to do now. Leave word for me to be called at two bells of Mr. Crabbe's watch, if you please."

Justin went below. He had stood the middle watch and taken the first boat ashore at six o'clock, and he was asleep within a few minutes of retiring to his cabin.

His peace was short-lived. A hand shook him to reluctant wakefulness, and he opened his eyes to find the master, Silas Crabbe, bending over him, and—behind the master's stooped back—the white, frightened face of Cadet Harris. Justin sat up, swinging his legs to the deck in swift alarm.

"What is it?" he demanded. "Is the captain in trouble?"

Harris nodded miserably. The old master said, "I'll leave the lad to tell you what happened, Mr. Broome. Your boat'll be manned and ready when you come on deck, and one o' the missionaries— the one called Kendall—is waiting for you. He says he'll help."

Justin started to don his shirt and trousers. "Tell me, Mr. Harris," he bade the boy. "Slowly and carefully. What sort of trouble is the captain in?"

Harris drew in his breath sharply. "They're holding him as hostage, sir. The chief Hongi . . . that is, sir. He—"

"Take it from the beginning, lad. You went ashore with the captain. He wanted to meet the chiefs, did he not?"

"Yes, sir, that's right." Young Harris made an effort to speak slowly. "Mr. Kendall introduced him to them, and they were very friendly. Hongi speaks some English, and he invited the captain to visit his village. We went there, sir—it was quite a way. The chief's hut was in the center, and it was—oh, it was marvelous." He started to describe the village, but Justin cut him short.

"I want to know what happened, Mr. Harris, and why the captain is being held hostage."

"Yes, sir. I'm sorry, sir." The boy took up his story again. "We went into Chief Hongi's hut—the captain was very keen to see what it was like inside. And there—there was a pole at the entrance, with a—a human head spiked on it. They'd shrunk it somehow, but it was a human head all right. Hongi saw the captain staring at it, and he took it off the pole and tried to give it to him, beaming all over his face, sir, as if it was the finest present he could offer. The captain shook his head and wouldn't take it, and Hongi said . . . Oh, it was awful, sir."

"What was awful?" Justin prompted, reaching for his watch coat.

Harris swallowed hard. "He said it was the head of a Captain Jones, sir—an Englishman, who was the master of a whaler called the *Eliza*. As far as I could make out—his English wasn't very good—Captain Jones led a raid on his village. There was a pitched battle, and Jones was killed—by Hongi himself, he claimed, sir. And he started rubbing his stomach and laughing. Well, what he meant was pretty plain, of course, and the captain lost his temper. He went red in the face, sir, and took his pistol out and . . . he shot the head out of Hongi's hand! After that all hell broke loose. Hongi's warriors seized the captain and tied him up, and Hongi sent me to tell you that the captain would—would be killed, sir, unless you pay a ransom for him."

The devil take it! Justin thought; this was worse, a hundred times worse, than he had anticipated. Jeffrey must have taken leave of his senses to behave in such a manner. "What," he asked, managing somehow to speak with a semblance of calm, "is the ransom? What's Chief Hongi asking for?"

Harris shuffled his feet nervously. "He wants muskets, sir. And a pistol like the captain's. They're to be delivered to him before sunset—ten muskets, he said, sir, with powder and shot. The captain gave me the key of the arms chest to give you. Here it is, sir."

So Jeffrey expected the ransom to be paid. . . . Justin was on his feet, his brain racing as he sought for the best means of dealing with the ugly situation.

"I'll talk to Mr. Kendall," he said. "You cut along, lad, and curl up in your hammock. There's nothing more you can do." There was a flask on the shelf behind his coat, and he gestured to it. "Take a few swigs of rum, Mr. Harris. It'll help you to sleep."

"I'm not tired, sir," Harris protested. "Let me come with you, sir, please. I can show you where they're holding the captain and—"

"Mr. Kendall can probably do that. If he can't, I'll send for you. Cut along to your berth, lad, and take that flask with you."

Kendall, a thin, studious-looking young man, was waiting on the quarterdeck with Silas Crabbe. He said at once, "I know Chief Hongi, Mr. Broome, and I can tell you he's making no idle threat."

"Then what do you advise?" Justin demanded. "Am I to give him the muskets he's asking for?"

"If you want to see your captain alive, I fear you will have to, sir. Your only alternative is to use force, and I cannot advise that. The situation is tricky enough as it is, and there will be hell to pay if you attempt to free Captain Jeffrey by force. He'd be the first to die, and Mr. Marsden—"

"Where *is* Mr. Marsden?" Justin asked sharply.

Kendall sighed. "He's gone to visit Ruatara's people at Rangihoura. It's ten miles away, and he's gone by boat, with Mr. King and Mr. Hall. He intends to spend the night there, and I'm afraid there is no chance of bringing him back here—in time, that is." He laid emphasis on the last few words, and Justin echoed his sigh.

It wanted only about three hours to sunset, and young Harris had said that Chief Hongi's village was—how had he put it?—"quite a way."

"Do you know the village, Mr. Kendall?"

"Yes, sir. I can guide you there. It will take us about an hour and a half to reach the place from here. But we should leave at once . . . it wouldn't be advisable to have to make our way back to the ship after dark."

"I see." Justin did not pretend to misunderstand the implication of the missionary's quietly voiced statement. "Will the chief test the muskets?" he asked, struck by an idea.

Kendall's smile was tight-lipped, lacking amusement. "If you are thinking of rendering them unusable, Mr. Broome, I can only beg you not to do so. If Hongi doesn't test them this evening, he will tomorrow, and it would undermine our relationship with all the tribes, if he found he'd been cheated. The Maoris are men of their word, and they expect us to be equally honest."

Justin looked at Silas Crabbe, who had been listening in silence to his conversation with the missionary, and the old master shrugged resignedly. "You'll have to give this Hongi what he asks, Mr. Broome—you've no choice."

And he had not, Justin recognized, since clearly a captain in His Britannic Majesty's Navy could not be left to die at the hands of Maori cannibals, if there was any chance of effecting his release. As he gave Silas Crabbe the required permission to unlock the arms chest, he found himself wondering whether the talk of the Reverend Marsden's gunrunning was true. If so, and if he had supplied tribes other than Hongi's with firearms, then the chief's eagerness to obtain the ten muskets was understandable . . . and perhaps even justifiable.

"How many men should I take with me?" he asked Kendall,

and was dismayed when he saw the missionary shake his head.

"None, Mr. Broome, if you will be advised by me."

"And if I won't? Ten muskets between two of us will be quite a load."

Kendall shrugged. "Then two, perhaps, with no weapons of their own. And let me carry the ammunition."

"Right," Justin agreed.

The boat was loaded, and on reaching the shore, Justin distributed the ammunition and the muskets—which were bound together in manageable bundles—among Kendall and himself and two seamen, and they set off. It took them just under the hour and a half the missionary had estimated to reach the village, following a narrow but well-defined track that climbed steeply up one side of a wooded valley. Justin was in no mood to appreciate or even to take in the natural beauty of their surroundings. That their progress was being observed by hidden watchers he had no doubt, and at times he even glimpsed a dark form, moving like a shadow among the trees, and heard—or imagined he heard—the soft pad of bare feet uncomfortably close at hand.

But they were not molested, and only when they came in sight of the village did any of Hongi's tribesmen show themselves. Then two venerable warriors, with white hair, their faces and arms heavily tattooed, came striding along the track to meet them. Both were armed with long spears tipped with bone points and had clubs suspended from their belts. Their manner was courteously dignified, but their dark faces were grave and unsmiling as each, in turn, thrust his spear, barbed point down, into the ground in front of him.

Kendall spoke to them; they examined the muskets and the ammunition with meticulous care and, Justin realized, with an attention to detail that, of itself, betrayed their familiarity with European weapons. Finally, having satisfied themselves that the ransom was, in every particular, what their chief had demanded, they signed to the rescue party to pick up their burdens once more, and led them into the village.

A small crowd had gathered to witness their arrival, and Justin looked about him with interest. Their huts, he saw, were primitive and flimsy, fashioned of reeds bound to light wooden frames and of a rounded shape that made them appear like so many beehives. All the adult males were grotesquely tattooed, and even the women, who kept in the background, had their chins and lips similarly ornamented. Despite this, they seemed to him a handsome people, with much lighter skins and a more European cast of features than the aboriginals of New South Wales, to whom he had been accustomed.

On his two previous visits, he had seen them only in their canoes or at a distance, but now, on closer acquaintance, he began to understand the Reverend Marsden's avowed preference for them and something of his admiration. They were, indeed—judging by appearance—vastly more intelligent and infinitely more noble than even their *Te Matenga* had claimed. But . . . Justin suppressed a shiver of apprehension, as they jostled about him. They were also undeniably warlike, and, by repute, they were cannibals.

Kendall touched his arm. "Hongi is awaiting us in the meeting house. Best move on, Mr. Broome."

Hongi's reception was staged with almost kingly ceremony. The meeting house, solidly constructed of wood, was much larger than the huts that surrounded it. Its roof beams and the posts on which they rested were elaborately carved, and its interior was cool and comparatively spacious.

The chief had discarded the scarlet military uniform he had worn at the early morning church service, and a shimmering cloak of feathers covered his broad shoulders, with more braided about his head. Thrust into his belt of woven flax was a curious carved ax made of a dark green stone, and his spear—held point down as the visitors entered—was tipped with the same stone.

There was a gleam in his dark eyes when they lit on the muskets. He questioned the two old warriors, and when both nodded vigorously, he turned to address Kendall in his native tongue.

"He asks whether you have brought the pistol," Kendall translated. "I told him that you had, but he wants to see it."

"Certainly," Justin returned. "He shall—when I have seen Captain Jeffrey and am satisfied that no harm has come to him."

Chief Hongi's understanding of English was seemingly better than he had intended to admit, for he burst out in angry remonstrance without waiting for the missionary to interpret Justin's reply to his question.

"He says," Kendall explained, "that he is a man of honor and has kept his word. Since it is not yet sunset, no harm has come to

Captain Jeffrey. You may see him, if you will hold out the pistol to prove that you have it. If I were you," he added, lowering his voice, "I should do as he asks, Mr. Broome. His warriors are outside, just waiting for the order to attack us. And, as I understand the situation, your ship came here to endeavor to prevent a war, not to provoke one. In that respect, sir, your captain is culpable, you know. His foolhardy action may well jeopardize our mission here and place all our lives at risk, unless we accept Hongi's terms and carry them out to the letter."

He was right, Justin knew. A score of feather-decked Maori tribesmen were standing about the entrance to the meeting house, and behind them smoke was rising from the nearby cooking place, a group of women moving with firewood to the ovens and making no attempt to conceal the nature of their activities.

This was no time for bravado. He took the pistol from his belt and offered it for the chief's inspection. Hongi looked at it and then compared it with another—Captain Jeffrey's, Justin recognized— which he had concealed on his person. He asked a question, which Kendall translated.

"The chief wishes to know if your pistol is loaded, Mr. Broome?"

Justin shook his head negatively. "Tell him, if you please, that I, too, am a man who keeps his word. I come in peace, and neither I nor my seamen are armed. As an expression of his good faith, ask the chief to permit me to see Captain Jeffrey and to speak to him before we proceed further with the matter of his ransom."

Kendall gave him an approving glance and obediently repeated what he had said. Justin had supposed that the captain was being held in one of the huts and that he would be taken to him, but instead Hongi waved a hand in a lordly gesture, and the two white-haired warriors took up their spears and left the meeting house, offering no sign that he should follow them.

"They will bring him here," Kendall said, in a tense whisper. "And whatever they do, betray no surprise. They have their own laws and customs, and Captain Jeffrey—whether intentionally or not—broke one of their taboos."

"What does that mean?" Justin asked, conscious that the two seamen were listening anxiously, although discipline held them silent.

"It means that, in their eyes, the spirits will mark him for

death—if not now, then later." The missionary sighed ruefully.
"We have not yet succeeded in teaching them Christian principles,
Mr. Broome." He grasped Justin's arm. "They're bringing the
captain now . . . remember, no surprise!"

But, in spite of this warning, Justin had difficulty in maintaining
a pose of indifference. The two old warriors returned, bearing
between them a trussed body suspended from poles, which were
balanced on their shoulders. It was, he realized unhappily, as they
cast their burden down at Hongi's feet, the ultimate humiliation for
the *Kangaroo*'s commander, for they were carrying him in a
manner more usually employed to transport inanimate objects
from one place to another.

Inanimate objects or . . . He tried to shut the hideous thought
from his mind, but it persisted, fueled by what the Reverend
Marsden had told him of the Maoris' way of life. Until the
missionaries had brought livestock to Whangaroa, these people
had had no domestic animals, save their dogs; Marsden's cows and
horses and pigs had been a source of wonder ever since the crew of
the *Active* had herded them ashore.

Sweet potatoes and taro roots, Justin knew, were the staples of
the native diet. The only animal food available to them, apart from
fish, were the dogs and what birds they could snare; so it was, he
supposed, small wonder that they had resorted to cannibalism. Yet
for all that . . . Sickened and appalled, Justin stared down at his
captain.

Chief Hongi might be attempting to force his hand by ordering
that the ovens should be lit and his captive tied up in a fashion that
suggested a trussed chicken; but on the other hand, he might
equally well be inflicting what he believed to be a just punishment
on one who had offended against tribal law. Whichever was his
motive, the unhappy Captain Jeffrey had surely suffered enough.
. . . Justin dropped to his knees beside the helpless man, who, he
saw now, had been gagged as well as pinioned.

Kendall's hand on his shoulder held him back. "No!" he
whispered urgently. "Not without the chief's consent. We have
only his word to depend on, Mr. Broome, if any of us is to get back
to the ship alive."

Again Justin had to concede that the missionary was right. Their
small, unarmed party would stand no chance against Hongi's
warriors; even if he and the two seamen seized the muskets, it

would take time to load and prime them . . . and they would almost certainly be given no time.

Kendall warned, as if Justin had spoken his thoughts aloud, "Our mission exists here on sufferance and because of the people's respect for Mr. Marsden. Do nothing, I beg you, to destroy their trust in us and in him!"

"There ain't nothin' we can do, sir," one of the seamen said, breaking his self-imposed silence. "Not against this lot there ain't, less'n we want to end up bein' butchered to fill their bellies!" He shuddered. "Gawd!"

Jeffrey was struggling impotently against his bonds, his blood-shot eyes rolling, and Kendall turned to plead with Hongi in his own language. The chief's headshake was emphatic, the spate of angry words to which he gave vent clear enough in their intent, and Justin rose to his feet, conscious that further argument would be futile.

"We are to give him the muskets and the pistol," Kendall said, his tone flat. "And two of his warriors will accompany us back to our settlement. They will release your captain when we reach there, and he is not to set foot on land again."

The return journey was fraught with tension. The warriors carried Jeffrey on their poles with scant heed for his dignity and less for his comfort, and as before, hidden watchers—the lengthening shadows affording them concealment—followed the band's slow, stumbling progress. The two seamen were sweating profusely, and despite their attempts to preserve a disciplined calm, it took several sharp reminders from Justin to keep them from panic-stricken flight. Both were young, and both were deeply shocked by the treatment meted out to their captain and what they had witnessed in Chief Hongi's village.

"Gawd knows why you stay 'ere, sir," the elder of the two observed to Kendall, when lights from the mission's huts came in sight, at last, through the trees. "I wouldn't, not for an 'undred guineas a week!"

"God *does* know why I stay," the missionary answered with conviction. "I'm here to preach His word to the heathen. I have thirty-four of their children in my school, and they are starting to listen to the word. When they grow up, they will not be heathens."

"Nor cannibals neither, Mr. Kendall?" the seaman challenged.

Kendall exchanged a glance with Justin. "If that is God's will, my friend."

At the edge of the missionaries' small patch of cultivated land, the two Maori warriors set down their burden without ceremony, removed their poles, and went padding off into the darkness without a word. With the aid of a seaman's knife, Justin cut Captain Jeffrey's bonds and removed the gag from his mouth. But he was beyond speech, so dazed and shocked that he seemed scarcely to realize where he was. He drank eagerly of the water Kendall brought him, and they carried him to the boat as gently as they could. As the boat's crew endeavored to make him comfortable, Justin drew Kendall out of earshot.

"I owe you my deepest thanks, Mr. Kendall," he said with sincerity. "Without you we should not have succeeded in bringing the captain safely back . . . and I doubt whether we should have got back ourselves, come to that. I am greatly in your debt, sir."

The missionary brushed his thanks aside. "You owe me nothing, Mr. Broome. Except perhaps . . ." He broke off, glancing across to the *Kangaroo*'s boat. "Your captain, when he recovers his senses, will be very angry, I fear, and that is understandable. But if he demands retribution, if he attempts to send his seamen under arms to avenge himself on Hongi's people, I beg you most earnestly to dissuade him. Such an action would put an end to all our work here, and it would undoubtedly lead to many deaths, of your men and Hongi's. It might even lead to the loss of your ship, for the other tribes would ally themselves with Hongi's. They are brave fighters, and they have canoes." He shrugged. "Our wives and children would not be spared, if it came to a battle."

Justin inclined his head gravely. "I understand, Mr. Kendall, and I shall do all in my power to avoid anything of the kind." Knowing Jeffrey, he thought, it would not be easy, but . . . He held out his hand. "You have my word. Like Chief Hongi, I'll keep it."

"Mr. Marsden will be back sometime tomorrow, please God," Kendall said. "He intends to return with you to Sydney, I believe, so perhaps if he . . ." He did not need to complete the sentence, for Justin again nodded his understanding.

Next morning, predictably, the storm broke. Justin was summoned to the captain's cabin and found him still lying weakly in his cot but in a rage he could barely contain.

"You are aware of what happened yesterday, Mr. Broome," Jeffrey flung at him, without preamble. "Those foul savages offered a grave insult to His Majesty's Navy and to my person, which cannot go unpunished. I want that self-styled chief Hongi seized and brought on board this ship, where I shall hang him." He silenced Justin's attempted interruption with a furious "Hold your tongue, sir, damn you! I'm about to give you your orders."

His orders were as predictable as the rage that consumed him, and Justin listened in stony silence. He was to muster and arm, with muskets and cutlasses, a party of sixty men, which he was to lead to Hongi's village for the purpose of effecting his arrest.

"If you meet with resistance, you are to open fire without hesitation . . . is that clear? Even if they have a few muskets, they will be no match for trained seamen, so I do not anticipate that you will have much difficulty. Do you understand, Mr. Broome?"

"I understand what it is you wish me to do, sir," Justin answered. "But, with respect, sir, do *you* understand what the consequences are likely to be?"

"To the devil with the consequences! I have given you an order—carry it out!" The captain raised himself on one elbow. "Devil take you, Broome! Are you afraid of a bunch of blasted savages? If you are, then Mr. Meredith had best go in your place."

This was what he had feared. Justin drew himself up. At all costs, he had to prevent Meredith from going in command of the party.

"I will go if you order me, sir," he said. "But I beg you to listen to me before you confirm your order." Before Jeffrey could refuse, he launched into the arguments Kendall had advanced, stressing the probability that all the tribes would unite against them, if Hongi were attacked, and stressing the danger to the ship if they were to do so.

The captain cut him short in mid-sentence. He said coldly, "I can take no account of such matters, nor, indeed, of any such dangers as you envisage, when His Majesty's flag has been insulted. You are a damned colonial, not a regular naval officer, Mr. Broome, and clearly you do not understand how an insult of this kind would be regarded by Their Lordships." He paused, eyeing Justin balefully, and then said, a sharp edge to his voice, "You will carry out my order and arrest Chief Hongi or face a court-martial. Which is it to be, Mr. Broome?"

Justin bowed. This would be the end of his brief naval career, he knew; all he could do would be to play for time and hope that Samuel Marsden would return before it was too late. He, at least—in the absence of Mrs. Jeffrey in Sydney—might be expected to change the captain's mind, if not by reasoning, then by the sheer strength of his personality and his civilian status. Jeffrey could scarcely threaten *him* with court-martial. . . .

He said flatly, "Sir, I will muster the landing party," and, without waiting for Jeffrey's reply, left the cabin.

Meredith was on watch. Justin instructed him to muster both watches and sent the master-at-arms to break out the required muskets. He took as long as he could over the selection of the landing party, and—the germ of an idea having occurred to him—he dispatched Cadet Harris in the gig to seek out the missionary Kendall.

"Tell him to meet the first boat at the landing place, Mr. Harris. And tell him it is very urgent that Mr. Marsden should come out to the ship the instant he returns—he'll understand why. Jump to it, lad!"

Harris's "Aye, aye, sir," was crisp. He asked no questions but obediently lowered himself into the waiting gig and made for the shore, yelling shrilly to his crew to put their backs into their rowing.

Meredith, by contrast, questioned every order he was given and expressed considerable resentment when Justin declined to assuage his curiosity. His sullenness led to delays, and Justin, meeting Silas Crabbe's inquiring gaze, shook his head in warning.

"Let him be, Mr. Crabbe. The longer we take, the better. I've been given orders I cannot, in the circumstances, carry out."

The old master shrugged resignedly.

"I can put two and two together, Mr. Broome. Let me come with you."

"And chance losing your warrant for dereliction of duty? You'd be wiser not to volunteer, Mr. Crabbe," Justin warned.

Crabbe gave him a slow, amused smile. "I was never a wise man, sir, and I never could get my bearings on land. I'm volunteering."

"Then thanks," Justin acknowledged wryly. "That makes two of us, does it not? Be so good as to call away the longboat, if you please."

Kendall was waiting, with young Harris, when the longboat grounded on the sandy beach, and it was evident, from the grimness of his expression, that he had gleaned enough from the boy to be fully aware of the situation. The armed seamen, mustering on the beach, were confirmation enough, and he said unhappily, "Mr. Marsden isn't back. I've sent a canoe to look for him."

"Then let us hope it finds him," Justin returned. "Let us *pray* it does!"

"Do you intend to march on Hongi's village, Mr. Broome? Did you not give me your word that you would not?" The bitter reproach in Kendall's voice was not unexpected, and Justin suppressed a sigh.

"I'll keep my word, Mr. Kendall. But I shall need your assistance. Can you organize divine service, where Mr. Marsden preached yesterday?" The second boat grounded, to discharge its cargo of armed men, and he gestured to them. "For my party?"

"For your sailors?" The missionary stared at him in disbelief. "In—in God's name, why?"

"It will keep them occupied and give Mr. Marsden more time to get here. And it might disarm suspicion as to our intentions . . . I imagine Hongi will have us under observation, will he not?"

Understanding and gratitude succeeded the bewilderment in Kendall's eyes. He inclined his head. "Yes—yes, he will. I . . . give me half an hour. I will summon some of the children to join with them, if you march your sailors to our settlement."

The service, when it took place, was unexpectedly moving, the Maori children singing tunefully and the seamen, their muskets laid on the ground beside them, adding their deep voices to the rendering of the English hymns.

To Justin's heartfelt relief, Samuel Marsden returned while the service was still providing occupation for his landing party, and a few words from Kendall sent him, in his canoe with his Maori companions, paddling across to the anchored *Kangaroo*.

He had been on board for less than twenty minutes when Cadet Harris brought Captain Jeffrey's countermanded orders. The landing party was to reembark forthwith, and the ship would sail for Port Jackson on the evening tide.

"Then all's well that ends well," Silas Crabbe observed, as he and Justin walked together to the boats. "Eh, Mr. Broome?"

"Is it?" Justin countered grimly. "I wonder, Mr. Crabbe."

He was not left for long in doubt. When he boarded the *Kangaroo,* he found Lieutenant Meredith awaiting him, a smirk of triumph on his sallow young face.

"The captain has ordered me to place you under arrest, Mr. Broome," he announced loudly. "I am to inform you that you will be confined to your cabin until we reach Sydney, when it is his intention to bring charges against you before a general court-martial."

The smug satisfaction in his voice irked Justin, but he said nothing, until Meredith added, "Your sword, if you please."

"I'm not wearing a sword. But"—Justin unslung the heavy musket he had been carrying and planted it, none too gently, with the butt on Meredith's foot—"you may relieve me of this, if you wish, and be damned to you, Mr. Meredith."

Leaving Meredith gasping with pain, he went below, hearing, behind him, a subdued cheer from the men who had overheard their exchange.

CHAPTER XIII

Sydney Cove was gay with flags and bunting when the *Kangaroo*, having fired the customary salutes from her signal gun, nosed her way into the anchorage as dusk was falling.

Justin, taking his permitted hour of exercise on deck, recognized the sloop of war *Emu*, arrived at last from Hobart, and was able to make out the name *Barden, London*, on the stern of a big three-masted convict transport lying at anchor nearby. Both ships were dressed overall, the *Emu* displaying a continuous array of signal flags from her jackstaff to her masthead and thence to her ensign staff—a sign that she was celebrating an occasion of national rejoicing. And the small, Sydney-owned traders and even his own *Flinders* lying off Robert Campbell's wharf were, Justin saw with astonishment, wearing every flag they possessed.

On shore, as darkness fell, bonfires were lit and the strains of military band music could faintly be heard, as the usual afternoon concert in Hyde Park came to an end and the band marched back to their barracks or . . . no, the sound was coming nearer. Ignoring Lieutenant Meredith's scowl of disapproval, Justin crossed to the starboard rail. Government House, he realized, was now brightly illuminated, with colored fairy lanterns, suspended from trees and bushes in the garden and festooning the great Norfolk pine near the gates, springing to flickering life.

"What the devil's going on?" Meredith exclaimed, forgetting, in his bewilderment, the animosity he had chosen to display since Justin's arrest. "Do you suppose I should inform the captain?"

Captain Jeffrey had kept to his cabin since leaving Whangaroa Bay; he had not even come on deck to bid the Reverend Marsden farewell, when the chaplain had decided to leave the ship and wait for his own brig *Active* to give him passage back to Sydney. The gig had been sent to pick up Mrs. Jeffrey, but it had not yet returned, and . . . Justin shrugged.

"Perhaps we had better find out first what *is* going on," he suggested. "And it might be as well if you were to prepare to dress ship, Mr. Meredith, so that you're ready when the captain gives the order."

"Yes," Meredith said. "That might be as well." He bawled a string of orders and then returned to Justin's side. "How the deuce can we find out what all the excitement's about? Perhaps I should send a boat across to the *Emu*."

"It shouldn't be necessary. There's a boat from Robert Campbell's going out to her now." Justin pointed. "That looks like one of her officers, does it not?"

"Yes, so it does," Meredith agreed with relief. When the boat came within hailing distance, he called out an eager inquiry. "Boat ahoy! What are you celebrating?"

"A great victory over Boney at Waterloo! The frogs running for Paris and the Duke after them!" The *Emu*'s lieutenant had evidently been celebrating with the hospitable Campbells, for his reply was roared out and his enthusiastic cheers were interspersed with loud hiccups. "The *Barden* brought the news, and Sydney's *en fête*, my boys! Get that ship of yours dressed, and look lively about it! The Governor's signal is splice the main brace!"

An answering roar went up from the men on the *Kangaroo*'s deck, where both watches had gathered. Forgetful of discipline, they stamped and hooted and cheered, and Meredith's attempts to restore them to order went unheeded or unheard.

"I think," Justin told him dryly, "that you should report to the captain now, Mr. Meredith, and request his permission to dress the ship overall."

"Aye, aye," Meredith began, and then, in a belated endeavor to reassert his authority, he added unpleasantly, "You are still under arrest, Mr. Broome, and your hour for exercise has expired. Be so good as to return to your cabin."

Justin said nothing. Lieutenant Meredith's animosity was, he knew, the least of his troubles, and as he went below, he wondered how long Captain Jeffrey intended to keep him under arrest and confined to his cabin. Jessica would have seen the ship come in— or, if she had not, no doubt someone would have told her—and she would worry if, when the ship's company were given shore leave, he was not among them. Besides, there was his little son. The boy would have grown during his absence, and he was eager to see him again. . . . Disconsolately, Justin took off his watch coat and lay down on his cot.

He did not sleep; he had slept too much since his arrest, and sleep eluded him. Lying there, his head pillowed on his locked hands, he listened to and tried to interpret the various sounds that filtered through to his small, airless prison.

Shouted orders and the tramping of feet on the deck told him that Meredith had sought and obtained the captain's permission to rig the ship with celebratory flags. While the topmen were still engaged in this task aloft, he heard a boat come alongside and guessed, from hearing young Harris's high-pitched treble, that Mrs. Jeffrey had come finally to join her husband—a supposition that was almost instantly confirmed when the sound of her voice, coupled with Meredith's sychophantic tones, reached him faintly from the entryport.

On shore, the festivities were evidently in full swing; he could hear the hiss of ascending rockets and glimpse their reflected trails in the dark water beneath his porthole, and the music of fife and drum continued at intervals, often almost drowned by bursts of cheering, which suggested that an enthusiastic crowd had gathered outside Government House to add their plaudits to the band's tribute.

Old Billy Onslow, the ship's cook, brought him a meal when the watch changed, and Justin questioned him as to what was visible from the deck.

"Seems like there's a mighty fine spree on shore, Mr. Broome," the old man answered sourly. "But we shan't see nothin' of it, more's the pity. No shore leave, the cap'n told Mr. Meredith, an' he passed that bit o' bad news on, grinnin' all over his face! An' 'twas just the usual tot at grog time."

Justin tackled his meal without appetite. Most of the ship's company would have heard about the Governor's signal to splice the main brace, he thought—the *Emu*'s lieutenant had announced it at the pitch of his lungs—but Captain Jeffrey had decided to ignore it, in addition to refusing shore leave, even to the watch below. Which would scarcely add to his popularity . . . He pushed his plate away.

"Beg pardon, sir," Billy Onslow said diffidently, "but where is Waterloo? That's where this great victory was won, ain't it?"

"Yes, I believe so, Billy. But I'm afraid I've no idea where it is." Justin frowned, suddenly reminded of the odd behavior of the aborigine boy, Winyara, on the night when he and his brother, William, had made camp on his land grant, in the new territory beyond Bathurst.

The episode had made a lasting impression on him, and . . . his frown deepened. He could recall the date—Sunday the eighteenth of June—and Winyara's strange, prophetic words. He had seen a mountain, the boy had insisted, on which a great battle was raging. *"Many men die,"* he had said *"I see fire, hear thunder . . . men fighting, killing."* And then quite clearly, in English, he had added, *"Two great warriors lead them."*

The French Emperor Napoleon and the Duke of Wellington fitted that description well enough, Justin told himself—they were the two most famous military commanders in Europe. And as to the date, if the *Barden* had made a fairly fast passage—or if she had picked up the news from a naval dispatch vessel in Rio or at the Cape—then Winyara's strange, dream-time vision had been closer to the truth than even he had supposed. The *Barden* was a three-master, of perhaps six or seven hundred tons burden . . . she could have sailed from England at the end of June and made the passage in—what? A hundred and forty days. Both the *Catherine* and the *Three Bees* had logged similar passages the previous year, he recalled, and today was November the nineteenth. Or the twentieth; he had lost count of time, and . . . Justin sighed.

"You feelin' all right, sir?" the cook asked solicitously, bending to pick up his tray.

"Yes—yes, I'm perfectly all right. And thank you, Onslow. You've looked after me well."

Old Billy Onslow bared his almost toothless gums in a friendly smile, pleased by the compliment. "There's officers and officers," he observed judiciously. "Some I got respect for, an' some I ain't. You an' Mr. Tempest, now—you're both prime seamen, Mr. Broome, an' you know how to command a ship an' how to treat the ship's company. But there's others, sir, what don't, an'—"

"I think you had better pipe down, Billy," Justin warned. "Though I appreciate what you've just said. Cut along back to your galley now. And if shore leave is granted tomorrow, perhaps you would be so good as to take a note to my wife."

"Gladly, sir," Onslow agreed. "If you're still here, that I will."

He had been gone for only a few minutes when Cadet Harris made an unexpected appearance, bearing a summons from the captain.

"He said he wants to see you right away, sir. He's going ashore with Mrs. Jeffrey, and I'm ordered to stand by with the gig."

The boy was breathless and, for some reason, excited, and Justin, rising to don his shoes and watch coat, asked curiously, "You look pleased with yourself, Mr. Harris. Have you been given shore leave?"

Harris shook his head. "No, sir, not that. But the captain's told me to put up my white patches—I'm to be rated midshipman, Mr. Broome. And Mrs. Jeffrey, sir—she promised to sew them on for me!"

"Did she, by George! Well, congratulations, Midshipman Harris." Justin spoke with genuine pleasure. Harris was a good lad, and it was no more than he deserved, but . . . He was struck by a sudden thought, and his pleasure faded. "Tell me, Mr. Harris . . . did the captain say anything else?"

"Anything else, sir?" Harris echoed. "Apart from sending me to fetch you, do you mean?"

"Yes, that's what I mean."

"Well, sir, he did warn me to keep a still tongue in my head and not say anything to anyone about what happened at Whangaroa." The boy's eyes were innocent of guile as he added earnestly, "And of course I wouldn't have dreamed of talking about it, Mr. Broome. I mean, sir, it's not the sort of thing one would—well, bandy about, is it? And the captain is going to make a full report to the Governor, he said, and to Their Lordships—which makes it official, does it not, sir?"

"Yes, most certainly it does," Justin confirmed. He buttoned his jacket and picked up his watch cap. An officer under close arrest was not permitted to wear a sword, he reflected; and in any case, he had no sword—nor a proper uniform yet, for that matter. He tucked the cap under his arm. "Were you instructed to escort me to the captain's cabin, Mr. Harris?"

"Oh, no, sir," Harris denied. "I'm to stand by with the gig—as I told you, sir, Captain and Mrs. Jeffrey are going ashore. The

Governor is holding a reception to celebrate the victory in France, I understand. Captain Forster of the *Emu* sent a boat across, sir, to inform the captain. And Mrs. Jeffrey told me, when I picked her up, sir, that she had received an invitation from Their Excellencies."

"I see. Thank you. Carry on, Mr. Harris."

"Aye, aye, sir." The boy sped off, and Justin made his way, deep in thought, to the *Kangaroo*'s great cabin. Harris, he reflected, had been present when Captain Jeffrey had become embroiled with Chief Hongi, and were the youngster to talk of the scene he had witnessed, his account of the incident would scarcely redound to his commander's credit. So . . . he had been given the coveted midshipman's rating—at least six months before it was due—and told, in no uncertain terms, to keep a still tongue in his head. Why? Justin asked himself. *Why?*

The influence of Mrs. Jeffrey, perhaps? She was the daughter of an admiral and conversant with naval tradition and practice, anxious to further her husband's career, and . . . had not Rick hinted that Jeffrey paid great attention to her views and advice?

He halted outside the cabin door, hearing the sound of voices coming from its interior. Was he, too, to be offered some kind of compromise in return for his silence, he wondered . . . perhaps even the withdrawal of the charges against him, and the consequent removal of any threat of a court-martial? If that were so, then . . . dear heaven, he would accept such an offer thankfully! Let Captain Jeffrey further his career; let him seek post rank, if that was what he wanted, and be damned to him!

Justin squared his shoulders and knocked on the cabin door.

As on the occasion of his first interview, Mrs. Jeffrey was with her husband. She was in an evening gown, her hair elaborately dressed in ringlets, and the captain—to Justin's surprise, for Jeffrey had kept to his bed throughout the passage from New Zealand—had donned his full-dress uniform, with sword and cocked hat lying on the table beside him. He looked pale and somewhat haggard but, apart from this, appeared to have recovered from his ordeal at Chief Hongi's hands; and his tone, when he spoke, was confident and forceful.

"Ah, Mr. Broome, I sent for you because there is a matter I wish to discuss with you. I can't spare long, I'm afraid—Mrs. Jeffrey and I have received an invitation from His Excellency to join in the official celebration of our victory at Waterloo. But . . . ah, the question of your trial by court-martial. I wonder if you realize that this could not take place in the colony?"

Justin stared at him, taken by surprise. But it was true, he recognized; naval courts-martial were held in England, a fact he had forgotten and now faced with the utmost dismay.

"It is possible," the captain went on, "that since you are a colonial by birth, your trial might be permissible if it were held in the criminal court here. Then, as you will doubtless be aware, your judges would be officers of the army garrison . . . Colonel Molle's officers." He paused, as if expecting some response, but Justin said nothing. Jeffrey glanced across at his wife, who inclined her head approvingly, and he continued, "However, I am reluctant to—ah—to create a precedent, since I have always adhered to the belief that breaches of naval discipline should be dealt with by naval courts. Do you agree?"

Justin kept a tight hold on his temper.

"As a colonial, sir, I have no experience of such matters," he answered quietly. "But, sir, may I be permitted to point out that you ordered me to be placed in arrest without informing me of what breaches of naval discipline you hold me guilty. I am not aware of the charges you wish to bring against me. If you will tell me what they are, I—"

"A pox on it, Mr. Broome!" the captain interrupted irritably. "I can list half a dozen, under the Articles of War. Insubordination, failure to carry out the orders of your superior officer, refusal to act in defense of His Majesty's flag, and—yes, damme!—cowardice in the face of an enemy, because that's what your infernal hymn singing with a bunch of savages amounted to, did it not? I had sent you ashore, in command of an armed party, for the purpose of seizing the person of a native named Hongi and bringing him to justice, had I not?"

"Yes, sir, you had," Justin admitted. "But it was necessary to wait for the return of the Reverend Marsden, so that he might guide my party to Hongi's village. I believed, sir, that he could intercede with Chief Hongi and avoid needless bloodshed. I sought Mr. Kendall's advice, and—"

This time it was Mrs. Jeffrey who interrupted him. She said, in a placatory tone, "Mr. Broome, it is really unnecessary to go into all these details. What is done cannot now be undone, and as it happens, Captain Jeffrey sent for you in order to tell you that he has decided to withdraw the—er—the charges, did you not, my dear?" She appealed to her husband, and he scowled resentfully but finally nodded.

"Yes, yes—that was my decision. I realize that one cannot expect a colonial, with no naval training, to accept naval discipline. Their Lordships made an error in granting you a commission, Mr. Broome, as I fancy I told you at our first meeting."

"You did, sir, yes. But I—"

"I have written to the Secretary to that effect," Jeffrey said, as if Justin had not spoken. "But I'm aware that it would be an injustice to compel you to go to England for trial, when your home and family are here, and I'm unwilling to request that you be tried here, by the criminal court. You do, after all, hold a commission in His Majesty's Navy at the present time. So . . ." He looked up, fixing Justin with a glassy stare. "Provided that you keep this—ah—this unhappy affair in strict confidence, Mr. Broome, I will withdraw my charges and release you from arrest. You may proceed on indefinite leave, pending a decision by Their Lordships as to your appointment to this ship. But I can tell you now that I shall not again require you to serve under my command. Do you accept my decision?"

It was the most he could hope for from such a man, Justin thought, and . . . anything was preferable to making the long journey back to England for a trial, of whose outcome he could not be sure. If he agreed, he would be free. He drew himself up and said evenly, "Yes, sir, I do."

Mrs. Jeffrey whispered something he could not hear, and the captain answered her angrily. He recovered himself, however, and said coldly, "I should like your promise that you will regard this whole—ah—matter as confidential, Mr. Broome. I shall be making an official report, of course, both to His Excellency the Governor and to Their Lordships, and, no doubt, Hongi will eventually be required to answer for his crimes against me." He rose. "Your word, Mr. Broome, so that I may order your release."

"You have my word, Captain Jeffrey," Justin assured him. "It is an episode that I am only too eager to forget. Have I your permission, sir, to leave the ship at once?"

"Certainly," Captain Jeffrey conceded. "Mr. Harris can bring the gig back, after he has set me ashore." He nodded in curt dismissal and turned to his wife, offering her his arm. "Come, my dear. We are, I fear, late already."

Justin returned to his cabin to bundle together his meager belongings, paused to tender a word of thanks to old Billy Onslow, and then sought out Silas Crabbe, who was on watch.

"So he's letting you go, Mr. Broome," the master said dryly, when Justin informed him of his impending departure. "Nothing else he could do, though, in the circumstances, is there? But I'll be sorry to see you go, and that's the truth. Without you and Mr. Tempest, well . . ." He shrugged. "Perhaps we shall stay here for a while and indulge in the social life."

"If you do," Justin assured him, "you will be most welcome at my house, Mr. Crabbe."

They shook hands warmly, and Justin went ashore in the gig.

There was a light burning in his small, waterside cottage when he reached it, but it was Kate Lamerton who came to the door in response to his knock.

"Mrs. Broome is at Government House," she said, then smiled, seeing his look of disappointment. "Don't worry, Mr. Broome. She's expecting you there, only she weren't sure if you'd be given leave. Her Excellency sent for her to help with all the preparations for the reception—still depends on her, Her Excellency does, you know, and it's a right do up there tonight, as you may have seen. Fireworks an' bonfires an' everyone that's anyone invited to a buffet supper. The town's gone mad, too . . . just needin' the excuse, most of 'em. But me"—her smile widened—"why, I'm lookin' after that son o' yours whiles his mother's gone. Not that he's no trouble—fast asleep in his cot, he is, and young Dickon in your bed, 'cause Miss Abigail an' Miss Katie an' Mr. Tempest are invited to Government House. You want to peep at them two little ragamuffins 'fore you go, Mr. Broome?"

"Yes," Justin said, after taking all this in. "And I'll have to spruce myself up a bit, if Jessica wants me to join her at Their Excellencies' reception." Captain and Mrs. Jeffrey, he thought with wry amusement, would not be pleased to see him in such august surroundings. But if Jessica was there, then . . . He patted Kate's ample shoulder. "Have no fear, Mrs. Lamerton, I'll not waken the lads."

Kate followed him into the bedroom and stood beside him as he peered down at his sleeping son, seeing his face dimly in the light of a single candle burning there.

"Murdoch," he said softly.

Kate chuckled. "Mrs. Broome don't call him that, sir."

"Does she not? It was the name we'd settled on, before I had to leave. What *does* she call him?"

"Well, sir, Murdoch may be his given name right enough. But 'tis Red his mother calls him. And look—here's the reason." Kate brought the flickering candle nearer and, careful not to waken him, drew the covering blanket aside to reveal the thatch of wispy red hair that had started to grow on the infant's small, shapely head. "Like his grandma," the stout midwife suggested. "Like your mam, Mr. Broome. If he takes after her, he'll be a real fine little fellow."

And indeed he would, Justin thought, conscious of a pang as he pulled back the scrap of blanket and moved away. "All right if I hunt for a clean shirt in the closet, Mrs. Lamerton?"

"No need to hunt for nothin', sir," Kate chided him gently. "Mr. Tempest left his uniform for you—the one that you didn't have time to take with you when the *Kangaroo* sailed. We altered it to fit you between us, an' Mrs. Broome laid it out for you on a chair in the sitting room, just in case you did get ashore this evenin'. You change now, an' I'll heat you up some shavin' water."

Justin did as she had suggested. It was the first time he had worn the uniform of a commissioned officer in the Royal Navy, and when he had shaved, he donned the braided tailcoat, Rick's full dress, pleased to find that—despite the difference in their height and chest measurements—it fit him well.

The uniform earned him a salute from the sentry on guard at the Government House gates and a polite greeting from two young officers of Colonel Molle's regiment as he crossed the lawn to the large marquee in which the buffet supper was being served. It was crowded with officers in uniform, civilians in evening dress, and their ladies, most of whom were elaborately gowned, as if for a ball. As he made his way through the chattering throng, Justin recognized quite a number of the wealthier emancipists, among them Simeon Lord, Dr. Redfern and his wife, Sir Henry Brown Hayes, Lawyer Crossley, the deputy government surveyor, James Meehan, and the Governor's clerk, Michael Robinson. Brown

Hayes was with the Molles and Captain and Mrs. Jeffrey in a small, tight-knit group of 46th officers, with Ellis Bent's widow, in deep mourning, advancing slowly on the arm of her brother-in-law, the judge, with the intention of joining them.

Justin instinctively stepped aside to avoid them, and glimpsing Jessica at last, standing behind Mrs. Macquarie's chair at the far end of the marquee, he moved forward in an attempt to make his belated arrival known to her. He contrived to catch her eye and wave, but before he was halfway across the marquee, he was brought to a halt when a toast was proclaimed and drunk with loud acclaim by the assembled company.

The toast was to "our victorious army," and the Governor, resplendent in Highland dress and his kilt of the Macquarie tartan, led the cheering, his glass held high and his gaunt, sallow face wreathed in smiles. Silence was called for, and Robinson, the government clerk, perspiring freely, read a poem he had composed for the occasion.

It began:

> Hail Britannia's warriors glorious,
> Still unrivaled, still victorious . . .

Justin heard little of it but, hemmed in by the crowd, had, out of courtesy, to remain where he was until the somewhat lengthy ode was brought, with muted applause, to its conclusion. The final verse, departing from the original purpose of the toast, appeared to be in praise of the colony and the Governor.

> A place
> Of golden vales and verdant hills,
> Sheltered from the martial storm,
> Where worth with dignity presides,
> Where truth directs and wisdom guides,
> Where mercy bends with graceful mein,
> And hope looks on with smile serene . . .

Some loud guffaws from the group that had Colonel Molle at its center upset poor Michael Robinson's composure and caused a frown to displace the Governor's happy smile, but Major Antill, ever sensible of his chief's feelings, stepped swiftly into the breach with a new toast.

"Let us drink to His Majesty's military forces in this colony!" he called out loudly, and Molle, red of face and taken by surprise, had no choice but to respond. He did so by pointedly raising his glass to Captain Jeffrey, who returned the compliment after a brief hesitation, both with their backs to the Governor.

Justin saw his wife slip away in the direction of the rear exit from the marquee and the kitchens and was about to go in pursuit of her when a hand came out to detain him by grasping his arm. He turned, to find himself confronted by a tall, fair-haired officer in the uniform of a naval commander, who gave him a friendly and humorous smile.

"I had not, until now, realized the undercurrents in this place," he said. "Is Sydney society always so openly divided?"

Justin echoed his smile, liking him at once. "The divisions exist, sir, and alas, they always have. Elitist against emancipist, the free against the felon . . . but perhaps the fact that we have a Governor who believes in according a fair and equal chance to those he deems to have earned it makes for—well, more open dissent. Privilege, when under threat, is jealously guarded."

"A most profound assessment of the situation," the commander observed with approval. He studied Justin's uniform thoughtfully and then looked up to meet his gaze. "I take it you've been here for some time? You're not from His Majesty's ship *Kangaroo*?"

"I was born here, sir," Justin answered. He reddened. "I was appointed to the *Kangaroo* when she arrived in Sydney and served as acting first lieutenant until—until this evening. But now I—"

"Ah! And now you are on leave, I understand." The commander held out a lean brown hand, a speculative gleam lighting his keen blue eyes. "I've placed you now—you are Lieutenant Broome, are you not? Lieutenant Justin Broome? I'm James Forster, commanding His Majesty's ship *Emu*, lately arrived here from Van Diemen's Land and the Derwent. I've heard a good deal about you, Mr. Broome."

"Have you, sir?" Justin shook the proffered hand, but eyed its owner warily. Forster must have spoken to Captain Jeffrey—and Captain Jeffrey, he thought glumly, had wasted no time in damning him. Although perhaps . . . He asked, his color deepening, "May I be permitted to inquire from whom, sir?"

"You may," Commander Forster answered readily. "Initially from Captain Pasco and then from Captain Case—William Case, who was out here with the *Semarang*. We served together in the *Centaur*, under Admiral Hood's command, in that nice action off Rochefort in eighteen six when the poor admiral lost an arm but captured four French frigates. Billy Case was loud in his praise of you—said he'd tried to persuade you to join the *Semarang*, but to no avail. I gathered, though, from various persons that his people were not exactly popular here?"

"No, sir," Justin confirmed noncommittally, recalling the riotous behavior of Case's ship's company during their stay in Sydney. "They were not."

"Least of all with His Excellency," Forster said. "Or so he informed me, when I first called on him." Another toast was being proposed, this time by Dr. D'Arcy Wentworth, and the *Emu*'s commander motioned to a servant to refill their glasses. Colonel Molle's party, augmented by a number of other officers of the 46th, talked loudly during Wentworth's brief speech; and as he lowered his glass, Commander Forster observed shrewdly, "I take it that, for all he's the colony's principal surgeon and a magistrate, Dr. Wentworth was originally one of the underprivileged?"

Justin shrugged. Jessica, he saw, had come back to the marquee, ushering in a posse of Government House servants with fresh supplies of food and drink, but she was absorbed in her task and did not look in his direction. Clearly this was not an opportune moment to approach her, and he turned back to answer his companion's question.

"There are rumors that Dr. Wentworth was convicted of highway robbery in his youth, sir, but he has always denied it, and the rumors were—well, spread by those who played a prominent part in the rebellion against Governor Bligh."

"I see. And now? He's been out here a long time, has he not?"

"About twenty-five years, sir. He bears an impeccable reputation."

"As you do yourself, Mr. Broome," Commander Forster suggested. "His Excellency the Governor speaks most highly of you and assured me that you enjoy his patronage. And yet . . ." The keen blue eyes subjected Justin to a further searching scrutiny. "Captain Jeffrey told me just now that although Their Lordships appointed you to his ship, to fill the vacancy left by Lieutenant

Tempest, he does not intend to employ you. And Tempest, as I understand the position, is to become a settler here, so there is no question of his being reappointed to the *Kangaroo,* is there?"

Justin shook his head. "No, sir, none. He's taking a land grant."

"Can you tell me the reason why Captain Jeffrey has refused to employ you, Mr. Broome?" James Forster's smile robbed his words of any intention to cause offense, and he added, still smiling, "I have a good reason for asking this question, and had I not so fortuitously met you this evening, I should have sought you out, in order to ask it. Is your captain's decision due to the fact that you were born here, of emancipist parents—and that fact sticks in his gullet?"

"Partly, sir, yes." Justin tried to answer honestly. "But only partly, I'm afraid. While we were at Whangaroa, I failed to obey an order Captain Jeffrey gave me. And, I'm sorry, sir, but I'm not at liberty to say more."

"Not at liberty? For the Lord's sake, why?" When Justin was silent, the commander went on, his tone suddenly cold, "Failure to obey an order from a superior officer is a serious crime in the Royal Navy—surely you know that? Captain Jeffrey could have sent you home and applied for your trial by a naval court-martial."

"Yes, sir, he could," Justin agreed evenly.

"But he doesn't intend to do so?"

"No, sir." On his guard now, Justin was puzzled by Commander Forster's persistence. He said, a faint edge to his voice, "Sir, I am junior to you in rank, but I am not under your command, and this, if I may venture to remind you, is a social occasion. I beg you, sir, to ask Captain Jeffrey for what reason he decided to terminate my employment. I'm obeying his instructions in the matter, and—"

To his surprise, Commander Forster gave vent to a rueful laugh. "Damme, Broome, I *did* ask him! All he told me was that you are a competent sea officer and a first-rate navigator, but not having been educated in the naval tradition, you are inclined to be insubordinate and to act on your own initiative. This he put down to the fact that you've held your own command, as master of a trading vessel, and— You there, one moment, if you please!"

Once again Forster broke off to summon a passing servant to replenish their glasses, and then he went on, as if there had been no interruption. "That was how Captain Jeffrey described you, when he was endeavoring to persuade me to agree to exchange my present first lieutenant for you. He is my senior, as you'll realize, so that a request from him is not one I can easily refuse . . . nevertheless, I said that I must meet you before agreeing to the exchange. The *Emu* is a happy and well-disciplined ship, Mr. Broome, and an insubordinate first lieutenant would undermine discipline. Tell me truthfully—*are* you insubordinate?"

Justin hesitated, and the *Emu*'s captain said, lowering his voice, "This matter is strictly between ourselves. I want your honest answer, and whatever it is, it will go no further, I promise you."

"Then, sir, I am not insubordinate," Justin asserted. "I have never, in my past service in His Majesty's ships, refused to obey an order from a superior officer, and I am not likely to do so again. I can only give you my word on that, sir."

"And I'm inclined to take it. That is unless you're willing to tell me, in confidence, why you refused to obey Captain Jeffrey's order at . . . what's the name of that place? Whangaroa, is it not? When your ship was at Whangaroa?"

Justin sighed. Finally, choosing his words carefully, he answered, "Because I feared that it would lead to needless bloodshed, sir."

"Whose blood did you fear might be shed?" Commander Forster challenged dryly. "Your own, your men's, or the Maoris'?"

"All of them would have been involved, sir, and also Mr. Marsden's missionaries and their wives and children. We should have had to evacuate them and Mr. Marsden—"

"Did Mr. Marsden agree with your reading of the situation?" Justin nodded. "I understand he did, yes. The order was canceled, after Mr. Marsden had talked to Captain Jeffrey. I . . . that is, sir, I *delayed* carrying out the order, in Mr. Marsden's temporary absence, in the belief that, when he returned, he would request its cancellation. And that is what happened. I truly thought, you see, that Captain Jeffrey did not appreciate the danger the missionaries were in."

"Thank you, Mr. Broome," the commander acknowledged. He paused, brows furrowed, again studying Justin's face, and finally he said, "Very well, you may take it that the exchange Captain Jeffrey has proposed will be given my immediate consideration. I can see the advantages of it—I carry no sailing master, so that your

skill and local knowledge would be useful to me. I anticipate that
we shall be ordered back to Hobart in the near future. His
Excellency is anxious about the situation there and, in particular,
about the depredations caused by the gangs of bushrangers. He
wants to send an officer on his staff to take command of the
military garrison and endeavor to put an end to the lawlessness
now prevailing. A Captain Hawley, I understand—a onetime
captain in the Royal Marines. Do you know him?"

Justin smiled. "Very well indeed, sir, as it happens. Captain
Hawley is my stepfather."

"Is he, by George! Well, that is another point in your favor, Mr.
Broome. I take it you'd be ready to sail as soon as His Excellency
orders my ship to Hobart?"

Justin glanced up, to see Jessica coming toward him, and bit
back the impulse to deny his readiness. "Sir," he answered flatly,
"I await your decision."

"You shall have it within a day or two," Forster promised. "Do
you know the present Lieutenant Governor of Van Diemen's Land,
Major Davey, by any chance?"

"I know *of* him, sir," Justin admitted warily. "But—"

"And nothing greatly to his credit, I imagine? All right, Mr.
Broome"—Forster's tone was clipped—"you need say no more—
but *I* shall. Davey is a drunken sot, who is letting the place go to
rack and ruin. Whilst I was there, a whaler brought news of a
convict transport—an Indiaman, the *Conway,* on passage here, I
was led to understand. She was hove to, the whaler's master
reported, and there were the corpses of three men hanging from a
yardarm. The skipper of the whaler hailed her, but all he could
learn was that there had been an attempt at mutiny. I wanted to go
out and investigate, but Davey would have none of it. He kept
shouting ' Pondicherry!' for some obscure reason and ordered me
away to Sydney to report to the Governor. And . . . the *Conway*
had not made port when I left the Derwent, so the Lord knows
what's happened to her—" He broke off, with a quick smile, as
Jessica approached them. "Your wife, Mr. Broome?"

"Yes, sir." Justin made the introduction, thinking how lovely
his wife looked, with her shining dark hair and her slim, erect
figure. Her dress, worn with a tartan shawl, was plain, and it could
not match the elegance of most of those worn by the Governor's
female guests, yet Jessica stood out from among them, and heads

turned in her direction as she moved gracefully to her husband's side.

"Mr. Tempest is looking for you, Justin," she said, as Commander Forster excused himself. "And Captain Hawley and Rachel are here. Have you spoken to them?"

Justin shook his head. "No, my love. And for all I've been trying to get near you for the past half hour, I've not spoken to *you* as yet."

"But"—she gestured to the uniform he was wearing—"you've been to the cottage, evidently. The uniform becomes you well, husband."

Justin smiled and bore her hand to his lips. Time enough, he decided, to tell her how close he had come to forfeiting the right to don the King's uniform. And perhaps, if the *Emu*'s commander agreed to accept him, there would be no need to tell her anything at all.

"You saw the boy?" Jessica questioned.

"Yes, indeed. He's a fine-looking fellow . . . and aptly named!"

"Oh, because I call him 'Red,' do you mean? I . . . it seems to suit him. But he's to be properly christened, Justin, at St. Philip's Church. I was only waiting until your return to arrange for it." Jessica looked up at him, her cheeks flushing with pleasure. "Mrs. Macquarie wants to give a party for the christening, and she . . . oh, Justin, she's offered to be his godmother. It's a great honor, and I . . ."

"You accepted, I suppose?" Justin challenged, with mock severity.

"No, I said I must await your return for that, too. But I . . . Justin, it is an honor, and—"

Justin put his arm round her tartan-clad shoulders, wishing that the marquee were not so crowded and that he might embrace her openly.

"My dearest love," he whispered softly, "I know it is, and I am more than proud to accept the honor on young Red's behalf. Perhaps you will accompany me to pay my respects to Her Excellency and thank her for her kindness? And then we will seek out Rick Tempest and Andrew and my little sister. What does Rick want, do you know?"

"He wants to go out to the land grant," Jessica said. "And to start building on it." She slipped from his embrace and held out her hand to him. "He is impatient to get married, you know, but says that he will not ask little Katie to wed him until he has a house to take her to. And the partnership papers are prepared, needing only your signature to them."

"I'll sign them tomorrow," Justin assured her. He took her hand and let her lead him across to where Mrs. Macquarie was seated. Major and Mrs. Antill were with her, and, to his dismay, he saw that the Jeffreys were about to join the group, with Colonel Molle and his adjutant. He sought to hold back, but Jessica, oblivious of the dictates of social protocol, pressed on. The Governor's lady had always treated her more like a daughter than as a serving maid, and it did not for a moment occur to her that her husband, in the glory of his naval uniform, might by his mere presence cause offense to any of the group now gathered to pay their respects to their hostess.

Captain Jeffrey gave him a forbidding glare, his wife affected not to see him, and Colonel Molle, with an incomprehensible growl, planted his stout body between them.

Justin came abruptly to a halt. He freed his hand from Jessica's light clasp and bowed stiffly. He was in the act of turning away when the Governor appeared at his side.

"Ah, Justin my boy!" General Macquarie's greeting was warm. He laid a hand on Justin's arm and led him adroitly to one of the tables. "Let us take a dram together," he invited. "I am most anxious to hear your account of Mr. Marsden's mission at Whangaroa. Your—ah—your esteemed commander appears singularly ill-informed on the essential details, but he tells me he did not set foot ashore, whilst you did. So . . ." He motioned to a servant, and as the man poured out two glasses of the Governor's own scotch whiskey, Justin glanced back at Captain Jeffrey's white and furious face.

He hesitated for an instant, and then said, loudly enough for Jeffrey to hear him, "The captain was unwell, Your Excellency. He was unable to go ashore. I will tell you all I can, sir. But . . . there is not a great deal to tell."

CHAPTER XIV

The transport *Conway* was plowing through heavy seas, six weeks after leaving Capetown, when Murdo was summoned unexpectedly to the master's cabin. It was after midnight, and he had been sleeping soundly; he wakened, bleary-eyed and resentful, to find Sergeant Holmes roughly shaking him.

"The devil fly away with you, Sergeant!" he exclaimed irritably. "What do you want at this hour?"

"It's not me that wants you, sir," the big sergeant returned, unperturbed by his reception. " 'Tis Captain Barlow. And you'd best bestir yourself, Mr. Dean, for the matter's urgent. There's mutiny afoot!"

Murdo swore under his breath but, with visible reluctance, climbed out of his cot and reached for his breeches, shivering as he donned them. It was bitterly cold in these southern latitudes, and even belowdecks the icy wind struck chill into his bones.

"Captain Barlow, Sergeant," he said, thrusting his feet into his boots and standing up, bracing himself against the ship's roll, "has claimed that the prisoners were about to mutiny no less than a dozen times since we sailed. It may be even more—I've lost count. But on every occasion in the past, his fears have proved to be groundless. The poor bloody prisoners are fettered and half starved."

"Not this time, sir," Sergeant Holmes asserted with grave conviction. "This time they mean it—one of 'em brought warning to the captain. I've turned our men out and posted 'em under arms, with full pouches."

He went into careful detail of the precautions he had taken, but Murdo scarcely listened. On each of the previous occasions, the precautions had been precisely the same—the sentries doubled, every hatchway leading from the prisoners' quarters on the orlop guarded, and two men, with loaded muskets, posted outside Captain Barlow's cabin, at his specific request.

It was, however, a wonder that the poor devils of convicts had not attempted to take the ship long before this, Murdo reflected grimly, as Holmes handed him his damp, salt-encrusted short coat and he struggled into it. Heaven knew, they had been provoked almost beyond endurance during the past months. Barlow's cargo of trade goods occupied space that should have been theirs, with the result that all one hundred and seventy of them were confined in foul, verminous darkness in the bowels of the ship, heavily chained, permitted little exercise, and compelled to exist on food that bore an unpleasant resemblance to hog swill.

George De Lancey had protested strongly and demanded improvement in the prisoners' conditions, but Barlow had done little to meet his demands. True, he had ordered the orlop fumigated before the ship made port at Rio, but rather because he feared the censure of the port health authorities than because of De Lancey's condemnation. The two men were no longer on speaking terms, and the atmosphere in the cuddy was, in consequence, somewhat strained, with the mate, Henry Fry, taking De Lancey's part but afraid to do so openly, and the other ship's officers ranging themselves aggressively against him.

He himself . . . Murdo sighed, regretting the cowardice that, he freely acknowledged, led him to take a neutral stand. He liked and, indeed, greatly admired George De Lancey, but he had too much at stake to risk his neck; the danger was too great, the consequences—should his true identity be discovered—too hideous to contemplate. For God's sake, they would throw him in among the convicts without a moment's hesitation, were they to learn who he really was and what he had done!

Buckling on his belt, Murdo glanced uneasily at Sergeant Holmes. The sergeant, he sometimes feared, suspected him of duplicity. Certainly Holmes was prone to watch him, even at times to test him, and was a mite too ready to question his authority and to meet legitimate orders with a dumb insolence that fell just short of insubordination. His behavior tonight was typical . . . Holmes had posted the guard before coming to him to report and receive the order to post extra sentries. Probably, had Captain Barlow not sent for him, the sergeant would have let him sleep on, in ignorance of what, if anything, was afoot, in the hope that he might thus incur Barlow's displeasure.

"Where is the captain?" Murdo asked, his tone deliberately sharp. "On deck or in his cabin?"

"In his cabin. I took the feller who brought the warning to him there. Had to smuggle 'im out, you see, sir, 'cause them Irish swine would've cut his throat if they'd had any inkling of what he was goin' to do." Holmes's expression was smug, his manner self-satisfied, as if what he had acomplished had been a minor miracle. "He hinted early this afternoon that he'd somethin' of great importance to tell the captain, but he was dead scared o' the others, so I made out I was arrestin' him for possession o' intoxicating liquor, an' his mates was wringing their hands an' promisin' to speak up for 'im. They—"

Murdo cut him short. "All right—I don't want his whole history, Sergeant. What is his name?"

Sergeant Holmes drew himself up, looking offended. "MacBride, sir—Peter MacBride. Like I told you, he's with the captain, and—"

"Then let us go and wait on the captain," Murdo said, again cutting him short.

The two scarlet-coated sentries came to attention outside the door of Captain Barlow's day cabin, and Holmes knocked on it loudly.

"Sar'nt Holmes, sir, and Mr. Dean," he announced.

"And not before time," Captain Barlow greeted sourly. He was only partially dressed, a thick flannel nightshirt tucked into the waistband of a pair of soiled white duck trousers, from which his stockinged, but unbooted, feet protruded in an oddly obscene manner. There was a pewter beaker of rum at his elbow—already almost empty, Murdo noted with contemptuous disapproval. The second mate, Charlie Lawrence, stood alert and fully clothed at his back, a pistol in his hand; and the convict informant, filthy and unshaven, crouched between them, eyes darting from one to the other, as if pleading for their compassion.

"Thanks to your sergeant's vigilance, mister," Barlow went on, addressing Murdo, "a dastardly plot to seize the ship and murder us all has been uncovered." He gestured to the cowering prisoner. "This man risked his life to bring us warning, but you, I venture to suggest, will try to tell me it's a false alarm and you knew nowt of it."

"I knew nothing of it," Murdo conceded. "But with my men posted under arms and the hatches closed, what can the convicts do? They're fettered and unarmed . . . they've no hope of taking the ship, Captain, still less of murdering anyone. They—"

The captain interrupted, red with annoyance. "The swine *are* armed, mister! Tell 'im, MacBride—tell this disbelieving King's officer what you told me, for God's sake! I want action, and I want it now!"

The convict responded with ingratiating eagerness. He was a thin, slovenly-looking man of uncertain age, his appearance rendered the more unpleasant by the privations he had endured and by the fact that, although all the prisoners were permitted to hose themselves down after exercise, he had clearly not taken advantage of this concession for a long time.

" 'Tis a God's fact, yer honor," he asserted. "Like I'm after tellin' the sergeant here, more dan a score o' men have armed themselves. They've made clubs, sorr, so they have, wid slats taken from the bunks—and the priest, Father Joseph, has a pistol. Sure, he keeps it hidden, but I've seen it wid me own eyes. An' some o' dem have filed through their leg-irons, an' honed them, to make knives and de loike. . . ." The whining, heavily accented voice went on, naming names, making accusations for which, when pressed, he could offer no proof, and Murdo listened with unconcealed skepticism.

"How do they plan to break out?" he asked coldly. "Did they tell you that?"

Unhappily, MacBride shook his head.

"I was never in dere confidence, sorr. But I've seen what they're doin' an' heard them whisperin' amongst themselves. Seamus Burke an' him they call Mr. Fitzroy and the father—they're the ringleaders. Holy Mother of God, sorr, ye must believe me! 'Tis de truth I'm tellin' yez."

"I reckon it is, sir," Sergeant Holmes put in forcefully. "You don't go amongst the treacherous rogues down there like I do, when the rations are issued, so you'll not have heard the whispers. But *I* have and I know they're up to no good." He turned to the captain. " 'Tis my belief, sir, that they intend to break out when we sight land. And that will be very soon, will it not, sir?"

"Aye, within the next twenty-four hours we should pick up South Cape of Van Diemen's Land," Barlow confirmed. He drained his beaker and set it down, his lips tightening. "The wind's easterly and rising. And the glass is falling," he added glumly. "We're in for some dirty weather, and if it turns out to be as bad as I fear, we'll maybe have to put in to Adventure Bay for shelter. If we do, Mr. Dean, you and your damned lobsterbacks will need to be on the alert day and night, you understand? No skulking in your berth—because, if Sergeant Holmes is right, the sight of land could incite those infernal Irish rebels to mutiny."

"I know my duty, sir," Murdo assured him stiffly.

"It's to be hoped you do, mister," the *Conway*'s master retorted. He jerked his head at the second mate and ordered gruffly, "We'll show the swine what's what, Mr. Lawrence. Give 'em a warning they'll understand. Before you send the morning watch below, muster all hands to witness punishment, the way a King's ship would do it. D'you think you can do that, eh?"

"Aye, sir," Lawrence acknowledged. He passed his tongue nervously over his bearded lips. "But . . . who is it that you intend to punish, if I may ask, sir?"

"You dimwit!" Barlow exclaimed, losing patience. "Use what brains the good Lord gave you! One o' the ringleaders, of course—the papist priest, what's his name? Father Joseph, ain't it? Well, if MacBride's telling the truth, he has a pistol concealed on his person or in his bedding. Get down there with Ensign Dean an' a brace o' his redcoats and *find* that pistol. Then bring Father poxy Joseph to me and I'll sentence him to a flogging. That'll teach them a lesson."

Everyone in the cabin, with the sole exception of Sergeant Holmes, regarded him in dismay. Murdo started to protest, but Holmes interrupted him.

"Leave it to me, Captain Barlow, sir," the sergeant offered. "I know how to handle the matter. If Mr. Lawrence will accompany me, as a witness, sir, an' MacBride show me where the priest sleeps, it can be done without causing no disturbance. Indeed, sir, I'll see to it that—"

The wretched MacBride gave vent to a squeal of terror. "Holy Mother o' God, Sergeant, ye promised! Ye gave me your word that I'd not be sent back to the prison deck if I tell't yez what ye wanted!" He was on his knees, trembling and wringing his bony hands, appealing to the indifferent Holmes, who eyed him scornfully and said nothing. "For pity's sake, sorr," the Irishman begged, directing his plea to the captain. "Dey'll kill me for sure if I go back dere! I'll work de ship, sorr, I'll do anything you ask, so I will. But don't send me back, sorr, for Christ's sake don't send me back!"

Captain Barlow shrugged. "Can you find the priest without the help o' this miserable rogue, Sergeant?" he asked. Holmes nodded confidently, and the captain said, with contempt, "Very well—get him out o' here, Mr. Lawrence. He can be put to work with the idlers. Send him below to the mess deck."

As Lawrence was obeying these instructions, Murdo again attempted to voice his protest, but Barlow silenced him with an angry roar.

"I'm master o' this ship, Mister Ensign, an' don't you forget it! I'll not stand for a scurvy bunch o' Irish scum threatenin' to mutiny an' take my ship from me. There've been too many o' their blasted threats all this voyage, devil take them! Enough's enough, an' I'm goin' to teach them a lesson they won't forget."

"But, Captain, flogging their priest will incite them to violence," Murdo persisted despairingly. "Choose anyone except the father, sir, I beg you, if you are set on teaching them a lesson. If you hope to deter them, then—"

"Are *you* a bloody papist, mister?" Barlow sneered unpleasantly.

He had been brought up in the Catholic faith, Murdo recalled guiltily, but it was a long time since he had practiced it. Before he could utter either assent or denial, the captain went on harshly, "Whatever you are, damn your eyes, you'll obey my orders! Off with you down to the orlop, you insolent young puppy, and give your sergeant the backing he needs. I want that infernal pistol found in front of witnesses and the priest brought up here, understand? And if the Irish scum offer any resistance, you are to order your soldiers to open fire on 'em. Is that quite clear, mister, or must I spell it out for you?"

"That will not be necessary, sir," Murdo managed stiffly. "Your instructions are clear enough."

It was, he knew, useless to argue. Throughout the long, weary voyage, the *Conway*'s master had feared the possibility that the prisoners might attempt to seize his ship; he had admitted it openly, and had gone to brutal lengths to prevent any such occurrence. But now . . . Murdo frowned in bewilderment as he left the cabin.

Now, it seemed, Captain Barlow was hell-bent on provoking a showdown; indeed, he appeared actually to want the wretched prisoners to resort to mutiny, and if they did, it was evident that he would show them no mercy. He intended to put down any attempted insurrection with a ruthless disregard for the Irishmen's lives or, come to that, for the lives of the soldiers whose duty it was to carry out his orders. And carry them out without question, God help them!

For a moment, standing there in the dimly lit passageway, Murdo was tempted to leave the priest's arrest to Sergeant Holmes. The infernal sergeant had started it all; it was he who had brought MacBride from the prison deck and taken him to the captain, with his wild and—yes, his unsubstantiated tale.

But . . . Holmes was waiting for him, he saw, with mock deference and an odd smile curving his lips. The fellow was not to be trusted down in the dark confines of the orlop, with armed men under his command . . . he himself would have to accompany the arresting party, Murdo thought bitterly. He would have to be there, if only to stop Holmes from carrying out whatever sadistic plans he had made.

For Holmes *had* made plans; every instinct he possessed told Murdo that he had. A pox on the bastard! He was grinning now, clearly deriving perverse pleasure from the crisis he had brought about. Damn it, Murdo thought, why had he been so blind? It was not Captain Barlow who was seeking to provoke a mutiny . . . it was Sergeant Holmes who had tricked him into believing that the prisoners were planning to break out!

As if to confirm his suspicions, the sergeant said, with unwonted solicitude, "No need for you to trouble yourself further, Mr. Dean, sir. Mr. Lawrence and I can do what's necessary. It shouldn't take us above ten minutes, and the orlop's no place for a gentleman with sensitive feelings or a weak stomach."

Usually he avoided the prison quarters like the plague, Murdo was forced to admit, conscious of shame. He hated the befouled air and the sight of the fettered convicts, and try as he would, he could never escape from the knowledge that—had fate not ordained otherwise—he might himself have been condemned to make the long voyage in similar conditions. The bumbling old judge at the assize court had sentenced him to deportation for the term of his natural life, and . . . He thrust the bitter memory from his mind. He was Ensign Michael Dean, commissioned into His Majesty's 46th Regiment of Foot, and, he reminded himself, he—and not Sergeant Holmes—was in command of the regimental draft.

Murdo braced himself and snapped, an edge to his voice, "I shall come with you, Sergeant, in accordance with Captain Barlow's instructions. He requires witnesses when the priest is searched."

Holmes's dark brows lifted in surprise, but he shrugged and said nothing, and when Lawrence reappeared, they both followed him to the midships companionway. The two sentries posted at its foot fell in behind them in obedience to the sergeant's gruff command; Lawrence took a lantern from its hook on the deck beam, and by its flickering light they descended in single file to the orlop deck.

It was in virtual darkness, the stench—even in Captain Barlow's purloined cargo space—so vile that Murdo was hard put to it not to retch, as a wave of nausea swept over him. A stout bulkhead, loopholed and studded with nails, cut off the prison quarters from the main hatchway, by which they had descended. The door was reinforced by iron stanchions, secured by three separate metal padlocks for which three different keys were required. Waving the two sentries posted in the narrow passageway to stand aside, Holmes produced the keys from his pocket with something of a flourish. He said, after glancing through the barred spy-hole in the door, "The priest has a bunk to himself—third or fourth on the starboard side, lower tier, if I remember rightly. There's none o' the scum stirring that I can see, so if we go in fast and I grab 'im, they shouldn't give us no trouble."

He addressed Lawrence, ignoring Murdo, and as he and the second mate started to unlock the door, Murdo found himself wishing that he had taken the time to rouse George De Lancey and prevail upon him to serve as an additional witness. But it was too late now, and in any case, De Lancey was a civilian passenger, with less authority even than himself. He was a lawyer, it was true, but . . . The heavy door creaked open, and Lawrence went into the prisoners' quarters, holding the lantern at arm's length in front of him.

Several inches of water, a relic of the last gale, covered the timbered floor and swished sluggishly from side to side with the ship's roll, adding to the foulness of the air inside, which hung heavy and lifeless, since both air scuttles were closed. Two rows of wooden bunks, one above the other, extended forward from the mainmast, each six feet square and occupied by four men, a continuous chain running between them, to which the men's leg-irons could, when necessary, be attached . . . one of Barlow's brutal refinements, Murdo recalled.

Roused by the creaking of the door and the mate's lantern, the convicts began to stir, some sitting up in bemused silence and others greeting the unexpected intrusion with surly complaints and growled obscenities. Sergeant Holmes ignored them. He strode forward, deaf to abuse and question alike, and, with Lawrence at his heels, made for the bunk where the priest was sleeping. Father Joseph was a young man, thin and pale, with a shaven head and a scar across one cheek. Huddled beneath the single thin blanket that was each convict's allocation, he struggled vainly to free himself as the sergeant's big hands seized him roughly by the shoulders and dragged him from his berth.

"What do you want of me, Sergeant?" he asked, startled, and then, remembering his calling, he added quietly, "If any man is dying and has need of me, I will come willingly. You have no call to use force. I know my duty to God, even in this hell ship, and—"

Holmes's fist silenced the mildly voiced complaint, and the priest staggered back, his fettered hands raised to protect his face from further blows. Lawrence was searching the bunk, ripping the sodden straw mattress with his seaman's knife, and he grunted his satisfaction when the object of his search came to light.

"Here we are!" he exclaimed. "A pistol—this scoundrel of a priest has a pistol! What price his duty to his God now, eh?" He held out his find for Murdo's inspection, bringing the lantern closer, a taunting smile playing about his lips. "Witness it, mister—'tis a pistol, right enough, is it not?"

It was an old dueling pistol, Murdo saw, rusty and in all probability liable to burst if, by some miracle, it could be fired, and he wondered, when a prolonged and diligent search failed to reveal either ball or powder for its use, why the young father should have troubled to retain it. But, for all that, he was compelled to admit that it was a weapon and that it had been found in Father Joseph's possession and undoubtedly concealed.

Pressed by Lawrence, he unwillingly stated as much, and Sergeant Holmes, without waiting for an order, grasped the priest by the collar of his ragged black robe and started to propel him toward the door of the prison.

Those convicts near and wakeful enough to realize his intention voiced angry demands that the father be released; others took up their cry, and pandemonium broke out, the Irishmen yelling wildly and beating their chains on the wood of their bunks. But the sight of the sentries' leveled muskets deterred all but a handful of braver spirits, and Sergeant Holmes's stern warning that they would open fire sufficed to discourage even these.

In tense, bitter silence, they had finally to watch their priest led away, but as the door slammed shut and the heavy padlocks were once again secured, they began to sing, and Murdo's heart sank as the sound of the defiant voices echoed from end to end of the ship.

> We trust in God above us,
> And we dearly love the green;
> Oh, to die it is far better
> Than be cursed as we have been!

And then, gaining in volume as more voices joined in,

> But we've hearts, oh, we've hearts, boys,
> Full true enough, I ween,
> To rescue and to raise again
> Our own immortal green!

With sullen reluctance, Murdo attended the brief trial in the master's cabin, gave his evidence, and heard Father Joseph sentenced to fifty lashes.

The savage sentence was carried out the next morning in the presence of the ship's company and twenty of the convicts, heavily ironed and mustered under strong guard on their exercise deck for the purpose.

The priest was cut down, unconscious, and before going below to break his fast, Captain Barlow warned those on the exercise deck that there would be worse to come at the first sign of trouble.

CHAPTER XV

The first George De Lancey knew of the unhappy affair was when he came on deck to observe the flogging in progress.

Sickened and appalled—as much by the calling of the victim as by the punishment—he sought out Ensign Dean for an explanation and listened, with growing indignation, to the younger man's account of what had led up to it.

He had slept through it all—his sleep induced by an overliberal consumption of Cape brandy, in which he had, of late, taken to indulging—and his conscience plagued him unmercifully as the sorry tale unfolded.

"In heaven's name, Michael, you should have wakened me!" he exclaimed reproachfully. "Why did you not?"

"What could you have done, sir?" the ensign countered, with a rueful shrug. "The father *had* a pistol—it was hidden in his palliasse. I was there when the second mate found it. And for all I know, some of the others have arms. The informer claimed they had. Truly, Mr. De Lancey, what could you have done?"

What indeed, George thought, unable to find an answer. He was a civilian and a passenger; and on board his own ship at sea, Captain Barlow had absolute authority. If he chose to order the flogging of a convict—priest or layman—he was within his rights to do so, particularly if the convict in question was proven to have committed a crime.

"All the same," he said, "Captain Barlow is inviting trouble, I fear. What was the mood of the other prisoners when you took the father away?"

"It was ugly, sir," Ensign Dean answered without hesitation. "And they were not then aware that Father Joseph was to be flogged. It will be a damned sight uglier now, I dare swear."

"Ugly enough to spark off violence?" George suggested. "Or an attempt to take the ship, do you suppose? That was what the informer claimed, was it not?"

"I don't know—but it wouldn't surprise me. MacBride said they have been improvising weapons for some time past, and if they have, I fancy they'll try to use them. They're Irish, sir, and the Irish know how to hate."

And with some reason, George was ready to admit. "The Irish regiments were among our best and bravest troops in the Peninsular campaign," he said thoughtfully. "Damme, you could not have asked for better regiments than the Eighty-eighth or the Royal Irish Dragoons, and the Sixth were magnificent at Waterloo—we charged beside them. But . . ." He sighed. "When they are denied freedom and privilege in their own country and condemned as rebels if they attempt to fight for these rights, then I suppose the result is inevitable. But it is not justice, is it? I wonder if it would help if I were to try to talk to them?"

"You'd be putting your head into a lions' den, sir," Ensign Dean returned with conviction. "And the master won't listen, either."

He was probably right, George thought regretfully, but in spite of it, he made an attempt to talk to Barlow later that morning, only to be met with ill-tempered abuse and an obstinate refusal to make even the smallest concession to the Irishmen's outraged feelings.

" 'Tis blowing up a gale, mister, and I've no time to waste on you or them convict scum. Likely they'll be too wet an' seasick to cause trouble before the day's out . . . three or four feet o' salt water floodin' their quarters ought to keep 'em quiet. They can have their pulin' priest back, but that's all. I've told Barney Shea to deliver 'im, as soon as he's back to his senses."

Father Joseph had taken his punishment with stoical courage and, until he had lost conciousness, had scarcely emitted a cry; but Surgeon Shea—supposedly present to call a halt to the flogging when the victim lost his senses—had not done so, George recalled with disgust. Instead he had caused buckets of salt water to be thrown over the unfortunate man and, when this had revived him, had waved permission for the lashing to be continued. By the time the full fifty lashes had been administered, the priest's back had been reduced to a bloody pulp and, barely breathing, he had had to be carried below to Shea's hospital in the fore part of the ship. And

Shea had broken his fast and imbibed his customary half bottle of liquor before going below to attend to him. . . .

Turning his back on the *Conway*'s master, George controlled his rising anger with difficulty. He had seen men flogged before—the Duke had been a stern disciplinarian, and looters, thieves, and deserters in the ranks of his motley army had been punished with the full severity of military law. But they had been tough, physically fit soldiers, not half-starved prisoners, at the end of a five-month voyage in a convict ship, whose bodies were skin and bone. And if the priest died . . . He swore in exasperation, shocked by the realization that his sympathies were almost exclusively with the Irish rebels and that, of the *Conway*'s entire company, only Henry Fry, the first mate, and Lewis, the steward—and yes, young Michael Dean, the guard commander—had deserved his respect.

Perhaps, he reflected wryly, for all he had supported the loyalist cause in America, at heart he, too, was a rebel. At all events, he set a high value on justice and freedom for the individual; these were the only causes for which it was worth dying.

With this conclusion in mind, he sought out Surgeon Shea and found him, as usual, in the cuddy with a half-empty glass in his hand and his cravat stained and awry, his speech already a trifle slurred. But Shea was sufficiently alert to reject his request to be permitted to visit the priest in the sick bay.

"I'm sending the rogue back where he belongs after dinner, De Lancey," he stated coldly. "If you happen to run into young Dean, perhaps you would be so good as to tell him that I'll need a guard." He pushed his bottle of brandy in George's direction and added, suppressing a hiccup, "Have a drink, man, and forget the damned rogues of convicts. We're in for the father and mother of a storm, if Captain Barlow's to be believed—and he usually is. Told me he intends to run for Adventure Bay, in Van Diemen's Land, as fast as the old tub will carry us. You'll not be able to stand on deck in an hour."

In this gloomy prediction the surgeon proved right. Within less than an hour, the *Conway* was battling against mountainous seas, which the wind, rising rapidly to gale force, whipped to fury. At the best of times, the ship was a slow sailer, answering sluggishly to her helm; in anything approaching bad weather, she shipped water in tons, burying her blunt bows beneath the frothing whitecaps, so that they surged over her from stem to stern, menacing any and everything on deck that was not secured. The men on watch moved at their peril, clutching the lifelines that had been hurriedly rigged, and the two men at the helm were compelled to lash themselves to their dangerous post in order to maintain their footing and keep the ship's head to the wind.

Anxious to reach shelter before conditions worsened, Captain Barlow kept as much sail on as he dared, and the old ship heeled under the wind's savage assault as he tried vainly to keep her on course. An upper sail split, with a report like that of a distant gunshot, and two seamen were lost when the topmen were ordered aloft to take it in. In such a storm, no boat could be sent to their rescue, and the *Conway* lurched on, leaving them to their fate, their bobbing heads soon lost to sight in her hissing wake.

For all his corpulence, Captain Barlow was everywhere on deck, wind and water seemingly powerless against his bulk, and George, watching from the comparative safety of the chart house, was forced to admire the stout master's courage and seamanship. Even when the foretopmast crashed down in a welter of torn rigging and shattered spars, Barlow did not lose his head. His bellowed orders, magnified by his speaking trumpet, sent men staggering across the heeling deck, George himself among them, to tear the wrecked and twisted cordage free with axes, knives, and even their bare hands.

At the height of the storm, even the soldiers were called into service, to man the braces and work the pumps, but to George's gasped suggestion that he enlist volunteers from the prison, Barlow swore wrathfully and shook his oilskin-covered head.

"Let them rogues loose? And with no soldiers to watch over 'em? By God, mister, that's the last thing I'll do! The swine can rot in hell, but they're not being made free o' my deck so long as I'm alive and in command! We'll be out o' this and in Adventure Bay in another couple of hours, if the wind don't shift. Go and take a turn at them pumps, if you've nowt better to do than offer me bad advice."

George did as he had been ordered, and with young Dean and his panting soldiers, he toiled at one of the pumps until close to dropping with exhaustion. The mate, Fry, relieved them at last.

"Not much longer, Mr. De Lancey," he yelled, his mouth close to George's ear, so as to make himself heard above the roar of the wind. "There's land in sight, and if my calculations are correct, we're not above ten miles from the bay. If we can keep her afloat for another hour, we'll be safely inside and out of this."

The lowering, windswept gray skies were yielding to the gathering darkness when the old ship, with her pumps creaking, limped into the shelter of the landlocked bay and came at last to anchor. A ragged cheer rose from the sorely tried men as the bower anchor splashed down into the black water and the *Conway* brought to, the tall, wooded hills rising steeply on either hand to cut her off from the gale, still raging furiously to seaward. There was much to be done before she could continue her voyage—a jury foremast to be rigged, damage to shrouds, halyards, and sails to be attended to, lost spars to be replaced, and the water she had shipped to be pumped out. . . . Henry Fry gravely listed these and a score of smaller defects that had to be made good. And it would take time, he warned.

But, for once, the taciturn master permitted his people to relax and celebrate their deliverance. The steward issued rum to the seamen and soldiers; and Barlow himself, changed into dry clothing and in a buoyant mood, came to the cuddy, inviting his officers and the passengers to drink with him and accepting their congratulations with gruff pleasure.

Only the surgeon, Dr. Shea, and Fry, the mate, were absent from the convivial gathering, but no one questioned the reason for their absence. George, aching with weariness and on his third brandy, was dimly aware of the fact that the surgeon's chair was empty— almost for the first time since the ship had sailed from Cork.

It was Sergeant Holmes who brought an abrupt end to the cuddy's celebration. He came staggering in, bleeding from an ugly head wound and ashen-faced with mingled pain and anger, to make the alarming announcement that the prisoners had made a bid to seize the ship.

"The treacherous bastards called for the surgeon, sir," he told Barlow. "Claimed there was several of 'em badly injured. Surgeon Shea went down with Mr. Fry and one o' my men, sir, and they jumped the lad, took his musket an' bayonet, an' seized the other two. Holding them hostage, they say, an' threatenin' to kill them, unless you come down an' parley with 'em." He paused to regain his breath and then gestured to the wound on his head. "I was by the bulk'ead door when some o' the sods rushed me. 'Twas all I could do to get the hatch closed an' the padlocks secured."

Leaving the hostages inside, George thought, to save his own skin . . . but perhaps he was being unjust. To have done anything else would have been to liberate the convicts, giving them the opportunity to overrun the ship and her exhausted crew. He glanced at Ensign Dean and saw that he was white with dismay.

"Will you parley with 'em, sir?" Holmes asked.

"No, by God I will not!" the master thundered, and his gaze went, as George's had, to Dean. "Well, mister?" he demanded harshly, all trace of his earlier benevolence gone. "Are you going to get your damned redcoats down there to deal with this? I want an end to it, even if you have to open fire on the bloody Irish scum, understand?"

Before Ensign Dean could reply, the big sergeant, recovering his lost bombast, put in quickly, "I've mustered our men, sir. They're ready." He added vindictively, " 'Twill be a simple matter to bring the swine to heel. The bulk'ead's loopholed. No need to risk opening the door."

Captain Barlow nodded. Impatiently, he challenged Dean. "Well, Mister Ensign? You're in command o' the convict guard, ain't you?"

"Yes, I am, sir," Dean acknowledged unhappily. "But what of the hostages? What of Mr. Fry and the surgeon? Will you not at least listen to whatever the convicts have to say—what terms they're offering, in exchange for the lives of the hostages? If we fire on them, even if we attempt to rush them, sir, they could still murder both men, and we'd be powerless to prevent it."

"Mr. Dean is right, Captain Barlow," George said, aware that his intervention would be resented, but unable to restrain himself. He held no brief for the drink-sodden Shea, but Henry Fry was a good man and a fine seaman, and neither Holmes nor the captain appeared to recognize the danger in which precipitate action would place them. "I'd be willing to parley with the prisoners and inform you of their demands, if you—"

Barlow's clenched fist crashed onto the top of the bar in angry frustration, cutting him short. "I'll strike no bargain with blasted convicts, Mr. De Lancey! But you can tell 'em my terms, if you've a mind to—you can warn 'em that they'll hang, every man jack o' them, if they harm my mate or my surgeon." His eyes blazing, he turned to Dean. "If they won't listen to this gentleman, then *you* warn the scum—fire over their heads! Go on, get down there, Mister Ensign! Or are you too lily-livered to do what His Majesty pays you to do?"

Dean flushed indignantly, but George grasped his arm. "Come on," he urged, in a tense whisper. "Let's see what we can do to make the Irishmen see reason."

In the malodorous confines of the orlop, an unexpected silence prevailed. But the convicts were on the alert, George realized, when a hoarse challenge halted him at the foot of the companion-way and the lantern he was carrying revealed the barrel of a musket protruding from one of the loopholes in the door of the prisoners' quarters. The spy-hole was open, and from behind it a voice with only a faint trace of an Irish accent bade him state his business.

"Stand where you are and tell us why you have come. We are asking to parley with the ship's master. You'll be aware that we are holding two officers and one of your redcoats as hostages, no doubt?"

"I'm aware of that, and the master has been informed of it." Conscious of Holmes's big body pressing impatiently against him, George took a pace forward.

"I have you in my sights. Come no closer," the Irish voice warned. "Have you the authority to negotiate the release of the men we hold?"

"I've been given no such authority," George admitted. "But I—"

"Then, faith, man, why have you come?"

"In the hope that bloodshed can be avoided. And to acquaint you with the consequences if any of the hostages are harmed. Release them to me now, unharmed, and no action will be taken against you. But if you do not . . ." George started to repeat the captain's threat, but with a muffled oath the man on the other side of the bulkhead interrupted him.

"If that is all you have to say, then you are wasting your breath. In the name of God, man, we are not fools, and we are not playing games! We've no intention of harming our hostages unless we are driven to it. And we are not engaged in a mutiny or in an attempt to take the ship. We've all of us had experience of English justice, by heaven, and we know all too well the consequences—you've no need to spell them out! Sure you'd hang as many of us as you could, and you'd flog the rest, would you not? Well, we have borne enough. We will release your officers and the soldier, if the master agrees to our terms."

"What are your terms?" George asked. Against all reason, his hopes rose, and beside him he heard Michael Dean expel his breath in a long-drawn sigh of relief.

"They're simple enough," the Irishman answered. "We want decent food and the removal of our chains and fetters for what remains of the voyage. We want clean water and adequate time and space for exercise in the fresh air . . . all things we've a right to and of which we've been deprived. We've sick men in here who've been given no treatment." His tone changed, taking on a note of bitter irony as he added, "The longest your miserable surgeon has spent with us has been since we seized him forcibly this evening! I fancy he'll agree now that our quarters are verminous and foul and, when we release him, he'll send us all the vinegar and sulfur we've begged for in vain since we left Rio. We're asking no more than to be able to land in Botany Bay like human beings instead of animals . . . and that is all we are asking."

"He's lying," Sergeant Holmes growled. "Don't you believe him, Mr. De Lancey. They're armed and they'll be on us the first chance they get. They—"

George silenced him sharply. He moved closer to the door, and this time the menacing musket remained still. "I will convey your terms to the ship's master. In the presumption that you speak for the rest, may I know your name?"

"Sure, for what it is worth, sir. I am Patrick Fitzroy, brother of the poor young priest your people flogged almost to death this morning." The Irishman paused, to let his words sink in, and then he went on evenly, "I should warn you that if the master is unwilling to accept our terms, Mr. De Lancey—"

His quick ears had picked up Holmes's mention of his name, George realized, and he prompted warily, "What then, Mr. Fitzroy?"

"Why, then, sir, we shall carry out our threat. The surgeon will be shot . . . and after him, if necessary, the other two. And damning the consequences, we shall try to take the ship."

His reply, firmly uttered, carried conviction. Patrick Fitzroy was no wild rebel from the Irish bogs but an educated man, and George felt both sympathy and respect for him. He was turning away, with the intention of going to report the result of his attempt at mediation to the captain, when, to his shocked dismay, Barlow himself came bounding down the companion ladder, thrusting the waiting soldiers aside in his haste to reach its foot.

Evidently he had overheard Fitzroy's last words, for he repeated them at the pitch of his powerful lungs. "Shoot my surgeon, will you, you cursed rogues! Try to take my ship! I'll see you in hell first, the whole scurvy lot o' you! Get his musket, Sergeant Holmes—grab it, I say!"

Holmes needed no second bidding. He hurled himself forward, keeping to the left of the pointing barrel, and George's attempt to intercept him was met with a heavy shoulder charge that left him on his knees, winded and gasping for breath.

The musket went off, but Holmes had his hand on the barrel, and the ball lodged itself harmlessly in the upper-deck beams. The explosion of the charge, unnaturally loud in so confined a space, reverberated like thunder, and instantly the prisoners' voices, silent until now, rose in shocked and angry protest. Then, as suddenly, they again fell silent and George, struggling dazedly to his feet, heard Fitzroy's voice yelling urgently.

"No! You crazy fool, *no*! Leave him be!"

A second shot rang out—but inside the prison this time—followed by an agonized scream and the thud of a falling body.

Fitzroy spoke again, his tone shamed and apologetic. "De Lancey . . . I am sorry. Your surgeon has been shot—in error. I regret to tell you that he is dead. But the others are safe. They'll not be harmed if—"

Whatever proposal he had been about to make was cut off by an imperious bellow from the captain.

"Man the loopholes, Mr. Dean!" he ordered. "By God, I'll hang the murdering swine! Fire a volley over their heads and tell 'em to release the mate. If they don't, get that door open an' rush them!"

"They will release him, sir," George began. "Let me—"

But Barlow ignored his plea. "Get on with it, Mr. Dean!" he roared. "You heard me!"

Dean, George knew, had no choice but to obey. He gave the order, having to shout it above the hubbub of shouts and curses coming from inside the prison. From where he stood, held back by the captain's heavy hand, George had no means of knowing whether or not the soldiers obeyed Dean's instruction to aim high with their first volley, but more screams and cries of pain led him to doubt whether all of them had done so.

Then they reloaded, and the door was unlocked to reveal a crowd of ragged convicts, shadowy, scarecrow figures in the dim light of the lanterns suspended from the deck beams above their heads. Fitzroy had clearly lost control of them or else, in desperation, had yielded to their decision to risk their all in an attempt to break out. They surged forward in a struggling mass, but despite their numbers they stood no chance against the armed and disciplined soldiers. Dean's men went in, the front rank opened fire, and as the thunderous echoes died down, the rest charged in after them, using their musket butts like flails.

They emerged, minutes later, bearing the body of Surgeon Shea and with Fry, the first mate—apparently unscathed—in their midst, leaving the prison quarters a shambles in their wake. George caught a brief glimpse of it before the door clanged shut, and he turned away, his stomach churning, to find himself confronted by the *Conway*'s master.

"They'll not mutiny now, mister," Barlow observed, with thinly disguised satisfaction. "And they'll not take my ship, damn them to perdition!" His gaze lit on Dean, who was standing, white of face and badly shaken, by the prison door, the keys to it in his hand. "Did you get your sentry out?" he asked curtly. The ensign nodded.

"Yes, we got him, sir. He wasn't hurt."

"Then put them padlocks back an' lock 'em, mister. What are you waiting for?"

"Sir, there are dead and dying men in there—a score of them, maybe more. Can we not attend to them?"

"Attend to bloody mutineers?" Barlow exclaimed contemptuously. "Give 'em the chance to take more hostages, for the Lord's sake? You're out o' your mind, mister! In any case, the scum murdered the only man who could bind up their wounds, did they not? They killed the surgeon, so let 'em rot. They brought it on themselves, the devil take them."

Once again, George attempted to intervene.

"Captain Barlow, they killed poor Shea in error . . . one man got out of hand; it was not intended. They were willing to release all three hostages unharmed, in return for a few concessions, which you could have granted them, sir, with no risk of trouble whatsoever. I beg you, allow me to go in—with Ensign Dean, if he's willing, and a guard of his men. To remove the dead, at least, and give the wounded fresh water and bandages and what succor we can."

Captain Barlow eyed him suspiciously from beneath scowling brows. "A veteran o' Waterloo, and you want to give succor to blasted rebels?"

"In common humanity, Captain . . . yes."

Barlow's mention of Waterloo sparked off the memories George De Lancey had sought vainly to erase from his mind . . . memories of the dreadful carnage that had been the aftermath of victory, of suffering men and mutilated horses and of his own predicament, pinned down beneath the body of his charger and powerless to help himself. As helpless as the unfortunate Irish rebels were now . . . He said tautly, "They are human beings, damn it, Captain Barlow."

To his credit, young Dean came to his support. "I'm willing, sir. And I can post a strong guard at the door."

Barlow's scowl lifted. "Very well, then. But let them rogues make a concession in return. Tell 'em they'll be given succor if they hand over the man who murdered my surgeon, so's I can hang him. And make sure they know he'll hang, mister. Punctually at eight bells o' the morning watch."

With extreme reluctance, George called Patrick Fitzroy to the door of the prison deck and explained the captain's conditions. The convicts' spokesman groaned when he heard them.

"The surgeon's death was never intended," he said. "I beg you to believe that, Mr. De Lancey. But . . . your captain leaves us no alternative, does he? We've three dead men in here and over twenty wounded, some of whom will die if they're left untreated. We need bandages and surgical instruments and laudanum. . . ." He listed their needs with a bitterness he did not attempt to hide.

"Have you the skill to use them?" George asked.

Fitzroy's eyes glinted behind the spy-hole's narrow aperture. "In times past, sir, I was a surgeon. My skills are rusty, but I've not entirely forgotten them. And . . . as to yielding up the man who killed your surgeon, I believe that can be arranged—but you must give me a little time. Ten minutes, perhaps, or maybe a mite longer, whilst I talk to the others? Thank you, sir."

Ensign Dean went with two of his soldiers to the hospital to fetch what medical supplies he could find, and George, returning to report to the *Conway*'s master, found him in what seemed to be angry conversation with the mate.

"They were ready to surrender, Captain," he heard Henry Fry say accusingly. "I swear, sir, they never had any intention of trying to take the ship, and they were treating us well. The man Fitzroy is a gentleman, and he—"

Captain Barlow cut in angrily, "Treating you well, were they? By God, I don't fancy that poor devil Barney Shea would agree with you, if he could talk now! They murdered him in cold blood, did they not? 'Twas his corpse the soldiers carried out, mister— shot through the back o' the head."

"That was the act of one young hothead, sir," Fry protested. "It wasn't intended. But when they heard you threaten them, there was a panic and they lost their heads. Barney Shea had antagonized them . . . the poor fellow wasn't sober, and he kept saying he'd see they were all sent to some place he called Coal River when they landed, sir. And he swore that none of them would leave it alive."

Barlow grunted. "If you say so, mister. But they're scum, the whole boilin' lot of them, and the man that murdered him shall hang." He turned to George and inquired with heavy sarcasm, "Well, now, Mr. De Lancey, what has the rebel gentleman Mr. Fitzroy to say for himself, eh? You made my conditions known to him . . . is he going to hand over the murderer to justice?"

Controlling an impulse to smash his fist into the master's round, red face, George answered him coldly. "He has asked for time to talk the matter over with the others. But as a lawyer, Captain Barlow, I question your right to bring the man to summary justice—and I question it strongly. He should be taken to Sydney and tried before a properly constituted court. You—"

"I have the right to deal with mutiny on the high seas," Barlow retorted angrily. "And no damned lawyer will talk me out of it. A pox on it, I've wasted enough time down here! I've my ship to put to rights tomorrow, and I'm dog tired. Tell them to hurry."

But there was no one at the spy-hole. They waited, Barlow yawning and tapping his fingers impatiently on one of his provision casks, and Henry Fry talking in a low voice to one of the sentries, watched balefully by Sergeant Holmes, who had attempted several times, without success, to engage the captain's attention.

Fry left, with evident reluctance, to stand his watch—Barlow shouting a spate of orders after him—but pausing at George's side, he said in a hoarse whisper, "He *has* the right to hang mutineers, Mr. De Lancey, and to shoot them in self-defense. But these are not evil men, believe me. Do what you can for them."

He was gone, without waiting for a reply. A few minutes later, Dean returned, he and his men laden with such medical supplies as they had been able to find in Shea's ill-stocked hospital. George was examining them when Fitzroy called through the spy-hole.

"Are those the supplies I asked for?"

"Yes," George told him. "And Dr. Shea's instruments." He was starting to enumerate them when Barlow intervened.

"Hell's teeth!" he thundered. "That's all they're getting. What about them keeping to their side o' the bargain—I want Shea's killer, and I want him handed over before they get any blasted medical supplies!"

"The bargain will be kept," Fitzroy asserted. "But not now, if you please—the man in question is needed." He hesitated, and then went on slowly, "I give you my solemn word that he will yield himself up as soon as the injured have been cared for, Mr. De Lancey. That may take a little longer than your captain has specified, but I'll not go back on my word. Will you accept it?"

Captain Barlow, craning forward to listen, started to shake his head, but George said angrily, "I will take his word, Captain. Damme, I—"

"*You* will? The word o' another gentleman, eh—even when this one's a scurvy Irish rebel! That's not good enough, mister, by God it's not!"

"What have you to lose, for pity's sake?" George argued hotly. "A few hours, perhaps. If Fitzroy fails to keep his word, then you can send Mr. Dean's soldiers in and bring the man out by force, can you not?"

"True," Barlow conceded. "But I want no more shooting. I have to deliver some o' these swine alive to Botany Bay, or the government won't pay me for 'em." He paused, frowning, and then a slow smile spread across his face. "Put your gentleman to the test, if you wish, Mr. De Lancey. Take 'em their medical comforts and stay in there till they're ready to keep their promise. Let 'em surrender the murderer to you—that's fair enough, is it not?"

It was evident, from the malicious gleam in his eyes, that the *Conway*'s master expected him to reject the outrageous suggestion, and George hesitated, taken momentarily by surprise.

"You will be in no danger from us, Mr. De Lancey. And I'd be eternally grateful for your aid, believe me." From the other side of the padlocked door Fitzroy's voice was pleading, and George responded to it, the anger that had filled him a few moments before slowly draining away.

Ignoring Barlow, he turned to Dean and said crisply, "Open the door, Mr. Dean. Send four men in with me to deliver the medical stores and remove the dead. And then—"

"Then, sir?" the ensign questioned. He licked at dry lips. "I'll stay, if you need me. I—"

"You'll get out an' lock the door, mister!" the captain growled. "In command o' the guard, ain't you? Then your place is commanding the sodding guard, not playing the hero. Leave that to Mr. De Lancey—he volunteered for it."

"I'll post a strong guard, sir," Dean promised, lowering his voice to a whisper. "And I'll be at the door. You'll only have to call me."

"Thank you, Mr. Dean," George acknowledged.

But it was unlikely that he would have to call on Dean's guard for help, he realized, when he stepped into the prisoners' quarters, carrying Surgeon Shea's bag of instruments. The men inside— gaunt, ragged, half-human in their degradation—were cowed and beaten, with no fight left in them.

With lackluster eyes they watched their dead being carried out, and they moved out of the soldiers' way and raised no protest when Sergeant Holmes uncovered a few roughly fashioned clubs, tucked away in one of the bunks without any real attempt at concealment. He confiscated them triumphantly, inviting any opposition, but they gave him none, simply shrugged sullenly and turned away.

"You see, De Lancey?" Patrick Fitzroy said, with bitterness. "We are not mutineers."

He was revealed as a tall, dark-haired man with a thick growth of beard, and he was as thin and scantily clad as the rest. In the flickering, uncertain light of the only lantern the orlop still boasted, he looked, to George's shocked and pitying eyes, as if he were ready to collapse from exhaustion . . . but he swiftly dispelled any such notion.

There were badly injured men to be treated, he pointed out—men with severe head wounds caused by the soldiers' flailing muskets, several with broken limbs, and half a dozen more with musket balls lodged in their bodies. In addition to these, as the onetime surgeon also pointed out, there were the chronically sick, many of them displaying the unmistakable ravages of scurvy.

"And Seamus Burke will have to lose his right arm," Fitzroy ended bleakly. "God help me, I hope I'm not too long out of the way of my profession to take it off for him."

He worked tirelessly throughout what remained of the night and into the next morning, grasping Shea's rusty, blunted instruments in his fetter-scarred hands, stitching up wounds, probing for bullets, and arresting bleeding as best he could, cursing his lack of practice and sometimes praying aloud. While the rest sank into apathy, a dozen or so of the men endeavored to help him. Among them were his brother, Father Joseph, obstinately making light of his own pain, and a fair-haired boy with a white, moon face and blankly staring eyes, whom he addressed as Christie and who hovered at his elbow, holding the lantern for him as he worked.

George, in his shirtsleeves, applied dressings and doled out laudanum. He was soon as filthy as the convicts about him and unhappily conscious of the vermin crawling over his skin and of the foul stench of the bilge water lapping about his feet. Many times, a violent nausea threatened to overcome him, but he fought it down, ashamed of his weakness in the face of suffering that was so much greater than his own.

The worst moment came when big Seamus Burke's shattered arm had to be amputated. Dean had included a small keg of rum in the medical supplies, and Burke was given a liberal dose of it and a plug of leather to bite on. But his agonized screams could not be stilled, and the sleepers, rudely awakened, joined their frightened cries to his until, mercifully, he lapsed into unconsciousness and Patrick Fitzroy, sweating freely, managed to complete his bloody task.

The captain did not appear again, but from time to time Ensign

Dean hailed George through the spy-hole, to reinforce his promise of continued vigilance. The pumps started up again, clearing most of the foul-smelling water the storm had left behind and improving conditions a good deal. Later, Henry Fry came down, to hand in some spirits from his own store and to warn that it wanted barely half an hour to noon . . . when the captain, at present sleeping, had ordered his steward to rouse him.

"He'll not allow you much more time," he told George, who answered his summons to the spy-hole. "Our repairs are progressing apace, and the gale's blown itself out. We shall be putting to sea again before dark, with a jury rig on the foremast. The old man intends to call at Hobart Town, he informed me, in the hope of obtaining a mast and to take on water and fresh supplies. Maybe he'll put the poor devils of injured ashore there and in hospital."

"What are the chances that he will?" George asked wearily.

The mate shrugged. "I can't tell you, Mr. De Lancey. But I do know that he intends to have his hanging before we sail—he ordered me to rig the main yardarm in readiness. The rope's waiting for poor Christie O'Dowd . . . Fitzroy will have to give him up or take the consequences."

"Christie O'Dowd?" George echoed, shocked out of his weariness. "The boy with fair hair?" He glanced over to where the boy was standing, still holding the lantern, and recalled his blank, uncomprehending stare and the curiously patient gentleness with which Fitzroy treated him. "But damme, Mr. Fry, he's half-witted! He's—"

"Half-witted or not, he shot Barney Shea. I was there; I saw him." Fry avoided George's gaze. "Better pass the word to Fitzroy, Mr. De Lancey. The captain will be along very soon, and that bloody man Holmes is issuing arms to his redcoats."

George did as the mate asked. Patrick Fitzroy, deep in conversation with his brother, Father Joseph, nodded with seeming indifference and said quietly, "Very well. I shall keep my word, have no fear of that. And thank you for the help you have given us, De Lancey. May I beg you to do one thing more?"

"Of course. Whatever I can do, I'll do gladly. For this isn't justice, and as a lawyer, it appalls me. I—" George swore.

Fitzroy's hand, still bloodstained, reached out to grasp his. "It is as a lawyer that I am asking for your aid. When this hell ship reaches Sydney, will you bring charges against her master? Will you make out a case in defense of these poor souls he has so cruelly abused?"

"I will indeed. By God, I will!"

"I thank you again, sir," Fitzroy acknowledged gravely. "Now, if you will forgive us—there is little time left, and I must speak with my brother. Alone, sir, if you please."

George left them and, sick with pity, went to endeavor to talk to the moonfaced O'Dowd. But the boy shrank from him, seemingly unable to understand, and from a bunk nearby, one of the injured men called out, "The lad's an ejet, sorr. You're wastin' your breath. Mr. Fitzroy's de only one he listens to."

And Fitzroy, George saw, was still talking with great earnestness to his brother. He saw the young priest make the sign of the cross and Fitzroy drop suddenly to his knees, the bloodstained, surgeon's hands clasped in front of him as if in prayer.

Even then, the significance of what he was seeing eluded him, and it was not until the door of the prison quarters opened once more, to reveal the captain, with Dean's soldiers ranged at his back, that, very slowly, understanding dawned. But by then it was too late. . . .

He heard Barlow's shouted demand for the killer of the ship's surgeon to be handed over and saw, with dismay, the bearded figure of Patrick Fitzroy step forward in answer to it.

"I'm ready to give myself up, sir," the gaunt Irishman said. "For all I deny your right to try me for any crime."

Galvanized into action, George flung himself through the press of men to reach Fitzroy's side. "No!" he exclaimed. "For God's sake, no! O'Dowd will be no loss, but *you*—don't do it, man!"

Fitzroy smiled, an oddly resigned yet almost pleased smile, and said softly, lapsing into an exaggerated brogue, "Ah, now, the boy's an ejet, so he is. He'd no notion, don't you see, and I can't let him die for that, can I? And sure, 'twas Shea's own pistol he used, so the man only got his just deserts. A surgeon should not come armed to treat sick men, should he, now?"

He freed himself from George's outstretched hand and murmured something to his brother. What he said was inaudible, but as he moved to meet the soldiers, Father Joseph brought the heel of his hand down in a skillful, crushing blow to the back of George's neck. He fell, as if poleaxed, and heard, as his senses left him, the priest call out anxiously, "Over here, two of you—Mr. De Lancey has fainted! 'Tis the foul air has overcome him, poor gentleman."

George was in his own cabin when he recovered consciousness, with Henry Fry and the steward, Lewis, bending over him. They had stripped him of his befouled garments, and Fry, with unexpected gentleness, was engaged in washing his naked body.

Seeing his eyes open, the mate raised a cautionary finger to his lips. "Stay where you are for a while, Mr. De Lancey. You'll not like what's being done on deck any more than I do, I dare swear. Maybe it would be as well if you were to drink this."

A beaker was held to his lips, but George pushed it away. "The priest hit me, for God's sake!" he protested indignantly. "He laid me out!"

Fry dismissed the steward. "Aye, for your own good, Mr. De Lancey. They knew what they were doing, the pair of them, and you couldn't have stopped them."

"I could have tried. Fitzroy might have listened to me." Finding some difficulty in holding his head up, George lay back, rubbing his neck. "The devil take it, I'm as weak as a kitten!"

Henry Fry eyed him with concern. "I doubt if he would have listened—his mind was made up. The Irish know the value of martyrdom. They build their legends on it . . . and their history. They always have, and that's the reason we'll never get the better of them. I know what they're like, Mr. De Lancey—my father was in the army, and I spent most of my boyhood in Irish garrisons." He again offered the beaker and urged quietly, "Come on, sir—drink this. It will put you to sleep for an hour or two, and from the looks of you, sleep's what you need. You did all you could. Fitzroy acted of his own free will."

"Is he dead, Mr. Fry?" George asked bitterly.

"By this time I fancy he is. The old man's not one for delay."

The rim of the beaker pressed against his lips, and conscious of a feeling of intense sadness, George gulped down the draught.

It was dusk when he awakened, and the motion of the ship told him that she was under way. He dressed and went on deck, to see—as he had dreaded—the body of Patrick Fitzroy, onetime surgeon, suspended from the main yardarm.

Two other bodies hung on either side of it, forming a curiously symbolic trio against the darkening sky, and George said bitterly, as Henry Fry, now on watch, came across to join him, "Three martyrs, instead of one, Mr. Fry? How did that happen, for pity's sake?"

The mate lowered his head in a gesture of resignation. "Two of them tried to do what you were going to do, Mr. De Lancey—they tried to intervene. Sergeant Holmes shot one, and the captain hanged the other for mutiny." He sighed. "A new legend to take with us to Botany Bay, I fear, but . . . what the devil can we do?"

He strode off to resume his duties, and George echoed his sigh. But there *was* something he could do, he told himself grimly. He could invoke the law and bring the *Conway*'s master to trial. . . .

CHAPTER XVI

Katie O'Malley reined in her horse at the top of the wooded slope and, glancing back at Rachel Broome, who was riding just behind her, called out persuasively, "Shall we stop here for a while and let the horses rest?"

"They're not tired," Rachel answered, evidently taken by surprise at the suggestion. "And William says the view is better from the summit."

"All right," Katie said, conceding defeat. Her stiff New England pride would not allow her to admit that she was saddlesore, aching with weariness, and at once awed and apprehensive, taken aback by the sheer vastness of this place in which Rick was expecting her to make her home.

Its isolation was daunting to one accustomed to the bustle of city streets. And the journey from Emu Crossing, on the Nepean River, to what her companions were pleased to call the township of Bathurst, had been . . . Katie's fingers tightened convulsively on her horse's rein. It had been frankly alarming, and, she reflected wretchedly, not since her father's ship had foundered had she been in greater fear for her life.

Although it had begun easily enough—even pleasantly, with a gentle ascent through a forest of lofty ironbark trees, which they had told her had been named Springwood by the Governor. Once clear of the trees, however, the climb had become steeper, and the road, rough and stony, had wound on and on, traversing hills, with only a timber rail between the riders on their scrambling horses and a sheer drop of hundreds of feet into the riverbed below.

Chasms had to be crossed by means of seemingly flimsy wooden bridges, and some of the descents were so precipitous that their supply cart could only negotiate them by their using drag ropes to slow its momentum. Rick, William, Rachel, and even little Dickon—whom Rick had insisted on taking with them—appeared impervious to danger, Katie recalled, conscious of unreasoned resentment. They were all accustomed to riding on horseback, of course, which she was not, and she had not dared to express the apprehension she felt, lest they should deem her guilty of faintheartedness—or even cowardice.

The journey had taken six days. They had halted each evening, an hour before sundown, and slept in huts left behind by the road builders, when these were available, but otherwise in the tents they had brought with them, cooking their meals on the glowing embers of bivouac fires.

The evenings and the nights, although chill and sometimes wet, had come as a welcome respite so far as Katie was concerned. Then Rick had fussed over her, making sure that she was dry and warm, whispering eager words of love to her, out of earshot of their companions, and assuring her, again and again, that she would need only to see Pengallon to agree that its situation was one of the most beautiful in the entire colony.

"When our house is built," he had said, "and we've brought the stock up, we can be wed, my dearest, and I'll bring you back as my wife."

Well, Katie thought, as Rachel cantered easily past her to lead the way, she had seen Pengallon; they had ridden out from Bathurst's cluster of primitive huts the previous day, bringing with them the two convict laborers Rick had engaged to work on the building of their future home. Certainly there was no denying that it was beautiful, with its acres of rich, undulating grassland, the sparkling river running through it, and lofty mountains in the distance, range upon range of them, each as blue as the sky above their awesome rocky peaks.

But it was lonely; apart from their small party and a few aborigines, it was deserted, a wilderness, devoid of any sign of civilized human habitation. And until the Governor decided the time had come to open the area for settlement, so it would remain. . . . Katie shivered.

Wildlife abounded, as Rick had pointed out—kangaroos, opossums, emus, ducks, in such numbers that they would never go hungry, and also wild dogs, called dingoes, that were predatory and had been known to carry off livestock in other parts of the colony. The natives used them, semitamed, for hunting. . . .

"Here we are, Katie!" Rachel's voice broke into her thoughts, and Katie forced a smile. She kneed her horse forward to cover the last few yards and then, thankfully, slid from her saddle to join the younger girl, who had already dismounted. "Look! Is it not worth the ride to obtain so fine a view?"

Perhaps it was, Katie was ready to admit, shading her eyes and gazing in the direction her companion was indicating . . . but only if one were able to find beauty in limitless desolation. She liked Rachel; the girl, not yet sixteen, was extremely pretty, intelligent, and well mannered, and from the beginning of their acquaintance had gone out of her way to be friendly and helpful—unlike Abigail's stepdaughter Julia, who had been quite the reverse, continually seeking to provoke her with barbed references to the recent war and her American nationality, in the face of which it was difficult not to take offense.

"See," Rachel invited. "There is Pengallon, Katie . . . oh, I do envy you! It will be lovely when your house is built and the stock pens and storehouses are completed. I hope that William will let me come with him when he drives your first flock up here . . . I can just imagine what it will look like, when there are sheep grazing everywhere and Rick harvests the first crop."

"Can we tie the horses up and sit here for a little?" Katie asked. "The horses may not be tired," she added ruefully, "but I am. And stiff . . . I'm not accustomed to horseback riding."

Rachel flashed her a warmly sympathetic smile. "Why, of course we can," she assented readily. "I'm sorry, I hadn't realized that you were tired or that you weren't used to riding. You should have told me." She relieved Katie of her horse's rein and led both animals away, to tether them to a nearby tree. Returning, she squatted cross-legged on the rock-strewn ground and, taking two apples from her skirt pocket, offered one to Katie.

"From the orchard my mother planted at Ulva. I brought them for the horses, but—there's plenty of grass for them, and our need is greater. They're tart but quite refreshing . . . try one."

"Thank you." Katie bit into the apple and stared down at her future home with doubting eyes. At present, the only building it boasted was a small bark hut, fashioned for his own use by the native boy Winyara, whom Justin Broome had employed to guard the holding. She tried to visualize what it would look like when the building work was done, remembering Rachel's description and her expression of envy, but found that the effort of imagination this required was quite beyond her.

Rick and William, accompanied by Dickon and the two laborers, had left their camp at first light, intending to make a start by cutting timber with which to supplement the meager supply of building material they had obtained in Bathurst. Pens and fences would go up first, Rick had told her, to enable the stock to be housed; he would engage a shepherd and purchase a ram and two hundred breeding ewes from Ulva. After that would come the house. . . . Recalling the pleasant dwelling house at Ulva, where she had spent a night before crossing the Nepean, Katie looked up to meet Rachel's gaze and asked uncertainly, "What will it look like—the house, I mean?"

"Well . . . ." Rachel hesitated, as if fearing to disappoint her. "It will be small—just two rooms, probably, and a cooking place. Built of logs, with a stone foundation and a stringy-bark roof. They will have to use whatever material is to be found here, because the road is too hazardous to bring up bricks from Sydney, even by oxcart . . . you've seen what it's like. But Bathurst will grow, Katie. The Governor has said he wants it to become a major settlement once he opens these lands and allocates more grants, and then, I am sure, craftsmen will be sent up—smiths and carpenters and stonemasons—and they will start making bricks. They will improve the road or even find a better route, through the Cow Pastures, perhaps. . . ." She talked on, brightly and eagerly, but Katie's heart sank as she listened.

The weeks she had spent with the Dawsons at Upwey had not prepared her for this. Why, she wondered miserably, had Rick set his heart on coming to this wilderness, when there were farms being offered for sale in Parramatta, Windsor, and Richmond— some even a few miles from Sydney?

Properties with farmhouses, like the one at Long Wrekin, with pleasantly furnished rooms, brick-built and solid; houses that had verandas and glazed windows and neighbors—above all, neighbors, close at hand.

Rick was so enthusiastic; he talked so hopefully of the future— *their* future here—expecting her to share his enthusiasm. And the Broomes, particularly William, were as keen and optimistic as he was. . . . Katie felt tears come into her eyes and quickly turned her head away, pretending to look in the direction Rachel was indicating. Even Rick's adored little nephew, Dickon, despite his handicap, was better adjusted to these conditions than she was, she told herself regretfully.

Sensing her discomfiture, Rachel asked diffidently, "Have you always lived in a town? Does all this seem very strange to you?"

Katie blinked away her tears. "Yes," she confessed. "I lived in Boston. I'd never been anywhere else until I sailed with my father in the *Providence* . . . I'd never wanted to leave Boston, but he was alone and he said he needed me. Boston is a wonderful city, Rachel, you've no idea."

"Tell me about it," Rachel invited, settling herself more comfortably, her back propped up against a moss-covered rock.

Nothing loath, Katie did as she had been asked, nostalgia lending her eloquence, and as she described the sights and sounds, the busy streets, the graceful buildings, and above all, the great seaport around which the town had grown to its present size and importance, she closed her eyes and let the memories come flooding in, blotting out the scene about her.

"They say that our squares and public buildings resemble those of London. The houses are built of mellow red brick, with balconies and tall mullioned windows and stone steps leading up to each front door. Our house was like that, only smaller, of course . . . but it was three stories high, and we had a wonderful view from the top floor. My bedroom was on the top floor, and I had a beautiful four-poster bed, which came from England. If I sat up very straight, I could see the roof of the customs house and the masts of the ships that were tied up to the wharves."

"Is Boston an old city?" Rachel asked curiously. "And how was it settled? By the Pilgrim Fathers?"

Katie shook her head. "No, by a man named John Winthrop, who was a Puritan separatist. He obtained a royal charter for the Company of Massachusetts Bay in New England, and sailed in March, sixteen hundred and thirty, with one thousand people of the Puritan faith. They were good, hardworking folk, and they established their prosperity by trading in furs and fishing. The success of the fishing industry led to the building of ships, and now, if people talk of a Boston man," she added, with conscious pride, "they mean a seafarer. All the men in my father's family were seafarers."

"My father's were, too," Rachel asserted. "And Rick's. It's odd that they should have become enemies, isn't it?"

"We had to fight for our independence," Katie defended.

Rachel eyed her thoughtfully. "We were taught in school that the War of Independence started in Boston . . . wasn't what was called the Boston Tea Party the—the incident that began it all?"

"There was what *we* call the Boston Massacre long before that, in seventeen seventy, when British soldiers fired on an unarmed civilian gathering and killed five of them. And then"—Katie sat up, waxing indignant—"the British ordered the closure of Boston Harbor, after Samuel Adams led a party of fifty men, dressed up as Indians, to the customs wharf . . . and they threw three hundred cases of tea into the water. All they were doing was staging a protest against the duty Lord North had imposed on the tea. But the port was closed—and you can imagine what effect that had— and an English general named Gage was appointed Governor of Massachusetts, and he was sent, with four regiments of redcoats, to subdue Boston. To add insult to injury, he quartered his troops in private houses, commandeered the public parks for his tents and his artillery, and patrolled the streets with armed men. The people of Boston were incensed by such tyranny—can you wonder that they rebelled?"

"No," Rachel responded doubtfully. "I suppose not, Katie. But the Irish always claim that they were driven to rebel against British tyranny, and when they are sentenced for treason and transported out here, they continue to rebel. Very few of them become good settlers, because they don't *want* to, even when they are given the chance. They would sooner try to escape or make trouble, whatever concessions the Governor makes to them."

As she might be tempted to, Katie thought—to escape, if not to make trouble. But could she ever hope to see her home again, to go back there, take up life again, as she remembered it . . . the happy, carefree life of her childhood and her youth?

It had seemed so secure, even when the war with England broke out again. She had never imagined living anywhere else, save when the time came for her to marry and she would move from her father's house to that of her husband. And . . . She bit back a sigh. She had always supposed that she would marry George De

Lancey, to whom Boston, too, was home, and the law—not the army or the navy—his chosen profession. But George had been drawn into the war, and on the British side. . . .

"Shall we move on?" Rachel said, breaking into her thoughts. "If you are rested. The men will be back at sunset, and they will be ready for a meal after hacking down trees all day. I hope they will bring some game with them; otherwise we shall have to depend on Winyara's fish."

Katie climbed stiffly back into her saddle, conscious once more of her own unsuitability for the sort of pioneering life Rachel and the others seemed to adjust to without difficulty. It was Rachel, for all her youth, who did the cooking; her sturdy, somewhat taciturn brother William who provided the wood and most of the game; and even Rick could make the unleavened cakes they called damper, and could fish with skill and considerable success, when Winyara was absent.

"I'm more of a liability than a help to you, where cooking is concerned," she said apologetically.

"It's all strange to you," Rachel assured her kindly. "I'm used to it; and you'll learn, Katie. Camp cooking is easy because it is simple. I never could produce elaborate dishes like the ones they serve now at Sydney dinner parties, but Abigail says that *you* can. And she told me you were an expert at making preserves." She smiled, kneeing her horse into a canter when they reached a patch of level ground. "We must exchange skills."

They lapsed into silence until faced by the next downhill slope, and when Rachel prudently reined in, Katie was able to catch up with her.

"I wish I could ride like you," she said enviously. "That's another skill I shall have to acquire before I can become a settler out here."

"I've ridden all my life," Rachel reminded her. "But my mother was the real horsewoman in our family. She was one of the first to breed horses in the colony—she bred and broke them to the saddle herself, and there was no young animal she could not handle, however wild. The horse I'm riding was hers . . . she called him Young Sirius, after his sire." Once again she talked on, and hearing the pride and affection in her voice as she spoke of her mother, Katie warmed to her anew.

They were in sight of the river when Rachel said suddenly, "It frightens you, doesn't it, the prospect of coming out here when you marry Rick?"

Katie hesitated, reddening. But there was nothing to be gained by pretending, and she answered honestly, "Yes, it does, Rachel. It scares me to death. The loneliness, the isolation, the thought of being cut off . . ." She tried to put her fear into words, but failed miserably. "I cannot explain it, and . . . I'd no idea that I would feel as I do. I didn't know what to expect, I suppose. And Rick is so keen, he can't wait to make a start here, and . . . I owe him so much. I . . . He saved my life, you know."

"Yes," Rachel said. "I know—Abigail told me." There was an odd note in her voice, and for no reason that Katie could understand, she seemed almost to withdraw from the intimacy they had established during their ride together. "I'll help you in any way I can, Katie. You might care to spend a little while at Ulva before your wedding. I could help you with your riding, perhaps, and teach you how to make damper and cook game."

The offer was spontaneously and generously made, yet Katie was left with the impression that Rachel had forced herself to make it, from a sense of duty, perhaps, or because hospitality to a stranger required it of her, for she added quickly, "But I expect you would prefer to stay in Sydney for as long as you can."

"No," Katie began. "No, I'll do whatever Rick wants. I—"

Rachel cut her short. She burst out with unexpected vehemence, "You shouldn't marry Rick if you don't love him—if you're only grateful to him for saving your life! And if you're afraid of the loneliness and isolation . . . don't let him bring you here, Katie. Don't!"

Bereft of words, Katie could only stare at her in shocked silence. They reached the riverbank, and Rachel said, in her normal, quiet voice, "They'll be back soon. Why don't you walk along beside the river to meet them? I'll take your horse. You and Rick haven't had much time alone together, have you? William and the convicts can bring the timber in, and I'll attend to the cooking."

She trotted off with their two horses, leaving Katie at the river's edge, dismounted and more than a little bewildered. The sound of men's voices in the distance told her that Rachel had been right— the men were returning, although the thickly growing timber, in which they had been working, hid them from her sight.

But was Rachel also right about her feelings—her true feelings for Rick Tempest, she wondered? Was it gratitude, rather than love, that had prompted her to accept his proposal? She clambered down to the river and, finding a sheltered spot, slipped down to her knees and crouched there, letting the cool water trickle over her blistered hands as she wrestled with the doubts that Rachel's words had engendered.

Rick was handsome; he was a gentleman, kind and considerate, with a fine record as a King's officer and excellent prospects in the colony . . . a catch for any woman, as a husband. Katie drew in her breath sharply. Certainly he was a catch for an orphaned American girl, friendless and alone, set ashore in a British penal colony, many of whose inhabitants—like Colonel Molle—regarded her as an enemy and went out of their way to show her that she was unwelcome.

Had this fact, allied to her gratitude, influenced her, Kate asked herself . . . had expediency, rather than love, been the real reason for the promise she had given Rick, the promise to wed him? He had proposed to her before she had set foot in Sydney, it was true, but . . . Honest with herself always, Katie did not seek excuses. Mrs. Jeffrey's attitude, during the *Kangaroo*'s passage from the Cape, had given her an insight into what was to come when she disembarked in the colony. It had shown her the value of Rick's protection and her need for protection, but that, surely, had not dictated her decision.

The awareness that George De Lancey had gone out of her life had been, as much as anything, the reason why she had agreed to marry Rick. She remembered the anxious, inarticulate prayer she had voiced, in the privacy of her cabin, and . . . Katie caught her breath on a sob, as she remembered also what Rick had told her of his future plans. He had talked then of his intentions to apply for a grant in the new lands beyond Bathurst, and . . . what had he said? That it would be a challenge . . . a challenge he would accept only if she came with him. She had felt proud to think that he needed her; she had prayed that God would make her worthy of him . . . and yet, here she was, faced by the reality of that challenge and ready to fly from it in cowardly dismay at its magnitude.

And Rachel, who was a child, barely grown to womanhood, had sensed her dismay, recognized her cowardice, and had implored her not to let Rick bring her here, after their wedding, unless she really loved him.

Tears welled into her eyes. The sun was setting in a blaze of glory behind the distant hills, its red glow reflected in the river water murmuring at her feet. Katie leaned forward, newly resolute, and scooped up water with her hands, dashing it over her face and her tear-filled eyes. It was quite shallow where she was kneeling, and, with the droplets of water, she scooped up a handful of small pebbles. She was about to throw them back when she saw that they possessed a glitter that might—or might not—be the reflection of the sinking sun.

Her curiosity aroused, she wiped them dry on her skirt and examined them again, holding them carefully on the palm of one hand and, with the other, shading them from the direct sunlight. The pebbles glistened back at her, dulled now, yet still seeming to possess a strange, glowing life of their own. She was so intent on studying them that she did not hear Rick's approach and, until he came slithering down the stony bank to join her, had not realized that the timber cutters had returned.

"We've done a good day's work," he told her with satisfaction, planting a kiss on her cheek. "The men are stacking the timber now, ready to be sawn. But Rachel said you were here, and . . . What's that in your hand, Katie my love? Treasure trove? Not a fish, surely?"

"No, not a fish." Katie laughed at the absurdity of his suggestion, her flagging spirits restored when he held her to him, making her once more aware of his strong male attraction. "But it may be . . . what did you call it? Treasure trove. Rick, I—I think it's gold. Look!"

Rick obediently looked down at the glowing pebbles in her hand, his eyes widening in surprise. "Where did you find these? In the river?"

"Yes." Bending forward, she scooped up a second handful, but these, to her disappointment, were just brown pebbles, worn smooth by the flowing water. A third attempt proved equally disappointing, but the fourth brought to light a pebble the size of a small apple, crystalline and white, with strands of what looked to her like gold running through it.

"Is it gold, Rick?" she asked eagerly, dropping it into his hand.

"If it is, all our troubles are over, my sweet love," Rick

answered, smiling. "But I think it's what is called fool's gold—pyrites. Anyway"—he took the pebbles from Katie's hand and put them into his breeches pocket—"I'll have them examined when we go back to Sydney, but don't pin your hopes on the result. Nothing ever comes easily in this life. All the same, I shouldn't say anything in the convicts' hearing, just in case I'm wrong and you're right." He rose, holding out his arms to her. "Katie my darling, will you be able to face the challenge of this place with me? Because, quite honestly, I'd not be able to face it without you, now that I've seen it. Tell me, my love . . . it's up to you."

Katie hesitated for only a moment and then went into his arms, her doubts fading. She *would* face the challenge, she told herself; for Rick's sake, she would overcome her fears. What she felt for him was more than gratitude, and the little glittering pebbles were surely a happy augury, even if they did turn out to be fool's gold.

She lifted her face for his kiss.

"If we're together, Rick dear," she told him softly, "I can face anything. And I'll learn how to cope—I promise you, I'll learn!"

Rick held her close. "Bless you, Katie," he said. "In the light of that . . . let's be wed when we return to Sydney. It may take two or three months to get this place shipshape and the stock brought up here, and . . . I don't think I can wait two or three months to wed you."

"If you wish," Katie assented. "But I want to spend a few weeks at Ulva first. Rachel has offered to teach me how to be a settler's wife. There's a great deal I don't know, Rick."

"I'll teach you," Rick retorted firmly. "When you're my wife."

CHAPTER XVII

Justin was on watch when, off the coast of Van Diemen's Land, His Majesty's sloop of war *Emu* sighted the laboring Indiaman. He hailed her, and on receiving the reply that she was the convict transport *Conway*, on passage to Port Jackson, he sent a midshipman to summon Commander Forster.

"I'm not sure whether she's the vessel your sealer skipper reported, sir," he said when Forster came on deck. "If so, she must have spent quite a time in port at Hobart. But I thought you would wish to be informed."

"Yes, indeed, Mr. Broome. The sealer's master reported seeing corpses hanging from her yardarm, I recall." James Forster raised his telescope to his eye and studied the other ship with some care. "Jury rig on her foremast, patched canvas, and the paint peeling off her . . . that suggests storm damage, does it not? Did she make mention of a mutiny?"

"No, sir," Justin assured him. "No mention at all. And she seems in a mighty hurry to distance herself from us. Do you want me to come about and close her?"

Forster shook his head. "If she's spent any time in Hobart, we'll hear all there is to hear about her when we make port. You have a friend there, didn't you tell me? A newspaper man?"

"Yes, sir—Damien Hayes, by name. He came out as a correspondent of the London *Chronicle*, but I believe he started a weekly news sheet in Hobart a year or so ago. He's an enterprising fellow. In fact"—Justin smiled—"he courted my wife before I had the good sense to do so."

And the Governor's wife, he recalled, had even encouraged the young journalist's courtship when he had accompanied the viceregal party to Van Diemen's Land for the Macquaries' first tour of inspection.

Commander Forster lowered his glass and, clicking it shut, restored it to the breast pocket of his gold-laced coat. "No doubt," he said, "if Mr. Hayes is a good journalist, he will have obtained whatever story the master of the *Conway* had to tell. Perhaps you should seek him out, Justin—or, better still, invite him to dine with us on board. Mutiny on the high seas is a damnably serious matter . . . and so is hanging men who take part in it."

Puzzled by his commander's interest in the matter, Justin turned to look at him.

"I will, sir, of course," he agreed. "But surely the *Conway's* master will have made a full report to the Lieutenant Governor?"

Forster snorted. "Good God, Justin, have you forgotten who is Lieutenant Governor?"

"Major Davey, sir?"

"The infernal fellow is never sober. You tell him something and it goes in one ear and straight out of the other." Forster, himself the soul of efficiency, started to discourse indignantly on the subject of Hobart's present ruler and then broke off, forcing a smile. "Perhaps I'm prejudiced, but we shall see. The people of Hobart call him Mad Tom—and that's when they are being charitable. Frankly, Justin, I don't envy your stepfather his new posting."

"What don't you envy me, Commander?" Andrew Hawley, tall and white-haired but still an impressive figure in his well-fitting marine uniform, strode across the *Emu's* narrow quarterdeck to join them. He was, Justin thought with admiration, ageless, despite the white hair and the maze of tiny lines etched into the tanned skin of his face. He had been in the colony for almost ten years now, serving as one of Admiral Bligh's aides and then, under the present Governor, commanding a company of the veteran corps, acting as port naval officer, and, when Governor Macquarie needed him, again acting as aide.

And, prior to this, he had served in two of Admiral Nelson's greatest battles, at Copenhagen and Trafalgar, and had seen action under Pellew, Duncan, and Hood, before being commissioned, on Admiral Hood's recommendation, for gallantry. What terrors could command of the garrison of Hobart Town possibly hold for a man like Andrew?

Justin grinned and took off his hat in salute. "My revered

captain does not envy your having to play second fiddle to Mad Tom Davey," he elaborated, since Forster seemed disinclined to explain his remark.

"Did I come upon you at an inappropriate moment?" Andrew suggested. "Because if I did—"

"You did not, sir," James Forster assured him. "Although no doubt I should keep a rein on my tongue! However, since I've been speaking freely to your stepson, I'll be equally frank with you and admit that, in my considered opinion, this fellow Davey is a most unfortunate choice for the position he holds. I am astonished that Governor Macquarie ever countenanced his appointment as Lieutenant Governor of Van Diemen's Land."

Andrew shrugged his broad, scarlet-clad shoulders. "He neither countenanced nor wanted it, Commander. The appointment was made by the Colonial Office, against His Excellency's recommendation . . . and he has made repeated requests for it to be terminated." He hesitated, and then went on, "This is in confidence, you understand . . . I'm being sent here to relieve Major Geils, who has had charges of corruption brought against him. He's to be recalled to Sydney. As his successor in command of the garrison, I have been instructed to endeavor to curb Davey's excesses until he, too, is relieved. It's probable that he will be— the Colonial Office is said to be sending out a Colonel Sorrell, but as yet the appointment has not been confirmed."

"I still do not envy you, my friend," James Forster observed, shaking his head. "Davey is an infernally awkward fellow to deal with, apart from his drunkenness. He trades on having been one of Governor Phillip's officers in the First Fleet. And his solution to practically everything, from the bushrangers to the aborigines, is armed raids by the military, intended to end their depredations by wiping them out! And"—he laughed, without amusement—"I'll wager that the first thing he asks me, when I report my arrival, is that I should land a party of armed seamen to assist his garrison to launch an effective raid on one or the other of them—you see if he doesn't."

At first light the following morning, the *Emu* entered the Derwent River and brought to off Hobart Town some two hours later, aided by a brisk following breeze.

The town had grown considerably over the years since its foundation, in 1804, by Colonel Collins's disillusioned settlers from Port Phillip, on the mainland. Yet, Justin reflected, as he moved about the *Emu*'s deck supervising her mooring, for all the breathtaking natural beauty of its surroundings and its splendid harbor, Hobart still wore an oddly primitive air.

The number of white-painted weatherboard cottages and huts had increased, but they still seemed to huddle haphazardly along the shoreline or cling, almost transiently, to the low hills beneath the snowcapped peak of Mount Table. There were more ships in the harbor—sealers, for the most part, and two whalers—and the wharf had been enlarged to give space for a new bonded warehouse, built partly of stone.

The prison, too, appeared to have been extended, and the barracks now boasted an impressive parade ground, made from what appeared to be a mixture of pounded rock and clay, bleached white by the sun. The church was there, Justin saw—the church in which his mother had married Andrew Hawley—but it still lacked a steeple, and only the burial ground had been extended, to include what his glass revealed as more rows of wooden crosses than he recalled seeing on his last visit, delivering mail in the *Flinders*.

The port formalities were swiftly and somewhat cursorily dealt with; Andrew's baggage was sent ashore in the care of a sergeant from the garrison, and Commander Forster, with a regretful smile, ordered his gig lowered.

"We had best not delay our call on His Honor the Lieutenant Governor," he said, "though I fear we shall have to search for him, since he's seldom to be found at his official residence. You, I take it," he added, addressing Andrew, his smile fading, "will have to acquaint Major Geils with the unpleasant prospect that lies before him?"

Andrew inclined his head. "Yes—and I don't relish doing it."

"Will he take passage to Sydney with us?" Forster asked. "We're not staying, you know—or at least no longer than it takes Davey to hand over his dispatches."

Andrew eyed him gravely. "My instructions are to give Geils an option. He can either elect to resign his commission and go home, or he can face the charges against him in Sydney—it will be up to him to decide which he does. My guess is that he'll go to Sydney and try to refute the charges."

"Then we shall have the doubtful pleasure of his company,"

James Forster said ruefully. "As a matter of interest, Captain Hawley, who is bringing the charges? The Governor?"

"No," Andrew denied. He flashed Forster a quizzical smile. "The Lieutenant Governor—Davey, backed up by the deputy commissary, a fellow named Fosbrook, whose own reputation is none too savory. They've accused the major of purloining spirits from the government stores for his own use and plundering the government's supplies of building materials. But as I understand it, Commander, Geils intends to bring countercharges against them, so they'll all be on their way to Sydney before long . . . though I trust not on board your ship. In any event, there will have to be a delay until Mr. Justice Bent agrees to reopen the courts in Sydney, since it will be a civil action, not a military trial."

"Good God!" Forster exclaimed disgustedly. "I begin now to sympathize with His Excellency the Governor, as well as with you. How can any man govern a colony, with such subordinates? And these people appear to consider themselves superior to the deported felons . . . even when the felons have served their sentences and expiated their crimes!" He sighed. "Is my gig ready, Mr. Broome?"

"Alongside, sir," Justin answered. "And Captain Hawley's kit has been sent ashore, sir."

He would miss Andrew, he thought, as the gig headed for the landing stage. True, they did not see a great deal of each other when he himself was at sea and Andrew at Ulva; but latterly his stepfather had been in attendance on the Governor in Sydney, with William left in charge at Ulva and their young sister, Rachel, keeping house and enjoying the social life of Sydney Town, as a change from rural isolation. And—thanks to Captain Jeffrey's reluctance to employ him and his procrastination on the proposed transfer to the *Emu*—he, too, had been able to spend more time than usual ashore and in Andrew's company.

Andrew and Jessica got on well, and Jessica had gone out of her way to make it a family reunion, which all of them had appreciated . . . and which, Justin reflected with a pang, his mother would have gloried in. It had been she who had kept Andrew at Ulva, the memory of her that had bound him to the place, even after her death. Perhaps he was wise to break with memory and accept this new challenge to his military skills, however taxing it might prove. He was a soldier by choice and training—a man of Mad Tom Davey's caliber would not ride roughshod over Andrew Hawley.

The gig came alongside the steps leading to the wharf, and they disembarked. Since Governor Macquarie's initial visit, almost five years before, the streets of Hobart had been named in accordance with the plans he had drawn up. Yet, although the street signs proclaimed George's Square, Macquarie, Elizabeth, Liverpool, and Collins streets, the straggling rows of ill-assorted shops and houses scarcely lived up to the grandiose titles the Governor had bestowed on them.

There were taverns at every street corner now, Justin observed, as ramshackle in construction as the dwelling houses they neighbored, and—although it was not yet noon—few were devoid of customers, and some were even crowded. Seamen from the sealing vessels and whalers, men in rough homespuns who looked like farmers, a sprinkling of women, and—meeting with Andrew's stern disapproval—quite a number of soldiers could be seen through the open doors and unglazed windows, their scarlet jackets vivid splashes of color against the drab garments of their companions.

In one dirty, down-at-heels alehouse, a gang of convict laborers, wearing leg-irons, disported themselves, strictly against regulations, under the apparently uncaring gaze of their overseers, and moved Andrew to exclaim wrathfully, "By heaven, if Governor Macquarie could see this, he would have Davey before a court-martial, no matter what influence he has with the Colonial Office!"

Inquiry of a passerby elicited the information that the Lieutenant Governor was likely to be found at Petchy's place. This proved to be a tavern on the corner of Collins Street, with a crudely painted sign hanging from the shingle roof proclaiming it "The Sealers' Rest."

Inside, Major Thomas Davey was holding court, his small, stout body enthroned on a padded leather chair in the center of the ill-lit taproom and a frothing tankard in his hand. To an audience of about a dozen—among whom Justin recognized the chaplain, the Reverend Robert Knopwood—he was seemingly affording entertainment by acting the buffoon and singing, in a cracked, untuneful voice, a bawdy song that had its origins in the Portsmouth gutters.

He broke off at the sight of the unexpected newcomers and, recognizing Commander Forster after a moment's puzzled scrutiny, called out a welcome.

"So you've come back, have you, Forster! Well, come in, man, come in—we don't stand on ceremony here, as you should know. A drink for these gentlemen, Mr. Petchy. You're acquainted with the commander, are you not?"

The young tavern keeper bowed obsequiously, but before he could comply with the Lieutenant Governor's order, James Forster shook his head.

"I have come only to report the arrival of my ship, Major Davey, and to introduce Captain Hawley to you. His Excellency Governor Macquarie has appointed him commandant of your garrison, in place of Major Geils."

"Geils has gone," Davey growled. "Sailed with the *Conway* a day or so ago, and good riddance." He eyed Andrew from beneath frowning white brows and then brightened perceptibly. "Ah, a real soldier, I see—an officer with presence! And—er . . . His Majesty's sloop of war *Emu*, that's the name of your ship, ain't it, Forster?"

"It is, sir," Forster confirmed coldly.

"Capital, capital!" Mad Tom exulted. "Means I can deal with the blasted Indians effectively at last and lay some of the damned bushrangers by the heels. Governor had a change of heart, did he? Sent me the reinforcements I asked him for finally, eh?"

Commander Forster exchanged a quick glance with Andrew and then again shook his head. "I have brought you no reinforcements, sir. My orders were to give passage to Captain Hawley and to return immediately to Sydney with mail and the officer Captain Hawley has relieved. And since you say he has already left, then I—"

Davey interrupted him with a stream of obscenities. "God damn you to hell, Forster! How many blasted sailors have you got on board your ship? Over a hundred, I'll warrant . . . well, you can spare me fifty o' them, can't you? This officer—what's his name? Hawley can command 'em. Only take three or four days, for God's sake . . . you can wait that long, surely?"

"I am afraid not, Major," James Forster answered, with finality. The Reverend Knopwood started to speak and then thought better of it, bowed stiffly, and took his leave with undignified haste. Several others, after a brief hesitation, followed his example.

"Deserting me, are you?" Davey bawled after them. "Devil fly away with you . . . you're the ones that own land. You're the ones that come crawling to me, demanding that I do something to stop your blasted farms being raided by the natives! Always complaining that your stock's being stolen and your damned crops burnt . . . and if it's not the Indians, it's the escapers, the bloody bushrangers! But what can I do, for God's sake, when I'm not given enough troops to stop 'em? When the Governor ignores my requests and sends me one officer—one infernal officer—when I asked for a company?" He glared at Andrew, shaking with impotent rage. "Well, Captain Hawley, what have you to say for yourself, damn your eyes? You going to rid me of the Indians single-handed, eh? Or teach my troops to shoot 'em, like they deserve?"

Standing beside him, Justin was aware of Andrew's growing tension. But his stepfather controlled himself and answered without heat, "It is not His Excellency's policy to permit the aborigines to be slaughtered indiscriminately, sir. On the contrary, he is endeavoring to educate them and to see that they are provided with suitable means of livelihood—to bring them into the community, not drive them outside it. He—"

"That won't work here," Major Davey retorted. "They're bloody savages in Van Diemen's Land—thieves and killers. The only thing they understand is when the troops raid the woods and drive 'em out. But . . ." His anger faded and he seemed suddenly to collapse like a pricked balloon. "Give me another drink, Petchy," he demanded, and waved a limp, heavily veined hand in weary dismissal of them all when Commander Forster attempted to support Andrew's statement.

As they took their leave, Forster could barely contain his anger. "Well, Hawley," he said, "now that you have seen Mad Tom for yourself, do you wonder that I said I didn't envy you? The fellow is quite impossible. He's got to be removed before he lets the whole colony go to the dogs!" Letting the tavern door slam shut behind them, he set off down the street at a rapid pace, as if anxious to put the sight and sound of Hobart's Lieutenant Governor behind him. Andrew laid a hand on Justin's arm, bringing him to a halt.

"I think," he said grimly, "that I had best start on my unenviable task at once, Justin. No point in putting it off, is there? I'll go to the barracks and take a look at my new command—the officers in particular. Make my apologies to your captain, if you please. I'll see you both before you sail."

He strode off, making for the squat barrack buildings and the shining, deserted parade ground, and Justin's heart went out to him in wordless pity. But, he told himself, if anyone could save this beautiful, ill-governed place from going to the dogs, it was Andrew, and perhaps, God willing, he had an even chance of doing so . . . provided Davey stuck to his drinking and raving and let him alone.

James Forster had cooled down when Justin caught up with him. "Davey said very little about the *Conway,* Justin, bar mentioning that Captain Hawley's predecessor had taken passage in her, did you notice? Not a word about a mutiny. I'd intended to ask him, but"—he shrugged—"he's probably forgotten all about it, as he forgets most things. Let us look up your *Chronicle* correspondent, shall we, and find out what he can tell us?"

The office of the Hobart *Chronicle* was a small, partly stone-built house in Liverpool Street, and appeared also to be the home of its proprietor. A large, old-fashioned printing press occupied most of the room that opened onto the street, with an editorial desk squeezed into one corner and piled high with printed sheets, while from the rear came an appetizing smell of cooking. But the office, for all its congestion, was clean and well lit, and the girl who came in response to Justin's knocking was nicely dressed in a checked gingham frock and a frilled apron, and very pretty.

She dropped the visitors a curtsy before shaking her shining fair head to their inquiry for Damien Hayes.

"I am so sorry, gentlemen, my husband has gone out. There has been another bushrangers' raid on a property at Harrowby, and he has gone out there to investigate the damage. It is about fifteen miles from here, and I am not expecting him to return until late afternoon. But . . . I can give him a message, if you wish." She eyed their uniforms and smiled. "You are from the King's ship, of course. Are you friends of Damien's?"

"I knew him well in Sydney," Justin answered, echoing her smile. Damien, he thought, had done well for himself, with a lovely, obviously intelligent young wife and his own newspaper.

On his last call in the *Flinders,* the newspaper had been a single, hand-printed weekly sheet, with a small circulation, and there had been no Mrs. Hayes.

As if guessing his thoughts, the girl blushed prettily and, avoiding Justin's eye, confessed that they had been married for only three weeks.

"My father's name is Triffit," she added. "He has a property in New Norfolk, and only last April, the notorious bushranger Michael Howe—who calls himself the Lieutenant Governor of the Woods—robbed him of stock and provisions to the value of seven hundred pounds. That was how I met Damien . . . he came to investigate, as he has done today. So some good came of my poor father's misfortune."

"And the culprits have not been apprehended, I suppose?" Commander Forster put in cynically.

"No!" the girl returned, indignation overcoming her shyness. "Howe has been at large for years, leading a gang of more than a score of the villains. And all Governor Davey did was offer them an amnesty—free pardons, sir, for the whole wicked gang, if they would agree to return peaceably to Hobart. He allowed them seven months' grace before they need do so, and of course they took that as a license to pillage and plunder to their hearts' content, free of all penalties for their misdeeds. Howe even sent a message to the Governor, by a soldier he kidnapped—a most insolent message, sir, in which he threatened to send some buckshot through Major Davey's old paunch!"

Forster caught Justin's eye and sighed.

"And what," he wanted to know, "did Major Davey do about that, Mrs. Hayes?"

Mrs. Hayes spread her small hands in a gesture of despair. "Oh, he sent the troops after them, but it was no use—some of the soldiers are in league with the rogues, Damien says, and instead of hunting them, they steal on their own account, and lay the blame on the bushrangers. Major Davey—the Governor, I mean—talks of demanding more troops from Sydney and introducing martial law, but nothing has been done. Damien writes leading articles, urging action, but I fear he is wasting his time . . . and making himself unpopular into the bargain. The high-ups take no notice—they are interested only in feathering their own nests, you see. And Major Davey is almost always tipsy. But . . ." She brightened. "Damien has sent some of his articles to the London *Chronicle,* and perhaps, if the editor publishes them, it will cause the Colonial Office to take action."

"Perhaps it will, Mrs. Hayes," Forster said, without conviction. He took out his watch, frowned, and replaced it in his pocket. "We must not take up any more of your time, and we have work to do, for I intend to sail in the morning. But I should like to talk to your husband, if that is possible. Will you ask him to dine with us, on board the *Emu,* if he returns in time?"

"Certainly, sir," Mrs. Hayes promised. "I'll be sure to ask him, the minute I see him."

She was as good as her word; a little after dusk had fallen, Damien Hayes presented himself, looking spruce and smart in a green cutaway coat, his cheeks freshly shaven and his manner alert.

Over the meal in Forster's stern cabin, he talked freely of the miserable state to which the settlement had been reduced during Mad Tom Davey's three years of misrule. He added to his wife's account of the bushrangers' depredations with a vivid, firsthand description of the raid on the farm he had visited only that morning.

"Mr. MacCarty, the owner of the farm, sir, with five of his laborers armed with fowling pieces, endeavored to drive them off. But there were too many of them, all carrying muskets and led by Howe himself, with a blackfellow they call Mosquito, whom he employs . . . a bloodthirsty devil if ever there was one. They killed one of MacCarty's men and wounded him and two others, looted the stockyard and house, and then made off into the timber, after cruelly abusing his womenfolk."

"Shocking," Commander Forster said, with genuine feeling. "Your wife told us that you were campaigning in your newspaper for drastic action to be taken against these lawless rogues. Has any good come of it?"

Damien Hayes shook his head. He glanced across the table at Justin, who had been listening in silence to his unhappy recital, and said bitterly, "Justin will tell you, sir, that I've tried to campaign against injustice and corruption before, by means of articles I send home to the London *Chronicle.* In Sydney, His Excellency Governor Macquarie gave me his wholehearted support, but here . . ." He mopped his heated brow. "The corruption that exists here, Commander Forster, passes belief, with Governor Davey at the heart of it. I tell you, sir, he is not only dissipated and profligate in his private life—he is privy to and sanctions the smuggling into Hobart of vast quantities of spirits, for his own profit! The last convict transport to call here, the *Conway*, landed all that her rogue of a master was carrying. I don't know how much, but I do know it took two nights to unload, and it was done under cover of darkness."

At the mention of the *Conway*, Justin saw his commander's brows come together.

"Ah, yes, the *Conway*, Mr. Hayes . . . tell me, did you hear anything concerning a mutiny by the convicts she was transporting?"

"A mutiny?" Damien looked puzzled. "No, sir, not a word. One of the surgeons was called, and a man whose arm had been amputated was transferred to the hospital. But that was all I heard, except that the man died—of some sort of virulent fever, apparently, and the ship was put in quarantine as a result. None of her people were permitted to come ashore, and after her cargo of spirits was unloaded, she lay at anchor in Double Bay for . . . oh, for the best part of a fortnight. Her master was hoping to obtain a mast, I believe, to replace one damaged in a storm. But he didn't get it, and the ship sailed yesterday, I think, or the day before, for Sydney, with the garrison commandant, Major Geils, on board." Hayes hesitated. "Do you know why he left, sir?"

"Yes," Commander Forster said shortly. "We landed Captain Hawley, his relief, this morning."

"He must have been in a great hurry," Justin observed. "To take passage in a fever ship, for heaven's sake!"

"He was," Damien Hayes confirmed. "He and Governor Davey fell out, and Davey was threatening to arrest him. They've made countercharges of peculation against each other . . . an example," he added, "of the pot calling the kettle black!"

He lapsed into glum silence, which Justin broke by offering congratulations on his marriage. Damien's young face was instantly transformed.

"I'm the most fortunate man in Hobart," he asserted, beaming. "My lovely Sarah is a prize . . . equaled only by the one of whom *you* robbed me, Justin my friend! You'll convey my warm regards to Jessica, I trust?"

"Most gladly," Justin assured him. They talked of mutual friends in Sydney as the steward cleared away the remnants of their meal, and Commander Forster offered port and cigars, making no attempt to interrupt their reminiscences until Damien started to speak of news he had recently received from England.

"My good friend and mentor, Mr. Deighton, of the London *Chronicle*, told me in his last letter that Mr. Macarthur is seeking a dispensation from the Colonial Office to enable him to return to Sydney. And Mr. Deighton seems to think that Lord Bathurst is disposed to permit him to do so."

"Macarthur?" James Forster put in. "The infamous John Macarthur, of whom one hears the most extraordinary stories still? Was it not he who plotted the Rum Corps' rebellion and engineered Admiral Bligh's downfall?"

"The same, sir, yes."

"And Lord Bathurst is disposed to permit him to return? Heavens, after all our talk of corruption in high places, Mr. Hayes, I should have supposed that the gentleman would be unwelcome! Particularly so to Governor Macquarie, who is the most upright of men."

"His Excellency probably was not asked," Damien said, with conscious cynicism. "Colonel Johnston, whose court-martial I attended before I left England, was made the scapegoat, of course. As a civilian, Mr. Macarthur can be tried only in the colony, you see, sir, so he's safe so long as he remains in London. But his wife, most of his family, and all his property are in New South Wales . . . small wonder that he should wish to return. And although poor Johnston was found guilty on all counts and sentenced to be cashiered from the army, he was allowed to return, was he not, Justin?"

"Yes," Justin confirmed flatly. "As plain Mr. Johnston. But he now leads an exemplary and useful life with his wife and sons at Annandale, and the Governor is on friendly terms with the whole family." He shook his head to Forster's offer of another glass of port. "I'm on watch in half an hour, sir. And if you want to sail at first light—"

"Damme, be assured that I do!" Forster said. He lit a fresh cigar and inhaled on it deeply, before motioning to Damien Hayes to refill his glass. "I am ill at ease in this place," he went on pensively. "It is as if I am sitting on a powder keg, with that outrageous drunken fool Davey ready to light the fuse that will blow Hobart sky-high, whilst the rest of Van Diemen's Land lapses into anarchy. How do you contrive to stand it, Mr. Hayes?''

Damien smiled thinly. "By continuing to campaign against the corruption, sir, and for Major Davey's removal. And if my friend Mr. Deighton is to be believed, the Colonial Office is about to appoint a Colonel Sorrell in his stead. Have you heard aught of it?"

Justin glanced across at his commander. Andrew, he recalled, had spoken of Colonel Sorrell's appointment in confidence, but . . . He saw James Forster incline his head.

"We have heard rumors, Mr. Hayes. And"—he smiled at Justin—"you will find a staunch and loyal ally in Captain Hawley, the new garrison commandant. He has Governor Macquarie's trust and his instructions, and I fancy things may improve now that he is here."

"Thanks be to God!" Damien exclaimed. He drained his glass and rose. "It is time that I take leave of you, Commander, lest my continued absence cause my wife concern. She has been nervous when left alone at night—the raid on her father's property had, alas, a bad effect on her. But it has been both a pleasure and a considerable source of encouragement to talk to you and Justin. I thank you, most sincerely, for inviting me to partake of your hospitality."

Justin escorted him to the entryport, and they shook hands warmly before Hayes descended to the waiting boat.

"Don't forget, Justin . . . my best regards to your charming Jessica. And, if belated, my congratulations on your naval commission. I shall hope to see you again one of these days, if your naval duties permit."

"I share that hope," Justin said. "Fare you well, Damien! God go with you."

The boat pulled away and was soon lost to sight in the darkness. Justin relieved the deck; the watch changed, and his young second, acting lieutenant Mercer, went yawning below.

After a while, a trifle to his surprise, Commander Forster joined him on deck.

"Let's walk a little," he suggested. "Your friend Hayes has given me much food for thought."

"Has he, sir?" Justin fell into step beside him. He liked James

Forster, he reflected, and they had formed a friendship, based on mutual respect and trust, that he was coming increasingly to value. By contrast with the arrogant Captain Jeffrey, he was an exemplary commander—a taut hand, where the discipline and efficiency of his ship were concerned, but not one who punished severely for minor offenses or who demanded the impossible from his men. The *Emu,* as Forster had claimed at their first meeting, was a happy ship, and he enjoyed the esteem of virtually her entire company.

"You were probably unaware of it," James Forster said, as they completed a turn of the brig's quarterdeck, "but I came out to this colony with the notion of following Rick Tempest's example and becoming a settler."

"You, sir?" Justin halted involuntarily, to stare into his shadowed face in disbelief. "But you're a commander, with every chance of being made post with your next command. Surely you would not contemplate abandoning your career at this stage?"

"My career in the King's Navy was blighted, Justin my boy," the *Emu*'s captain answered bleakly, "when I lost my ship to a damned Yankee privateer, who refused to believe that the war was over when he encountered me. I was under orders not to fire on the American flag, so I had no choice but to surrender . . . or so I supposed. But Their Lordships thought differently. You may credit this or you may not, Justin, but when our erstwhile colonists released us and I returned to London, I was accused of cowardice in the face of the enemy!"

Shocked, Justin continued to stare at him, scarcely able to believe the evidence of his own ears.

"Did they charge you with cowardice, sir?"

"No. In the circumstances, they could not. However, it was made clear to me that when my present appointment is terminated, I need expect no other seagoing command. So I shall *not* be made post, and I did not much fancy the coast guard service or command of a receiving ship in the Thames." Forster resumed his steady pacing of the deck, and after a momentary hesitation, Justin caught up with him.

Why, he wondered, was the older man telling him this? He had known that the *Emu* had been taken when on her way out to New South Wales . . . she had been long overdue, and despite the cessation of hostilities with America, the fact that an American ship had made her prize had been talked about and widely deplored in Sydney. But Forster himself had never spoken of it before, and . . . He ventured uncertainly, "Do you still intend to settle out here, sir?"

"By God, no!" The denial was emphatic. "After what I've seen and heard, that's the last thing I'd do. I admire Governor Macquarie more than I can tell you, but I fear for his future, both as Governor and man. He's made enemies, Justin, and they'll not rest until they've ruined him."

"He's made friends, too, sir," Justin countered. "Far more friends than enemies."

"Aye, friends without power or influence, friends who lack the patronage that dissipated rogue Davey enjoys. Macquarie's friends are the poor devils of emancipists, are they not? And—what do they call your kind?—currency kids like yourself, lad." Forster's arm round his shoulder robbed the words of any malice, and Justin took no offense, though he felt the color rising to his cheeks as it always did when the term was applied to him.

"There are a good many of us now," he defended.

"I know—and they're the backbone of the colony, the ones on whose sweat and toil its future prosperity depends. The other faction, the damned elitists, are mainly interested in amassing fortunes, and they don't care how they do it." Commander Forster shrugged, his tone abrasive. "Macquarie's too honest for their taste, Justin. For God's sake, look at the Bents—look at Molle and his conniving, upstart officers; consider what harm they've done to him already! And the tales they're telling, behind his back, to the Colonial Office. Remember how others of their stamp destroyed Admiral Bligh . . . devil take it, boy, you were there when they deposed him, weren't you?"

"Yes," Justin conceded reluctantly. "I was there, sir. But . . ." He caught his breath, seeing again, in memory, the red-coated ranks of the Rum Corps marching, with bayonets fixed, on Government House, their colors flying and Colonel Johnston riding at their head.

Only Governor Bligh's daughter, Mary Putland, had found the courage to defy them and to seek to deny them entrance, armed only—ludicrously—with a parasol. And they had brushed her aside, as the bonfires they had prepared leaped into life and the fifes and drums beat out the rhythm of "The British Grenadiers," almost in mockery, and voices were raised, shouting, "Down with the tyrant!"

"For heaven's sake, sir," he burst out. "Surely you don't imagine that Colonel Molle's regiment will rebel? Why—"

"No, of course I don't. But there are subtler ways of achieving the same end, I fear." James Forster halted by the starboard rail and looked out across the moonlit water of the wide harbor to the darkness beyond. He went on, with an abrupt change of tone, "I received an offer from the Brazilian Navy when we were in Rio— they offered me post rank and command of a seventy-four, Justin, and the offer is still open. At the time, it did not occur to me to accept, since I was planning to settle here. But our time on this station is limited. Governor Macquarie told me that the colony cannot afford to keep either the *Kangaroo* or this ship on the station for much longer, and when the *Elizabeth* sloop is ready for sea, she will take over our duties." He turned from the rail to look at Justin, his eyes suddenly bright. "The *Kangaroo* is to leave first, and we'll not be long after her—a month . . . six weeks, perhaps."

"Yes, sir," Justin acknowledged, his bewilderment returning. The *Elizabeth* had been built in Robert Campbell's yard, from materials shipped out from England, which had delayed her completion, but she was, he knew, almost ready for fitting out.

She was much smaller than the two King's ships that, it seemed, she was to replace—a brig-sloop of similar design but of only one hundred and twenty tons burden and pierced for six nine-pounder guns, with a single eighteen-pounder bow-chaser, yet to be sent out. But Justin had long admired her graceful lines and the care and skill that had gone into her construction, and she would, he supposed, be adequate for her task, provided she was well manned.

No officer had so far been appointed to her command, and he found himself wondering whether perhaps the Governor had offered it to James Forster.

"Do you," he asked diffidently, "intend to join the Brazilian Navy, sir, after all?"

"Yes, I do," Forster answered, with crisp decisiveness. "Although, I confess, I only made up my mind to do so today . . . it was our conversation with Hayes this evening that caused me to come finally to the conclusion that I'm not cut out to become a settler. Which brings me to you. You are a good officer, Justin, and a fine seaman. William Case did not exaggerate when he told me that you possess exceptional qualities, which, in his view, are unlikely to earn the reward they deserve if you remain here. So . . . how would you like to come with me?"

"I . . . come with you, sir? To Brazil?"

"That's right. Return to England in the *Emu,* pay her off, and then accompany me to Rio, as first lieutenant of my seventy-four. I'm to be permitted to choose my own officers, and there are a number of our countrymen serving under the Portuguese flag. Good men, most of them."

It was, Justin recognized, a generous offer, and also a flattering one. He had not expected it—although looking back and recalling their conversation, he realized that James Forster had been leading up to it, ever since he had come on deck. He started to voice his thanks, but was waved to silence.

"The pay is excellent, and there would be accommodation for your wife and child, whom we can bring to England with us." Forster went into details. "Damme, you might well be given your own seventy-four in a year or two and end up as an admiral! You could make a fine career, Justin, as I hope to."

"Yes, sir," Justin echoed, without conviction.

"Before you decide," the *Emu*'s captain went on, "I am bound to tell you that there is an alternative . . . command of the colonial vessel *Elizabeth.* On my recommendation—which I would give you wholeheartedly—I fancy that she could be yours. Governor Macquarie mentioned the possibility to both Captain Jeffrey and myself. Jeffrey was—well, somewhat lukewarm in his reaction, and I did not know you then. I told the Governor that I would report on your fitness for the appointment on our return to Sydney. Jeffrey wants it for one of his officers—Meredith, I think his name is—but I feel sure that Governor Macquarie would prefer you to have it." He smiled. "So would I, except that I fear it would be a dead end for a man of your ability. You might advance no further, Justin."

"I . . . don't know what to say, sir. In all honesty, I . . ." Justin fell silent again, at a loss for words.

Command of the *Elizabeth,* he thought dazedly—God in heaven, it would be beyond his wildest dreams! While Commander Forster might consider it a dead end, how could he see it in that light? He might end his days in his present rank, never make post, never hold another command, but . . . was not his home here, in the land Governor Macquarie now officially designated Australia?

He remembered his mother's words, whispered as she lay dying in sight of the new lands beyond Bathurst.

"Only imagine what this will mean, to you and the whole colony! Think of the flocks and herds this land will sustain, the crops it will grow . . . look at it, children, for it is your future spread out down there. And it is for you to build on. . . ."

Conscious of a tightening of the throat as the words came back to him, Justin caught his breath on a sigh. He had a stake in those lands, he reminded himself; he and Rick Tempest. If the sea ever failed him, there would be the lush pastures and the wooded hills beyond the Blue Mountain barrier, in the existence of which his mother had believed so fervently for all of her life . . . and which he himself had helped to discover. Rick had planned to take his bride-to-be to see the site of the homestead he intended to build on their grant—indeed, they were probably there at this moment, or on their way back, with William and Rachel, making their plans for the future.

Plans that would include him . . . Justin turned to face his commander, his decision made, as Forster's had been a few minutes before.

"It is good of you, sir, to offer me the chance to accompany you to Brazil. I'm deeply grateful, and I wish I could accept, for there is no one I would rather serve under than yourself, believe me. But I—"

"But you're a currency kid?" James Forster suggested. "Or maybe I should call you an Australian? All right, Lieutenant Broome, I understand. The colony needs men of your stamp to counteract those who are doing their best to destroy it. And brave, well-intentioned visionaries like Governor Macquarie need support." He smiled and once again clapped a friendly hand on Justin's shoulder. "I will not pretend that I'm not sorry, but I shall do all in my power to obtain command of the *Elizabeth* for you. Well"—he stifled a yawn—"I'll turn in, I think. See that I'm called at the usual hour, if you please."

"Aye, aye, sir." Justin touched his hat. "And thank you, sir, more than I can say."

Commander Forster's smile expanded into an oddly boyish grin.

"I do not greatly like Captain Jeffrey," he confessed. "And I don't at all fancy young Meredith—and frankly, I do not believe the Governor does, either! I think you can take it that you'll be given the *Elizabeth*, Justin. Good night."

CHAPTER XVIII

Governor Macquarie sat at breakfast with his wife and young Lachlan, his two-year-old son, and as he listened to the little boy's laughter and watched his wife's glowing face as she bantered with him, he felt the cares of his office slip away.

It would not be for very long, the Governor was aware; soon John Campbell, his devoted and efficient secretary, would come into the dining room to remind him that there were papers to deal with, petitions to be heard, and people to see. There were always people waiting to see him—officials, officers of the garrison, private citizens, settlers, both free and emancipist, convicts—a variety of people, each with his own particular problems, his demands, his complaints.

And, Lachlan Macquarie thought regretfully, there was never enough time to spend with his wife and son, in whose company he could unwind and relax. True, the past week had been spent with them on a visit to the township of Liverpool and a tour of farms and new settlements in the area, but even there he had not been free; he and Elizabeth might steal a few hours to ride together to an outlying farm or take Lachlan with them in the carriage, but . . . He sighed. There were still people demanding his attention when their destination was reached, still others awaiting their return, however brief their absence.

And there were, it seemed, a growing number of people throughout the colony whom he must now recognize not only as critics and detractors, but also as enemies. Enemies who, with their pens dipped in venom, wrote lengthy and derogatory reports to the Colonial Office and to their influential patrons at home in an attempt to discredit him and undermine his authority.

"Oh, see, Lachlan dear, how the boy's table manners have

improved," Elizabeth begged, pride in her voice, and the Governor managed a thin smile, distracted from his thoughts, momentarily at least, by the sight of his son manfully coping with knife and fork. Young Lachlan was the apple of his wife's eye and a source of so much pride and happiness that the Governor could not bring himself to tell her that she spoiled him.

"He does you credit, my love," he told her. "Indeed he does." And that was true; not long since, the boy had been wont to throw plate and cutlery to the floor in a tantrum, if his horn spoon and the implement Elizabeth called his "pusher" were taken from him.

"I thought," Elizabeth said, eyeing their small son indulgently, "that I would take Lachie for a drive this morning and perhaps a picnic lunch. If you will not be needing the carriage and Sergeant Whalan, he could escort us and bring his boy Charley to play with Lachie. You will be busy all day, I imagine?"

"Yes, my dear," the Governor confirmed abstractedly. "Alas, I shall. But I shall not need Whalan, so take him with you, by all means."

Elizabeth talked on, listing the calls she intended to make on her way, but Macquarie, again busy with his own thoughts, scarcely heard her, and only when she mentioned Eliza Bent did he offer a disapproving comment.

"Surely that's not wise, is it, my dear? You know on what terms I am with her infernal brother-in-law, who continues to defy me and flout my authority in every way he can devise. Damme, Elizabeth—you heard what Dwyer and Cullen said only yesterday. Judge Bent and his bosom friend, the Reverend Nicholas, again refused to pay when they entered the turnpike. Bent actually threatened the men, claiming he would pay no toll, and that if they did not let him pass, he would send them to jail! He has no right to demand exemption from a duty everyone else in the colony has to pay."

"But poor Eliza is widowed, Lachlan," Elizabeth reminded him. "Widowed and sickly and, with all those young children, worried out of her mind. She is not, after all, responsible for her brother-in-law's behavior."

"She shares her house with him," the Governor pointed out sourly. "An official residence, furthermore, to which neither she nor Jeffrey Bent is any longer entitled. It is the judge advocate's residence, the judge advocate is dead, and his brother has refused to preside over the supreme court for the past six months! By the next mail, God willing, I shall receive instructions from Lord Bathurst to relieve him of office . . . truly, Elizabeth my dear, I should prefer you not to call on Mrs. Bent socially."

In the face of his cold resentment, Elizabeth yielded. "Very well, dear," she agreed. "If you feel so strongly about it, then I will not. I shall simply send Joseph Big round later, with a few small gifts for the children." She rose and bent to kiss him, before taking young Lachlan in her arms. "Try not to work too hard, dearest. Think of your health . . . you must spare yourself, for my sake, Lachlan, and the boy's. We need and love you."

The Governor watched her go, carrying the child perched happily on her slim shoulders, and as the door closed behind them, he expelled his breath in frustration.

How could he avoid working too hard, when there was never time enough in the day to do all that had to be done? he asked himself bitterly. How could he think of his increasingly frail health, when he was seldom permitted more than an hour or two to relax? His temper was suffering, as well as his aging body, of which his long service in India had taken a heavy toll; he was, he knew, becoming irascible and all too easily provoked. He acted too impulsively and—yes, perhaps even too autocratically at times, giving his enemies fresh opportunities to attack him.

There was the incident in which that odious young cleric, the Reverend Benjamin Vale, had chosen to involve himself, the repercussions of which were still plaguing him. Governor Macquarie refilled his coffee cup, frowning as he went over the details.

In February an American merchant ship, the *Traveller,* had come into port with trade goods consigned to a Sydney merchant from Canton. The American war was over, the peace treaty signed, and having received no instructions to the contrary from the home government, he had authorized her entry and then gone on tour. But, in his absence, and aided and abetted by William Henry Moore—the only free solicitor in the colony—Vale, the 46th Regiment's chaplain, had armed himself with a warrant and proceeded to place the *Traveller* under arrest, claiming her as a lawful prize. The warrant had, of course, been made out and signed by Jeffrey Bent . . . and Bent had endeavored to have an Admiralty court convened, in order to legalize the claim.

But Colonel Molle—to his credit for once—had not dared to

accede to Bent's demand and had taken action to terminate the arrest. The American captain had been permitted to deliver his goods and leave port, and . . . The Governor's frown deepened. He had ordered Benjamin Vale to be court-martialed; the court had found him guilty as charged and sentenced him to be severely and publicly reprimanded, whereupon the arrogant young chaplain had declared himself unjustly treated and threatened to leave the colony.

That, of course, Macquarie reminded himself, would have been a matter more for relief than regret. He had turned a deaf ear to Vale's threats and to Moore's expressions of fury when the lawyer found himself dismissed from the office of crown solicitor as a result of his part in the seizure. But, with diabolically unfortunate timing, weeks after the *Traveller*'s departure from Port Jackson, had come a dispatch from the Colonial Office, informing him officially that American ships were debarred from engaging in commerce with any British colony.

The Governor set down his empty cup, his hand trembling with suppressed indignation. Moore had promptly launched a petition on behalf of himself and Vale—whom he described as his "client"—and addressed it to the House of Commons. Jeffrey Bent had composed the infamous petition, for all it was in Moore's name; they had obtained signatures to it, mostly from intoxicated tavern habitués, and it would soon, presumably, be on its way to England.

He had written to Lord Bathurst in explanation of what had happened, but . . . Bathurst had, of late, displayed some incredulity, and if the infernal petition were to be put before the Commons, there was always a danger that some members of Parliament might give credence to its outrageous and malicious accusations.

And now, as if the *Traveller* affair were not enough, there was another ship lying at anchor in the cove—the transport *Conway*—whose master had hanged three convicts for mutiny and against whom countercharges of extreme cruelty and brutality had been laid by the officer commanding the escort and a civilian passenger, who was also a barrister.

The Governor frowned. He had ordered an investigation by a court of inquiry, presided over by Dr. D'Arcy Wentworth, Sydney's chief magistrate and superintendent of police, and—the devil! It had slipped his mind that John Campbell had been appointed, with William Broughton, to serve on the inquiry, and if the court were still sitting, Campbell would not be available to assist him with this morning's petitioners. He would have to make do with his clerk, Robinson, and that would result in muddle and delay. Michael Robinson was a fair poet and an Oxford graduate to boot, but he, alas, did not possess Campbell's tact or his memory for names, and on the occasions when he was required to take the secretary's place, Robinson almost invariably let his nervousness get the better of him.

Macquarie swore irritably beneath his breath and made his way, with reluctance, to his office—which, as he had anticipated, was already besieged by a motley and impatient crowd, with whom Robinson was already engaged in futile argument. He seated himself at his desk in dignified silence and called for the first petitioner.

At noon, to his relief, John Campbell returned, to announce that the court of inquiry had completed its investigation and given its findings.

"There are some matters that merit Your Excellency's attention," he added. "And Dr. Wentworth is anxious to make them known to you. He's here, sir. He came with me, so if you will receive him now, I will arrange for the rest of the petitioners to attend on Your Excellency tomorrow."

"Good," the Governor approved. He added his signature to an application for a land grant and laid down his quill. "Show Dr. Wentworth in, John."

The colony's senior surgeon came in briskly, a warm smile lighting his darkly sallow face as Macquarie rose to greet him. He was in his late forties, but despite advancing years and the numerous responsibilities he bore, D'Arcy Wentworth radiated both energy and good humor. The Governor liked him and made a point of inviting him to Government House functions, and he said now, before Wentworth could speak, "D'Arcy, my dear fellow, I'm about to lunch. You'll join me, I trust?"

"Thank you, sir. I shall be delighted to." He glanced at Campbell, and the secretary said, with mock gravity, "I took the liberty of anticipating His Excellency's invitation, Dr. Wentworth. An extra place has been set."

They went together into the dining room, exchanging pleasantries until the first course had been served; then, when the servants withdrew, Macquarie asked gravely, "What of the inquiry, D'Arcy? You've concluded it, I gather?"

"Yes, sir, we have." Dr. Wentworth supplied details of the charges and, with admirable brevity, outlined the evidence he had heard. "The master of the *Conway,* a fellow named Barlow, was found guilty, by a unanimous decision, of all save one of the charges brought against him. He was exonerated of the last—that he deliberately sought to provoke a mutiny by the convicts. But we found him guilty of neglect and extreme cruelty, exercised in a variety of forms toward unoffending prisoners, who were loaded with irons, closely confined, and strictly guarded. Barlow, sir, ordered the sentries to open fire on the prisoners, through loopholes in the door leading to their quarters. His defense for that act was that the ship's surgeon, Barnabas Shea, who was being held hostage by the convicts, was shot dead by one of them. But according to the prisoners—whose case was most competently and eloquently presented by one of the *Conway*'s passengers, a barrister of Lincoln's Inn named George De Lancey—the surgeon was shot in error, during a struggle for his pistol, by a half-witted young convict by the name of O'Dowd." Wentworth consulted his notes. "Ah, here it is, sir—Christian O'Dowd. The first mate, who—"

The Governor interrupted him. "Did you say De Lancey?" he asked.

"Yes, sir." D'Arcy Wentworth again leafed through his notes. "George De Lancey. He held a commission in the Royal North British Dragoons and fought with them at Waterloo. He was a captain, it seems, and—"

Again the Governor cut him short. "Damme, he must be a relative of Sir William De Lancey, the Duke's deputy QMG! According to the casualty list the *Barden* brought out, Sir William was killed at Waterloo, poor fellow. And you say that this De Lancey is now a barrister?"

"Indeed, yes," Dr. Wentworth confirmed. He smiled. "And, if I may offer a suggestion, Governor, he may well prove to be . . . how shall I put it? The answer to our crisis in the judiciary. Mr. Garling most reluctantly fills the office of judge advocate, pending the arrival of Mr. Wylde, as you're aware." The Governor nodded thoughtfully, and Wentworth went on, "There is another hero of Waterloo on board the *Conway*—the guard commander, a young ensign of Colonel Molle's regiment named Dean. He also gave evidence in the prisoners' defense, and so did the first mate, a reliable fellow, in my opinion—Henry Fry.''

The servants returned, bearing fresh dishes, and Wentworth shuffled his notes into order and passed them across the table to the Governor. "Perhaps you might care to glance through these, sir. John"—he gestured to the secretary—"in fact took them, so I am sure they will be complete."

Governor Macquarie read the closely written pages, occasionally exclaiming in shocked astonishment at what the evidence revealed. It was appalling, he thought, that a man like the *Conway*'s master should be entrusted with the command of a convict transport. The master of a ship at sea had absolute authority; he had the power of life and death, and if he abused it, as Barlow undoubtedly had, he must be made answerable for the deaths he had caused.

Plague take him . . . according to Ensign Dean's evidence, he had not only ordered the soldiers to fire on defenseless and fettered prisoners, who sought only relief from the unendurable conditions imposed on them, he had . . . Macquarie shook his head in disbelief. He had hanged an innocent man for the surgeon's murder, a man who had himself been a surgeon and who had tended the wounded whom the troops' fire had left in agony.

And . . . He read on, with growing horror, the food on his plate untouched. Barlow had apparently prevented any communication between his ship and the shore authorities, during the time the *Conway* was in port at Hobart, by declaring that the prisoners were infected with a contagious fever. The ship had been quarantined and sent to the anchorage in Double Bay—although not before her cargo of spirits had been landed. And that, in itself, was another black mark against the reprobate Lieutenant Governor, Major Thomas Davey, the devil take him! And probably against the commandant of the Hobart garrison, Geils, who had also, it appeared, given evidence to the *Conway*'s court of inquiry, although he had only taken passage in her from Hobart to Sydney.

Concluding his careful perusal of his secretary's notes, the Governor returned them. "The court has recommended that the master, Barlow, and the sergeant of the Forty-sixth . . . ah, Holmes, isn't it? That they should be held under arrest until given passage to England to stand trial," he observed. "Was that recommendation unanimous?"

Dr. Wentworth glanced at Secretary Campbell and waited for his nod of assent before replying. "Mr. Broughton felt very strongly that, in the present state of the judiciary, this would be the best course, sir. The sergeant could face a court-martial here, of course, but . . ." He sighed, leaving the sentence uncompleted, and tactfully making no mention of Colonel Molle. "It was agreed that the chief mate, Mr. Fry, should be given command of the *Conway*—she is under contract to return by way of Canton—and that he should give passage to the witnesses the court selected. But it seemed to us advisable that the two accused, Barlow and Sergeant Holmes, should not travel in the same vessel . . . although it is for you to decide, sir, whether or not to accept our recommendation."

The Governor grimaced. Past experience had taught him that, on the grounds of expense, the British Colonial Office did not welcome the sending home of persons accused of offenses on the high seas, although technically only crimes committed within the colony were subject to his jurisdiction. Major Geils's case was, alas; but the unspeakable Barlow's was not. He looked across at John Campbell, brows raised in unspoken question.

"In my view, sir, the court has recommended the best course, in the circumstances," the secretary said. He added, as if Governor Macquarie had voiced his doubts aloud, "The witnesses the court selected include a priest—brother of the unfortunate man who was hanged, Patrick Fitzroy—and the mate, Mr. Fry, who will in any event be returning to England. We took sworn depositions from Mr. George De Lancey and Ensign Dean."

"Good!" the Governor approved. "I must take the earliest opportunity to make the acquaintance of Mr. De Lancey. I imagine he will have brought letters of recommendation from the Colonial Office—although I have not received any prior notice concerning his arrival, have I, John?"

"No, sir, not that I recall. There is still some mail yet to be discharged from the *Conway*, though, and there may be some official letters still to come. I can send to the postmaster, if you wish, sir, and inquire."

"No, it does not matter," Macquarie said wearily. He pushed his plate away and rose. "Damme, I've still got to study the latest dispatch from His Lordship and draft my reply! But tell me—when is my wife arranging her next dinner party, do you know?"

"Tomorrow night, sir," John Campbell answered. "I haven't the full guest list here, but I know that Miss O'Malley has been invited, with Mr. Tempest. Since Mr. De Lancey is an American, shall I send him an invitation?"

An American, was he? But a barrister of the English bar? The Governor nodded his assent, recalling belatedly that, of course, Sir William De Lancey had been American by birth. He came of a loyalist family, however, and had served in the Peninsular campaign, where he had earned the great Duke's esteem. Such esteem was not easily won; if this relative of his were of the same stamp, he would be an asset to the colony. He—

"There is one other matter, sir," D'Arcy Wentworth said, with some reluctance. "I hesitate to trouble you with it now, but . . . it can't be glossed over, unfortunately, because Bent seems to have got wind of it, and he's out to make as much mischief as he can."

"When is he not?" Macquarie countered bitterly. "Well, you'd best tell me about it, I suppose."

The doctor produced a second set of notes from his jacket pocket. "You'll recall, sir, that you issued orders for a special watch to be kept for trespassers entering the Domain by way of the wall on the Woolloomooloo side?"

"Certainly—the shrubberies were being used for improper purposes by lewd and disorderly men and women. They were destroying the young trees and causing offense." The Governor spoke irritably and then, conscious that he had done so, changed his tone to a more placatory one. "A constable arrested three of the rogues last week, did he not? The order is clear enough—the public are free to enter by the main gate into the Domain, if they wish to use the grounds for recreation. Crossing the wall is forbidden."

"Quite so, sir," Wentworth agreed. He hesitated, and then went on with visible reluctance, "Constable Willbow arrested the three men in the act of scaling the wall. He took them to the jail, and on being informed of this, sir, you ordered them to be given twenty-five lashes apiece . . . unhappily without calling the men before you."

Macquarie's indignation was again aroused.

"The devil take it, D'Arcy, they were caught red-handed,

weren't they?" he demanded. "As a Governor, I am head of the
judiciary, civil and military. It's on *my* authority that magistrates'
sentences are waived or confirmed . . . damme, I'm surely
within my rights to order convicts to be flogged, if they flout my
orders?"

"Yes, Governor. But . . . these were not convicts, sir. They
were freemen. Hensall is an emancipist, and he works at the mint.
Blake is a free settler and a blacksmith, and Daniel Read, sir, is the
caretaker of Samuel Marsden's town residence."

The Governor groaned. "The constable—what's his name?
Willbow described them to me as low, vicious characters—he said
that Read had previously been charged with robbery and that
Blake, if I remember aright, was suspected of acting as a receiver
of stolen goods. I considered them proper objects, of whom an
example might—aye, and should be made. You recall the
constable's report, do you not, John?"

"Yes, indeed I do, sir," Secretary Campbell concurred. He
looked reproachfully at Wentworth, who excused himself apologetically.

"The floggings had been administered before I had a chance to
intervene, sir. But, in any case, I truly doubt whether any more
would have been heard of the matter had it not been for Bent. How
it came to his ears I don't know, but Constable Willbow told me
that as soon as the offenders were released, Bent's clerk came
sniffing round. And Marsden could have heard the story from
Read, I imagine."

"No doubt he could. Well"—Macquarie's tone was resigned
now, rather than angry—"what mischief is Judge Bent making of
it?"

Wentworth avoided his eyes. "All three men have made
affidavits, sir, and Bent is said to have added them to his damned
petition. I'm also informed that he promised all three of the men he
would put their cases, in the strongest terms, to Lord Bathurst.
It's . . . oh, the devil! It's unfortunate, sir, and I regret exceedingly that I must add to your difficulties, but I felt it my duty to
make you aware of what is going on."

"Thank you, D'Arcy," the Governor said. "I am grateful for
your loyalty."

And indeed, he reflected, he was—loyalty to his cause was at a
premium these days. There would, he knew, be no peace, no end

to the constant pressure being put upon him, until Jeffrey Hart Bent was officially relieved of his office and removed from New South Wales. Bent's malice was such that it could not be assuaged. . . . Macquarie's frown returned. He could only hope and pray that Lord Bathurst would give no credence to Bent's petition or to the spate of letters reaching the Colonial Office from his vitriolic pen.

D'Arcy Wentworth managed to strike a lighter note before taking his leave. "Bent and Nicholas have been summoned to appear before my bench charged, once again, with refusal to pay the toll when using the Parramatta turnpike." He chuckled with cynical amusement. "They will not appear, of course—they'll send Moore to represent them. But Dwyer and Cullen, the toll keepers, are ready to swear that the judge threatened to commit them to jail for demanding payment. I believe that they both spoke of the matter to Your Excellency yesterday?" The Governor nodded, and Wentworth's smile widened.

"On the last occasion that a summons was issued against Judge Bent and his friend, I fined them forty shillings apiece. This time, sir, their fine shall be doubled, and I will send a posse of constables to collect it!"

"Good," Macquarie said, but there was a tired, resentful edge to his voice, and again aware of this, he clapped a friendly hand on Dr. Wentworth's shoulder. "We try, do we not, to bring law and order to this colony? But it is not easy when the man who should enforce it goes out of his way to make mockery of our judiciary. But perhaps Mr. De Lancey may provide an answer. I shall be interested to meet him, at all events. You'll dine with us on Friday, I trust—you and your lady?"

"We shall be happy to, sir," Wentworth assured him.

When he had gone, the Governor, his secretary in attendance, returned to his office. He signed the necessary documents to signify his official agreement with the findings of the *Conway* court of inquiry and asked, as he gave these to the secretary, "What of the unfortunate convicts Barlow brought out? How many survived, John?"

"I'll check, sir," Campbell promised. "I have a note some-where . . . ah, yes, here it is. One hundred and seventy-two male convicts were embarked at Cork. Two died of natural causes before the *Conway* made port at Rio. Three were hanged for mutiny, four died of their wounds after the soldiers fired on them—including one man, landed at Hobart following amputation. Nine dead, in all, but . . ." He continued despondently. "I fear there are likely to be more deaths. Twenty-three were admitted to hospital here, sir, suffering from the scurvy. Those who were fit were transferred to Parramatta yesterday. At his request, Ensign Dean went in command of their escort."

The Governor was unable to conceal his outraged feelings. "After all my appeals to the Colonial Office and the Transport Commission, men like this dastardly fellow Barlow are still given command of convict transports. And there's no one on board with sufficient authority to ensure that the prisoners are properly treated. I've requested again and again that naval surgeons should be appointed and that responsibility for the prisoners should be vested in them, not the masters . . . but my requests are ignored."

"Do you wish to write again on the subject, sir?" Campbell inquired.

The Governor, in answer, reached for his quill. "I'll go further, damme, John! I'll draw up a set of regulations and demand that the commissioners adopt them." He wrote rapidly, anger driving him. First, in unequivocal terms, he advocated the appointment of a surgeon-superintendent to each and every convict transport leaving the United Kingdom:

> Such officers should be vested with adequate authority. And they, and the ships' masters, should be provided with written instructions for their mutual guidance at the commencement of the voyage.

He paused, lost in thought, and then wrote on:

> Convicts . . . should not be confined or punished without the surgeon-superintendent's authority. The master and officer commanding the guard should be obliged to obey the surgeon-superintendent's orders so far as they respect the convicts, in like manner as the commands of a civil magistrate, when given to suppress riots or to enforce the law.

After a while, the impetus of his anger lessened and he looked up, to meet Campbell's concerned gaze. "You think I'm tilting at windmills, do you not, John?" he said.

"No, sir, nothing of the kind." Campbell's lips tightened. "After sitting on the *Conway* court of inquiry, I feel as strongly as Your Excellency that this state of affairs must not be permitted to continue. Masters of Barlow's stamp are the exception, rather than the rule, sir—conditions on the transports *have* improved, there's no doubt. But I'm fully in agreement with your proposal to draw up regulations, so that even with a man like Barlow in command, prisoners cannot be treated as he treated those consigned to his care on this voyage. Their conditions were intolerable. When Dr. Redfern made his inspection, sir, he said that no windsails had been rigged and that he did not think the air scuttles had been opened for months!"

"Ah, Redfern . . . of course." Macquarie passed the sheet of closely written paper across the desk. "Show him these notes, John, and invite him to add to them. He's a most competent surgeon—let him draw up detailed regulations, and I will send copies both to Lord Bathurst and the Transport commissioners." He sighed heavily. "We will also forward copies of the evidence given at your court of inquiry. Perhaps, in the light of *that,* they will give serious consideration to my proposals, instead of ignoring them!"

"I hope most sincerely that they will, sir," Campbell responded gravely. He gathered up the papers. "I'll deal with the matter right away, unless Your Excellency requires me for any other reason?"

The Governor shook his head. He felt unusually tired and out of sorts, but . . . "My wife's not back, is she?" he asked.

"No, sir, not as far as I know."

"Then," Macquarie decided, making an effort to shrug off his weariness, "I shall study Lord Bathurst's last dispatch, John, and start drafting a reply . . . bearing in mind that Jeffrey Bent's damned petition will reach him by the same mail! And doubtless, because I had those three scoundrels flogged for trespassing in the Domain, I'll be accused of tyranny or worse. I've no appointments for this afternoon, have I?"

"One, at four-thirty, sir." Apologetically, the secretary opened the engagement book lying at his elbow, and the Governor read the name, his brow furrowed. "Young Richard Tempest? What the deuce does he want? Did he tell you?"

"He did not say precisely, sir, save that the matter was of some importance." Campbell hesitated and then added, "I understand that Mr. Tempest has lately returned from the land grant on the Macquarie River—the grant that was allocated to Lieutenant Broome, sir, in which they have entered into partnership. He told me that he had spent several days there, with Mr. Broome's brother and sister, and his betrothed, Miss O'Malley."

The Governor stifled a yawn. He was most infernally tired, he thought, and found himself hoping that Elizabeth would not linger over her picnic and the carriage drive for too long. She could join young Tempest and himself for afternoon tea and, perhaps, spare him a lengthy interview. The boy probably wanted a grant of his own, adjacent to Broome's, but . . . until the new lands were opened for settlement, it would not be possible. The government surveyors had more work to do on maps and measurements, and the road had to be improved before he could permit general settlement. He was planning to make fifty-acre grants to carefully selected applicants who had been born in the colony and who were of proven agricultural experience—a plan very close to his heart. Tempest could be included in it, of course, when the time came. He was an admirable young man, with a fine record of naval service—the type of settler who should obviously be encouraged, with sufficient means to compensate for his lack of practical experience on the land.

"If you would rather postpone the appointment, sir," Campbell began, "I can inform Mr. Tempest or—"

"No, no." The Governor shook his head resignedly. "I'll see him, since it's arranged. Have you His Lordship's last letter?"

"It's here, sir." The secretary laid the letter before him and withdrew.

Macquarie felt a twinge of annoyance as he scanned past the opening pleasantries. It was a strangely ambiguous letter, appearing to give support to the views of Jeffrey Bent concerning emancipist attorneys, while condemning both the Bents for the manner in which they had sought to enforce their ban. However . . . He found the section he was looking for:

> The remonstrances of Mr. J. Hart Bent against the employment of convicts in the confidential situation of

attorneys was equally proper, nor am I disposed to sanction
their employment in the colony under any other circumstances than those which existed at the time, *namely there
being but one other attorney in the colony* . . .

And now there was not even that one, Lachlan Macquarie
reflected, giving vent to a dry chuckle. Yet he had dismissed
Moore from office with reason enough to convince Bathurst—and
with a certain satisfaction. The unexpected arrival of George De
Lancey might, therefore, prove providential, since he must have
brought with him Colonial Office sanction to his employment in
the colony's judiciary.

He read on, deciding as he did so to postpone writing his reply
until after he had made the newly arrived barrister's acquaintance.
There were other matters, of even greater urgency, of which the
Colonial Secretary must be informed. . . . He reached for the
now-bulging folder of the architect Greenway's designs for a new
courthouse and the proposed lighthouse on South Head.

And . . . he cursed silently as, with predictable destruc-
tiveness, another shower of plaster from the ceiling of his office
descended to spatter the papers spread out on his desk. His official
residence was falling to ruin, but Lord Bathurst had not, as yet,
authorized funds for its repair.

CHAPTER XIX

Rick Tempest walked the short distance from his sister's house on Pitt Street to Government House at a brisk pace, anxious to be in good time for his appointment with the Governor.

In his pocket, carefully wrapped, were the pebbles Katie had found in the Macquarie River and, in addition to these, the larger one he himself had found, concealed in a crevice of rock a few yards farther downstream. The find had excited him, for he had not expected to discover more than Katie had done, but there, deposited by some previous spring or autumn flood, had been a nugget the size of a walnut, its soft yellow luster reflected in the swirling water of the river.

He had prized it out, the conviction growing that it was not fool's gold but the genuine precious metal. He had shown it to no one, not even to Katie, lest he raise false hopes, and as yet had not attempted to have it assayed, since the only man in Sydney capable of giving an expert opinion was an emancipist named Hensall, who worked at the mint. And Hensall was in trouble with the Governor. . . . Rick slowed his pace somewhat as he strode past the sentry at the Government House gates.

He wished that Justin Broome had been in Sydney to share the excitement—and the responsibility—of his find, but the *Emu* had been sent to Newcastle just before he himself had returned from Pengallon, and they had missed each other by twenty-four hours.

There were rumors that both the King's ships were shortly to be dispensed with and that the *Kangaroo* would be leaving almost immediately. Old Silas Crabbe had paid him a visit only that morning, with a tale of bad relations between Captain Jeffrey and the Governor—brought to a head, the *Kangaroo*'s master had asserted, by Jeffrey's refusal to permit his ship to be sent on errands he considered improper for "one of His Majesty's ships of war."

"The reason he would not permit the *Kangaroo* to convey reliefs for the Coal River garrison was not hard to find," Crabbe had said, with a dry chuckle. "It was starting to blow a gale, Mr. Tempest, and the commissary officer wanted a few tons of coal brought here, on the return passage. 'Twas that gave him the excuse, see—but 'twas the gale he didn't like! Commander Forster made no objection—he took the *Emu* out right away."

He would miss old Crabbe, Rick thought, but he would shed no tears when the *Kangaroo* hove up her anchor and set sail for England. Probably the only people who were likely to regret her going would be the Bents and Colonel and Mrs. Molle, with whom Captain Jeffrey and his wife had conspicuously allied themselves during their stay in the colony.

Reaching the door of Government House, he paused to remove his hat and then lifted the ornate brass door-knocker. A servant answered his summons and—evidently acting on instructions—ushered him into John Campbell's office.

"Ah, you're here, Tempest!" The secretary sounded agitated. "I'm not sure that His Excellency will be able to see you after all, but . . . I will ascertain. Is the matter urgent?"

"It is important, Mr. Campbell," Rick assured him. "And I do have an appointment, sir."

"Yes, yes, I know you have. But—" Campbell mopped at his heated brow with a handkerchief and hesitated, as if wondering whether or not the circumstances required explanation. Deciding finally that they did, he went on in a lowered voice, "There has been a most unfortunate accident. Mrs. Macquarie was returning in her carriage from an outing when a child ran out in front of the horses. Big, the coachman, had no time to pull them up—the poor young soul was struck and killed instantly. As you may imagine, Tempest, both Their Excellencies are gravely upset . . . Mrs. Macquarie is in tears. I . . . that is, I truly cannot say whether His Excellency will receive you. I will ask him, I . . . be seated, if you please."

Rick took the chair the Governor's secretary had indicated, in two minds whether to go or stay. He could, indeed, imagine Mrs. Macquarie's distress; she was a kindly and very softhearted woman who loved all children, and the fact that the victim of the accident had been a child would add immeasurably to her distress. Clearly no blame for the child's death could be attached to her, for she had not been driving the carriage, but . . . He waited, ready to accept his dismissal, should the Governor decide to cancel his appointment.

In one respect it might even be desirable, he decided. His marriage to Katie was to be celebrated in less than a week's time, which would preclude his returning immediately to Pengallon. But he would have to go back—and with Justin, if it could be arranged—in order to make a full and careful investigation, with the right tools, of the prospects their land possessed. Obviously the discovery of gold in any quantity would obviate the necessity to stock and farm the grant, and , . . damn it, they would both be rich men!

Rick's fingers closed about the small package in his coat pocket. If the Governor put off his appointment, he would show the small pebbles to the silversmith, Hensall, and obtain his expert opinion as to their nature. The fellow was said to be a rogue, but there was no one else he could consult, and if Hensall was in trouble, he could probably be coerced into keeping a still tongue in his head, since he would not want to invite more trouble. Indeed, it might be wise, on all counts, to delay reporting his find to the Governor, at least until he was certain that Katie's pebbles and his nugget were really gold.

John Campbell returned, looking anxious, and conscious now of relief, Rick rose to meet him.

"I'm sorry," the secretary began, "and His Excellency has asked me to apologize to you, but he cannot receive you now. A coroner's inquest will have to be arranged, and I am going now to offer condolences to the unfortunate child's parents. I—"

"It's of no consequence, Mr. Campbell," Rick assured him. "I should not dream of intruding at such a time."

"I can make another appointment, if you wish, Mr. Tempest. But"—Campbell brightened—"you have been invited to dine with Their Excellencies tomorrow evening, have you not? With your sister, Mrs. Dawson, and Miss O'Malley?"

"Yes, that's so, sir," Rick confirmed.

"Then you'll have an opportunity to speak to the Governor then, if that will serve?"

"It will serve admirably, sir. Thank you."

"Thank *you*, Mr. Tempest." Campbell was already searching through some papers on his desk, and Rick delayed his departure no longer.

He found Hensall about to leave work. He was a small, shifty-eyed man of uncertain age, who eyed his unexpected caller with suspicion and endeavored to excuse himself on the plea of a vague but urgent appointment. However, when Rick told him that he would be well paid for his time, his manner swiftly changed to obsequiousness, and he agreed readily to regard the matter as confidential.

His tests were thorough and competently carried out, despite a complaint that the pebbles were too small, and Rick resisted the temptation to produce the nugget. Hensall displayed a cautious curiosity, but on being told sharply to mind his own business, he lapsed into silence and worked on, albeit a trifle sullenly.

"It's gold all right, sir," he announced finally, putting his scales back into a drawer, and eyeing Rick speculatively. "But with such small samples, there's not much more I can tell you. And since you won't tell me where you found 'em, I can't even make a guess as to the chance of your finding more. Maybe you will, maybe you won't . . . but I'd say the gold's there for the finding." He asked several questions as to the geological nature of the site of the find, which Rick evaded, and on being paid the agreed sum, he grinned and thanked him courteously enough.

"Glad to see you're settling your debt in honest English money, sir, and not in mine."

"Yours, Mr. Hensall?" Rick exclaimed, startled. "Are you a self-confessed coiner, then?"

The shifty eyes held an oddly defiant gleam. "That's what the swine of a judge sent me out here for," the man admitted. "But what I meant was that I was the one who worked on them Spanish dollars the *Semarang* brought out . . . turned 'em into holey dollars and dumps, to serve as legal currency. Odd, when you come to think about it, sir, ain't it? In the bloomin' penal colony of New South Wales I'm paid for doing what I was convicted for back in the old country!"

"Very odd," Rick agreed noncommittally.

"And to top it all," Hensall went on, "I'm pardoned, and the sodding Governor orders me to be flogged without a trial for trespassin' in his precious Domain! But I'll tell you this, sir,

General Macquarie'll live to regret what he done. Sendin' a petition to the House o' Parliament we are, to ask for justice. And—"

"I think," Rick warned sternly, "that you had best say no more, Mr. Hensall. Talking out of turn, about this matter *or* about the assay you've just undertaken for me, will get you into more trouble than you can conceive of. I give you good day."

His conscience worried him, however, as he walked back to Pitt Street. The fact that his find had been confirmed to be alluvial gold laid an added burden of responsibility on him, which he longed to share. But the house in Pitt Street had been transformed into a purely feminine domain in which, he soon learned, his presence was unwelcome . . . for Katie was being fitted with her bridal gown.

Abigail was there, with Julia and Dorothea; Rachel Broome had come down from Ulva to stay for the wedding; and Jessica, with her baby son, had been there since morning—she and Kate Lamerton were, it appeared, assisting the seamstress in the fashioning of the gown.

"We had not expected you back so soon, Rick," Julia told him tartly when he encountered her in the hall. "And you surely know that it is unlucky for the bridegroom even to glimpse his bride's wedding dress before the day."

Rick, compelled to admit his ignorance of this superstition, suffered her to banish him to the garden, puzzled by the change in her. From the time of their arrival in Sydney, Julia had been offhand and even spiteful to both Katie and himself, but with their wedding day approaching, her attitude seemed to have softened, certainly toward Katie and, to a markedly lesser degree, to himself. Perhaps, he thought, as he made his way into the rose garden, which Frances Spence had created with such loving care, perhaps the fact that Katie had invited the two Dawson girls to act as her maids of honor had contributed to Julia's recent change of heart.

He found Dickon in the garden, playing with a ball, and the boy's face lit up at the sight of him. Rick grinned at him, holding out his hand for the ball.

"We're not wanted, Dickon old son," he said, miming the words in elaborately executed gestures. "So we'll have to bear each other company for a while."

Not that he minded. He was, Rick realized, inordinately fond of Abigail's handicapped son, despite his handicap—or possibly because of it. Dickon was an entrancing little character, possessed of a happy nature, courage, and more than ordinary good looks. He bore no ill will to anyone—not even to Julia, who teased and mocked him unmercifully—and, as he had proved when he had accompanied their small party up the hazardous road to Bathurst, he was an accomplished horseman, with a knowledge of bushcraft that verged on the uncanny.

With Winyara and others of his tribe, small Dickon had been surprisingly at home, seemingly able to make himself understood without the smallest difficulty. He went hunting with them, fished with them, and enjoyed an intimacy with each and every one that even William Broome had marveled at. These days, he and Alex, the Dawsons' son, spent most of their time at Upwey with Tim, while Abigail divided her time between Sydney and the farm . . . compelled to do so, Rick knew, by Julia's oft-expressed dislike of rural life. Dorothea, though more amenable than her elder sister, tended to side with her in such matters, and Abigail gave in to them in order to keep the peace.

Abigail had changed during the past few months; she had changed even more than Julia had done, but . . . Rick flung the ball high into the air, sending Dickon flying after it. Lucy's death and that of Frances Spence—now long since confirmed—had had a profound effect on his sister, making her . . . what? Stronger, certainly, and perhaps more conscious of her duty, both to her husband and to her stepchildren, which made her—although a year younger than himself—seem older, more mature than he was. Even a possible confidante, with whom, in Tim's and Justin's absence, he could share the burden of his momentous discovery?

Rick frowned and decided against it; Abby, bless her heart, had cares enough of her own, and Tim Dawson would be here in a day or so, in time for the wedding. Justin, too, Jessica had told him; the *Emu* was not expected to stay for long at Coal River.

Dickon retrieved his ball and hurled it back, but Rick's attention had wandered from their game and the catch slipped through his fingers. Laughing at his own clumsiness, he bent to pick the ball from among the rosebushes, and as he straightened up, he glimpsed Katie's small, piquant face in one of the upper windows. She had not seen him, and mindful of Julia's injunction, he looked quickly away, but the memory lingered and his heart quickened its beat, for she had looked so lovely and so desirable, with her golden hair entwined in the veiled crown of flowers that she would wear when she became his wife.

Dear God, Rick thought, how fortunate he was to have won her love, to be taking Katie to wife! He loved her so deeply and passionately—aye, and so jealously, too—that the next few days, the days of waiting, would seem endless. But . . . Dickon was beside him, tapping his arm and pointing. Supposing that the boy was reproaching him for his remissness in not continuing their game, he held up the ball, preparing to throw it, but Dickon shook his head and, running to the edge of the lawn, gestured excitedly toward the cove.

Rick followed him, to see the *Emu* come gliding into the anchorage, the topmen already aloft furling sail.

"Good lad, Dickon!" he exclaimed. "But how the deuce did you know how anxious I am to see that particular ship make port?"

The signal gun started to fire the customary salute; Dickon, unable to hear its echoing boom, grinned back at him delightedly, mouthing something that Rick could only guess meant that the boy shared his pleasure at the sight of the King's ship. The *Emu*, smartly handled, dropped anchor within hailing distance of the *Kangaroo*, and, a few minutes later, her gig was lowered . . . Captain Jeffrey, Rick surmised cynically, exercising his prerogative as senior officer to summon James Forster to report to him. Which meant that Justin, as the *Emu*'s first lieutenant, would have to remain on board.

He gave Dickon a parting hug, pointed to the *Emu* in explanation, and set off at a run for the Governor's wharf. The harbor master's boat took him out to the newly arrived King's ship, and as he had expected, he found Justin on her quarterdeck.

"You're in a hurry, Rick," Justin greeted him. "Not, I trust, bad news?"

Conscious of the nugget in his pocket, Rick shook his head. "The reverse, I'm happy to say. But I need to talk with you, Justin. And my sister's house isn't the place for serious conversation at the present moment . . . my bride is having her gown fitted there, aided by, among others, your wife and son."

"Then we'll talk in my cabin." Justin raised his voice. "Mr. Mercer, be good enough to relieve me of the deck, if you please."

He issued a few brisk orders and then gestured to the main hatchway. "After you, Mr. Tempest."

In the privacy of Justin's cabin, a beaker of claret in his hand, Rick unburdened himself, the nugget laid carefully on the cot blanket, together with Katie's small pebbles, in proof of his claim.

"And you say there's no doubt that these are gold?" Justin, who had listened without interruption to the account of their discovery, picked up the nugget and stared down at it in unconcealed astonishment.

"No doubt at all," Rick assured him. He repeated the details Hensall had supplied. "The fellow knows his trade, for all he's something of a rogue. This is alluvial gold, Justin, of high quality, but I cannot tell you the value of the nugget, because I thought it wiser not to let Hensall see it."

Justin nodded approvingly. "Have you told anyone else about it? Or reported your find to the Governor?"

Rick shook his head. "I was unable to see the Governor, although I called on him this afternoon with the intention of reporting it to him. Mrs. Macquarie had an accident with her carriage. . . ." Again he explained and saw Justin's brow furrow.

"You know, Rick," he said, after a moment's thoughtful pause, "I don't think you should tell anyone at all, including His Excellency, until we can be sure about the extent of the gold deposits. It could cause immense trouble, and we'd have every bad character in the colony—escapers, bushrangers, malcontents—starting a wild search for gold all over the new lands."

Rick's spirits lifted. Justin, he reflected gratefully, was a level-headed, practical fellow, and what he had just said made excellent sense. "I arrived at the same conclusion myself," he asserted. "Which was why I was in such a hurry to talk to you—to suggest that we go up to Pengallon together, just the two of us, at the earliest possible opportunity, and make a thorough investigation. The trouble is, though, I'm no geologist. Are you?"

Justin shrugged. "I picked up a certain amount from the *Investigator*'s scientists, but it was a long time ago, and my knowledge is a mite rusty. I'd recognize gold-bearing rock easily enough, but alluvial gold is another matter. Apart from finding the nugget the way you did, I fancy one would need to wash and sieve the sand from the river bottom, which should not be beyond us, should it? If there is gold in the Macquarie River, we'll find it, Rick. When could you come with me?"

"I'm being wed on Tuesday." Rick reddened. "And I've arranged to spend a week at the late Mr. Spence's farm at Portland Place—Katie is eager to practice her riding. I . . . well, I would not like to cut our stay there short."

"Of course not. But after that—you'll leave Katie here, will you not?"

Rick hesitated. He was reluctant to leave his bride, but she, he knew, would not view with any favor the prospect of a second trek out to Pengallon, so soon after her first, none-too-happy visit. He had taken the lease of an officer's house at Farm Cove for six months, during which time he hoped to have the building work on their grant completed and the stock driven up—a plan that would involve his periodic absence from Sydney. But Katie had agreed to this; she would understand, surely, if he told her why he must go up to the grant with Justin sooner than they had anticipated. And she need not remain by herself in the rented house in Sydney; if she preferred to do so, she could pay her promised visit to Ulva and Rachel Broome. It was on their way to the new road; he could leave her there and pick her up when he returned.

He glanced across at Justin. "I can fit in with you," he said. "Katie will understand—after all, it was she who discovered the gold before I did. When can you obtain leave?"

"Depending on the date of Captain Jeffrey's departure with the *Kangaroo*, we are hoping to get the caulkers to work on the *Emu*. That will allow us all—what? A couple of weeks, whilst she's careened." Justin hesitated. "The chances are, Rick, that I shall not be going with her to England."

"The devil you won't!" Rick was startled, even angry. "For God's sake, Justin, you are not resigning your commission, are you? That would be a great pity."

Justin shook his head. "No . . . no, I'm not. Commander Forster has promised to recommend me for the command of the *Elizabeth*. It isn't certain by any manner of means that I shall be given it, but I understand that my rival for the appointment is our mutual friend Meredith, on Jeffrey's recommendation."

"Then it's yours," Rick assured him, relieved. He consulted his pocket watch and rose, offering his hand. "Accept my congratulations, my dear fellow. And as to our visit to Pengallon, let us endeavor to make it within the next three weeks, shall we? At all events, as soon as possible."

"We'll do that, Rick. And keep the matter strictly between ourselves. I take it Hensall won't talk?"

"I warned him of the consequences if he did," Rick said. "But I do not believe I gave him enough information for it to matter greatly if he does." Justin handed him the nugget and they both smiled, as Rick returned it to its wrapping and then put it carefully into his breast pocket. "You're bidden to my nuptials," he added. "Jessica has the invitation. I trust the fact that—er—diplomacy compelled me to invite Captain and Mrs. Jeffrey also will not deter you from accepting!"

"It will not, you can take my word for that!" Justin laughed, with genuine amusement. "The reverse is likely to be the case, I fear. I'll call away a boat for you."

The gig, Rick saw when they emerged on deck, was still tied up to the *Kangaroo*'s midship chains. For whatever reason Jeffrey had summoned James Forster, they had been closeted together for almost an hour, and he wondered fleetingly whether Jeffrey was making a last attempt to secure command of the new colonial sloop *Elizabeth* for the unpleasant young Meredith. But he did not voice his thoughts. Justin was the first native-born Australian to be commissioned into the Royal Navy, and Governor Macquarie— just as he had with Dr. D'Arcy Wentworth's elder son, who had been given an ensign's commission in his own regiment—would see to it that his patronage met with the desired result . . . and was not challenged.

He glanced across the anchorage to Robert Campbell's yard. The *Elizabeth* was still in the stocks, but she was almost ready for launching, and just for a moment Rick felt a twinge of envy. The sea had been his life since he was twelve years old, and there were many times when he regretted having abandoned that life, but . . . He thrust the thought from his mind, and his fingers closed about the rail, the knuckles gleaming white.

For the Lord's sake, he reproached himself, the decision had been made; he could not go back on it now. He was a settler and about to marry the girl he loved, to make his home here and, God willing, raise a family and, perhaps, find gold on his land and make a fortune . . . this was no time to envy any man.

The boat was lowered and alongside, the bowman hooking his

boat hook to the chains and looking up expectantly. Rick wrung Justin's hand and climbed down to the waiting boat with the ease and speed of long practice. Seated in the sternsheets beside the *Emu*'s young midshipman, he raised a hand in farewell and the oars splashed into the water.

Ahead of them loomed the convict transport *Conway*, her dark bulk silhouetted against the golden glow of the sunset, and the midshipman said excitedly, "They arrested her master just now, sir, and took him to the jail. I was on watch, sir, and I saw them."

"Were you, now?" Rick was not particularly interested. He had heard that a court of inquiry was sitting, but, he reflected cynically, it was not the first time that the master of a convict ship had been guilty of maltreating his unwilling passengers, and it probably would not be the last. It might, however, serve as a salutary example to those who came after the *Conway*'s commander.

The boat came smoothly alongside the Governor's wharf, and with a word of thanks to the midshipman, Rick stepped ashore. He was passing the gates of Government House when a tall figure emerged, holding up a hand to attract his attention, and he halted, realizing that the man was a stranger. He was well dressed, his green coat of immaculate cut, tight-fitting gray overalls tucked into well-polished Hessian boots, after the manner of a soldier—a cavalryman—in civilian dress.

"Can I be of service to you, sir?" he inquired politely.

"Indeed you can, sir," the newcomer answered. He bowed, matching Rick's courtesy. "I am a recent arrival in Sydney— George De Lancey, a passenger from the *Conway*. And you, I take it, are a naval officer?" He gestured to the boat, now on the way back to the *Emu*. "But not, I trust, a stranger, from whom it would be of no use to ask directions?"

Rick introduced himself. "I'm no longer in His Majesty's Navy, but I'm no stranger, sir. Where is it that you wish to go?"

De Lancey smiled. It was a friendly, pleasant smile, and Rick found himself liking him instinctively. "I've been bidden to dine at the officers' mess of the Forty-sixth Regiment, Mr. Tempest, by— er—Colonel Molle, who is, I believe, their commanding officer. I should be most obliged if you could set me on my way. I found the Governor's residence easily enough and have just left cards on His Excellency, but I must confess that I am now lost. Is the mess far from here?"

"No distance at all, Mr. De Lancey. I'll walk with you."
Colonel Molle, Rick thought, as they fell into step together, had
wasted no time. The *Conway*'s passenger was clearly a gentleman
of some substance and the type whom Molle would be eager to
recruit to the elitist faction. The officers of the 46th were under
strict orders to permit no emancipists to darken the doors of their
mess or to sit at table with them, and even wealthy merchants and
shipowners, like Simeon Lord, had been pointedly excluded at the
colonel's stern behest. The sole exception was the Irish baronet,
Sir Henry Brown Hayes, whose crime—he had been accused of
abducting a Quaker girl—Molle had declared ought rightly to be a
matter more for congratulation than censure.

Wise now in the devious ways of Sydney society, Rick made no
mention of Molle's prejudices as they skirted the residence of the
judge advocate and that designated for Judge Jeffrey Bent and
crossed the Tank Stream, to emerge into George Street. Instead, he
pointed out landmarks and replied to his companion's questions,
learning no more about him than the fact that, as he had supposed,
George De Lancey had been a cavalry officer and had served in the
Peninsular campaign.

They parted amicably on the edge of the 46th's regimental
parade ground, both of them expressing the hope that they would
shortly meet again, and Rick set off for Pitt Street to find, when he
reached his sister's house, that the female celebrations were still in
progress and his presence an embarrassment.

A trifle put out, he ate his meal in solitary state and retired to
bed.

CHAPTER XX

Katie was conscious of a feeling of elation when she entered the reception room at Government House on Rick's arm. As they stood together, awaiting their turn to be announced, other guests crowded round them, to wish them well and offer congratulations on their forthcoming marriage.

Even Captain and Mrs. Jeffrey—for whom, it seemed, departure from the colony was imminent—voiced their approval, Mrs. Jeffrey going so far as to plant a chill little kiss on her cheek, which Katie accepted with forbearance and what she hoped was a convincing smile.

"It is a great relief to Captain Jeffrey and myself," she announced effusively, "that our little orphan of the storm should have found not only a home here but also a husband. Indeed, I take some small measure of credit for bringing the two of you together, Miss O'Malley."

Mindful of her manners, Katie offered no contradiction of this singularly exaggerated claim, and Mrs. Jeffrey passed on, bestowing her smiles like largess among those with whom she felt herself on terms of social equality and, very pointedly, ignoring the others.

By contrast, Mrs. Macquarie's greeting was genuinely warm and friendly, her kiss spontaneous. She shook Rick's hand and congratulated him on his good fortune, beaming at Katie as she spoke. The Governor was deep in conversation with a tall, dark-haired man in elegant evening dress, who had his back turned to the advancing line of guests, and as they continued to talk, Mrs. Macquarie touched her husband's arm.

"Lachlan dear," she reminded him gently. "Miss O'Malley and Mr. Tempest have arrived, and we are shortly to attend their wedding. I feel sure that Mr. De Lancey would wish to be introduced to Miss O'Malley, who is a countrywoman of his."

Katie heard his name an instant before George De Lancey turned to face her, but even so, the shock of seeing him again was so unexpected that it took her breath away. He had changed, she realized; he looked at once older and more assured—no longer the diffident young law student she remembered, but a man, with a sprinkling of silver hair at his temples and lines on his bronzed countenance that had not been there before. He wore a mustache and whiskers, and these, too, made him seem unfamiliar, like a vision—or a ghost—from the long-dead past.

This realization enabled Katie to regain her composure, to take his hand, to smile, even to murmur a greeting in response to his. But the look in his eyes set her heart beating wildly, and she could feel the color leaping to her cheeks as she met his gaze, read the question in it, and then hurriedly lowered her own, fearing that Rick might sense that something was amiss.

Rick, however, had his hand extended, and the two men acknowledged each other cordially by name.

"Introductions would appear to be unnecessary," the Governor observed, with some surprise. "You already know each other, do you not? See, Elizabeth my dear—so much for our efforts to make Mr. De Lancey feel at home. He has already done that for himself! Is the world shrinking, De Lancey? Did you make the acquaintance of Tempest and his betrothed in America?"

"Mr. Tempest was kind enough to give me directions yesterday evening, when I contrived to lose myself," George De Lancey said. "And Miss O'Malley and I are old friends, sir, from my student days. We both hail from Boston, by a happy coincidence."

He made it sound as if their relationship had been purely a youthful one, and Katie seized eagerly on his words, grateful for his swift reading of the situation and the pains he was taking to spare her embarrassment. But the mute question was still in his eyes, belying the casual tone of his voice, and she knew that he had not forgotten what they had once meant to each other, any more than she had, for all the intervening years.

The Macquaries were introducing him to some of their other guests—Abigail and Tim Dawson, Julia, Captain and Mrs. Jeffrey, and Simeon Lord among them. Dr. D'Arcy Wentworth, to whom he was evidently already known, greeted him affably and extended the introductions to his wife and younger son, and to Dr. and Mrs. Redfern. But when dinner was announced and they took their places at the long, candle-lit table, Katie found herself beside him, with Rick on her other side.

"What in the world," George asked, as if the question had been wrung from him, "what in the whole wide world brought you here, Katie?"

She started to tell him, but Captain Jeffrey overhearing his question, cut her short.

"My ship, sir, brought her here—His Majesty's ship *Kangaroo*. Miss O'Malley was the sole survivor of one of your Yankee traders, the *Providence*, which went down in a South Atlantic storm."

The *Kangaroo*'s commander launched into a graphic account of the rescue, holding the attention of the whole table . . . just as he had, Katie recalled, on the first occasion that she had been invited to a meal at Government House. This time, however, in Rick's presence, while giving his first lieutenant credit for the actual rescue, Captain Jeffrey was mainly concerned with the care he and his wife had lavished on their "orphan of the storm" and the fact that the bodies of the American longboat crew had been buried at sea, with full naval honors.

Katie sat, frozen-faced and fighting against tears, as Captain Jeffrey talked on, oblivious alike of Mrs. Macquarie's tactful attempts to interrupt him and the Governor's frowning disapproval.

Rick's hand found hers and held it in wordless sympathy, as Jeffrey concluded unctuously, "We did the right thing, Mr. De Lancey, by all your countrymen, I'd have you know. Miss O'Malley's father served against us in the American Navy—and God knows, sir, having been a prisoner of war and subjected to diabolical ill-treatment at their hands, I had no reason to honor them. Nonetheless, sir, on my orders, all the bodies we recovered were consigned to the deep under the American flag. Indeed, I—"

"Captain Jeffrey!" The Governor's interruption was forceful, his tone cold and brooking no argument. "You are laboring under a misapprehension. Mr. De Lancey served with our armies in the Peninsular campaign and at the glorious victory of Waterloo. His brother, Sir William De Lancey, was the Duke's chief of staff and quartermaster general, and he lost his life at Waterloo. No family served the King and the loyalists' cause with more distinction, I can assure you, in both conflicts with the American colonists. You will be good enough, sir, to tender Mr. De Lancey your apology for any offense your words may have caused him."

Captain Jeffrey stared at him, with jaw dropping, his round, red face draining of color. "Damme!" he exclaimed, attempting bluster. "I'd no idea. I understood that Mr. De Lancey was an American, I . . . the devil take it, sir, no one told me any different. I . . . ah . . . you have my apology, sir, of course. As His Excellency says, a misapprehension, for which I ask your indulgence."

To Katie's relief, George De Lancey accepted the proffered olive branch with quiet dignity, and the dinner progressed, the conversation, if initially a trifle strained, swiftly becoming general. Julia, who was seated on George's left, contrived to monopolize him, exerting all the charm she possessed and smiling demurely at his sallies. For once, Katie was grateful to her, conscious that her own ability to sustain any conversation—even with Rick—was sadly lacking.

The meal over at last, the Governor's kilted piper marched in, and under cover of his lively playing, she heard George say urgently, "Katie, for God's sake . . . I must talk to you! Please, my sweet Katie . . . is there anywhere in this place where we can be alone, even for a few minutes?"

There was the garden, Katie thought—perhaps they could be alone for a little while in the garden. It was the custom, in the heat of summer, for the viceregal guests to stroll out there in groups, in order to gain the benefit of the cool evening breeze blowing in from the cove, and if she chose her moment carefully, she might manage to slip away unnoticed. There was a small arbor, with a summerhouse to the rear, not far from the stables, where Jessica, she remembered, had told her that Mrs. Macquarie sometimes took tea.

In a tense whisper, she explained its location and saw George nod his understanding.

"I'll be there," he assured her. "And I'll wait for you to join me."

"I can't promise," Katie began. "But I'll try. I—" Mrs. Macquarie rose, signing for the ladies of the party to follow her, and the Governor and his gentlemen were left to their port and cigars.

Escape proved easier than she had anticipated. Coffee was served on the veranda, and Mrs. Jeffrey, exclaiming that she was overcome by the heat, led the exodus into the garden. Katie followed half a dozen others at a discreet distance and, as she had hoped, managed to slip away without anyone appearing to notice her absence. She entered the darkened summerhouse, and within minutes George De Lancey emerged from the shadows to join her.

"Is it true," he demanded abruptly, "that you are to wed Richard Tempest on—damn it, on Tuesday? Three days hence?"

"Yes," Katie confirmed, her voice not quite steady. "Yes, it is true."

"He saved your life, if one is to believe that insufferable fellow Jeffrey?"

"Yes. Most men would—would have left me for dead. My father was, and all the men in the longboat . . . but Rick wouldn't let me die. *He* cared for me, not Mrs. Jeffrey. I owe him everything, George, I—"

"Is that why you are marrying him, Katie?" George spoke gently, pleadingly, and Katie gazed up at him, seeing his face as a dim blur in the darkness and unable to discern his expression.

"No," she denied. "I care for him deeply. I—" Suddenly George's arms were around her, drawing her to him, and she was conscious, once again, of the attraction he had always had for her. She had tried to dismiss her love for him as a childish infatuation, she reflected miserably, tried to erase the memory of him from her mind and to accept the fact that he had gone out of her life forever, but . . . he was here, here in Sydney, not twelve thousand miles away, as she had supposed.

"You went away," she reproached him. "I did not know whether you were alive, even. Oh, I know it was difficult to write, when our countries were at war. But others did, George—letters were smuggled in, yet I had no word from you."

He did not attempt to defend himself.

"Yes," he conceded, "I know, Katie. But you were always in my heart. I thought of you so often, but I believed I had lost you. I—"

"You have lost me," Katie reminded him bitterly. "I am to wed Rick Tempest."

"Don't wed him—in heaven's name, Katie, I beg you not to! My love, by what seems to me a miracle, we've found each other again." George's arms tightened about her, and his lips found hers. Katie had not intended to yield to him, but the touch of his hands overcame her resistance, his kiss reawakened emotions she had imagined dead. She had loved him for so long, she thought, seeking an excuse for her weakness; she had dreamed, ever since she had been a schoolgirl, that one day she would become his wife, and the dream had faded, but it had never died.

"Please," she whispered, turning her face away. "Let me go. I am betrothed to Rick, I have given him my promise. I can't . . . I can't betray him. You have no right to ask me to."

George released her but retained his clasp of her hands, compelling her to face him.

"Katie, don't you believe in fate, in destiny?" he persisted. "What else could have brought me here, only days before your wedding? My decision to come out here was made almost on impulse, because I could not return to America and because my brother, when he was dying, talked of it to me. And I was weary of war, I . . . Oh, Katie, dearest girl, don't let the—damn it, the gratitude you feel for Rick Tempest blind you to the truth. We love each other, sweet . . . we always have."

Perhaps it was true, Katie thought despairingly, but her conscience would not permit her to believe it. She shook her head, seeing George De Lancey's face through a blur of tears.

"I have prospects here," he told her. "The Governor is to appoint me a magistrate, and he has offered me temporary employment as acting judge advocate, in place of a man who, it seems, does not want to serve in that capacity. And what can Tempest offer you? On his own admission to me this evening, he intends to take you to some primitive wilderness to breed sheep. For God's sake, Katie, is that what you want from marriage? If you loved him, it might be feasible, but if you do not—darling, you are condemning all three of us to unhappiness!"

Again, Katie was forced to admit, what he said might well be true, but again she shook her head. "No—no, I cannot change anything now. And I *do* love Rick, I—it isn't only gratitude. Perhaps it was at first, but now . . . now it is different. Oh, George, please try to understand. I love him too much to—to humiliate him."

"And do you love him enough to face the wilderness and the sheep?" George asked bleakly. "Can you honestly tell me that?"

Katie drew a shuddering breath. He had sensed her doubts, known that it was this she feared, and she could not give him the assurance for which he had asked, because . . . because she did not know. And the fact that he had come back so unexpectedly into her life added immeasurably to the uncertainty she had experienced since the visit to Pengallon. But it was herself she doubted, not Rick; her own ability to live the life he had planned for them, to overcome her terror of the isolation that she must face within a few months of their marriage.

George made to take her into his arms again, but she eluded him, seeking to free her hands from his.

"We must go back. People will have noticed our absence. They—" A sudden sound startled her, lending urgency to her plea. George heard it, too, and he spun round, with a smothered exclamation.

"What the deuce! Did you hear anything?"

The sound came again; the crackle of a twig, crushed underfoot, and then footsteps and the momentary glimpse of a white form, moving from the shadows into the moonlight and, as swiftly, back into the shadows again. Running feet, muffled by the clipped grass of the Government House lawn as their owner made a hasty retreat, shielded by the trees growing there. A woman, Katie thought, a woman in a white dress, who must have stumbled on their meeting place by chance and, whoever she was, must have overheard some, if not all, of their conversation. She looked up at George De Lancey in dismay, prepared to take flight, but he grasped her shoulders, holding her beside him.

"No, don't run away. Walk back to the house with me, on my arm, Katie. We've nothing to hide . . . what is more natural than two old and dear friends—two Americans, for God's sake—seizing a chance to walk and talk together?"

"They gossip here," Katie warned him miserably. "And clacking tongues will make something of it."

"Not if we behave naturally. We *are* old friends—we knew each other long before either of us came to Sydney." George took her arm, tucking it under his. He added, with a faint edge to his voice, "The eavesdropper could only have heard your avowal of love for the man you purpose to wed."

"I . . . I suppose so. But—"

"No buts, Katie. Do you still intend to wed Rick Tempest?"

What else could she do, Katie thought, her heart plummeting
. . . it was too late to go back on her promise, with the wedding
only three days away. And she owed Rick her life and her loyalty.
She said, her voice a faint whisper of sound in the darkness, "Yes.
Yes, I do."

"And nothing I can say will make you change your mind?
Think, darling—think what it will mean. I still love you, Katie!"

Tears ached in Katie's throat, but she managed a firm,
irrevocable, "No—no, I shall not change my mind."

"Then, so be it," George acknowledged. "But I wish it could
be otherwise."

They walked back together through the moonlit garden, joining
with other strollers and seemingly occasioning no particular notice
or comment. Rick was on the veranda, talking to Mrs. Macquarie.
He rose at once and came smiling to Katie's side; George
relinquished her arm, bowed, and left them together, and Rick
said, "I've been hearing about Mrs. Macquarie's carriage accident, Katie. Poor soul, she puts on a brave front, but she is
devastated by the child's death. There's to be a coroner's inquest,
and I think she intends to ask your friend De Lancey to represent
her, to ensure that the unfortunate episode is not blown up out of all
proportion . . . simply because it was *her* carriage. You know
how tongues wag here. . . ."

Indeed she did, Katie thought dully. She barely listened to
Rick's account of the accident. Abigail, she realized, was wearing
a cream silk dress; Mrs. Jeffrey was in pink—both colors that
might, in the silvery glow of the moon, have appeared to be white.
Julia's flounced muslin was white, with sprigged roses and a full
skirt that rustled as she moved, and both Mrs. Wentworth and Mrs.
Redfern were in differing shades of blue. Women tended to wear
light colors in the heat of Sydney's summer; it was impossible to
tell which of Mrs. Macquarie's female guests had been the
eavesdropper.

"It's time we took our leave, my sweet," Rick said, bringing
her abruptly back to awareness of her social obligations, and Katie
moved forward obediently to make her curtsy to the Governor and
his lady.

"I am looking forward so gladly to your wedding," Mrs.

Macquarie told her, including Rick in her warm and friendly smile. "Marriage is a blessed state, Miss O'Malley, and I wish you joy and happiness in yours. You are, I feel sure, ideally suited to each other and possessed of the courageous pioneering spirit that this colony needs. I trust, however"—she addressed her words to Rick—"that you will not deprive Sydney society of your bride for too long at a time, when you take up residence beyond the mountains."

"That will not be for several months, ma'am," Rick assured her. "It will take me a while to prepare a suitable home at Pengallon." He bowed to the Governor and linked his arm in Katie's as they moved toward the hall. "God grant that you *will* find joy and happiness when you are married to me, my love," he whispered. "I pray for it with all my heart."

Katie remembered that prayer when, three days later, she walked up the aisle of St. Philip's Church on Timothy Dawson's arm and Rick took his place beside her, his hand reaching out to find hers and, hidden by the voluminous folds of her bridal gown, clasping it gently.

"Dearly beloved, we are gathered together in the sight of God and in the face of this congregation, to join this man and this woman in holy matrimony, which is an honorable estate, instituted of God in the time of man's innocency, signifying unto us the mystical union that is betwixt Christ and His church . . ." The Reverend William Cowper, his tall, slim form enveloped in cassock and surplice, read the opening words with proper solemnity. He had a clear, resonant voice, and Katie listened attentively as he went on.

"Which holy estate Christ adorned and beautified with His presence and first miracle that He wrought in Cana of Galilee; and is commended of Saint Paul to be honorable among all men and therefore is not by any to be enterprised nor taken in hand unadvisedly, lightly or wantonly, to satisfy man's carnal lusts and appetites, like brute beasts that have no understanding. . . ." Rick's fingers tightened about hers, and Katie felt an odd tremor pass through them when the Reverend Cowper demanded of the congregation, "If any man can show any just cause why this man and this woman may not lawfully be joined together, let him now speak or else hereafter forever hold his peace."

In the brief ensuing silence, Rick's gaze was on the candle-lit altar, and turning to glance at him, Katie felt her conscience start to plague her anew. Was it possible, she wondered anxiously, that whoever had witnessed her clandestine meeting with George De Lancey had told her bridegroom of it? His sister Abigail perhaps, or . . .

"Richard Edmund, wilt thou have this woman to thy wedded wife, to live together after God's ordinance in the holy estate of matrimony? Wilt thou love her, comfort her, honor and keep her in sickness and in health and, forsaking all other, keep thee only unto her, so long as ye both shall live?"

Rick's answer, given firmly and without hesitation, brought the unbidden tears to her eyes. Seeking to stem them, Katie let her lids fall, as the chaplain asked her gravely, "Kathleen Mary, wilt thou have this man to thy wedded husband, to live together after God's ordinance in the holy estate of matrimony? Wilt thou obey him and serve him, love, honor, and keep him in sickness and in health and, forsaking all other, keep thee only unto him, so long as ye both shall live?"

Forsaking all other, Katie reminded herself . . . forsaking the land of her birth and the dreams of her childhood and her youth. She lifted her head, biting back the tears, and responded as Rick had done.

"I . . . will."

The service continued, its beautiful, age-old words striking an echo in her heart. Rick put his ring on her finger, the Reverend Cowper joined their hands together, and she heard him, moments later, pronounce them man and wife.

As they knelt in prayer, side by side, the sound of the chaplain's voice faded. Katie made her own, silent prayer from the depths of her heart.

"Please, Lord, let me be the wife my husband deserves. Let him find joy and happiness in me, so long as I live. Give me strength, Lord, so that I may not fail him, whatever he needs of me."

CHAPTER XXI

In one of the side pews, at the rear of the church, Murdo stirred uneasily. He was in uniform, inconspicuous among a number of other officers of the 46th attending the wedding, but for all that, he was nervous.

While the court of inquiry had been sitting, he had remained on board the *Conway* with the other witnesses and had only twice taken the opportunity to go ashore. The first time had been in order to report to Captain Sanderson, the adjutant of the 46th, who had instructed him to call and leave cards on their commanding officer while, almost in the same breath, assuring him that it would not be necessary to display a similar courtesy toward the Governor.

On the second occasion, he had spent several hours in a fruitless attempt to discover the whereabouts of his sister, Jessica, and it was by pure chance that, on his return from escorting the *Conway*'s surviving convicts to Parramatta, he had encountered the white-haired master of the King's ship *Kangaroo* in a tavern on George Street. Murdo frowned, recalling how, in the course of a casual conversation with the old master, Silas Crabbe, he had found out all that he wanted to know, without having to ask any questions that might have revealed his relationship to Jessica and thus the deception he had practiced.

Old Crabbe had been mildly intoxicated and very friendly in consequence. He had talked freely and with admiration of Justin Broome, who was, it seemed, Jessica's husband and the first native-born son of emancipist parents to be granted a commission in the Royal Navy. In addition and with very little prompting, the kindly fellow had not only described the location of Lieutenant Broome's house, he had guided Murdo to its very door, in the conviction that the new arrival intended to call on its occupants, which . . . Murdo felt the sweat break out on his brow. Which, when the moment came, he had been unable to nerve himself to do.

But Crabbe had mentioned the wedding, assuring him that all Sydney's society would be there. "Quite an occasion, sir, you can take my word for it," he had asserted. "Their Excellencies are to be present and, of course, all our ship's company. Mr. Tempest came out here as first lieutenant of the *Kangaroo*, see, and 'twas he who saved the young American lady he's to wed." The story of the rescue, told in minute detail, had followed, and then the *Kangaroo*'s master had added, "Lieutenant and Mrs. Broome will be at the church, sir, that's for sure. Everyone will be!"

He had not exaggerated, Murdo had realized when he entered the crowded church, to find scarcely a seat left, save for those reserved for the viceregal party immediately behind the bridegroom's. He had recognized Jessica without difficulty when she came in; six years had changed her little in appearance, although she had matured and carried herself with a degree of assurance that astounded him. And she was beautiful, he realized; the thin, dark-haired girl he remembered had grown into a striking young woman and one, he guessed, who would not now cower in terror from their brutal stepfather, were he suddenly to reappear.

Jessica had walked past him without a second glance or a flicker of recognition, to take her place in one of the front-row seats on the bridegroom's side, where, soon afterward, she was joined by an attractive woman of about her own age and a pretty, red-haired girl, with whom she was obviously on warmly intimate terms.

The arrival of the Governor and his wife, with an escort of uniformed staff officers, caused a stir, and Murdo's attention had been distracted when the whole congregation rose to stand respectfully until the viceregal party had taken their seats. Governor Macquarie was, he knew, a Highlander and a military officer of considerable distinction, who had commanded the 78th Highlanders, but he looked stooped and ill and, despite the resplendent trappings of his office, seemed to cut a singularly unimpressive figure, dwarfed by most of his staff.

Beside him, one of the 46th subalterns muttered as he sat down, "The old man appears a mite put out, does he not? No doubt there are too few of his emancipist friends present to make him feel at ease!"

Murdo stared at him, puzzled and seeking enlightenment, but the young officer closed one eye in an amused wink and said no more.

The bride appeared, on the arm of a broad-shouldered, handsome man whom he took to be her father; but beyond registering the fact that she was slim and graceful, Murdo took no interest in her and little in the service, his attention returning to Jessica and her two companions. Not until the service was over and the bridal procession was on its way to the church door did he, by the process of elimination, identify Jessica's husband as the tall, fair-haired officer in naval uniform who was acting as best man.

Wee Jessie, he thought, liking the look of Justin Broome, wee Jessie had done well for herself, that was for sure. The officers seated near him were rising, and Murdo followed their example, looking about him in the hope of seeing someone else he had known in the past. The 78th, he was aware, had left the colony for India, and presumably his mother and stepfather and the two bairns had gone with the regiment, but . . . An officer wearing the 78th's facings caught his eye, walking just behind the Governor.

Antill, he thought, with a glow of pleasure—Lieutenant Henry Antill, who had been so good to his mother, and to Jessie and himself, after their father was killed. A major now, and on the Governor's staff, with a pretty, buxom young lady on his arm . . . he, too, had done well for himself. They had not met for—Lord, it must be six or seven years, and there was little likelihood that Antill would recognize him, but . . . Instinctively, Murdo held back as his fellow officers edged toward the door, to find himself once more beside the youthful lieutenant of the 46th who had winked at him.

They emerged into the street to see the Governor's carriage moving off, with its escort of two mounted dragoons, and his neighbor observed regretfully, "Off they all go, to enjoy the finest hospitality in Sydney, which, alas, we must forgo! And damme, with the price of liquor in our mess, I cannot even afford to drink the bride's health!"

"Why not?" Murdo asked, surprised. "Surely you are invited to the reception?"

His new acquaintance eyed him pityingly. "Of course, you've only just joined, so you will not be aware of the—er—the regimental rules. On board the transport, prior to our arrival here, the officers of the regiment passed a resolution not to associate with convicts or emancipists for as long as we remain in the colony. That means, to all intents and purposes, Sydney society is barred to us. We even have to refuse invitations to dine at Government House now, since most of His Excellency's guests are damned emancipists.''

Murdo stared at him incredulously. "D'you mean we are forbidden to attend the reception? But for heaven's sake, the groom's a naval officer, isn't he? And''—he gestured to the seamen from the *Kangaroo*, being mustered by their petty officers after forming a guard of honor at the church door—"he's been given a guard of honor from his ship. Does that put him beyond the pale?''

"No, no—not Tempest," the lieutenant answered. "Or the Dawsons, who are giving the reception—Dawson is one of the richest landowners in the colony, and he keeps one of the best tables, so it will be a fine affair, I don't doubt. But half the guests will be infernal untouchables, including the colonel's *bête noire*, Dr. D'Arcy Wentworth. And the Governor will be there, of course. Colonel Molle has ordered us to put in an appearance at the church, which we did, and then disperse. I confess I am miffed, because one of Mr. Dawson's daughters is . . . well, she happens to be the object of my intentions. Julia Dawson—I expect you noticed her? She was one of the bridesmaids, and she is breathtakingly beautiful! But''—he shrugged resignedly—"the honor of the regiment demands sacrifice, so I shall perforce return to the mess house. Are you coming? I will introduce you, if you like, and you can stand me a glass of brandy in which to drown my sorrows!''

Murdo hesitated. He had intended to go to the reception and endeavor to make himself known to Jessica there, but in view of Colonel Molle's orders, he knew that it would not be prudent to do so . . . certainly not in uniform.

"Thank you," he said. "That will suit me admirably."

The 46th's regimental mess was typical of others he had been in since assuming Michael Dean's identity; the stand of colors in the entrance hall, pictures lining the walls and hanging beside the staircase, and a knot of officers gathered in the anteroom, to drink and gossip before luncheon. His new acquaintance, John Bullivant, duly introduced him to those present and accepted a glass of

Cape brandy, which he savored with obvious enjoyment, while complaining once again of its price.

"The old Rum Corps knew how to look after themselves," he observed wryly. "They chartered ships and imported their own liquor at ten shillings a barrel and sold it in the colony at three hundred percent profit. But we, for our sins, are forbidden to do so, and the Governor has slapped a tax on every drop that is brought in!"

Over luncheon, served at a long, highly polished table decorated with the regimental silver, there were more complaints concerning the high cost of living, the profiteering of the Sydney merchants, and the restricted social life. Captain Sanderson had brought a guest, whom he introduced as Captain John Piper, late of the New South Wales Corps and about to take up appointment as port naval officer.

Piper, a good-looking, self-assured man of about forty, announced with evident pleasure that his friend, John Macarthur, had at last received permission from the Colonial Secretary to return to the colony, but the announcement occasioned little comment from the assembled officers, who appeared unaware of its significance. The talk then turned to the building of suitable premises for a Masonic lodge, of which, it became clear, Captain Sanderson was the Worshipful Master.

Murdo took no more interest in the argument that ensued than he had in the imminent return of the unknown John Macarthur, and he was casting about him for an excuse to cut short his stay when he heard Captain Piper say, in authoritative tones, "There's only one man you can entrust with the building of your lodge, Sanderson. He's the fellow I've engaged to design and build my new residence at Eliza Point—Francis Greenway. The man's a genius."

"He's an infernal emancipist!" Sanderson objected. "Or a ticket-of-leave convict, I'm not sure which."

"He's the officially appointed government architect," Piper countered. His tanned face wore a faintly malicious smile as he added, "I'm aware of your commanding officer's social ban and, indeed, of his strong feelings in the matter, but . . . you do not require to invite Greenway to dine with you. Receive him in your orderly room, give him your instructions and agree to a fee for his services, and then let him go to work. But remember, if you please, that he has to complete *my* house before he'll be free to work for you."

Sanderson looked disgruntled, but he said no more, and the luncheon came, at last, to an end. Murdo approached him diffidently, as the senior officer present, to request permission to leave and to inquire about quarters, and found himself fixed with a steely glare.

"Who are you—Dean, eh? Oh, yes, you arrived in the *Conway*, I recall. Well, the mess isn't the place to discuss domestic matters. Report to me in my orderly room in half an hour. I've orders for you, if I remember rightly, but I can't bring to mind what they are."

It was his dismissal, and Murdo was about to accept it when Captain Piper intervened.

"Dean . . . the *Conway*? You gave evidence at the court of inquiry, did you not, Mr. Dean? You and a gentleman by the name of De Lancey, I believe?"

"That's so, sir," Murdo confirmed. Conscious that Sanderson was continuing to glare at him, he bowed and made to move away, but once again Piper addressed him.

"Hold hard, my young friend! I want to ask you about Mr. De Lancey. You were on passage together, so presumably you know him well? Indeed, someone told me that you were both at Waterloo. Not, I take it, in the same regiment—he was in the cavalry, was he not?"

"Yes, sir, in the Second Dragoons—the Scots Greys. I was in the Fifty-second Foot."

"Both fine regiments," Piper approved. He asked a number of questions about the battle and De Lancey's military service, to which Murdo replied as briefly as he could. Captain Sanderson's displeasure was uncomfortably evident, and he wanted only to make his escape, but the onetime Rum Corps officer had not done with him. A spate of questions followed concerning George De Lancey's legal status, to which he could only reply vaguely.

"I believe, sir, that he's a barrister of Lincoln's Inn and that the Colonial Office issued him with a license to practice here as an attorney. But that is all I know."

"Ha!" Piper exclaimed gleefully. He rounded on his host. "As a brother of the late and highly esteemed Sir William De Lancey, he'll have all the patronage any man could want. Your crony

Jeffrey Bent is in a foul temper, Ned. He's convinced himself that the Governor intends to appoint De Lancey to the high court in his stead—in a temporary capacity, of course, pending Colonial Office sanction. Or else as acting judge advocate, since Garling seemingly does not want the job . . . but either way, it would spell the end for His Honor Judge Bent, I imagine. He would have to resign, would he not? And quit the colony."

Captain Sanderson reddened angrily. "You may leave us, Dean," he snapped. "Wait for me in the orderly room." To Piper he said, a distinct edge to his voice, "For the love of heaven, John, don't spread such rumors! They can do incalculable harm, as you should know."

Murdo waited to hear no more, but the sound of Sanderson's voice, raised in belligerent argument, echoed down the passage after him as he beat a hasty retreat.

It was almost an hour later when the irate adjutant deigned to remember him and return to the orderly room. He shuffled through some papers, muttering to himself, and then looked up, to eye Murdo balefully.

"It is not done, in this regiment," he said, with severity. "To boast of military achievement in the mess—least of all is it the place for a damned whippersnapper of an ensign to do so. However, you'll not be given the chance to repeat your ill-mannered conduct. I have your orders here. You are posted to the Bathurst garrison, and you will take a draft of twenty men to relieve Ensign Critchley and his platoon of their duties in the settlement. He'll tell you in detail what those duties are, but I will tell you that the most important task you will be required to perform is the guarding of the road. Peaceful travelers are being attacked and robbed by escaped convicts, and it will be your responsibility to put an end to their depredations. Do you understand?"

"I . . . think so, sir," Murdo answered uncertainly. "But I . . . sir, I was only replying to Captain Piper's questions. I did not intend to boast or—"

Sanderson waved him imperiously to silence and went on, "You will leave first thing tomorrow morning, with an oxcart and driver, which will carry mail and supplies for the Bathurst garrison, calling on your way at the government farm on the Nepean River for more supplies. And you will require a horse. I have an animal that is surplus to my needs—you can have it for forty pounds, if you wish. Saddlery will be isued to you—my groom will see to it." He paused, frowning. "Mr. Dean, can you afford to pay me forty pounds, or shall I have that sum debited to your mess bill?"

Murdo, his dismay at these unexpected and unwelcome orders reflected in his face, controlled himself with a visible effort. He had purchased a very good young mare in Parramatta from one of the officers stationed there and, he thought rebelliously, for ten pounds less than Sanderson was demanding for what was, in all probability, a runt, since the big captain wanted to be rid of it.

He drew himself up and answered, with restraint, "I have a horse, sir, thank you."

Captain Sanderson looked disappointed, but, recovering himself, he shrugged. "Very well. Ah—one more point I must make, Dean. You are being sent to Bathurst—which, in case you do not know it, is not a particularly desirable posting—for a reason, which Colonel Molle instructed me to make clear to you. Your conduct on the passage out here and the evidence you gave at the recent court of inquiry into the treatment of the convicts brought out by the *Conway* did not—how can I put it? Did not redound to the regiment's credit, Mr. Dean. Colonel Molle wishes you to understand that you have incurred his disapprobation, and I must warn you that your future in this regiment will depend on how you conduct yourself now that you are here. Is that clear? Then you are dismissed, Mr. Dean."

He was allowed no protest, Murdo thought, given no explanation of precisely how he had incurred his commanding officer's disapprobation or in what way his evidence had discredited his regiment at the court of inquiry. He was tempted to ask for an explanation and then thought better of it. He was ordered to leave for Bathurst next morning, which . . . He stifled a sigh. Which left him only what remained of the day to seek out his sister and make his preparations for departure. His kit had been sent ashore from the *Conway* and dumped somewhere in the mess, presumably in whatever quarter had been allocated to him, but it should not take long to find both. And by the time he had done so, the wedding reception would no doubt be over and Jessica back once more in the white-painted cottage on the waterfront that Silas Crabbe had shown him.

He saluted woodenly and left the orderly room.

An hour later, he was outside the Broomes' cottage, still of two minds as to the wisdom of revealing himself. Jessie, his little sister Jessie, was surely to be trusted not to betray him, but . . . Murdo felt icy prickles of fear coursing down his back. Her husband, Justin Broome, was an unknown quantity—a "currency kid" now turned King's officer, who might have stern notions as to his duty. It was a thousand pities that he had not been able to contact Jessica when she was alone, but there was no time to choose his moment. It had to be now or never.

On the point of walking up to the door of the house, Murdo heard voices and drew back, finding concealment in an alleyway between the house and its immediate neighbor. Luck, he realized, was with him . . . Jessica appeared, on her husband's arm, with two young midshipmen weaving an erratic course a few yards to the rear. He heard Broome say, laughing, "I'll shepherd these two tipsy characters back to the ship, my love, before the captain sees them. You'll be all right? Kate will deliver young Red to you before dark, and—I'll see you in the morning, before we sail."

Peering out, Murdo saw him stoop to kiss his wife, and then he was gone, the two mids in tow, laughing their heads off, as Jessica opened the door of the cottage and turned to wave them farewell. He waited, his heart pounding, until they were out of earshot, and then approached the door. Jessica, on the point of closing it, waited politely, her brows raised in mute question as Murdo, his head bared, came up the short garden path toward her.

When he did not speak, she inquired, smiling, "You are newly arrived here, are you not? Do you seek directions, sir?"

"No." Murdo shook his head. Now that the moment had come, his mouth was so dry that he could scarcely utter the words he had planned to say, still less remember what they were. Instead he blurted out hoarsely, "Don't you know me, Jessie?"

She studied his uniform and then looked up, puzzled, to his face. "I do not think so. Who are you, sir?"

"Murdo," he managed. "Jessie, I'm your brother, Murdo, I . . . please, may I come inside? It is a long time, I know, but I . . . I'm not jesting."

Jessica stood aside, white-faced and deeply shocked, staring up at him incredulously.

"Murdo—you *can't* be Murdo! My—my brother is dead. He . . . they hanged him. He was condemned at the Winchester

Assize Court for robbing a mail coach over . . . over three years ago. You—"

"It was the Southampton Assize Court," Murdo corrected, "in June of the year eighteen thirteen, before Mr. Justice Devereux. Of his mercy, His Lordship elected to commute my sentence to one of transportation for life."

His tone, as much as his words, convinced her but, if anything, added to her dazed bewilderment. Like one in a dream, she crossed the small parlor and took a carved wooden box down from the mantelshelf to extract, from among the jumble of papers it contained, a yellowing scrap of newsprint, which she thrust into his hand. Murdo glanced at it and saw that it was a report of his trial:

> Mr. Justice Devereux pronounced sentence of death on Richard John Farmer, Septimus Todd, and Murdoch Henry Maclaine, and it is expected that all three will meet their fate at Winchester Prison on Tuesday of next week.

He shivered involuntarily, thinking of Sep Todd and Dickie Farmer, good friends and bosom companions—now, alas, poor devils, long in their unmarked felons' graves . . . as he might also have been, had old Judge Devereux not taken pity on his youth.

"Where did you get this?" he demanded, crumpling up the torn scrap of paper with an unsteady hand.

"Duncan Campbell gave it to me," Jessica answered flatly. "It was his farewell gift, before he left with the regiment for Calcutta."

"Then he did not change," Murdo suggested. "Damn his soul!"

"No," Jessica confirmed, "he did not change. But," she added, with a sudden flash of spirit, "I bested him, Murdo. I put him in fear of his life at the last, and he never laid a hand on me again."

"And Mam—did he treat Mam any better?"

She shook her head sadly. "Mam died on the passage out, Murdo. I never saw her again, and Duncan Campbell married after he came out here. A good, decent woman—the little ones loved her from the start, and they all went to India, with the regiment."

She told him what she could of their mother's death, of the two little girls and their new stepmother, and then of her own runaway voyage on board the Governor's ship.

"Major Antill helped me," she concluded. "He is here, Murdo, as major of brigade."

"I know—I recognized him at the wedding." Murdo smiled. "He hasn't changed."

"You were there—you were in church this morning?" Jessica exclaimed. "Oh, Murdo, why did you not make yourself known to me then? Why did you not come to the reception? I'm married, and my husband, Justin—Justin Broome, was best man. But he's had to go back to his ship and—"

"I know," Murdo repeated. "I waited outside your house until he had gone." He shrugged. "I did not know what sort of reception he would accord me, Jessie. It seemed best to try to see you alone first."

Jessica was silent, and watching her lovely, expressive face, Murdo could almost follow the thoughts flitting, in swift succession, through her mind. Certainly he could guess with what suspicion she must regard him, and her next words confirmed his fears.

"Murdo, you were spared from—from the death sentence; but if you were condemned to transportation, you . . ." She drew in her breath sharply, and gestured to his uniform. "How has it come about that you are an officer in Colonel Molle's regiment?"

Murdo hesitated. Even to Jessica, he decided, he dared not tell the whole truth, dared not admit that he was an escaped felon, with no right to the uniform he wore or the rank he held. A half-truth must suffice for the time being, and it was to be devoutly hoped that she would believe it.

"I volunteered for the army, Jessie," he told her. "It was just before Boney made his escape from Elba, and the Duke of Wellington needed men. The recruiting sergeants did not ask questions, but I had to change my name, in case they did. I'm Michael Dean now, and I obtained my commission after the battle of Waterloo." He added hurriedly, lest his sister doubt him, "Men commissioned from the ranks have to go to other regiments. I exchanged into the Forty-sixth in order to come out here . . . to see you, Jessie. And I'd hoped that Mam might still be here."

"Then you were at Waterloo—you fought at Waterloo?" Jessica looked at him with shining eyes, accepting his story without

question, and Murdo sighed his relief. She asked him about the
battle, and here he was on firm and familiar ground, able to give
her a graphic account of it that would, he knew, ring true.
Uninhibited by the disapproving presence of Captain Sanderson,
he even waxed lyrical on the subject of the long marches, the fierce
fighting, and the French cavalry charges, and Jessica had tears in
her eyes as he described the terrible plight of the wounded in the
aftermath of victory.

"I was well cared for in a private house in Brussels, Jessie," he
told her. "A Belgian surgeon saved my life."

"How could you suppose that Justin—that my husband would
not welcome you?" Jessica reproached him. "You have made
good, Murdo—you fought bravely and proved yourself, did you
not? Both Justin and I will be proud to welcome you. We—"

"But not as your brother, Jessie," Murdo put in quickly. "I
cannot admit to being your brother. I was never granted a pardon,
you see, so my sentence still hangs over me. The authorities here
would be bound to arrest me if that were known."

She looked at him in hurt surprise. "The Governor would
pardon you—" she began, but he cut her short.

"No—I dare not risk it. It would cause a scandal, which"—
ironically, he quoted Captain Sanderson—"would not redound to
the credit of the regiment. And I came out here in the *Conway*—I
saw, at first hand, how convicted felons are treated here. I have to
be Michael Dean, Jessie, to you and everyone else. I can be—oh,
damn it, your cousin, if you wish. But Murdoch Henry Maclaine is
dead. Please, Jessie, if you love me, promise that you will tell no
one who I really am . . . not even your husband."

"Justin is to be trusted," Jessica protested indignantly. "He is
the son of emancipist parents—he would never give you away. He
knows—dear heaven, no one knows better than Justin how felons
and their offspring are treated here! Besides—" Her tone changed,
and she rose and came to put her arms around him. "Dearest
Murdo, I am proud of my brother! You are a brave soldier's son,
and you proved it at Waterloo . . . let me, I beg you, tell Justin
that you are my brother."

"But only Justin," Murdo insisted. "No one else."

She gave him the promise he sought, albeit reluctantly, and
then, eager to fill in the gaps their long separation had left in its
wake, questioned him about his days on the road. Murdo told her

as much as he dared, careful to name no names and making more of the unhappy months when he had been in the employ of the crooked peddler than of the halcyon days with Nick, when he had lived life to the full, glorying in the triumphs and the narrow escapes that had been part and parcel of existence on the road.

A knock on the door interrupted them, and Jessica jumped eagerly to her feet.

"It will be Kate Lamerton," she explained, "bringing my son back. The kind soul cared for him whilst we were enjoying Rick Tempest's wedding festivities."

"Wait!" Suddenly anxious, Murdo caught her by the arm, turning her to face him. "Jessie, I'm ordered to Bathurst I have to leave here with a draft tomorrow morning. So perhaps I had better go before . . . well, before you have to lie about me to your caller. You could say—"

"I know what to say, Murdo," she reproached him gently. "And I have not forgotten my promise. Please stay where you are."

She slipped free of his grasp and went to the door, to return a few moments later carrying a lively child of about ten or twelve months old and followed by a buxom, gray-haired woman in the dark garb of a servant. But, servant or not, they were clearly on terms of friendship, Murdo realized, and he waited tensely for Jessica to introduce them.

She did so, after a barely perceptible hesitation. "Kate dear, this is my cousin, Ensign Michael Dean, of Colonel Molle's regiment, who is lately arrived by the *Conway*. Mrs. Lamerton, Michael— Kate, to all of us. And my son, whom we named Murdoch, after— after my brother, Murdoch Maclaine. But—" She smiled up at him and whisked the woolen cap from the little boy's head. "We call him Red because he has had the good fortune to inherit his grandmother's beautiful red hair. I'm sorry you never knew her, Michael—she was a wonderful woman. But you will meet Justin, my husband, whilst you are at Bathurst. He has a land grant on the Macquarie River, and he plans to go there when his ship, the *Emu*, leaves the colony."

Her smile widened, and she put the child into his arms.

Murdo, his throat tight, bent to kiss his namesake's curly red head. For a moment, he could not speak; then, without thinking, he blurted out, "I . . . thank you, Jessie, for not forgetting me. I—"

Kate Lamerton said practically, "I will fetch the brandy, Mrs. Broome. Likely you'll be wanting to drink Mr. Dean's health, will you not?"

She left them together, and Murdo swore softly. "It was I who forgot. Do you suppose she noticed my slip of the tongue?"

"If she did," Jessica answered, with conviction, "she'll say nothing. And Red will never know." She took the child back, and Murdo felt the tension drain out of him as Kate Lamerton came bustling in and beamed at him, offering the tray of glasses.

CHAPTER XXII

The prevailing drought, although its effect in the vicinity of the Bathurst Plains was much less severe than it had been on the Sydney side of the dividing range of the Blue Mountains, had reduced the level of the Macquarie River by several feet. In places it was little more than a trickle, but there still was deep water in the numerous creeks and gullies, and Rick was up to his knees as he waded the length of one such creek, which he had named Discovery. He was searching for Justin, who was somewhere on the high bank above him.

They had been at Pengallon for ten days now, but with each passing day their hopes had fallen. With improvised tools, they had endeavored to devise a method of washing the sand dredged up from the creek bed, but with little success, a few small particles being their only reward for hours of patient toil.

Stubbing his foot on a stone, Rick cursed irritably. It had been a painful wrench to leave Katie—his bride of only six weeks—by herself in the rented house at Farm Cove, and she had been upset by his decision, but he had had no choice. He sighed, squinting up into the sun to look for Justin. The *Emu*'s refit had, of necessity, dictated the date of their departure for their holding, since until the King's ship was handed over to the caulkers and carpenters, she had been almost continuously at sea and Justin with her, engaged in running the government's routine errands.

His friend and partner, Rick recalled, had suffered a shattering disappointment when, on the *Emu*'s return from the Hunter River, he had been informed by an apologetic John Campbell that command of the new colonial sloop *Elizabeth* was not to be his. Captain Jeffrey, exercising his prerogative as senior naval officer, had, prior to sailing for England, appointed Lieutenant Meredith to

the command, giving as his reason the fact that Meredith had
elected to marry the daughter of one of Colonel Molle's officers
and remain in the colony.

This had scarcely seemed a good enough reason to Justin, but
the Governor had accepted it, and Justin was now, alas, himself
thinking of quitting and joining James Forster, the *Emu*'s captain,
on his South American venture. Rick repeated his sigh. He had
counted on finding at least sufficient gold at Pengallon to induce
Justin to change his mind—even the hope of it would have done.
Poor little Jessica was far from eager to settle in Rio de Janeiro,
whether or not her husband were to become first lieutenant of a
Brazilian seventy-four . . . and Katie would miss them sorely, if
they did leave Sydney. They— He caught sight of Justin,
descending the slope above him, and cupping his hands about his
mouth, he called out a greeting.

"Justin—how are you faring?"

Justin turned to look down at him, lowering the pick he was
carrying. He had been investigating a seam of what had appeared
to be gold-bearing quartz running along a rock face at right angles
to the riverbank, but his expression told Rick that this, too, like all
their earlier efforts, was likely to end in disappointment.

His assessment of the seam was expressed in technical terms,
emphasizing the difficulties of following the seam and, with
inadequate tools, chiseling out and crushing the quartz.

"I have some quite promising specimens here, taken at random
over almost a quarter of a mile and consisting mainly of quartz,
but—I think the river offers our best chance. Maybe our only
chance, Rick. We could try digging into the clay banks above the
watermark."

"But you don't believe we'll find anything?" Rick challenged
glumly.

"I didn't say that. It was where you found that first sizable
nugget, was it not?" Justin paused to mop the sweat from his brow
and then came down to the top of the bank, below which Rick was
standing. With a grimace, he dumped the sack containing the
specimens he had gathered. "That weighs a ton! And I've wrecked
two chisels, not to mention my left thumb. Let's call it a day, shall
we? I could do with something to eat."

"Are you wanting to give up?" Rick asked, unable to conceal
his dismay. What would Katie think, he wondered, after all the

promises he had made, the hopes he had aroused? "Are you in such a hurry to go off to Rio and stake your claim to Forster's seventy-four, damn it?"

Justin's brows rose in surprise at his outburst. "No," he answered mildly. "You should know me better than that. And to be honest, Rick, I'm not entirely sorry that we have failed to find gold here. This is pastoral land, and I remember what my mother said, when she saw it for the first time. 'Think of the flocks and herds this land will sustain, the crops it will grow,' she said. 'It is your future, spread out down there.' And she was right—it is! We agreed, when you first told me of your find, that it could cause the most appalling trouble if word of it got out prematurely. You cannot raise stock or grow crops on land that is overrun by thousands of escapers—rogues and ruffians—searching for gold. This is a penal colony, don't forget, and the Governor—"

"I have not forgotten," Rick interrupted irritably. He climbed up beside Justin and flung himself down full length on the rocky ground, brushing the tormenting flies from his sweat-soaked face with an impatient hand. "And don't *you* forget, Justin, that I'd every intention of reporting my find to Governor Macquarie. I had even made an appointment with him, but Mrs. Macquarie's carriage accident prevented me from seeing him. So I told you instead, and we both agreed to wait until after we had made an investigation and confirmed that there's gold here. I still believe there is." He felt unreasonably angry but controlled himself, aware that Justin was eyeing him reproachfully. "Devil take it, the fact that we have failed to confirm it gives *me* no satisfaction, whatever your mother may have said about this land. I'd pinned my hopes on it!"

"Well, suppose we had been able to confirm it," Justin argued. "And we had informed the Governor—have you considered that his reaction might well have been the same as my mother's was?"

Rick sat up. "For God's sake, Justin! Do you mean that the Governor would insist on giving the land to the pastoralists for damned sheep rearing?"

"Yes," Justin returned quickly. "That's precisely what I mean. From what I know of him, Governor Macquarie is a man with very firm views as to the future of this colony. He wants to see us become self-supporting by means of our agriculture, and he wants those who came out here as convicted felons to be rehabilitated, by settling them on the land." He smiled. "You can't eat gold, Rick."

"You can buy food with it," Rick asserted.

"And reduce the entire colony to a state of anarchy in the search for it! There would be no other work done, don't you see? Assigned convicts would run away in hordes, settlers would desert their farms and seamen their ships. And how could they be stopped—with one regiment and a single King's ship?" Justin laid a placatory hand on Rick's arm. "I've been giving the matter a great deal of thought whilst we've been up here, and I say, in all truth, that I'm not sorry we've failed to find gold here, Rick. It's better so."

Rick's temper flared. "Plague take you, Justin, you're a fine one to talk so! You're leaving anyway, are you not? You're sailing with Forster in the *Emu*?"

Justin shook his head. "I've been giving that matter quite a lot of thought, too," he admitted. "And I've decided to resign my commission and stay. I still have the *Flinders*; she's only hired by Robert Campbell. And"—he shrugged—"Jessica wants to stay."

Rick was silent, digesting this; but he still felt aggrieved. There was undoubtedly logic in Justin's argument, yet he felt unable to abandon the hopes he had cherished. "I'm not giving up yet," he insisted. "I'm going to try digging into the bank. And damn it to hell, if I do find gold, no one is going to stop me from taking it!"

"Macquarie may," Justin reminded him.

"Then I shall keep a still tongue in my head," Rick snapped. He got to his feet, gesturing in the direction of the farm buildings. They and the small, compact log-built house were almost complete, lacking only the shingle roofs that would render them weatherproof. As a precaution, the convict laborers, who had worked all summer on the buildings, had been paid a bonus for good work and sent to Bathurst, where the money they had earned would, Justin had calculated, suffice to keep all three happily drunk until summoned to return to their labors. But now, unable to stifle the anger and disappointment he felt, Rick turned impatiently on his partner.

"You can leave me to it, if you want to, Justin. Go off to Sydney and reclaim your infernal *Flinders*—chuck in your commission, if that's how you feel! But don't send the men back here yet, for I tell you, I've not done. Not by a long chalk."

An instant after he had spoken, he regretted his words. Justin, he reproached himself, had done nothing to deserve his anger, but before he could offer an apology, Justin, too, was on his feet. Lifting the sack of quartz specimens onto his back, he said, without heat, "Very well. I'll fetch a musket from the house and see if I can bag a kangaroo for the pot before dark. I'll leave you the pick for your digging. But if you will forgive me for mentioning it, I think you'll be making a grave mistake if you leave a wife as beautiful as Katie for too long by herself."

Rick abandoned all thought of apology. It was not often that he lost his temper completely, but he lost it now, and Justin added fuel to the flames of his wrath by turning his back on him and making off, up the slope, seemingly indifferent to his shouted protests.

Left alone, his anger still simmering, Rick grabbed the pick and slithered down the bank, almost losing his footing on the greasy yellow clay and swearing aloud as he let the pick fall into the water.

What damned business was it of Justin's to warn him about leaving Katie in Sydney by herself? For God's sake, she was his wife and she loved him! Fumbling about in the deep waterhole to recover the pick, Rick let his thoughts return to the first few weeks of his marriage to Katie O'Malley. At Portland Place, the extensive farm once owned by Jasper Spence, they had occupied the luxuriously furnished bedroom that Tim Dawson's first wife had planned and decorated, with the exquisite taste for which she had been renowned.

Katie had been delighted with it, exclaiming over the velvet drapes and the flounced muslin bedcover, which reminded her, she had said, of her parents' comfortable bedroom in Boston. And . . . Rick caught his breath as he remembered how she had given herself to him, shyly at first, even painfully, because of her virgin state, but then with a passion that was a fervent response to his, her lovely body naked and pliant in his arms, her soft mouth joyously giving him kiss for kiss. He remembered, too, the first time he had held her thus, without passion, intent only on giving her the warmth that would restore her to life . . . and his anger swiftly faded.

He was the most fortunate man alive, he told himself, as he had done more than once since Katie had consented to wed him. It was for her that he wanted to find gold on these barren, lonely acres . . . not for himself. And she would understand, she would love him enough to understand if he stayed here, seeking the means to give her a house like the one at Portland Place, with a bedroom like Henrietta Dawson's, whatever Justin thought about it. Justin, for heaven's sake, left his wife for weeks and months at a time, when he was at sea! Rick's mouth tightened obstinately.

Recovering the pick, he started to hack away at the bank, dragging himself higher up, to the level the water normally reached when the rainfall was heavy and regular. He hacked until his arms were aching, using his bare hands to scrape away the squelching clay by which the rock was covered, and losing all count of time as he toiled doggedly on.

Then, as the sun was setting, his search ended, so suddenly and unexpectedly that he could scarcely believe his eyes. Lying on a bed of clay was a nugget, worn smooth by the water that had flowed over it, and emitting a dull glow as it caught the last, fading rays of the sinking sun. In size it was bigger than the palm of his hand, and as he lifted it carefully from its hiding place, Rick could only guess at its weight and value. There were two smaller pieces, revealed as he lifted the first, and his hands were shaking uncontrollably as he prized them out and laid all three on a flat rock at the top of the bank.

He had been right, he told himself exultantly—the land *was* auriferous, and there must be more, much more, gold to be found. He wrapped the nuggets in his kerchief and placed them in the pocket of his stained and soaking breeches, his first impulse to seek out Justin and acquaint him with the momentous news of his find. But then, as he set off for the farm buildings, he changed his mind. Justin—for God's sake, had not Justin made his views clear enough? Had he not insisted that the Governor must be informed, and given it as his opinion that Macquarie would use his authority in order to ensure that the land should remain agricultural?

To break the news to Justin would be tantamount to . . . damn it, to reporting the find to Macquarie, and thereafter losing all rights to what must be a fortune!

Rick halted, breathless, at the summit of the hill. From where he stood he had a clear view not only of the farm buildings but also of the river and the wide expanse of flat grassland through which it flowed. Dusk was falling, but he was able to make out the figures of Justin and the native boy, Winyara. They were both squatting by a newly kindled campfire, the smoke from which was spiraling slowly skyward, and—evidently their hunt had been successful—Justin was engaged in skinning a small kangaroo.

Rick was about to move on to join them when, in the far distance and on the opposite side of the river, he caught sight of a party of men weaving their way through a thin patch of woodland in the general direction of Pengallon. He counted eight of them, with four laden packhorses, and then recalled that George Evans, the deputy government surveyor, had gone out, three weeks previously, to plan the route for a larger exploration of the area by his immediate superior, John Oxley.

Evidently the Evans party was returning; they were, as nearly as he could judge, six or seven miles away, but with daylight rapidly fading, it was probable that they would halt and make camp before going much farther . . . certainly, they were moving at a leisurely pace, and were too far away to have seen the smoke of Justin's campfire.

Rick breathed a sigh of relief. It was one thing to keep silent about his find with only Justin present, but it would be infinitely more difficult to do so if the inquisitive Evans began to ask questions. He and Justin were friends; they had taken part in exploratory expeditions in the past, and worked together on the road from Emu Ford to Bathurst, two years ago. Justin, being the transparently honest fellow he was, would have no hesitation in revealing the reason for their presence here, if Evans asked him about it. And George Evans, whether or not he possessed the academic qualification, liked to dabble in geology; if Justin were to hint at a possible gold find, there would be no holding him. The secret would be out and the Governor made privy to it, for he, like Justin, was a Governor's man.

Somehow, Rick decided, brushing aside a momentary qualm of conscience, he must keep the two of them apart . . . perhaps by persuading Justin to leave for Sydney before Evans and his men crossed the river. He waited, watching to see if the surveyor's party left the shelter of the trees, and finally, satisfied that they had not done so, he descended from his vantage point at a brisk run, in the last of the fading light.

The appetizing smell of cooking meat met him, and Justin, apparently bearing him no grudge, looked up from the spit he was turning and said, smiling, "We bagged a nice young 'roo. Sit you down, Rick—it will be ready soon. Winyara's gone to fetch water for our tea. I take it you had no luck?"

Rick shook his head, his conscience once again worrying him, and he hesitated before voicing the lie. What was it about the prospect of acquiring a fortune that could turn a hitherto honest man into a deceiver, he asked himself, but could find no answer to the nagging question. He slumped down beside the fire, the weight of the nuggets in his breeches pocket hardening his resolve, as Justin observed consolingly, "Well, what of it, my dear fellow? Nothing has changed, really. You'll bring Katie up here and breed sheep, just as you originally planned, and it will not be long before you have neighbors. John Campbell told me that the first five who are to receive grants have been chosen, and they're all good youngsters, who were born here. One of them, Willie Lee, intends to breed shorthorn cattle, and Captain Lawson, of course, is already working on similar lines. There's talk of growing wheat up here, too, and when Oxley completes his survey of the Lachlan River, then—" He broke off abruptly and asked, with a swift change of tone, "What's that? Did you hear anything?"

"No," Rick began uncertainly. "I don't think so. I—" Winyara's lithe dark form came flying toward them out of the darkness, to whisper a sibilant warning in his own language. It was unintelligible to Rick, and he asked impatiently, "What's the matter? What did he say?"

"He says there are men, six or seven of them, on their way here," Justin told him. "And he says they're armed." He got to his feet, reaching for his musket. "Better take cover until we see who they are, Rick."

"It's probably George Evans's party," Rick said, without thinking, and then cursed his own carelessness. "That is—"

"What do you mean, George Evans's party?" Justin put in sharply. "Did you see them?"

"Yes, from the top of the hill, ten minutes ago. They were about six miles from here, on the far side of the river. Eight men and four horses. But, for the Lord's sake, Justin—"

"These men have no horses," Justin asserted. He did not look up from the priming of his musket, but went on levelly, "And Winyara says they are moving quietly, as if they don't want to be heard." He spoke to the aborigine in his own tongue, and Winyara nodded in confirmation of whatever suggestion he had made. "He spotted Evans's party too, Rick. They wouldn't have had time to get anywhere near us, and besides, they'd have been talking their heads off—no reason not to. Is your piece in the house?"

Infected by his urgency now, Rick jumped up. "Yes," he said. "I'll get it. But do you really think they mean trouble?"

"This is escapers' territory these days," Justin answered crisply. "And if there's been any loose talk of your gold find—by that fellow who did your assay, for instance—then maybe they do. Or they could be looking for food. The smell of that 'roo may have tempted them." He picked up the spitted carcass and grinned. "If so, they're not getting it. We'll go to the house, Rick, and wait and see, shall we?"

He led the way, carrying the meat in one hand, his loaded musket in the other. A whispered word to Winyara sent the native boy gliding off into the darkness, and leaving the fire burning, Rick followed him into the small, roofless cabin. He found his musket, loaded and primed it, and joined Justin at the unglazed rear window. They waited tensely, peering out into the blackness, but no sound came to disturb the stillness. The moon rose; casting a faint, silvery light over the fold yard and farm buildings to their right and the undulating, tree-grown land spread out in front of them, but still neither of them could detect any sign of movement.

Twice Justin went to the door at the front of the cabin to listen, but he shook his head to Rick's question.

"Not a thing. The fire's still burning. If there are men out there looking for trouble, they'll come this way"—he gestured to the rear window—"where there's cover, right up to the buildings."

"*If* there's anyone there," Rick retorted edgily. He was wet and tired, feeling the night chill and conscious of hunger, which the congealing kangaroo meat on the floor made more acute. "For God's sake, Justin, how can you be sure?"

"Winyara doesn't make mistakes," Justin said with conviction. "He said that the men had come from Kurrara—which is what the aborigines call Bathurst—two days ago, and that they had remained in hiding on the *omeo*—the mountain—west of here. He thinks they were watching us."

"But he can't *know*, Justin. He—"

"You would be surprised," Justin claimed, "by how much these people do know, merely from studying tracks that we can hardly see. In any event," he added, with finality, "this area is out of bounds to anyone but permitted settlers and their servants, Rick—or, of course, to authorized exploratory expeditions, like George Evans's. No one who has a right here would hide in the hills for two days. They have to be escapers."

"Well," Rick argued, "escapers or not, I can't see hide or hair of them now. Probably they've gone back to their blasted *omeo*! And I'm famished. Why don't we finish cooking that 'roo before the fire dies on us? We'll hear them, if they do try to sneak up on us, and we're both armed."

"So are they," Justin reminded him. "And there are half a dozen of them. Give it another half hour. They may be waiting until they think we're asleep—so let's keep quiet, shall we?"

Rick waited, with growing frustration, the cold eating into his bones and the pangs of hunger becoming unendurable. His earlier elation over the finding of the nuggets had faded, and as the silence remained unbroken, his impatience increased. How, he asked himself despondently, was he going to persuade Justin to leave their holding before George Evans and his party arrived? Now that he knew of their presence, he would almost certainly want to stay, in order to hear what fresh discoveries Evans had made . . . and it would never occur to him not to talk of their own search and its objective. Even if he were to insist that it had been abortive, George Evans's curiosity would undoubtedly be aroused . . . and Evans was a persistent fellow.

Rick moved back from the window, flexing his cramped limbs. "We've given your plaguey escapers half an hour, Justin," he said. "And there's not been a sound of them. I reckon they were a figment of Winyara's imagination or else they've taken themselves off." He bent to pick up the kangaroo's carcass. "I'm going to finish this off—damn it, we haven't eaten since early this morning. You can cover me from the door, if you want to."

Justin did not argue but followed him to the door in silence. Rick shouldered his musket and, with the kangaroo clutched awkwardly under his other arm, strode stiffly across to the fire. It was reduced to glowing ash but still alive, and he had started to pile fresh branches on it when, without warning, a shadowy figure darted out from the concealment of one of the nearby farm buildings.

Rick had just time to glimpse the leveled musket in the man's hand and fling himself to the ground before the weapon was fired, at point-blank range, and a shower of buckshot whistled over his head, sounding like a swarm of angry bees. He did not realize that he had been hit; there was no sensation of pain, but when he attempted to get to his feet, to his stunned dismay, he found he could not do so.

A fusillade of shots followed, coming from several different directions; he heard a howl of agony, close at hand, and saw a man fall within a few yards of him, clutching his stomach. And then Justin was beside him, grabbing his musket, firing it and, almost in the same movement, flinging it down and hoisting him to his feet.

"I . . . can't . . . walk!" Rick gasped. "I—" He choked, blood gushing into his mouth. Justin heaved him onto his shoulders and ran for the house, gaining it, Rick had no idea how, as booted feet came pounding after them and several more shots were fired—seemingly without hitting either of them.

The door was slammed shut; Justin dumped him unceremoniously on the wooden floor, and Rick heard him swearing as he sought to reload his own musket. Voices rose outside; there was an attempt to kick in the door, but its solid timbers held, and then a shower of buckshot spattered the further wall. Justin's shot answered it, fired through the window aperture, and there was another high-pitched scream from outside.

"Two of them won't trouble us anymore," Justin exclaimed breathlessly. His voice, although it was clear enough, seemed to be coming from a long way away. Rick endeavored to drag himself upright, but his legs still had no feeling and would not respond to the prompting of his brain. Finally, defeated, he managed to crawl across the room, using his hands, the lower part of his body an immense, insensitive weight that defied all his efforts to lift it.

He spat out blood and, exerting his last reserve of strength, hauled himself up by the sill of the rear window. Bright moonlight illuminated the fold yard now—where, he supposed dully, the bushrangers must have been in hiding, waiting, as Justin had suggested, for them to fall asleep. Or one of the scoundrels, anyway—the man who had fired the first round of buckshot at him had emerged from there.

What a fool he had been, to insist on leaving the house! He heard Justin fire again and turned, with infinite difficulty, to look at him. He was reloading, only his hands and the barrel of his musket visible in the light from the window, and Rick saw him jump back, with a strangled exclamation, as another shower of buckshot shattered the sill.

And then he heard shouts, coming from the direction of the river, and he turned back, his heart thudding, as he tried to identify the men from whom they had emanated. Whoever they were, they were running . . . dear God, more blasted convict escapers, or bushrangers or whatever the swine called themselves! Surely they could not be, surely they . . . Rick leaned as far out as he could, straining his eyes into the shadowy distance.

Then a small, solitary figure emerged into the moonlight, bent low and running, and he recognized Winyara with a shuddering gasp of relief. The next two men who followed were leading horses, a third was riding, and . . . Rick let his unwieldy body slide back to the floor.

"Justin," he called out hoarsely, "it's Evans—Evans and his people! And Winyara."

"They made good time," Justin responded. "But I'm afraid those rogues out there have heard them—they're making off, as if the devil himself were after them. But they've abandoned their wounded, so there'll be only three of them to round up. That should not be beyond the powers of Molle's redcoats, should it?" He propped his smoking musket against the window from which he had been firing and crossed to Rick's side, his voice concerned as he asked, "How are you, Rick old man? Are you in much pain?"

"No—no pain at all, I—" Rick stared up at him, filled with a nameless fear. "I don't know where I was hit. In the back, I think, but I—Justin, I can't feel my legs, devil take it! And I can't stand up."

Justin knelt down beside him. There was blood on his forehead, a thin trickle of it running down his left cheek, but he made no mention of his own injury. Instead, he put his arm under Rick's shoulders and gently lifted him into a sitting position, easing the tail of his shirt from his breeches, and moving him into the faint light from the window.

"I can't see much in here," he apologized. "And I don't imagine there are any candles, but you've caught it in the back, all right. The swine were using buckshot, damn them to perdition! They—oh, here's Mr. Evans. Lie here for a minute or two, will you, Rick, whilst I have a word with him."

He had no choice, Rick thought bitterly. Anxiously he felt his right knee with his fingers, then the calf of his leg, digging his fingernails deep into the flesh. There was no sensation, and it was the same when he tested his other leg—he could feel no pressure, no twinge of pain.

God in heaven, he thought, seized by sudden panic, suppose he were paralyzed, suppose he were never able to walk again . . . suppose he were never able to make love to Katie again? His questing fingers went to his thigh and encountered the hard bulk of the nuggets in his breeches pocket. Despairingly he pressed the rounded stones into the muscles with all the strength he could summon . . . and felt nothing. He lay back, clammy with sweat, praying silently.

"Not that . . . oh, please God, not that! Have mercy on me, I beseech thee, Heavenly Father. . . ."

George Evans and Justin were talking in low voices as they stood together at the door, and Rick ceased praying and endeavored to listen to them, able to catch only a word or two of their exchange.

". . . secured the three you hit . . . won't have gone far. Your blackfellow can . . ." Evans was speaking. Rick lost his next words and then heard him ask, "Badly hurt, you think?"

Justin's answer was only just audible.

"I'm afraid so . . . charge of buckshot in his spine . . . get him to Bathurst . . . first light. One of your horses if . . . I think the military have a dray."

Evans's answer was in a louder tone. "The road's very rough, Justin, and it will take days. Is he fit to stand it?"

Rick held his breath, waiting for Justin's verdict. Relief flooded over him when he heard his friend and partner say, "He's strong and tough, George. But we've got to get him to a surgeon as fast as we can. Once that damned buckshot is removed, I reckon his troubles will be over. Maybe a couple of days' delay for him to rest up . . . we can see how he is when we get him to Bathurst."

"What about informing his folk?" George Evans asked. "I'm going back to Sydney right away, to give the Governor my report. I could—"

Justin cut him short, before Rick himself could intervene. "No," he said, with finality. "He's only recently married. Better wait until we see how he stands up to the journey. Tell His

Excellency, of course, but not the family or his wife. I'll send someone ahead, when the times comes, to tell them."

Rick sank back, satisfied. Katie would be spared anxiety, he thought, and once the surgeons got to work on him, he would be all right. And . . . his fingers closed about the gold in his pocket. Justin had made no mention of their search to George Evans, and Evans was leaving for Sydney—in all probability at once.

The secret was safe, and as soon as he had recovered, he could devise a means of selling the gold outside the colony. Old Silas Crabbe would be going home with the *Emu*, and he was completely trustworthy. . . .

He heard Evans say, "I wonder what induced those rogues to attack you? Hunger, do you suppose?"

"I fancy it must have been," Justin agreed. "We'd shot a 'roo and were cooking it. There's not much up here for escapers to eat, is there?"

Rick closed his eyes, and this time his prayer was one of thankfulness.

A little later, having made him comfortable on a pile of blankets, Justin brought him tea and some slices of freshly roasted meat. To his own surprise, his appetite was as keen as ever, and he ate every morsel with enjoyment.

Soon after dawn, strapped onto one of George Evans's pack-horses and with Justin leading it, he was on his way back to Bathurst . . . and Evans had gone.

CHAPTER XXIII

Considerably to his surprise, George De Lancey received an invitation to luncheon at the judge advocate's official residence, still occupied jointly by Jeffrey Hart Bent and his widowed sister-in-law. Enclosed with the formal invitation was a request, fulsomely worded, that he time his arrival an hour before the expected arrival of the other guests.

He was anxious, the deposed justice stated, to call him in consultation on a highly confidential legal matter, as a fellow member of Lincoln's Inn. It was for this reason that, after a good deal of thought, George decided to accept the invitation.

His initial dealings with Jeffrey Bent and his first meeting with his fellow barrister had been, to say the least, unhelpful. Bent had been arrogant and discourteous, for which, perhaps, he could be excused, since he had supposed that his own, somewhat precarious, position was threatened by the advent of a man as well qualified as himself to administer the colony's supreme court. But the Colonial Office had ordered his dismissal from office only a few weeks later, and Lord Bathurst had informed the Governor that two new judicial appointments had been made. Mr. John Wylde, a brother of the Lord Chancellor and a barrister of wide experience, was to succeed Jeffrey Bent's dead brother as a deputy judge advocate, and a Mr. Barron Field was to replace Bent himself as judge of the colony's supreme court.

Since he had contrived to prevent the supreme court from exercising its functions for almost two years, Jeffrey Bent could hardly complain about his dismissal from office. Indeed, this would have taken place much sooner, had Governor Macquarie possessed the authority to terminate his appointment or had the Colonial Office in England acted more swiftly. Macquarie had

offered to appoint George himself on a temporary basis, but he had
refused both this and the suggestion that he relieve the present
acting judge advocate, Frederick Garling, of the office he
supposedly did not want.

Perhaps . . . George smiled wryly as he reread the cryptic
note that had accompanied his luncheon invitation. Perhaps, if
Katie had not married Rick Tempest, he might have accepted the
Governor's second offer, as a means of establishing himself; but
since the girl he loved was now Mrs. Tempest, there seemed little
point in doing so. He would have incurred Jeffrey Bent's enmity if
he had, and he was loath to engage in the colony's bitter legal
wrangling, if he could avoid it. Bent's longtime feud with the
Governor, prosecuted with such venom, had shocked him deeply,
and . . . George folded the note and put it into his pocket.

It was, of course, difficult if not impossible to remain neutral,
and his own sympathies were with the hard-pressed Governor, for
whom he had conceived both liking and respect. Lachlan Macquarie might not be the most tactful of men, but he was an
honorable and unfailingly high-principled ruler, who worked
tirelessly to improve the lot of those over whom he ruled. Whereas
young Mr. Justice Bent was possessed of no principles at all—a
malevolent, scheming rogue, prepared to stop at nothing in his
efforts to undermine the Governor's authority and increase his
own.

George rose and started to pace the room. He had taken lodgings
in Macquarie Street, using the ground floor room as his professional chambers and the three small rooms above as living accommodation, and his law practice was beginning to build up—
sufficiently, at least, to justify the purchase of a curricle and a pair
of horses and the employment of a young ticket-of-leave man,
named Rodney Akeroyd, as his clerk. It was, perhaps, a trifle
ironic that, once having ascertained that he offered no rivalry,
Jeffrey Bent had referred clients to him and endeavored belatedly
to enlist his support for what he termed "the respectable members
of our society."

And he had responded to Bent's overtures initially, George
reflected. The unexpected meeting with Katie at Government
House had left him deeply shaken. He had welcomed any
opportunity to lose himself in his work, and although no cases
were heard in the closed supreme court, the magistrates' courts

were busy, and there was no lack of litigation among the respectable members of the colony's society. He had found himself in demand as defense counsel in Parramatta, as well as in Sydney, doing wordy battle against the often harsh sentences imposed by magistrates like the Reverend Samuel Marsden and his colleague Hannibal Macarthur.

Colonel Molle's officers had come to his chambers for legal advice, and some of the wealthy merchants and free settlers followed in their wake, bringing him their land-grant and shipping leases to study and pronounce on, their debts for which to sue, or—more usually—their creditors to placate.

He had had plenty to occupy him, but . . . disillusionment had come, opening his eyes to Jeffrey Bent's true character and purpose, when quite unexpectedly William Moore—the crown solicitor, whom the Governor had deprived of office—had come to him with the casually voiced suggestion that he might care to append his name to a petition.

"It is to be sent to Mr. Grey Bennet, M.P., who will present it to Parliament on our behalf," Moore had explained. "As you will see, Mr. De Lancey, a substantial number of our foremost citizens have signed their names to it, and it—ah—occurred to Mr. Justice Bent that you might wish to do likewise. Oh, you need not trouble to read it in full," he had added, when George had put out a hand to take the document from him. "It is a plea for justice, setting out specifically numerous examples of the Governor's unjust and oppressive conduct in relation to ourselves and those of our social standing in this colony. All the claims have, I assure you, been exhaustively examined, and most are supported by affidavits, duly sworn by the injured parties."

He had said a good deal more, George recalled, while he himself, on the pretext of listening, had read as much of the petition as he could contrive to get his hands on. It was a vindictive catalog, contributed to by malcontents, but so adroitly worded that it held a faint ring—if not of truth—at least of plausibility.

Even his cursory examination of the document had revealed an extraordinary variety of complaints and accusations, some petty and unproved, but a number, as Moore had said, supported by affidavits. All were calculated to show that Macquarie governed the colony autocratically, deeming himself to be above the law and riding roughshod over those who dared to question his authority.

It was claimed that he had ordered the flogging of "free persons, without the formality of a trial," that he had interfered with court proceedings and overruled judgments. The court-martial of the Reverend Benjamin Vale had been dealt with at considerable length, but the most damning accusation of all was contained in a few lines. With nothing to substantiate its veracity, it was suggested that the Governor's instructions to the coroner, to inquire into the death of a child, had been intended to protect his wife—whose carriage had run the child down—from a serious charge.

This last accusation had been so flagrant a falsehood that, George recalled, he had flung the infamous document across his desk in cold fury. He had heard the story of the accident from Elizabeth Macquarie herself on the occasion of his first meeting with her and, having witnessed her distress, had, at her request, attended the inquiry in order to represent the coachman, Joseph Big. The verdict of accidental death had been quite properly brought in, confirmed by reliable eyewitnesses, who had attached no blame to Big.

William Moore had grown indignant when he had refused to sign the petition, and the onetime crown solicitor had been angrier still, George remembered, when he had condemned it as a gross distortion of the truth and advised that, as such, it should not be sent to England.

Moore's annoyance had been shared by Jeffrey Bent; for a time the affronted young judge had ceased to have any dealings with him. The flow of "respectable" clients had dried up, the invitations to dine with the officers of Colonel Molle's regiment no longer reached him, and, George was reasonably certain, the petition had been dispatched to London without regard for his advice. The Governor had been aware of this but had made no attempt to stop it, contenting himself with a lengthy report to Lord Bathurst, which, he naively supposed, would be all that was required in rebuttal.

And perhaps it would be, George reflected, although he took leave to doubt it. At all events, Governor Macquarie seemed unconcerned; Bent's dismissal had been authorized by Lord Bathurst, and in the weary Governor's view, that was the end of the matter. What heed would the British government pay to the distorted accusations of a disgruntled former official, who by the time his petition reached London would long since have departed from the colony?

Indeed, everyone had expected that Bent and his brother's widow would lose no time in leaving Sydney, but instead they remained, on the plea of business matters to be cleared up and claims for a pension for Eliza Bent and her children yet to be agreed.

To his embarrassment, George had found himself once more the recipient of Jeffrey Bent's favors. Not only had more litigation been channeled in his direction; Bent had come in person to his chambers, in order to consult him as to the validity of his sister-in-law's entitlement to a pension and of his own, more complex, claims against both the home and the colonial governments.

He had behaved with courteous restraint, paid flattering tribute to his colleague's knowledge of the law, and appeared to have forgotten that there had ever been any differences between them, real or imagined.

And now this. . . . George frowned over the invitation lying on the desk in front of him. Only once before had he been a guest at the Bents' house, and he remembered the occasion well, for it had been on the day of Katie's wedding. Seeking distraction from that, he would have dined with the devil himself, he thought ruefully. But . . . today was another matter, and he was not looking forward to renewing his acquaintance with Ellis Bent's widow. True, she was a good-looking woman, but one who held no attraction for him, with the black widow's weeds that she seemed almost to flaunt as a sign of her loss, and her bitter, ceaselessly complaining tongue.

He consulted his pocket watch. It was time to go, if he was going to walk to the judge advocate's residence and arrive there punctually at the appointed hour. He called young Rodney Akeroyd in and left him with a sheaf of notes to copy, then let himself out into the street.

It was a fine, warm day, with a pleasant breeze blowing in from the harbor, but the street was crowded and dusty from lack of rain, and George felt no disposition to linger. Head down, he was striding briskly along the shaded side of the street when a carriage emerged from the vicinity of the hospital and a voice called out to him by name.

"Mr. De Lancey—wait! Let us give you a lift."

It was a feminine voice, and as the carriage pulled up just ahead of him, he recognized Julia Dawson and her stepmother seated in its commodious rear. Like Eliza Bent, Timothy Dawson's elder daughter possessed more than her share of dark good looks, and in his search for distraction he had, perhaps, paid her too much attention when he had first arrived in Sydney.

With a reluctance he was at pains to hide, George approached the carriage, hat in hand. He had been every sort of a thoughtless fool, he was aware, for he had never intended the girl to take him seriously. Julia Dawson was young, little more than a schoolgirl, but with the dearth of marriageable young women in Sydney society, she was in demand at most social gatherings. She could have taken her pick of Colonel Molle's youthful subalterns, who vied hotly for her attention, but Julia had ignored them and, to his dismay, had showered her favors on him.

At a ball, given by the 46th to celebrate their colonel's birthday, he had asked her for a dance, and she had crossed all the other names from her program and partnered him for the rest of the evening. Her escort, a subaltern named Bullivant, had been left fuming at her desertion, and her stepmother, the charming Abigail Dawson, had seemingly been as perplexed by her behavior as he himself had been.

The last thing he wanted was a serious entanglement, George reflected ruefully, but Julia was setting her cap at him, and Sydney's gossips were waiting expectantly for a romance to develop between them.

"Mrs. Dawson—Miss Julia, good day." Purposely, he made his greeting formal, bending over Abigail Dawson's hand, as custom decreed, but bowing distantly to her eagerly smiling companion. Undeterred, Julia patted the seat beside her and repeated her invitation.

"We are on our way home for luncheon," she added, with a swift, questioning glance at her stepmother. "If you have no other engagement, Mr. De Lancey, perhaps you would care to join us?"

Abigail did not echo the suggestion; her slight frown, in her stepdaughter's direction, was disapproving. George said hastily, "Thank you, but I have a luncheon engagement, Miss Dawson, and I'm on my way to it now."

He stood back, expecting the carriage to move on, but Julia Dawson persisted.

"Perhaps," she said sweetly, "it is on our way, too, and we can, at least, save you walking. Where are you lunching, Mr. De Lancey?"

Disconcerted by the question, George was unable to dissemble. "At the judge advocate's residence, Miss Dawson. But I assure you, I find walking no hardship."

"In this heat?" Julia countered. "Oh, come, sir, it is no pleasure! And the judge advocate's residence *is* on our way, is it not, Abigail?"

"Yes," Abigail conceded. "Of course it is. So let us drop you there, Mr. De Lancey. It will be no trouble."

Realizing that it would be a breach of good manners to refuse, George thanked her and got into the carriage. The coachman whipped up his horses, and he did his best to make polite small talk as the vehicle bowled slowly along the dusty thoroughfare. Skirting the rear of the Government House garden, the road became unusually crowded, with people making in excited droves for the cove. The coachman was compelled to slow the carriage to walking pace.

"I'm sorry, ma'am," he called to Abigail, "but there's that many folk all over the road, I dursn't go no faster."

"What is going on?" Abigail demanded. "Ask someone, Thomas—ask why they're running."

The coachman bawled a question, and several passersby answered him in unintelligible unison. He said confusedly, "Near as I can make out, ma'am, there's a ship gone down at 'er moorin's in the cove. I reckon 'tis the *Elizabeth*, ma'am."

"The *Elizabeth*? But she was launched only two days ago." Abigail's distress was in her stricken face. "I was there when Mrs. Macquarie performed the naming ceremony! How terrible . . . I hope those people were wrong."

But when the carriage reached the end of the road and came in sight of the cove, George saw, with a pang, that their informants had made no mistake. The new government sloop lay on her side, with the water washing over her and half a dozen oared boats clustered about her, pulling frantically this way and that in search of survivors from her crew.

The King's ship *Emu*, back at the anchorage after her refit, had evidently acted with commendable speed, George realized, as he leaped down from the carriage, for two of the boats were hers, and they were fishing men from the water. He recognized, or thought he recognized, the tall uniformed figure of James Forster, her commander, in the sternsheets of one. "My God," he exclaimed hoarsely, "what happened?"

A man in the watching crowd, a seaman by his garb, answered him. "She just capsized, sir, for no rhyme or reason that I could see—less'n that mainmast o' hers weren't rightly stepped. Her new cap'n came aboard, with his wife, an' they was hoistin' tops'ls ready to take her out for her sea trials, and . . . over she went! I seen it all, standin' here. The King's ship didn't waste no time, but I fear there'll be quite a few o' them lost. Gone down with her, you see, sir. It happened so sudden, if they was belowdecks, they'd have had no warnin'."

George returned to the carriage with the tragic news. Abigail said sadly, "All the years it took to build her, and then to end like that! Poor Mrs. Macquarie will be so upset—the ship was named after her, you know—*Elizabeth Henrietta*. There was some question as to who was to be given command—Justin Broome wanted it badly. But Captain Jeffrey overruled the Governor, and it was Lieutenant Meredith who was chosen. Well"—she gave a despondent shrug—"Justin will have reason to be relieved that the ship did not go down when he was in command, I imagine." She glanced across at Julia, who was weeping ostentatiously, and bade her, a trifle sharply, to dry her eyes. "I'll call on Mrs. Macquarie at once and offer my condolences. You can make your own way to Mr. Bent's from here, can you not, Mr. De Lancey? It's only a stone's throw, and with this crowd, you'll probably be quicker on foot."

"Yes, of course, Mrs. Dawson." George thanked her and took his leave, the sobbing Julia making no attempt to detain him.

He found Jeffrey Bent in the room—built originally to house the supreme court—that he had taken over as combined chambers and reception annex. He, too, had been watching the rescue attempt in the cove, and he expressed his concern at some length, interspersed with criticism of the *Elizabeth*'s builders.

"They are all the same, these damned colonial merchants. Only interested in profit for themselves, never mind how badly the work's carried out. And Campbell's been in financial difficulties of late, I believe—some upset with the East India Company over cargoes. He probably skimped the work on the *Elizabeth*, and that's why she went down."

"As I had understood it," George demurred, "the ship was built to Admiralty specifications, of materials sent out for the purpose. That's what the Governor told me—and he blamed the delay in completing her on the time it took to obtain the materials from England. I should think Campbell's shipwrights lost heart—and small wonder!"

"That is no excuse for poor workmanship," Bent retorted smugly. "I believe they saved most of her crew, but there's a rumor—alas, quite a strong rumor—that poor little Mrs. Meredith has not been found. Please God we may not have yet another tragic death to mourn! I see every day, in the face of my poor sister-in-law, what effect my brother's loss, at so young an age, has had on her. At least the Merediths had not been married long enough to have children. Mrs. Bent, my dear De Lancey, has five, all under eight years of age, and the fifth born after my poor brother's demise! He wore himself out in the service of this benighted colony, and yet the Governor procrastinates over the granting of a widow's pension to her."

George studied the thin, pale face and petulant mouth of the man in front of him, more than a little repelled by what he saw. Jeffrey Bent was young—thirty-one or two, someone had said— but he had an oddly pedantic manner better suited to one of twice his age, and he made an aggressive assumption of authority that, in itself, was provocative and was probably intended to be. The deposed justice lacked dignity, yet he endeavored to give the impression that he possessed it, and his dark eyes were constantly darting this way and that, as if challenging confrontation and then seeking to avoid it.

"They buried my brother in the common burial ground," Bent was saying. "In the same place where lie the mortal remains of convicted felons and a host of ne'er-do-wells! It is quite inexcusable, a final, cruel insult to his widow and children. I am exerting all the influence left to me in the hope of persuading General Macquarie to have him reinterred in the chancel of St. Philip's Church, as befits the immense service he rendered. In this, I may say, De Lancey, I have the support of the Reverend Samuel Marsden, in addition to that of most of the respectable citizens of Sydney. And, sir, if it is the last thing I do before I leave here, I shall see to it that my brother's poor bones lie in a tomb that is worthy of him. He—"

George quietly interrupted the flow. "Did you invite me here, sir, to discuss the question of your late brother's reinterment?"

Jeffrey Bent's gaze met his for a moment and then darted to the papers on his desk. "No," he denied. "I invited you here for a different purpose. It is a matter that, in the present circumstances, I cannot deal with myself. But it is a serious matter, sir, I assure you." He selected a roll of heavy cartridge paper from the pile in front of him and went on gravely, "No doubt you have heard of the infamous practice here of circulating the so-called pipes, by means of which the honor and integrity of decent persons are attacked in doggerel verse? No one is immune to such attack, and successive Governors have suffered it . . . indeed, most prominent officials have been subjected to it, at one time or another. I have myself. The offensive verses are inscribed on paper such as this, which is then neatly rolled and placed in some conspicuous public place, where it is easily found and, of course, passed around to all and sundry."

"I have heard of the practice," George answered, again endeavoring to halt the flow of Bent's pedantry. "But I should not have supposed—"

"That it would merit calling you in conference, De Lancey?" The roll of heavy paper was waved impatiently in front of him. "Normally it would not—normally the verse is the work of barely literate rogues, or it is made to seem so. But this—this truly malevolent attack on Colonel Molle's honor and loyalty was composed by a person with a classical education and with a knowledge of Latin and Greek. And it has been copied and widely circulated, but . . . glance at the scurrilous aspersions the author casts. See for yourself, De Lancey, what harm it can do!"

George unrolled the paper. The verse ran to several pages, he saw, and was headed with a Latin tag—"*In foro conscientiae*"— which he translated as "judged by one's own conscience." The unknown poet, confessing himself "irresolute of choice amidst the numerous votaries of Vice," went on:

Till thou, G___ge M_ll_, high o'er the rest art seen.
Thou of the stately port and haughty mien.
Who would not say that such a portly gait

Revealed a mind aspiring, noble, great?
Who would imagine that contemptuous smile,
Which seems so keenly others to revile,
Conceals a Soul so attached to filthy pelf,
One undivided mercenary self . . .

Astounded, George turned the closely written pages. Verse
followed verse, all in the same or similar vein, now pouring scorn
on Colonel Molle's friends and associates—who included Bent
himself and the Reverend Samuel Marsden—now deriding the
colonel's military prowess in words of searing, contemptuous
mockery. One stanza in particular caught and held George's
attention, and he read it through twice, astonished by the poet's
intimate knowledge of Molle's apparent betrayal of Governor
Macquarie's friendship:

See him, on days of state, with joyful haste,
Attend the Ruler's summons to the feast;
Hear him with three times three in bumper toast,
Propose 'The Health of our Illustrious Host,'
Then, in oration ready cut and dried,
Wish that the helm of State he long may guide.

With what effrontery he makes the prayer.
And can it be that he is not sincere?
Yes! While he feigns with friendship warm to glow,
He is his greatest, bitterest, deadliest foe;
He seeks his power and influence to thwart,
By every dirty, sly, insidious art . . .

The pipe ended:

And now farewell, thou dirty, groveling M_l_e!
Go with thy namesake, burrow in thy hole!

"Well?" Jeffrey Bent challenged, when George laid the sheets
of stiff paper back on his desk. "It's a pretty iniquitous piece of
work, is it not? And, as may be imagined, it has greatly angered
Colonel Molle, who is determined to trace the perpetrator."

"Does he have any idea who that might be?"

"The colonel has his *suspicions*, certainly." Bent whisked the offending papers away, thrusting them hurriedly into a drawer, as if their mere touch might contaminate him. "Initially he feared that one of his junior officers might have been responsible, due to an excess of high spirits perhaps, or a warped sense of humor. But to a man they denied it, and all agreed to permit a search to be made of their quarters for any sign of incriminating material. This was duly carried out and nothing found. All the officers of Colonel Molle's regiment are cleared of suspicion, their loyalty beyond doubt. In proof of this, they have jointly offered a reward of two hundred pounds—no small sum, De Lancey—for information that will lead to the unmasking of the author of this foul and libelous poem."

His dark, glowing eyes fixed momentarily on George's face, Bent waited expectantly for a reaction. Reluctant to commit himself, George hesitated. Strictly speaking, the offending poem was libelous, since the truth it contained could not easily be proved; but from what he knew of the 46th's unpleasant commanding officer, the unknown poet had not been guilty of any gross exaggeration—and Molle would have his work cut out to convince any court that he had.

"In what way do you suppose that I can assist you?" he asked. "I am, as you know, newly arrived here, and my acquaintance is limited. I can offer no suggestion as to the author, but if he is discovered, does Colonel Molle propose to sue him?"

"Of course he does!" Bent was indignant. "Damme, sir, it was for that reason that I invited you here. In the unhappy circumstances in which Governor Macquarie has placed me, I cannot act for the colonel myself. He wants *you* to act for him."

George stared at him. "My professional advice, sir, would be that Colonel Molle should *not* sue. In any court of law, he would have difficulty in proving libel, and even if he were able to do so, the resulting publicity would be harmful to him, would it not? His best course, in my view, would be to treat the poem as laughable. If he does, it will soon be forgotten, surely? A joke in poor taste, a lampoon—"

"It is more than that!" Bent said furiously. "And a great many people have already seen it. Devil take it, De Lancey, you read enough of the miserable effusion to realize that it impugns George Molle's honor! It accuses him of hypocrisy, of perfidy in his relations with the Governor."

"He is no friend to the Governor, Bent," George pointed out dryly.

"The infernal Governor has few friends amongst the respectable inhabitants of the colony. But . . ." Jeffrey Bent paused and, for all they were alone in the spacious room, lowered his voice. "He has his adherents, of course, particularly amongst the lower ranks of society. The popular belief is that his upstart secretary, Campbell, wrote the poem, and certainly he's quite capable of having done so. He's attacked Marsden and myself in the infernal *Gazette* before now, though admittedly he's avoided libel and made his comments anonymously, like the cowardly creature he is. Molle himself suspects a fellow named Murray—you probably know him. He once held a commission in the First Dragoons, but I fancy he was cashiered . . . at all events, he came out here under a cloud."

"You cannot mean Robert Murray, who acts as clerk to the Sydney bench?" George was startled.

"That's the fellow—a toady of Wentworth's. Calls himself *Captain* Murray. I don't think he has the education, but . . ." Once again the erstwhile judge paused, and his wayward gaze was briefly focused on George's face. "I have a much more likely suspect, De Lancey. A young officer who betrays his caste by associating too freely with pardoned felons and their like. He has even gone into partnership with one such person in a land grant, in the new territory beyond Bathurst." There was another wary pause, but this time Bent kept his gaze averted. He went on accusingly, "The pipe was left at the entrance to the officers' mess of the Forty-sixth three weeks ago. Three weeks—and my suspect took himself off the very next day to his land grant and hasn't been seen here since! You know, I feel sure, to whom I refer."

George shook his head, his temper rising, anticipating the suggestion that was about to be made. "No," he managed woodenly, "I don't think I do, sir."

"Oh, come now, sir!" Bent urged. "He is not a fellow *you* have cause to respect greatly, I've reason to believe. Newly wed and he leaves his poor bride to languish alone, whilst he vanishes into the mountains, leaving that iniquitous poem to be found and suspicion to attach itself to others! I refer, sir, to Richard Tempest."

George's brain was racing. Why, he wondered, aghast, should Bent infer that he had any reason to dislike Rick Tempest? Why, for that matter, should he attempt to attribute authorship of the pipe to Katie's new husband? Merely because he had left Sydney the day after the infernal thing had been deposited outside the 46th's mess? It was ludicrous. He started to say so, controlling his indignation, but Bent waved him to silence.

"Sydney is not a place where secrets are easily kept, De Lancey. Your previous attachment to the beautiful Mrs. Tempest is known, and—er—it has aroused some speculation. Despite your attempt to pull the wool over our eyes by the attention you have seen fit to pay to . . . what is her name? The little Dawson girl. No, wait—" he protested as George rose wrathfully to his feet. "I've not done, my friend. I—"

"I think you have said more than enough, sir," George managed coldly, keeping a tight rein on his temper.

But he recalled, with dismay, the eavesdropper who had overheard his brief, impassioned plea to Katie a few days before her wedding . . . the woman in the white dress, whom neither of them had been able to identify. Mrs. Jeffrey had been at Government House that evening . . . she had been a close friend of Colonel and Mrs. Molle and of the Bents also, he supposed. Certainly some woman had been privy to his clandestine meeting with Rick Tempest's bride, and whoever she was, she had talked of what she had seen and heard and had set tongues wagging.

Jeffrey Bent smiled. He said, as if there had been no interruption, "It occurred to me that you are in a unique position to prove—or disprove—my suspicions, in this particular case. And I can offer you a guarantee that, should you give him proof, Colonel Molle would see to it that you receive the two hundred pounds reward . . . this being, of course, conditional on a successful prosecution of the culprit, brought on the colonel's behalf by yourself. Well—what do you say, De Lancey? It is a fair proposition in these circumstances, is it not?"

Sickened, George reached for his hat. Bent, he thought, was trying both to bribe and to blackmail him, but . . . determined not to be provoked into an outburst he might afterward regret, he bowed stiffly.

"Your proposition is beneath contempt, sir, and I reject it with the scorn it merits." It took every vestige of self-control he possessed to speak calmly, but somehow he contrived to do so. "I cannot bring myself to accept your hospitality, Justice Bent.

Perhaps you will convey my regrets to your sister-in-law for my absence from her luncheon party."

He was still shaking with barely suppressed anger when he emerged into the street. Cramming his hat on his head, he started to walk blindly away, intent only on putting as great a distance as he could between himself and the man he had just left. There were people still gathered round the vantage points overlooking the anchorage, and George let himself be carried along by the crowd, scarcely conscious of where he went.

The sloop *Elizabeth Henrietta* had been righted, and men were on board her, hauling out guns, he saw, as he came nearer to the cove, his anger slowly starting to cool. Ex-Justice Bent was not worth troubling about, he told himself; like his damned proposition, he was beneath contempt, he— A bright golden head, moving with difficulty through the crowd, caught his eye, and he drew in his breath sharply, recognizing Katie.

She was alone or appeared to be and, it seemed, in some considerable haste, but constantly impeded by the press of curious onlookers through whose ranks she was attempting to pass. He had not set eyes on her since her marriage to Richard Tempest, and prudence dictated that he should avoid her now, in view of Jeffrey Bent's insidious remark concerning their previous relationship, but . . . he saw her stumble and almost fall, and all thought of prudence was swiftly erased from his mind. In a few impatient strides he was beside her, elbowing aside a pair of drunken convict women who barred his path.

"Take my arm, Katie," he bade her, "and let's get clear of this mob."

She did as he asked, and he led her into the comparative emptiness of Bridge Street. It was then, when they came to a breathless halt, that George realized she was weeping.

"What is it, Katie?" he asked, resisting the impulse to take her into his arms. "Did the crowd alarm you?"

Katie shook her head. "No—no, it wasn't that." With trembling hands, she replaced her bonnet on her head. "I hadn't expected so many people. I would not have gone that way if I'd known."

"The new government sloop capsized," George told her. "That was what brought them. God knows where they all came from!"

Katie mopped her tear-stained face, and he felt her shudder. "I

did not see her go down, but . . . I saw them bring in two—
bodies. One was Mrs. Meredith's, George. She—poor young soul,
she hadn't been married as long as I have, and she was drowned.
Someone in the crowd said that she had been below when the ship
turned over."

George reached for her hands, taking them gently in his own.
"Yes," he confirmed. "I heard that, too. But where were you
going in such haste, Katie? And why were you on foot and
alone?"

"Oh!" It was as if she had suddenly been recalled to her
mission, and the tears returned, streaming uncontrollably down
her cheeks. "To the—to the hospital, that's where I was going. A
soldier came about—oh, more than an hour ago. He said that my
husband, that Rick had been injured, and they were bringing him
down from Bathurst in a dray. He didn't know any more than that.
He couldn't tell me how badly Rick was hurt."

"Or when he would reach here?" George suggested.

"No. He—he said I should stay where I was, in the house, and
I'd be sent for. But I couldn't . . . just wait, George. I had to
come. Even if he's not at the hospital yet, I can wait there and be
there when he arrives." Katie bit back a sob and looked up at him,
bravely attempting to smile. "I came by myself because we have
only one servant, and I had sent her to the market. I . . . stupid-
ly, I didn't even change my shoes. I just ran out and—and straight
into that crowd. I did not want to come through the Domain, you
see, I—"

"I'll take you to the hospital, Katie," George offered. "And
we'll wait there together until they bring Rick in."

But Rick was already there when they reached the hospital, and
inquiries elicited the fact that the surgeons were about to operate,
to remove shot from his back.

"It seems he was attacked by some damned bushrangers," a
young surgeon told them. "Dr. Redfern is caring for him. But I
think you'll be permitted to see him, Mrs. Tempest, if you would
like to come with me."

Katie was gone for only a few minutes, and when she returned,
she was white with shock.

"Justin was there," she whispered unhappily. "His partner,
Justin Broome. He—he's staying with Rick whilst they take out

the—the buckshot, he said it was. Rick can't walk, George. He has no feeling in his legs, he—'' She was choking with sobs.

George put his arm around her. "He'll be all right once the buckshot is removed, Katie,'' he assured her, with a confidence he did not feel. "Let me take you home. I'll come back here and find out how he's faring, and—''

"No," Katie said obstinately. "I'll stay here till—till the surgeons have finished with him. I—I have to know. To be with him when they've done. Justin promised he would tell me.''

George waited with her in the small, bleak room that was put at their disposal, doing his best to comfort and reassure her. The time passed with agonizing slowness, as Katie wept softly and the shadows lengthened.

The tall Justin Broome came finally to take her to her husband's bedside.

"He's fine, Katie, and wanting to see you," he said, but his eyes, meeting George's over her bent head, held no such promise. When she was out of earshot, supported by the kindly Dr. Redfern, Justin added, with terse bitterness, "Devil take those swine of escapers! Some of the buckshot can't be removed—it's too close to the spinal cord. Redfern's afraid he'll never walk again." He expelled his breath in a long sigh. "You—you're Mr. George De Lancey, are you not? I'm Justin Broome. You need not stay any longer, sir. I'll look after that poor girl. I'll bring her back with me. My wife is a good friend of hers; she'll know how to break it to her, when the time comes."

George thanked him and accepted his dismissal with the best grace he could muster. But, as he walked out into the dark, deserted street, he cursed the fates that had timed his arrival in Sydney so ill that honor demanded he must walk away from the woman he loved, leaving strangers to care for her, because he could not.

A carriage drew up a few yards away, and in the semidarkness he recognized Abigail Dawson and Julia. They alighted quickly, and he stood aside as they hurried into the hospital, seemingly without seeing him. He watched them go, with a heavy heart, his own isolation suddenly unendurable.

CHAPTER XXIV

"Lieutenant Broome, Your Excellency," John Campbell, the Governor's secretary, announced. He stood aside, smiling, for Justin to precede him.

"Justin, my dear boy!" Governor Macquarie's greeting was, as always, affable. "Sit down. You've come, I take it, to tell me that the *Elizabeth Henrietta* is now seaworthy; but I have the advantage of you. . . . I watched you take her out for her sea trials early this morning. I also, I confess, watched somewhat anxiously for your return."

Justin took the proffered chair. "She came through her trial with flying colors, sir," he answered. "I'd like to do a little more work on her and try her in storm conditions when the opportunity arises, but . . . she's ready for service, if you require her."

"Good!" Macquarie approved. "Have you formed any conclusions as to what caused her to capsize, with such tragic results?"

He had come to some very firm conclusions, Justin thought, but in the circumstances he had decided not to voice them. Poor Meredith had relinquished his command and returned to England with the *Emu*, and what had been done could not be undone. In any case, Meredith's errors had been due to lack of experience, in that he had failed to observe the faults in the sloop's construction— and for that he could scarcely be held culpable.

"I am compiling a full report, sir," he said guardedly. "There were a number of causes, of which the most serious were the size and positioning of her mainmast and the weight of her guns. These have all been put right now, sir. We've stepped a shorter mast."

The Governor seemed satisfied with his brief explanation and again expressed his approval.

"Do whatever you deem necessary," he added. "The command

is yours, Justin, as I had decided initially it should be. But, as you're aware, Captain Jeffrey insisted that it was his right to appoint a commander . . . for all I am His Majesty's viceroy and commander in chief, I do not always get my own way."

"No, sir," Justin acknowledged, without rancor. He shifted uneasily in his chair, conscious that the real reason for his call on the Governor would not be so easily explained. Rick Tempest had told him only two days ago of his gold find at Pengallon, and . . .

The Governor gave him, unintentionally, the opening he sought. "Tell me—how is Richard Tempest faring? That was a most unfortunate business, and even though the miscreants who injured him have been apprehended, it scarcely compensates for his sufferings, I fear. Dr. Redfern told me that the poor young man may never walk again."

"Yes, sir, he told me that also. The surgeons have been unable to remove all the buckshot from close to his spinal cord. Sir, Tempest was shot at point-blank range, you see, and the men who attacked him were—"

"Why *did* they attack him—attack you both?" the Governor asked sharply. "Were they after food, do you suppose?"

It was his chance, and Justin took it.

"No, sir, they were after gold." As briefly as he could, he repeated the details of Rick's gold find. "A whisper must have got out. Tempest tried as hard as he knew how to keep his discovery a secret—indeed, sir, he has only just informed me of it. He entrusted these nuggets to me, so that I could show them to you." Carefully, he unwrapped the nuggets and laid them on the desk for the Governor's inspection. "It's alluvial gold, without any doubt, I believe, sir."

Macquarie stared down at the gleaming objects, his dismay mirrored in his thin, lined face. His reaction, Justin thought, was precisely what he had warned Rick it was likely to be, but even so, he was unprepared for its intensity.

"God in heaven!" the Governor exclaimed harshly. "If word of this should be allowed to spread, the consequences could be disastrous! The convicts could not be controlled—there would be mass escapes, and every escaper would be up in the mountains, in the new grazing lands, searching for gold. And not only the convicts—free men, too, the emancipated settlers, men of the garrison." He picked up the larger nugget and weighed it in the palm of one hand, the expression on his face one of mingled shock and anger. But, controlling himself, he went on more calmly, "You did well to bring this to my attention, Justin. Has it been examined by an expert—has it been assayed?"

"Only some of the smaller pieces, sir," Justin answered. "Tempest took them to a man named Hensall, at the mint."

"The rogue I had flogged . . . well, I suppose a way can be found to ensure his silence. Or better still, I will have an official statement issued, to the effect that samples of rock from the Bathurst area have been analyzed and found to be worthless. The truth *has* to be suppressed."

Macquarie sighed deeply, motioning Justin to pick up the nuggets. "Keep them well hidden. You understand why, Justin, do you not? The future prosperity of this colony lies in making it self-supporting by means of its agriculture and, once the new lands are opened for graziers, in meat and wool. The people would starve if they were permitted to squander the bounties of nature in a wild quest for gold. As it is at present populated, this colony could well become ungovernable, with all that we have worked so hard to achieve in danger of being destroyed. I cannot permit that to happen, or even run the risk of it."

"I understand that very well, sir," Justin assured him. Indeed, these were the same arguments that he himself had advanced to Rick, but which Rick had not understood and probably would never understand. He had revealed his find with extreme reluctance, because it had been forced on him by his present incapacity, but he had done so in the obstinate belief that Governor Macquarie would grant him a license to prospect for gold at Pengallon.

"Mr. Evans has done splendid work, exploring the Lachlan River," Macquarie went on. "James Meehan and young Hamilton Hume are spreading our frontiers even further to the south and west. When Mr. Oxley completes his investigation of the land and the rivers beyond Bathurst, I intend to open the Bathurst Plains to settlement. I intend also to give grants of agricultural land in the Illawarra area and found a settlement at Jervis Bay and in the Bargo Valley. These plans are too important, too essential, to be jeopardized." He paused, eyeing Justin gravely. "For that reason, Justin, the terms of your land grant must be altered to exclude the right to mineral deposits for . . . well, how long do *you* think it will take to bring my plans to fruition? Ten years, twenty? . . . I shall not be here to see it, but you will—and, please God, your friend Tempest also. In the meantime, you must both keep silent concerning the gold and rest content to rear sheep and cattle on your grant."

"Yes, sir," Justin acknowledged. "I expected that would be Your Excellency's decision. I'm arranging for my brother to bring up a small flock of sheep from Ulva, as soon as the buildings are completed and I can obtain the services of a reliable shepherd."

The Governor nodded his approval.

"Excellent. Mr. Cox, as I imagine you know, has established a small military post on the Lachlan River, as a prelude to John Oxley's expedition, which I trust will set off in March or April. It might perhaps be advisable to post a corporal's guard on or near your holding, whilst it remains unoccupied. If any whisper does get out concerning the gold, that will discourage the curious and the escapers . . . the guard can be deemed part of Oxley's preparations. And John Campbell shall prepare a suitable statement for publication in the *Gazette*, calculated to scotch any rumors. I think that is about all we can do at present, Justin. Be so good as to call Mr. Campbell from his office, will you, please?"

Secretary Campbell entered with a broad smile on his face.

"I was just coming to inform Your Excellency that the transport *Lady Elizabeth* has been sighted off the Heads, with Judge Advocate Wylde on board, sir. The wind is favorable, and her master signaled for the pilot to bring her in. Do you wish me to go out to meet Mr. Wylde, sir?"

Governor Macquarie's thin, austere face lit up. "Thanks be to God," he said, more to himself than to his two listeners. "Now, perhaps, I shall be able to rid myself and this colony of that designing blackguard whose sole delight it is to sow the seeds of discord and insubordination!" He recalled himself to his surroundings and offered a smiling apology. "I let myself be carried away, gentlemen—forgive my outburst. By all means, go out to bid Mr. Wylde and his family welcome, John. And explain, as tactfully as you can, that his official residence is in the continued occupation of his predecessor's widow and the late judge of the supreme court, Mr. Jeffrey Hart Bent. Tell him we shall endeavor to place temporary accommodation at his disposal with all possible speed, and . . . yes, ask His Honor to give us the pleasure of his company at dinner this evening."

"Very good, sir. Rest assured that I shall do my best to be tactful, but"—John Campbell spread his hands helplessly—"it is not an easy situation to explain to a newcomer, is it, sir?"

"No," Macquarie agreed grimly. An idea suddenly occurred to him, and his expression relaxed. "Take Mr. De Lancey with you, John—send round now to ascertain if he is at liberty to accompany you—and leave the explanation to him. He's a barrister, and he's been here long enough to be aware of our situation in regard to the Bents. And Justin—"

"Sir?"

"Take command of my barge and convey the two gentlemen to the *Lady Elizabeth*, if you please. Mr. Wylde shall be welcomed in style."

Less than an hour later, the government barge, its smartly uniformed crew at the oars and Justin seated in the stern, was waiting alongside the steps from the wharf when first Campbell and then, a few minutes later, George De Lancey made their appearances.

The barge put off while John Campbell was still explaining the reason for the unexpected summons, and Justin saw a gleam of sardonic amusement in De Lancey's eyes as he listened.

"I see," he acknowledged quietly. "Well . . . I shall do my best, Mr. Campbell. Has the new judge advocate a family, do you know?"

"A wife and child, I believe," the secretary answered. "And his father, Mr. Thomas Wylde, who, we were informed, is to act as clerk of the peace."

"And is there no immediate prospect of Mr. Bent vacating his official residence?"

Campbell sighed despondently. "At a price, sir, at a price. I received a list of the articles Mrs. Bent requires us to compensate her for, before she will consent to vacate the premises. They range from her venetian blinds, valued at sixty pounds, to her fire irons and pantry fittings—in total, the sum of two hundred and thirty-eight pounds. I have not yet summoned the courage to present her demands to His Excellency."

"That is tantamount to extortion," De Lancey said, his brows raised in surprise.

"Indeed, sir, it is," Campbell agreed. "When you take into account the sum of two thousand nine hundred and fifty pounds of government money, which was advanced to the late Ellis Bent to enable him to build his official residence. And," he added sourly, "it was to include a courtroom. I don't know whether you've ever seen the room he allocated for that purpose, but . . . it was a mere twenty feet square!"

"I was in it a few days ago," De Lancey answered. He caught Justin's eye and shrugged. "It would barely have held the bench and the court officials."

"Quite," the Governor's secretary said, pursing his lips disapprovingly. "And all the fuss Mrs. Bent is making about a pension and allowances for her children is driving the poor Governor to distraction. Her late husband was given a grant of twelve hundred acres of prime land on the Nepean River for the benefit of his two sons, land that was to be held under covenant for five years. He sold it within six months!"

"I think, Mr. Campbell," De Lancey begged, "that you had best tell me no more. If I divulge the half of it to our newly arrived judge advocate, he's liable to take passage on the next ship bound for England!" He turned to Justin. "How is your friend Richard Tempest, Mr. Broome? Have the surgeons managed to remove the buckshot from his spine, or have they abandoned the attempt?"

"I understand they've abandoned it for the time being," Justin told him. "He is to be sent home, in the hope that rest and careful nursing may improve his condition—or that the shot may move of its own accord into a more accessible position." He hesitated, remembering George De Lancey's presence at the hospital, the evening when they had brought Rick in. Julia Dawson had expressed annoyance over the familiarity De Lancey had shown to Rick's wife, but . . . he had scarcely listened. And Jessica had dismissed it as jealousy, plain and simple. "Poor Rick is very despondent, as might be expected. I understand Dr. Redfern has told him that his paralysis is temporary, the consequence of a damaged nerve. But the poor fellow can't walk."

Campbell joined in, asking for details of the bushrangers' attack, and Justin answered him with crisp brevity. "We wounded three of them, and the others gave themselves up to the military search party the next day. They had all escaped from the government farm at Emu Crossing, and they told Ensign Dean that—"

"Do you mean young Michael Dean?" De Lancey put in. "Was he there?"

"Yes," Justin confirmed cautiously. Since Jessica had confided in him, he had been careful to say as little as possible about his newfound brother-in-law, and he regretted having inadvertently mentioned him by name now. But De Lancey, it seemed, had a high regard for Michael Dean.

"We traveled out together in that hell ship, the *Conway*. Dean conducted himself extremely well, in very trying circumstances. Indeed, it was largely thanks to his evidence at the court of inquiry that the swine of a master got his just deserts. Dean's a most promising young officer, in my view—but why in the world has he been banished to Bathurst? Whose toes did he tread on?"

Justin smiled, recalling the boy's indignation at his unexpected posting. "It would appear that Colonel Molle did not think so highly of his conduct as you did, Mr. De Lancey—or of his conduct during the *Conway*'s passage out."

"Good Lord, why not?"

"The colonel claimed that it did not redound to the regiment's credit, I gathered. However, now that he's there, I don't think Dean regards being posted to Bathurst as banishment. He's enjoying an independent command and seems to be in his element. Captain Lawson, the commandant, is seldom there. He owns an estate at Prospect and has a thousand-acre grant near mine and Rick's, on the Macquarie River, which he's busy stocking."

"Was he not one of the party that made the first successful crossing of the Blue Mountains?" George De Lancey asked, with interest. "Lawson, I mean?"

"He was," John Campbell supplied. "And so was Justin himself. Contrary to any impression you may have formed after your first few months in Sydney, Mr. De Lancey, we're not solely engaged in squabbling amongst ourselves or concerned with legal wrangling and the like. Captain Lawson, Mr. Gregory Blaxland, and Dr. Wentworth's younger son, William Charles Wentworth, led the expedition. . . ." He launched into a lengthy account of the crossing, George Evans's subsequent explorations, and the building of the road to Bathurst.

Justin, embarrassed by the lavish praise being heaped on him for his part in the enterprise, at last interrupted.

"There is your ship, gentlemen," he announced, pointing ahead of them to where a tall three-decker lay at anchor off South Head. "The pilot cutter's just getting under way. I'll put you aboard before she makes sail."

He brought the Governor's barge alongside the looming dark side of the *Lady Elizabeth* with practiced skill. As his passengers clambered up to her entryport, he glimpsed a tall figure watching with interest from the upper deck. It was the merest glimpse, but what he saw heartened him—the new judge advocate appeared young and vigorous, a dark-haired man, with an unmistakable air of dignity about him, which Jeffrey Bent, for all his posturing and claims to distinction, would find it hard to match. If, indeed, the Governor permitted him the freedom to try . . . Justin smiled to himself.

"Very well, cox'un," he said, as the bowman released his boathook from the *Lady Elizabeth*'s lee chains. "Let's have the mains'l on her and head for home."

Under the brisk southwesterly breeze, the barge made swift progress, the weary oarsmen thankful to relax after their six-mile pull against it.

It wanted about an hour to sunset when they entered the cove, and Justin paid a brief call at the shipyard before going home. The long nine-pounder bow-chaser gun was due to be mounted in his new command the next day, and he was anxious to make sure that the yard's preparations were complete. Another disaster such as the one that had followed the sloop's naming must, he knew, be avoided at all costs. Meredith had insisted on a long eighteen on a heavy traversing carriage, which had contributed to the sloop's instability, and Justin was determined to take no chances when his own gun was mounted. Reassured that all was in readiness for the following morning's work, he walked the short distance to the small, white-painted cottage on the waterfront, to find Jessica awaiting him and his meal ready.

Little Red greeted him with delight and sat happily on his knee, wielding his spoon with more enthusiasm than skill and helping himself to any plate but his own, an angelic smile curving his lips when his mother chided him for his greed. When, finally, he was packed off to bed, protesting tearfully, Justin lit his pipe and settled in his favorite chair, and Jessica seated herself opposite him, with her sewing box and a pile of mending.

So had his mother sat, he thought nostalgically, in the old days when he, too, had been a child, and with a sudden surge of tenderness, he leaned forward and, capturing his wife's small hands, drew her into his arms.

"I love you, Jessica India," he whispered, lips on hers. "And I thank you for giving me such a fine son."

"A rogue, if ever there was one," she answered indulgently, and then pulled away from him, color leaping to her cheeks, as she added softly, "Red will have a brother or a sister, Justin. I didn't tell you before because I was not sure. But—"

"And are you now, my love?" Justin asked, pleased. "And do you know when the happy event will be?"

She nodded, smiling. "Yes, I'm sure now. And it will be in March or early April, Kate Lamerton says. Are you glad?"

"You know I am, sweetheart. Very, very glad." He drew on his pipe and added, teasing her, "And it will do Red good, for you'll have less time to spoil him."

"He's not spoilt," Jessica defended. She reached into her sewing box for needle and thread, her smooth brow furrowed. "I could wish that Katie Tempest were in the same state as I am, Justin. I helped her to prepare for Rick's homecoming . . . she went to so much trouble to have everything ready for him. A splendid meal, a chair and footstool on the veranda, to enable him to have a view of the harbor and incoming ships . . . but he seemed scarcely to notice any of it, he was so bitter and angry."

"That's understandable," Justin began. "The poor fellow is paralyzed, and—"

"There is more to it than that," Jessica asserted unhappily. Head bent over her sewing and needle flying, she went on in a low voice, "I fear that Julia Dawson is making trouble. Oh, I know I told you that she was indulging in jealous tantrums over Mr. De Lancey without reason, but—I believe she has been dropping hints to Rick. And it has upset him, as might be imagined."

"What the deuce can she hint?" Justin objected. "De Lancey struck me as a most high-principled gentleman. Admittedly, I don't know him well, but I took him out to meet the *Lady Elizabeth* this afternoon . . . the new judge advocate is on board, and he and Mr. Campbell went to receive him with due ceremony. De Lancey was—"

"The new judge advocate?" Jessica looked up, momentarily distracted from her anxiety on the Tempests' behalf. "Oh, Justin, does his arrival mean that the Bents will go? Poor Mrs. Macquarie will be so relieved when they do! She and the Governor have suffered sorely at their hands, and yet, I declare, no one has shown the Bents more kindness, from the day they arrived here. *Will* they leave now?''

Justin shrugged. "Campbell says they are clinging like limpets, my love—to the judge advocate's official residence and the judges' chambers. It was in order to explain the situation that His Excellency sent De Lancey to meet the new judge advocate, before he comes ashore and finds himself without a roof over his head. But as to De Lancey and Katie Tempest, I truly cannot see what Julia can possibly accuse them of.''

"They knew each other in America," Jessica said. "And Julia insists that they were betrothed." She gave him the details she had gleaned. "It may be true; I don't know, and I've no idea from whom or where Julia obtained her information. But she is out to make trouble, Justin. I think you should try to talk to Rick. He is your friend, and . . .''

He had less pleasant news, even than this, to impart to Rick Tempest, Justin thought ruefully. The Governor's decision to alter their leasehold would have to be made known to him, and—he felt for the nuggets in his pocket. The gold would have to be returned to him, and it was all the gold he would be permitted to own for . . . the devil! For twenty years, if the Governor had his way.

"All right, sweetheart," he promised. "I'll do what I can.''

They talked of Rick's injuries, and then Jessica said, "You know that pipe that so enraged Colonel Molle? Copies are being printed and circulated all over town. I bought one for you; I thought you might want to see it." She got to her feet and took the sheets of printed paper from a drawer in the dresser. "Here it is . . . and there's much speculation as to the author.''

Justin read through the doggerel verse, smiling at first and then laughing uproariously as he quoted some of the lines aloud.

"For the Lord's sake, listen to this, my love: 'With grin triumphant, and malicious sneer, his joy he whispers in his partner's ear.' It's Molle to the life! And heavens, he's even had a tilt at Samuel Marsden and his like! '. . . the lads in black, thy chosen crew, the canting, preaching tribe,' he calls them. Oh, this is a masterpiece, Jessie my sweet—thank you for buying it for me. I'd heard it was good, but I'd not realized *how* good!''

"And can you hazard a guess as to who wrote it?" Jessica inquired.

Justin flashed her an amused glance. "My love, I don't need to guess—I know. There's only one person who could have written it . . . my absent friend William Charles Wentworth. And because he knew he would be absent and well on his way to England when the pipe was planted, he really gave the perfidious colonel a broadside!"

"A number of people say it was Mr. Campbell," Jessica reminded him. "Or . . . Rick. But—"

"No," Justin denied emphatically. "Campbell has no sense of humor, and Rick—good heavens, Rick can't rhyme to save his life! And he would have told me if he had contrived to write it. Besides, this has Willie's hallmark. See how he opens it: 'Vice and Folly reign in every place.' That's taken from one of his favorite couplets: '. . . hail at once the patron and the pile, Of vice and folly, Greville and Argyle.' Campbell's a dour Scot; he would never have used it." He rose, tapping out his pipe and stifling a yawn. "We must see to it that your brother—that is, your cousin—Michael Dean, receives a copy of this, Jess. He had little reason to love old Molle or, for that matter, the odious Captain Sanderson, had he? Come—" He offered her his hand. "Let's go to bed, my love. I've an early start in the morning—we're mounting guns."

Jessica obediently started to put away her mending. "There's another scandal brewing about Captain Sanderson, Justin. Did you hear about it?"

"No." Justin put his arm about her waist. "And I'm not sure I want to, but . . . what poor unfortunate has the gallant captain got his knife into now?"

"Into poor Mr. Greenway—the architect. It seems he took overlong in carrying out some Masonic work he had undertaken, and rumor has it that Captain Sanderson horsewhipped him. He could not lift a hand to defend himself, because he is still on ticket-of-leave, but the story is that he—that is, Mr. Greenway—intends to make a criminal court case of it and sue."

"A fine beginning for our new judge advocate," Justin observed dryly. "Well, be damned to Colonel Molle and his crew! Like Willie Wentworth, I trust he'll go with his namesake and burrow in his hole . . . I've better things to do than worry my head about any of them. Not even about Rick." He drew Jessica to him and held her close. "Sweet Jess, I want to make love to the mother of my sons. Do you suppose she would welcome my overtures?"

Jessica's arms crept around his neck, and she raised her smiling face to his. "I fancy she would, Justin. Indeed, I'm sure of it."

It was as he was undressing that the nuggets fell from his breeches' pocket, making a soft thud on the wooden floor. Justin did not bother to pick them up, and to Jessica's whispered question he answered flatly, "Some pebbles Rick found in the river. Fool's gold, my sweet—dross, of no value."

He pulled his shirt over his head and slipped into the bed beside her, his hands feeling gently for her swelling breasts. . . .

CHAPTER XXV

"For pity's sake, Katie—go and leave me be!" Rick exclaimed impatiently. "I have all I need—Jonas and Mary to wait on me, Dickon for company, and this damned chair in which to sit, watching the world go by. So have no qualms—go and enjoy yourself."

"Oh, Rick," Katie pleaded, in a choked voice. "You know I don't want to leave you. I—"

"What can you do for me, if you stay?" Rick retorted. "Rumple my pillows? Fetch more blankets to cover me?" He was, he knew, being both ungrateful and unjust. Katie meant well; she did all that any woman could do to help him pass his endless, helpless days, but her mere presence was a source of exasperation, a reminder of what she had once been to him and was no longer.

"Without you," Katie began, "I shall not enjoy myself. Truly, Rick, you—"

Rick cut her short, a harsh edge to his voice. "Fiddlesticks, of course you will! You'll hear all the latest gossip, and you'll be able to repeat it for my benefit this evening. You'll hear whom—apart from myself—the gallant Colonel Molle suspects of engaging in scurrilous satiric verse. And how the equally gallant Captain Sanderson has reacted to being fined five pounds—by a court of his fellow officers—for having assaulted the felon, Francis Greenway. Oh, and of course what His Excellency has to say concerning the vulgar lampoon of him in the Forty-sixth's guardroom . . . that's all they talk about at these Government House luncheon parties, is it not?"

Katie reddened. "You know it's not," she protested. "How can you be so unkind, Rick?"

How could he indeed, Rick wondered bitterly. How could he

stop himself from goading Katie, from tormenting his unfaithful wife, when she refused to confess her infidelity, but instead insisted on playing the role of nurse to him, fussing over his comfort and well-being, as if it were he who commanded her devotion, not her lover?

Times without number he had tried to trick her into an admission, but always she evaded his carefully slanted questions, refusing to be provoked into a loss of temper or a single unguarded answer. But the most galling aspect of the whole miserable business was the knowledge that she—his adored bride—had seized upon his brief absence at Pengallon to betray him. She had not known then that he would be shot and paralyzed . . . perhaps, if she had, she could have found it in his heart to forgive her. If she were unfaithful now, at least it would be understandable, since he was chained either to his bed or to this chair on the veranda, and incapable of being a husband to her—incapable of even walking more than two or three steps unaided.

Rick swore under his breath as Katie moved away from him, hiding her face so as not to let him see that she was weeping. A plague on George De Lancey, he thought savagely. Why had the infernal fellow come to the colony and back into Katie's life? And why, damn it to hell, had Katie married *him*, if she was still in love with her former betrothed?

"Is there anything you want?" she asked. "A book, perhaps, or a drink?" Receiving a brusque headshake, she added in a muffled voice, "Very well, then, I'll go. I'm early, but I want to call on Jessica on my way. She's lonely without Justin, and the baby is due soon."

Rick, with conscious sarcasm, again urged her to enjoy herself. He had watched Justin's departure, ten days ago, the *Elizabeth* under full sail, looking like a graceful seabird from his vantage point on the veranda, with Colonel Sorrell, the new Lieutenant Governor of Van Diemen's Land, on board. The drunken, incompetent Major Thomas Davey had been superseded at last, but the Colonial Office had softened the blow by ordering Governor Macquarie to grant him two thousand acres of prime grazing land in the Illawarra area.

And Macquarie had done so without a murmur, Rick reflected rebelliously, while depriving Justin and himself of the mineral deposits on their grant for twenty years. If only he could get back there; if only he— A small voice, mouthing an unintelligible request, broke into his thoughts. His brief resentment faded, and he held out a hand in welcome to his nephew. Dickon was his closest companion these days. The little boy came daily, rain or shine, to be with him, and in such innocent and undemanding company, Rick found himself not only at ease but, to his own surprise, oddly content.

Alone together, they played childish games, throwing a ball back and forth between them, aiming at birds with a slingshot, making decorations from seashells, which Dickon picked up on the narrow expanse of sandy beach half a mile away, in Palmer's Cove. Sometimes Rick fashioned tiny model ships, carved from driftwood, with twigs for masts and scraps of paper to serve as sails, and the boy would scamper down to the end of the garden and set them adrift.

He was oddly frightened of the high water lapping about the rocks, however, and—unable to swim, according to his mother— would throw the little vessels in from some distance away, and come running back to Rick's chair with high-pitched squeals of mingled fear and pride in his achievement.

The veranda, for all Rick hated it as a prison, was a fine vantage point, and from it he could see right across the harbor to the signal station and the sprawling, rocky mass of South Head, on which a lighthouse was taking shape, designed by Francis Greenway prior to his unfortunate brush with the Worshipful Master of the Masonic Lodge, Captain Sanderson.

In the six months that he had occupied his prison, he and Dickon had watched the ships entering and leaving Port Jackson and Sydney Cove, and Rick had kept boredom at bay by observing them through his naval glass and attempting to identify each one, for Dickon's benefit. Lately, at the boy's behest, he had started to make more elaborate models for him to keep, based on each new arrival to drop anchor in the cove and land her cargo of convicts and trade goods, mail and newspapers, from far-off England.

They now had five in their collection—the transport *Mariner,* of four hundred and fifty tons burden and Whitby built, had come early in October, carrying male convicts; the *Surry* had arrived five days before Christmas; and in February 1817, the four-hundred-ton *Lord Melville,* bearing a hundred female malefactors and the new supreme court judge, Mr. Barron Field, had arrived after a voyage of a hundred and sixty days. Two others had made port quite recently, within days of each other—the *Fame,* built in Quebec; and a fine Indiaman, the *Sir William Bensley,* a week ago.

Dickon, to Rick's surprise and delight, had taken to sketching the ships in charcoal and was showing a remarkable aptitude as an artist, which put his own roughly carved models to shame. The boy had a sketch now held in his thin, grubby little paws, and he was gesturing to it, an eager expression on his face.

"What is it, lad?" Rick asked, mouthing the words slowly to enable him to understand. The drawing was recognizable as the *Sir William Bensley,* but under head and topsails only, as she had backed her wind, preparatory to working into the anchorage in the cove, and Dickon, it seemed, was not satisfied with her thus. "You want to show her under full sail, is that it?"

Dickon nodded vigorously, and Rick took the drawing from him. "Right, then here's what you do. She's on the larboard tack, so her courses will be at this angle, see? Upper tops'ls so, and . . . oh, the devil!"

A gust of wind ripped the flimsy sheet of paper from his hand and lifted it, like some wayward leaf, high into the air. Dickon tore after it, leaped up, but his clutching fingers failed to grasp it, and it floated away from him, now dipping, now rising again, as if possessed of a life of its own. It was being carried toward the water, and realizing the danger, Rick yelled at the boy to have a care.

Dickon could not hear his warning; he slithered down the grassy slope, lost his balance at the water's edge, and as Rick watched in horror, the scrap of paper fluttered over the edge and the boy fell headfirst after it, a shrill cry of alarm and a faint splash confirming his fears.

Without conscious thought, Rick hurled himself from his chair, took two unsteady paces, and then crashed down, dragging himself along with his hands, too short of breath even to call for the servants to come to his aid. Somehow he reached the end of the slope and was able to see Dickon threshing wildly in the water below, mouth open in a soundless cry and eyes tightly closed, as if in a vain attempt to blot out his terror, as a wave washed over him, driving him under.

Exerting all the strength he could muster, Rick went in after him. He had always been a strong swimmer, and buoyed up by the water, he found to his infinite relief that his useless legs were, once again, obedient to the demands he made on them. He reached the struggling boy, turned him onto his back, and, grasping him by the shoulders, struck out for a rocky promontory some thirty yards away. His legs miraculously did not fail him; he gained his objective and lifted Dickon onto a ledge of rock, where the boy lay gasping and spluttering but seemingly unharmed.

Scarcely able to believe in his good fortune, Rick levered himself onto the ledge and attempted to stand up. His leg muscles, weakened by six months of disuse, caused him to stagger unsteadily, but he managed to get his balance and remain upright and then to take a few tentative steps. Dickon watched him with round, astonished eyes, and then, with an inarticulate cry, the little boy jumped up, shook himself like a puppy, and offered his thin, damp shoulder as a crutch.

Rick grinned at him, accepting the offer, and together, very slowly, they made their way back to the garden, to be met by Jonas, with the female servant, Mary, close at his heels.

"You're *walking*, Mr. Tempest! Oh, praise be to God!" Mary, Irish and devoutly Catholic, crossed herself and burst into tears.

Rick said nothing. Transferring his hand from Dickon's shoulder to Jonas's, he stumbled into the house, holding himself stiffly erect and expecting that, with every step, his legs would buckle under him. When they did not, he offered up his own silent prayer of thankfulness and then said, aloud, "Find us both some dry clothes, Mary, if you please. And, Jonas—"

"Sir?" Jonas was staring at him, still unconvinced that he had, indeed, witnessed a miracle. "What can I do, sir?"

"Go to the hospital, Jonas," Rick bade him. "And ask Dr. Redfern to bring his probes and remove the shot from my back. Tell him it must have shifted, because I'm walking again. And hurry, lad!"

"Yes, sir. Shall I fetch Mrs. Tempest, sir, when I've told the doctor? Shall I tell her?"

Rick hesitated and then shook his head. "No," he said firmly. "Just Dr. Redfern."

Elizabeth Macquarie looked around the room at her assembled guests a trifle anxiously. Her luncheon party was exclusively female—what Lachlan called one of her hen parties—and, on the surface at least, the gathering appeared the picture of harmony, as over a score of well-dressed ladies greeted each other with every appearance of pleasure.

But Elizabeth was unhappily aware that appearances were deceptive. There was little Katie Tempest, for example, looking a wan, sad shadow of herself . . . though making a courageous effort to talk animatedly to Mrs. Wylde, wife of the new judge advocate.

Elizabeth sighed as she watched the girl. They had met by chance an hour ago, she recalled, at the house of Jessica Broome. She had called to offer congratulations to Jessica on the birth of her second son, born in the early hours of the morning, and Katie had arrived on the same errand. They had admired the sturdy, contented baby in the arms of a proudly smiling Kate Lamerton, and had gone together to Jessica's bedroom to express their pleasure and relief at her safe delivery, but . . . Katie had, throughout, been perilously near to tears.

No doubt her chagrin had its roots in her own childlessness; her poor young husband's long illness, which had rendered him a paralyzed cripple, must—coming so tragically soon after their wedding—have placed a great strain on her and on their relationship. Elizabeth glanced at her again and saw that she had moved away from Mrs. Wylde, and as she did so, Mrs. Molle and— predictably—Mrs. David Allan, wife of the deputy commissary, pointedly turned their silk-clad backs on her. Katie was left standing, frozen-faced and alone, the color slowly mounting her thin cheeks as she realized that both ladies had deliberately cut her.

Indignantly, Elizabeth started toward her, with the intention of drawing her into conversation, but to her relief, Abigail Dawson intervened and led the girl over to a group in the center of the room, chatting cheerfully, a friendly, supporting hand on her arm.

She had heard the gossip concerning Katie Tempest, of course; the Governor's wife repeated her sigh. Malicious tongues had been clacking for months, savoring each small tidbit of scandal that linked her name with that of George De Lancey, yet—knowing from whom most of the talk stemmed—little, if any of it, was convincing.

Certainly, Elizabeth thought, turning to greet two more of her guests as Moore, the Government House butler, announced them . . . certainly *she* had not been convinced, or Lachlan, either. True, both Katie and Mr. De Lancey were Americans, but that meant nothing at all now . . . save perhaps to Colonel Molle, who persisted in adopting a hostile attitude to those he was pleased to describe as "rebel colonials."

George De Lancey's record in the late war should surely have given the lie to any suggestion of the kind in his case, but apparently, in Colonel Molle's eyes, it did not . . . and some of his arrogant young officers followed his lead, regardless of the truth. Perhaps for that reason Katie had been tempted to seek solace from her fellow countryman, and perhaps, when she and the girl had driven together from Jessica Broome's to Government House a little while ago, a warning of what the gossips were saying might have been timely. But that would have been to accuse the girl, to imply that she herself believed the malicious talk. . . .

"Mrs. Robert Campbell, Your Excellency," Moore declaimed. "Mrs. Thomas Reiby."

Elizabeth smiled and shook hands warmly with the new arrivals. Sophia Campbell was a charming woman, sister of Commissary John Palmer, and Mary Reiby the pretty emancipist wife of Robert Campbell's new trading partner, a onetime sea captain and now a leading merchant and shipbuilder.

Their husbands were among the staunchest of the Governor's supporters, but, Elizabeth was unhappily aware, it was scarcely necessary to look around to see the effect that the announcement of their names had had on Mrs. Molle's group by the window. Once again, she knew, backs would be turned, the insult no less painful for its familiarity to the recipients than if it were being delivered for the first time.

And, for all this was her own house and she the wife of the appointed Governor, she was quite powerless to prevent it. What a relief it would be to both herself and Lachlan, Elizabeth thought, when Colonel Molle's regiment was replaced by the 48th! Under the command of Colonel Erskine, the 48th was at sea and expected to reach Sydney within a month or so. They could not come too soon for her liking . . . but why, oh, why did protocol demand that, if she gave a luncheon or a dinner—even for a hen party—she must invite both opposing factions, lest one or the other feel slighted by their omission and stir up fresh trouble?

Heaven knew, the Molle and the Bent factions stirred up trouble whether invited to Government House or not, and the deposed

Justice Bent's recent actions had come close to sending her poor, harassed Lachlan into a serious decline.

Matters had come to a head just before Christmas, when Jeffrey Bent had issued a writ against William Gore, the provost marshal, and attempted to reopen the supreme court by summoning the magistrates Alexander Riley and William Broughton to the bench. Poor Mr. Broughton, in an earlier quarrel over an assigned servant, had been treated very badly by the deposed judge, and had refused to obey the summons, and Mr. Riley had followed his example. Jeffrey Bent had threatened both with arrest, and the Governor—laid low by an attack of his old bowel trouble—had been compelled to rise from his sickbed in order to deal with the matter.

But he had done so with firm authority, Elizabeth recalled proudly. Advised by Mr. Wylde and George De Lancey, he had exempted the two magistrates from court service, ordered Jeffrey Bent ejected from the judges' chambers in Macquarie Street, and published a government order declaring that his appointment had been terminated and that he was forbidden, at his peril, to assume the functions of a supreme court judge within the colony.

A less insensitive man would have recognized defeat and taken steps to relinquish the official judge advocate's residence, of which he had, for so long, deprived the Wyldes. Indeed, Elizabeth told herself indignantly, had he possessed the instincts of a gentleman, Mr. Bent would long since have shaken the dust of Sydney from his feet. There had been ships in plenty in which he might have taken passage back to England . . . but he had not done so. He and his sister-in-law Eliza were still here, demanding the reburial of the late Ellis Bent's remains in St. Philip's Church, arguing over the amount of compensation to be paid for Eliza's furniture and for their fares and, she was virtually certain, determined to ruin George De Lancey's reputation, as a final act of spite before they finally departed.

But for the continued tittle-tattle concerning Katie Tempest, Lachlan would have appointed him to the supreme court. . . . Again Elizabeth's uneasy gaze went to Katie's face. The girl had perked up a little under Abigail's influence; Mary Reiby was talking to her, and Mrs. Wylde seemed about to join the group. The buffet luncheon was ready, with Moore and his wife, Nancy, assisting Mrs. Ovens with her preparations for serving the first course. Thrusting to the back of her mind the fear that a buffet luncheon had not been a wise choice, Elizabeth invited those nearest her to partake of it.

They did so, moving slowly toward the laden tables but, as she had feared they would, keeping to their groups. As she passed that of Mrs. Molle, she heard the colonel's wife say in an audible voice, "Sir Thomas Brisbane, who, as you will be aware, was one of the Duke of Wellington's *best* generals, is being talked of everywhere in London, I'm told, as likely to be appointed our Governor in place of the present incumbent."

Elizabeth stepped back, flushed and resentful, missing the next few words, but Mrs. Molle glanced over her shoulder and, as if noticing her for the first time, said with cloying sweetness, "I was just telling Mrs. Allan that General Brisbane is shortly to marry a cousin of my husband's, Mrs. Macquarie. A charming girl— indeed, a lady born and bred, and well suited to support Sir Thomas in any high office he may be called upon shortly to assume."

Elizabeth managed to retain the cool dignity expected of a Governor's wife. She had had over seven years' practice in the art of hiding her feelings, she reminded herself, and she would not allow Mrs. Molle, of all people, to provoke her into revealing her hurt. The infamous poem, which had shown Colonel Molle for the perfidious man he was, could have applied, with equal truth, to the woman he had married, but . . . Elizabeth drew herself up to her full height.

She would not put herself in the position of the unhappy target—the "luckless butt" of whom the poet had so aptly written. She tried to remember the lines: *"And should some luckless butt perchance draw near,"* Molle would, she recalled, *"mark his coming with a wink and sneer . . ."* And—how had the pipe continued?

And should the fool, to 'scape his scoffs, sneak off,
From the circle bursts a hoarse-horse laugh,
Which draws the eyes of all to his retreat . . .

Lachlan had been deeply shocked by the now widely circulated pipe, but she had not. Far from it . . . Elizabeth's lips curved into a smile.

She said, matching Mrs. Molle's sweetness, "I am delighted for

Sir Thomas and for your husband's cousin, Mrs. Molle. It is to be hoped that, with the great Duke's influence to aid him, the general will be given a post worthy of his talents. He will need all of them if he comes out here, as I feel sure you will agree . . . and not least an exceedingly thick skin!"

She swept on, not waiting for Mrs. Molle to reply and satisfied that, for once, her tormentor had been left with no excuse for laughter.

And, she decided rebelliously, whatever Lachlan said concerning the demands of protocol, neither Colonel Molle nor his wife should again be invited to any Government House function. Like the Bents, the Sandersons, and the Reverend Samuel Marsden, their names should be crossed from Secretary Campbell's list, and invited to the next dinner should be . . . Elizabeth considered, her smooth brow thoughtfully puckered.

The Wyldes, the new young supreme court judge, Barron Field, George De Lancey, and—yes, Mrs. John Macarthur, for whom, whatever her husband might have done in the past, she had the greatest admiration and liking. The poor soul had been left alone to bring up her family and manage the Macarthur farms during the nine years of her husband's enforced exile from the colony, and she had done both with impressive success. Now that Mr. Macarthur had been given permission by the Colonial Office to return to Sydney, the past must be considered the past, just as it was where other ex-officers of the Rum Corps were concerned. Many of them—notably Captain Lawson and Mr. Cox—had performed most valuable services in the colony since their return; all were landowners, with wives and growing families, who contributed to the general prosperity in agriculture and trade.

All were—what was it that Lachlan liked to call them? Australians. A proud title, surely . . .

Behind her, a piping little voice called out eagerly, "Mama! Mama!" and breaking away from Mrs. Whalan's restraining hand, her own little son came running to her, resplendent in kilt and silver-buttoned velvet jacket.

Elizabeth dropped to her knees to grasp his outstretched hands, her throat suddenly tight.

Their precious boy, she thought, her son and Lachlan's, was also an Australian.

CHAPTER XXVI

Katie slipped away from Government House when Mrs. Macquarie's other guests prepared for the customary evening promenade in Hyde Park, the only difficulty she experienced being that of evading Abigail's kindly offer to take her to the band concert in the park.

She was grateful for her sister-in-law's staunch loyalty, but the party itself and the attitude of the little clique led by Mrs. Molle had become more than she could bear with dignity. Mrs. Macquarie, too, had been kind . . . when, come to that, had she not? But the unexpected encounter with the Governor's wife, when they had arrived almost simultaneously at Jessica Broome's, had unnerved her, and . . . Katie felt tears aching in her throat.

Had she shown her feelings too clearly, she wondered wretchedly, when she had been called upon to admire Jessica's fine, healthy new son? Had Elizabeth Macquarie sensed her unhappiness and, for that reason, talked lightly of any and everything else, seeking to spare her?

Katie paused by the gate leading into the Domain, tears obscuring her vision. She was on foot, as she usually was—the curricle and pair, which Rick had purchased without telling her of his intention, she regarded as his and left for his exclusive use. The fact that he had not suggested she do otherwise was, she supposed bitterly, a measure of the deterioration in their relationship, if measurement were needed.

Rick had claimed to be hard up, yet after a visit from an emancipist named Hensall, he had found the money to pay for the smartly painted trap and two matching carriage horses, and had added a groom to their small establishment. . . . Katie's teeth closed fiercely about her lower lip. He had taken Dickon with him, when he had first tried out the new acquisition, but had told her nothing of how he had fared. . . .

It could not continue, she told herself. Rick had shut her out of his life, and at first she had tried to understand, to explain by making allowances for his paralyzed state; but he had exhausted her last reserves of pity and tolerance and, by his failure to utter a single word in defense of her reputation, had encouraged the cruel and unfounded gossip that was destroying it.

For it *was* unfounded; she had done nothing of which she need feel ashamed. Katie halted, the tears blinding her. Julia Dawson, she knew, had been the first to spread the rumors linking her name to that of George De Lancey, but—Julia had not been the only one.

Someone else—she had no idea who it could be—had added to the tale, more with a view to discrediting George than herself, she had lately come to realize. Exaggerated, bearing little resemblance to the truth, this latest rumor had spread in the manner that bushfires spread, when the native blacks raided a farm at harvest time and set light to a field of ripened corn. There was even said to be a pipe about it in circulation, although she had not seen the noxious thing.

She had seen George, however, two days ago. She could stay away no longer, unable to endure any more of Rick's thinly veiled accusations, his ill-tempered outbursts, or the evident preference he now showed for any company save hers. In sheer desperation, she had gone to George's chambers and asked his clerk for an appointment, but George himself had heard and recognized her voice and had come out at once, to usher her into the book-lined room in which he worked. . . . Katie dabbed at her swimming eyes and slowly, reluctantly, resumed her journey, choosing one of the less frequented paths, in the hope of avoiding other passersby.

And . . . she sighed, remembering. She had intended to make the meeting formal, to ask his advice, seek his aid, even planning precisely what she would say.

"I want to go home—home to Boston. I cannot stay here; my marriage was a mistake and it's over. Please, I need your help, George, to find an American ship and book my passage. . . ." That had been all she had planned to say, but . . . suddenly all the pent-up misery of the past six months had loosened her tongue, and she had told him the truth in a spate of bitter, heartbroken words.

"I've been judged and condemned for something I never did . . . and not only by women like Mrs. Molle and Mrs. Allan. *Rick* has condemned me. He believes that I betrayed and cheated him—he supposes that you and I are lovers. But he has never asked me outright or given me the chance to deny it. I've tried to make him talk about it, but he always shies away, as if he's afraid of knowing. . . ."

There had been more, and George had listened gravely and then come to take her into his arms.

"My poor little Katie, I did not realize what you were going through," he told her contritely. "Oh, I heard the talk, but since I was very well aware that there wasn't a word of truth in it, I decided to ignore it. I was reasonably sure from whom it stemmed and who was keeping the wretched gossip alive—and I thought I knew why. But . . ." He had stroked her tear-stained face with gentle fingers, Katie recalled, and added, just as gently, "I never for one moment imagined that your husband would believe it. And—well, in view of his injuries and the fact that he was paralyzed, I convinced myself that the only honorable course I could pursue would be to stay out of your life. If we were never seen together, I supposed that the talk would stop, that having nothing on which to feed, it would die a natural death."

"It hasn't," she had reminded him.

He had held her close in firm, strong arms and promised that he would arrange passages for them both, in the first American ship that came to Sydney.

"Without you, I'd not want to stay here. I love you, Katie. Rick Tempest does not deserve you, and if you say that the marriage is over, then that is enough for me. We'll go home, my dearest love—we'll go home together and live as man and wife, and the good folk of Boston will never know what either of us did. Why should they?"

She had inclined her head in eager, wordless assent, Katie remembered, feeling as if she were waking from a nightmare. George had kissed her with a lover's passion and talked of the resumption of trade with the United States and the probability that a trading vessel like her father's *Providence* would give them passage.

"If not we can go to China with one of the transports and take passage from Canton in a tea ship," he had promised, and, the decision made, she had felt only relief.

Until she had seen Rick again, and the irony of his silent accusations—now that, at last, they had some basis in truth—had become too much to bear. Her resolution had faltered, as it was faltering now. . . . Katie drew a sobbing breath as, unbidden, the vows she had made on her wedding day came flooding back into her memory.

"Wilt thou have this man to thy wedded husband?" the Reverend Cowper had asked. *"Wilt thou obey him and serve him, love, honor, and keep him in sickness and in health and, forsaking all other, keep thee only unto him, so long as ye both shall live?"*

She had vowed that she would—vowed to God the Almighty, in front of His holy altar, that she was taking Rick as her husband for as long as they both should live. She had no right, in the eyes of God, to desert him, she . . . Biting back her sobs, Katie picked up her skirts and started to run. A youthful couple, hidden by the bushes and indulging in clandestine lovemaking, sprang apart at her approach, but she did not notice them or hear the girl's shrill reproaches, or the curse the man shouted after her.

Dickon met her in the street, just before she reached the house, and in a series of excited gestures and attempts at mime, he endeavored to tell her what had occurred during her absence. Katie, her patience worn thin and her conscience plaguing her, gave him scant attention but contrived to register the fact that he had fallen into the water and nearly drowned.

"That was bad of you, Dickon," she chided him, and the little boy's eager smile faded. But he shook his head, rejecting her censure, and, seizing her hand, urged her to hurry into the house. She did so, worried now lest his escapade had upset Rick, and was quite unprepared for the shock of seeing her husband walking without aid.

"Oh, Rick!" She stared at him incredulously. "Rick, you're well again—you can walk!"

"Yes," he confirmed curtly. "I can walk, and Dr. Redfern's removed the buckshot from my spine—it hardly took five minutes of his time. I'll be riding a horse in a day or so and able to attend to my own affairs. And that includes our marriage, Katie. I . . . have you seen this?" He thrust a rolled-up sheet of paper into her hand. "One of those infernal pipes—Jonas brought it to me. It was pushed in between the palings at the front of the house. Read it, for God's sake! Read it and tell me how much truth there is in it.''

Katie opened the roll, her fingers shaking. There were several verses of doggerel, but a glance at the first sufficed to reveal its malicious purpose, and she felt the color flooding her cheeks as she read it.

> George De Lancey's taken a fancy
> To the spouse of a poor sick man.
> He won her affections despite the objections
> Of that sorely mistreated man . . .

"Well?" Rick's tone was harsh, the expression on his gaunt face accusing and devoid of pity. "Has De Lancey been your lover whilst I've been lying here like an accursed log? Has he, Katie?"

Katie shook her head. "No. No, he has not. I—"

"But you've been seeing him, haven't you?" Rick interrupted. "Damn it, you don't need to cover it up for fear of retarding my recovery! I *am* recovered, so you don't have to pity me any longer or sacrifice yourself for my sake. Redfern says I'll soon be as good as new—thanks to young Dickon." His gaze went to the boy, who was watching both of them in mute, unhappy bewilderment, and his expression relaxed. "Of course, you don't know how he wrought the miracle, do you?" He told her, and Dickon responded with a smile.

"So that was it!" Katie exclaimed, with swift contrition. "And I scolded him. . . . Oh, Dickon, I'm sorry. I did not realize, I—"

"He'll get over it," Rick said curtly. "He's used to being misunderstood. Cut along home now, Dickon lad," he ordered, mouthing the words slowly. "Give your mama that note from me, will you, please? And you can tell her that I'm on my own two feet again. Right—you've got that, have you?"

Dickon hesitated and then inclined his small dark head, indicating the folded note in the pocket of his jacket. He touched Katie's arm in farewell, flashed her a forgiving smile, and was gone.

Rick shrugged. "It's better that he doesn't stay. I'm afraid the poor little devil was expecting us to fall into each other's arms, and we've disappointed him. He's an innocent—he has no idea how a husband feels about an unfaithful wife.''

"I have not been unfaithful to you, Rick," Katie protested bitterly.

"But you're not in love with me, are you?" Rick challenged, with a bitterness that matched hers. "You never were—it was always De Lancey, was it not?"

"He was the first man I ever loved," Katie admitted. "But I married you, and I've tried to be a good wife to you, Rick. Truly I—"

"Oh, yes, I know that!" Rick flung at her. "Dear God, you have driven me nearly mad with your wifely devotion and your damned pity! Whatever I did, however hard I tried, I could never escape from your pity—or from the thought that it was De Lancey you loved and wanted, not me. That wretched pipe put it in a nutshell when it described you as the wife of a poor sick man, devil take it!"

"You made it very hard for me, Rick," Katie defended. "You shut me out; you wouldn't let me come near to you or—or even talk to you. You must believe me, you—"

Again he cut her short. "All right, I concede I've been difficult to live with, but it has been hell lying here, day after day, night after night, never knowing when—or even if—it was going to end. And you *have* seen De Lancey, haven't you? Katie, I know you went to his rooms in Macquarie Street on Tuesday—you were seen, so don't trouble to deny it."

Taken by surprise, Katie met his gaze without flinching. "I don't deny it. But it was the only time, and I went there because I—"

"Because you'd decided to leave me?" Rick accused. "Because you'd had your fill of being married to a poor sick man—was that it, Katie? I want the truth, damn it!"

It was time for the truth, Katie thought miserably. "I had decided to go home," she said, in a voice that was choked with tears. "Back to America, to Boston, Rick. I felt so despairing, so alone—I could not endure any more. I—it wasn't only that you had rejected me, it was the awful gossip, the way some of the women behaved to me. Even at Government House, they turned their backs on me. And none of the gossip was true—I wasn't having an affair with George De Lancey. I never saw or spoke to him after you were brought to the hospital, I swear I did not."

"But you intend to leave with him, do you not?" Rick challenged furiously. "De Lancey's going with you, isn't he?"

"Life here has been made impossible for him, too," Katie managed. "He is an honorable man, Rick, but the talk goes on and neither of us has done anything to deserve it. Without a shred of proof, his reputation is being ruined, as well as mine. People believe the—the stories. Even you believe them."

Rick eyed her for a long moment in silence. Then he said, "Yes, I believed them. Oh, I take your word for it that you have not been unfaithful to me. But you don't love me, Katie . . . and I don't want a wife who—damn it, who can only give me pity. Leave with De Lancey if you wish—I'll not stand in your way. There are two ships in harbor now in which you could take passage, but I'd advise the *Fame*. Rumor has it that Justice Bent and his sister-in-law are leaving in the *Sir William Bensley*, and they'd hardly be congenial fellow passengers, would they?" His anger had subsided, and he went on evenly, "Abigail told me that Colonel Sorrell—the new Lieutenant Governor of Van Diemen's Land—traveled out with a lady who was not his wife, and there's talk about them. If you shrink from it, you might be wise to travel separately."

Katie could only stare at him, bereft of words. This, she thought despairingly, was the end of her marriage—Rick was sending her away, coldly and calmly, making no attempt to persuade her to stay. But was he right, was pity all that she could give him now, all that was left? She remembered, with a pang, the days they had spent together at Portland Place, immediately after their wedding . . . Rick's lovemaking, at once tender and passionate, the manner in which they had talked and laughed, enjoying their shared companionship and wanting no other. They had loved each other then, and she had seldom thought of George De Lancey but only and always of the man she had married . . . her husband, whom she had vowed to love, honor, and keep, in sickness and in health, for as long as they each should live.

She expelled her breath in a pent-up, unhappy sigh, and Rick said, without apology, "I am going to call on Abigail. Don't wait dinner for me—I'll have mine there."

He drove off in the curricle, with his convict groom, Shelford, and it was long past midnight when Katie heard him return. Next day, he left the house before she was up and, as before, did not return until the early hours. On the morning of the third day, the sound of the curricle's departure wakened her at dawn, and shortly afterward the maid, Mary, brought her tea tray and a disconsolate and tearful Dickon, with a note.

" 'Tis from the master, ma'am," the girl said. "He's away to the mountains, taking Rob Shelford wid him. An' he asked me to keep an eye on the wee boy, since he's like to fret by himself."

Katie poured a cup of tea for Dickon and settled him at the foot of her bed before reading the note. It was brief and businesslike and oddly chilling. Rick had written:

> I am going to Pengallon permanently. I shall take the curricle and Shelford as far as Ulva, where William Broome has some more stock to drive up for me and a shepherd by the name of Jethro Crowan, who is being lent to me by Tim Dawson.
>
> The house is yours for as long as you are likely to need it, since you will presumably be taking passage home within the next few weeks.
>
> I have arranged to hire a dray to bring up supplies and furniture and the two house servants—Mr. Riley will make this available at the end of the month. Perhaps you would contact him or his warehouse manager in order to give him a firm date for the departure of the dray.

Katie turned the page over, tears pricking at her eyes. Only in the last few lines was there anything in the note to express Rick's personal feelings or to suggest that he felt some regret at the ending of their life together.

> I could not bring myself to bid you farewell, Katie. Whatever you may or may not feel for me, I still love you.
>
> Should you have a change of heart, and wish, after all, to share life with me at Pengallon, the way is still open for you to join me. Dickon, with Abigail's consent, will be doing so for a time, and he will travel up here with the dray.

Katie laid down the sheet of paper, blinking back her tears. Dickon looked at her with a strangely adult expression of sympathy in his bright dark eyes. He said something she could not understand and, putting down his cup, reached for the note. Katie had never been sure whether or not he could read, but she did not attempt to take it from him, and he studied it carefully, his lips moving soundlessly as he did so.

Then, with a shrill cry, he jumped off the bed and ran out to the veranda, to come scampering back excitedly, a few minutes later, half carrying, half dragging a heavy wooden box. It was Rick's sea chest, Katie realized, with his name painted across the lid in inch-high letters. Dickon produced a key and, setting the box down on the floor beside her, opened it. Inside were a dozen or so of his charcoal sketches of ships, and supposing he wanted her to admire them, she said, mouthing the words slowly, "They're lovely, Dickon. But I've seen them before, you know, and I ought to get up."

Dickon shook his head with an odd show of impatience, and like some small dog in search of a buried bone, he started to delve into the interior of the chest, thrusting the sketches to one side and finally bringing to light a bundle of letters. A pleased smile lighting his face, he thrust the letters into Katie's hand and, by signs, indicated that she should read them.

She hesitated, recognizing Rick's handwriting, and then, with astonishment, saw that they were addressed to her. There were a dozen in all, each bearing a date and each beginning "My darling Katie." Still puzzled, she studied the first and saw that the date it bore was almost six months old—and the last had apparently been written only a week ago.

Dickon replaced his sketches in the chest, locked it and, with another beaming smile, dragged it back onto the veranda and vanished.

Left alone, Katie started to read the letters, a knife twisting in her heart as the realization dawned on her that they were love letters, written to her by Rick during the time that he had been paralyzed and helpless and tormented by doubts as to her fidelity.

One of them began,

If you no longer love me, if you want to be free, then it would be kinder to tell me. The torture lies in not knowing

. . . yet I dare not ask you, because I am afraid of what your answer would be . . .

Two or three of the letters were bitter outpourings of the jealousy and frustration he had felt:

De Lancey knew you before I did, he loved you and wanted you for his wife long before I did, so it is natural, I suppose, that he should retain his sentiments where you are concerned. And he is a man, possessed of those powers that render a man desirable to a woman, whereas I . . . oh, Katie, my love, my darling, I am a useless vegetable, a log, selfishly clinging to you because I married you, yet incapable of being your husband. . . .

You do your duty, you act the loving wife, but what is in your heart, Katie—what are your thoughts as you tend me? Do you dream of the man you did not marry and of what might have been, had you never set eyes on me? Gratitude, pity, duty—are these the frail bonds that bind you to me?

Is the talk true or false? Are you seeing De Lancey in secret, is he your lover? I want you so, Katie, and I need you . . . did you know that desire—yes, even lust—can still be in the mind, all-pervading, tormenting, whilst beyond fulfillment?

The closely written pages blurred before Katie's eyes, but she bit back a sob and read on:

You will never read these letters, Katie, because I shall never show them to you. At least I am still man enough to keep my shame hidden, and it is some measure of relief to write them, for all they can serve no other purpose.

But why must you be so kind, so patient and uncomplaining when I rant at you and display my foul temper in your presence? I try, at times, to drive you away—to drive you into De Lancey's arms—but then I draw back. I continue to hope that this paralysis is temporary, that it can be cured, yet with each day that passes, the hope grows fainter.

Julia came this afternoon, with Abigail, and they said that the talk never ceases. Abigail believes that Justice Bent and that miserable sister-in-law of his are the ones who spread the lies. But when Abigail left, Julia told me that you *are* seeing De Lancey . . . she gave me chapter and verse, adding to my doubts.

Why should Julia want to harm you, why should she lie? And if she is telling the truth, oh, Katie, my wife, my love, you are playing me false . . . yet I cannot blame you.

Perhaps I should let you go. That is the honorable thing, the honest, generous way to treat the woman I love. Yet I cannot, Katie. And . . . still I am tempted to bargain with God. I say, in my prayers, "Give me back the use of my paralyzed body, dear Lord, and I will let her go free." It is an unworthy, blasphemous prayer, and the Lord, in His wisdom, does not hear it.

Katie buried her face in her hands and wept, unable to stem the tears that came to overwhelm her. She had not understood, she chided herself. She had not attempted to understand what Rick was going through, and . . . she had not realized how deeply he loved her. But . . . there was still time to make amends, still time for them to begin their life together anew—God, in His infinite mercy, had vouchsafed them time. And in the clean, fresh air of Pengallon, away from the clacking tongues and the bitter feuds of Sydney, they would be able to start again. Rick was her husband, and the vows she had made bound her to him.

And . . . had he not given her the opportunity for—what had he termed it? A change of heart.

She read the last letter again. "Whatever you may or may not feel for me, I still love you," he had written, in the one letter he had intended her to read.

But . . . there were the others, the letters he had never meant her to see. In feverish haste, Katie dressed and, carrying the bundle of letters, went in search of Dickon.

It was not easy to make him understand, despite taking care to face him and speak slowly, and at first he only stared back at her blankly. Finally, however, his puckered brow cleared and his lips curved into a smile. He took the letters from her and went to unlock the chest.

"No!" Katie exclaimed. "Don't put them in the chest again, Dickon. They must be destroyed. Like this—look!" Snatching one of the letters, she tore it into shreds. "Uncle Rick must never find out that I read them. You must not tell him, ever . . . oh, Dickon, try to understand!"

The little boy nodded gravely. From the unlocked chest, he took his sketches and, carrying these and the remaining letters, motioned her to follow him. She did so uncertainly, still fearing that he had failed to grasp her meaning. He led her to the water's edge and to the point from which, only a few days before, he had fallen and almost drowned. As Katie watched, his small brown fingers tore letters and sketches into a thousand pieces, and then, greatly daring, he leaned out as far as he could and scattered the shreds of paper into the air. The breeze took them, carrying them out beyond his reach, and then let them float slowly down, to be lost in the glistening blue water at his feet.

Turning to her, Dickon smilingly mimed the motion of a ship under sail and then gestured to the empty sea chest. Realizing that he had fully understood both her meaning and her intention, Katie hugged him. When—if ever—Rick were to look in the chest for his letters, he would find it empty, and Dickon would tell him that he had used them, and his own precious sketches, to make sails for the little model ships they had been accustomed to set afloat in the cove.

"Dickon," she told him shakily, "we will go to Pengallon as soon as the dray is ready to take us." Dickon nodded happily, and Katie sent him off to find Jonas. There was one thing more she must do, she reminded herself. She would have to write a note to George De Lancey, and Jonas could deliver it.

CHAPTER XXVII

"You will attend the colonel," the 46th's new adjutant, Lieutenant Madigan, said crisply. "He is going to the civil court this morning and may be there all day. The magistrates are to inquire into the guilt or otherwise of a character named Murray—who is an ex-officer of the Royals, incidentally, but a thoroughly bad lot. At present he's acting as clerk to the bench, which adds to the interest . . . indeed, I envy you the opportunity of hearing the case. I'd go myself, if I didn't have all this infernal paperwork to plague me."

Murdo eyed him warily. "What is Murray accused of, do you know?" he asked.

Madigan clicked his tongue impatiently.

"Yes, of course I know—the whole damned regiment's known for months! But I was forgetting— you've been up in the wilds for the past six months, haven't you?"

"Eight," Murdo corrected. "Eight months."

The adjutant grunted and reached for his clay pipe. He filled it with meticulous care, lit it, and, when it was going to his satisfaction, prepared to reply to Murdo's question with equal care.

"A scurrilous piece of doggerel verse, which impugned the honor of our revered commanding officer, was given wide circulation in the form that the people here call a pipe. Suspicion fell initially, I regret to say, on the more high-spirited of our junior officers, but their innocence was, of course, swiftly established. The regimental mess combined to offer a reward of two hundred pounds in return for proof positive of the insolent rogue's identity. It has not been claimed, but Colonel Molle has accused Robert Murray of having written the defamatory verse, and on his insistence, the bench of magistrates are to hear and investigate the charge. Not, may I add, without considerable pressure being brought to bear." Madigan puffed hard on his churchwarden. "Indeed, my dear Dean, the chief magistrate, Dr. D'Arcy Wentworth, was the reverse of eager to agree to a hearing. So you can expect a few sparks to fly!"

Murdo suppressed a smile. "You would not have a copy of the poem, I suppose?"

The adjutant shook his head. "Damme, it's not the sort of thing to keep floating about in the orderly room—the mere sight of it is likely to give the colonel apoplexy! But I don't doubt that extracts from it will be read in court, as part of the evidence, so you'll hear it then."

"No doubt I shall," Murdo agreed. "Thank you, sir. I'll report to the colonel, shall I?"

"You can wait for him here. The court does not open until nine-thirty. And there's another matter I have to discuss with you." The 46th's adjutant searched among the papers on his desk. "Ah, yes—here it is. You've put in an application to exchange into the Forty-eighth, in your present rank, have you not?"

"Yes, sir, I have. I—"

"For heaven's sake, Dean, why? You surely don't want to stay here, do you? We're posted to Madras, which is an excellent station. Lord!" Madigan waved his pipe in an expressive gesture. "I can hardly wait to quit this infernal penal colony, with its jumped-up ex-felons and its feuds and factions in what passes for society. In India, one mixes with one's own kind; one does not have to worry as to whether or not they're socially acceptable. And besides, with the extra year's service you will be allowed for Waterloo, you are eligible for promotion to a lieutenancy without purchase if you stay with us. You should think about it, you know."

"I have thought about it," Murdo assured him. "And I want to stay."

"You'll be telling me next that you liked garrison duty in Bathurst!" Madigan exclaimed, his dark brows lifting in unconcealed astonishment. "Good lord, with no women and no social life and a veritable spate of plaguey escapers and bushrangers . . . you must be out of your mind!"

"Perhaps I am, sir," Murdo conceded. He grinned. "It was far from dull, I give you my word."

And that was the truth, he reflected. The eight months he had spent in the Bathurst garrison—while they had presented neither the thrills nor the dangers of life on the High Toby in England— had nevertheless offered scope for energy and initiative. And they had opened his eyes to the colony's future prospects, when the new lands beyond the mountains were explored and surveyed and finally opened for settlement. He had done some exploring on his own account, when escapers had had to be tracked down and apprehended, and, with Captain Lawson, had assisted in preparing the way for the official expedition led by the government surveyor general, John Oxley, which was endeavoring to trace the course of the Lachlan River.

William Lawson—known disrespectfully as Old Ironbark—the commandant of the garrison, combined farming with his military duties. He had over two hundred head of horned cattle now on his grant on the Macquarie River; his fellow veteran, William Cox— who had built the road from Emu Ford to Bathurst—had almost as many, and recently Rick Tempest had driven up a flock of at least five hundred sheep to his property in the same area. The land was being opened up, and several smaller grants, of fifty and a hundred acres, were to be allocated to new settlers.

Murdo's grin widened. There had been rumors of a gold find, too, and although this had been officially denied, he did not entirely discount the possibility that it might be true. Not that Lawson had encouraged speculation. Old Ironbark was a rich man, with a large property at Concord, a delightful wife, and eleven children, and Cox was of the same stamp. Both had made their fortunes on the land; both had been at the forefront of the exploration and development of the area beyond Bathurst, and both thought of it exclusively in terms of agricultural value.

He liked and respected William Lawson, Murdo thought, and it had undeniably been a privilege he had not anticipated to serve under his command. All the same . . .

Madigan said, uncannily as if he had read his thoughts, "Shall I tell your new commanding officer to send you back to Bathurst, then? That is, of course, provided that your transfer to the Forty-eighth is approved. The Autocrat may not permit it."

"The Autocrat?" Murdo questioned, puzzled.

"His Excellency Governor Macquarie." The adjutant's smile was thin. "I fear he's not enamoured of our regiment, Dean. In fact, I've been led to believe that he has informed the colonel that he doesn't want any of our officers to exchange into the Forty-eighth. He intends to make a clean sweep. But maybe you can pull a few strings.''

"Maybe I can," Murdo returned, his tone deliberately noncommittal. Lawson would speak up for him if need be, he told himself; they had got on well, and, indeed, the veteran captain had encouraged him to apply for a transfer, with the promise that, if he did so, he could expect to take part in future exploratory expeditions. He might even obtain a land grant eventually, although Governor Macquarie had ordained that serving officers of the garrison regiment were ineligible.

"You're an odd fish, Dean," Madigan observed, not unpleasantly. He seemed to remember something and frowned. "But of course—you have relatives here, have you not?"

"A cousin, sir, yes," Murdo admitted. He had returned to Sydney only the previous evening and had not, as yet, had time to call on Jessica, but her husband's ship was at anchor in the cove, so presumably she would not be alone. He liked Justin Broome well enough, and for all he was a seaman, he had acquitted himself singularly well when the gang of bushrangers had attacked Tempest's farm at Pengallon, but . . . Murdo stifled a sigh. He could never feel entirely at ease in Broome's company. Jessica had insisted on telling him of their real relationship, and that could mean disaster if he ever inadvertently let out the truth.

"The colonel's coming now," Madigan warned, gesturing to the window. "Step outside and wait for him in the passage. I'll tell him I've detailed you to attend him in the court. Keep a still tongue in your head and just do whatever he tells you. It should be plain sailing, but you never know with these blasted Sydney magistrates—they acquit when proof of guilt is staring them in the face!"

He tapped out his pipe and rose, straightening his well-cut scarlet coat. Lowering his voice, he added, "Pity it's not a court-martial, really, but Justice Bent advised against that—and then left before the case could be heard.''

"Justice Bent has left Sydney?" Murdo echoed, unable to conceal his surprise. He had heard a great deal about Judge Jeffrey Hart Bent from both Lawson and Cox, little of it to his credit. But neither had expected him to leave. . . .

"He sailed in the *Sir William Bensley*," Madigan supplied shortly. "And Murray has engaged De Lancey to represent him."

Colonel Molle's heavy footsteps sounded on the stone staircase, and the adjutant jerked his head in the direction of the orderly room door. Murdo hastily absented himself and was standing at attention in the corridor when Molle swept past him.

He emerged a quarter of an hour later, thrust a bulky leather satchel into Murdo's arms, and, with no other acknowledgment of his presence, led the way out to a waiting carriage. They turned out of the parade ground and into George Street and proceeded at a rattling pace to the end of Phillip Street, the colonel maintaining an austere silence. When the coachman drew up at the entrance to the courthouse, Molle said curtly, "Go in and find me a seat. I've someone I want to see first. Oh, and—" He opened the satchel and extracted some documents from it. Quickly glancing through them, he gave them to Murdo. "See that Judge Advocate Wylde gets these at once. At once, you understand?"

"Yes, sir," Murdo acknowledged woodenly. "Very good, sir."

The courtroom, when he entered it, was crowded, most of the seats being occupied by officers of the 46th. Captain Schaw, who had led a punitive expedition against native raiders in the Appin area the previous year, was seated by himself, a vacant chair beside him. His expedition, Murdo had been told indignantly by William Lawson, had resulted in the mass suicide of most of the tribe's women and children, after the soldiers had slaughtered their chief and almost a score of his warriors, and Schaw had been censured by the Governor and ostracized by his brother officers as a result. Nevertheless, since the only vacant seat appeared to be the one beside him, Murdo placed Colonel Molle's satchel on it, requested him politely to retain it for their commanding officer, and, not waiting to learn whether he had any objections, went in search of the judge advocate.

Wylde, an impressive figure in wig and gown, accepted the documents without comment. A few minutes later the magistrates filed in, led by Dr. Wentworth, and took their places on the bench, the defendant facing them, with George De Lancey—also in wig and gown—at his side.

Murdo made his way to the back of the courtroom, to stand with some of the late arrivals. The preliminaries were dealt with, and he identified the other two magistrates as Simeon Lord and Alexander

Riley, both well-known Sydney merchants. Judge Advocate Wylde detailed the nature of the inquiry and the charges at considerable length, his deep voice echoing from end to end of the crowded court.

"It is claimed that the accused, Robert Lathrop Murray, late captain in His Majesty's Royal Regiment of Dragoons and presently clerk and constable to this court, did with willful malice attempt to defame and vilify the character and good reputation of Lieutenant Colonel George Molle, officer commanding His Majesty's Forty-sixth Regiment of Foot, by the device of circulating a pernicious and libelous verse, of which he was the author."

To Murdo's cynical delight, extracts from the pipe were read, and he saw Colonel Molle's face suffused with angry color as he listened to the offending words.

Wylde next addressed the accused, inviting him to make reply to the charge brought against him. Robert Murray, a small, thin man with graying hair, offered a vigorous denial.

"The first I saw of the verse to which you refer, sir," he stated, "was when it was in circulation throughout Sydney Town. I am not the author of it, I do most earnestly assure Your Honor."

His reply predictably caused no surprise, but when the bewigged figure of George De Lancey was seen rising, a hush fell over the packed throng. Murdo, recalling De Lancey's skill in cross-examination from the *Conway* inquiry, waited expectantly.

"Your Honor, I crave the court's indulgence to enable me to call a witness who can refute the charge against my client and ensure that he goes free of all further suspicion of involvement."

"Your request, sir, is in contravention of the normal court procedure," the judge advocate cautioned. "We have not yet heard Colonel Molle's evidence in support of the charge."

"I'm aware of that, Your Honor," De Lancey assured him. "But since this is an inquiry and not a trial, the waiving of normal procedure is, I believe—with the court's agreement—permissible. Furthermore, sir, it will save the court's time."

"In what way, sir?" Wylde demanded, with a hint of irritation.

"The witness I propose to call, sir, will name the author of the offending verse," De Lancey stated quietly. Behind him, the spectators let out a concerted gasp of mingled astonishment and anticipation.

"Do you mean, sir, that your witness will offer the court a

confession?" Wylde was as astonished as the rest, Murdo realized; clearly he had not expected De Lancey's request and was at a loss to know how best to reply to it. "Does he intend to admit to authorship of the verse?"

"No, Your Honor. As I stated, he will name the author."

Colonel Molle could contain himself no longer. He was on his feet, voicing a furious protest, but the judge advocate ignored the interruption, and Captain Schaw laid a restraining hand on his commanding officer's arm. Molle sank back into his chair, muttering angrily to himself, and Wylde, after a brief consultation with the three magistrates, signified the court's agreement.

"You may call your witness, Mr. De Lancey."

"I thank you, sir." George De Lancey paused, savoring the moment and fully aware that he was about to cause a sensation. "I call Dr. D'Arcy Wentworth!"

Wentworth rose at once, clearly prepared for the summons, but his two fellow magistrates stared at him in openmouthed bewilderment, and the advocate general exclaimed in shocked tones, "For heaven's sake, De Lancey, you cannot call any of the bench to give evidence! Damme, it is most irregular!"

Recovering from his shocked surprise, Simeon Lord echoed his protest, but De Lancey put in firmly, "May I remind you, gentlemen—this is an inquiry, not a trial. And since Dr. Wentworth has vital evidence to give this court, and since he has, of his own free will, agreed to be called as a witness, I submit that he should be sworn in without further ado."

Above the hubbub of voices these words provoked, Colonel Molle roared, "If it will enable us to get to the bottom of this outrageous affair, let Wentworth be sworn! As the injured party, I've no objection."

Order was restored; Dr. Wentworth took the oath, and when he had done so, De Lancey asked formally, "Sir, do you know the identity of the author of the verses that are the subject of this inquiry?"

The surgeon inclined his head. "I do, sir, yes. It has only lately come to my knowledge that my son William wrote them. He did so a few days prior to his departure for England. He is not here in person to make this admission, but I make it on his behalf, in order to avoid a miscarriage of justice. The gentleman who has been accused of publishing the verses, Mr. Murray, is innocent. As to my son's culpability, I can say no more than plead indulgence. He is young and high-spirited, and—"

He got no further. Murdo watched in amazement as Colonel Molle leaped from his seat and, rushing forward, seized Dr. Wentworth's hand and wrung it warmly.

"Sir," he shouted, "you have taken a great weight off my mind! I applaud your honesty and courage in making this confession and thus clearing all others on whom suspicion has, from time to time, fallen—including the officers of my regiment. I . . . I thank you, sir."

He crossed to Robert Murray's side with hand outheld and, after a brief consultation with him, announced that both were agreed that the proceedings should close. Alexander Riley, still looking bemused, moved to adjourn the court.

There was jubilation in the regimental mess when the colonel and his officers returned there. Toasts were drunk with enthusiasm; Colonel Molle made an emotional speech and was cheered lustily, and Captain Sanderson replied, assuring him that he commanded and would continue to command the admiration, respect, and loyalty of every officer and man who proudly wore the uniform of the 46th Regiment of Foot.

"Our only regret, sir," the stout captain asserted, "is that the perpetrator of the foul libel should have gone unpunished."

"He's in England, damn it," Molle said. "And cannot be punished, more's the pity."

"His father is here, Colonel," Sanderson suggested slyly. "And, as the Autocrat is always reminding us, Dr. Wentworth holds a surgeon's military commission. You let him off deuced lightly, sir."

"He did the right thing with his admission," Molle demurred. Murdo, watching him intently, saw his eyes narrow, but no more was said, and after another toast, the colonel departed to tell his wife the good news.

When he had gone, Sanderson called the other officers together.

"Gentlemen, we have all languished under the cloud of suspicion ever since that pernicious poem was circulated. Having today been cleared of complicity, I believe it would be appropriate if we were to publish a declaration to that effect, together with an expression of regard for our esteemed colonel."

A roar of approval greeted his suggestion. Lieutenant Madigan was dispatched to find pen and paper, and, most of them affected by their liberal consumption of alcohol, they gathered round, eagerly offering contributions to be embodied in the declaration.

"Can we publish it in the *Gazette*?" a young lieutenant asked excitedly.

Sanderson shook his balding head. "The Autocrat would never permit us to do so. But we can print handbills and see to it that they are widely circulated. Come now, John—read us what you have taken down so far."

Madigan flashed him a wry smile. "It's pretty strong, Ned. But here goes: 'We, the officers of His Majesty's Forty-sixth Regiment of Foot, are desirous of expressing our jubilation at the discovery that the foul libel against our commanding officer issued from the pen of a man so much our inferior in rank and situation that we know him not. We learn that he comes from that promiscuous class which—with pride we affirm—have ever been excluded from intercourse with us. Had the effusion been the work of a respectable person, our hurt would have been more grievous.'" He paused for breath, and his assembled listeners clapped enthusiastically and urged him on.

"This is yours, Ned." The adjutant picked up a fresh sheet. "'We request that our commander allow us to approve and applaud still more that system of exclusion, wisely adopted prior to our arrival in this colony, the benefits of which we have reaped with advantage to ourselves, as officers and gentlemen, and which, although it may have prompted the malignity of those from whom we have kept aloof, has established the name of our regiment on a most respectable basis. Our mess table has come to be regarded as the standard of society in this colony, and we feel that we have established a salutary rule for the regiments that succeed us.'"

"We must see to it that the Forty-eighth receive copies," Captain Schaw said. He hiccuped loudly. "You said it was strong, John—devil take it, my dear fellow, it's not strong enough! Not by a long chalk . . . let's have an expression of our contempt for the foul venom of the upstarts who compose such libelous doggerel in the guise of satire! Let's name the rogue responsible for this one, for God's sake!"

"That might lead to trouble," Sanderson cautioned. "But I see no reason why his damned father should not be brought before a military court-martial. I'll speak to the colonel about it when the excitement dies down. It would really rile the Autocrat, would it not, if his esteemed Dr. D'Arcy Wentworth were laid low? And it would square the account for poor Bullivant."

Murdo pricked up his ears, recalling the friendly young officer who had first introduced him to the mess. "What happened to Bullivant, sir?"

Sanderson eyed him coldly and seemed, at first, as if he were disinclined to answer, but finally he said, with a thin smile, "He was foolish enough to draw a caricature of His Excellency the Governor in a—how can I describe it? An ignominious position, on the wall of the guardroom, to which some damned amusing labels were attached . . . not all of them by Bullivant. However, he was given the blame, and the Governor ordered him to be sent home." He turned back to John Madigan. "Include the colonel's toast, John. He expressed the hope that 'the regiment's hearts and hands will ever be united in friendship, esteem, and emulation, equally cordial in the hours of private and social intercourse, as in that field which our speedy removal from this colony may afford us an opportunity of enjoying.'"

Madigan wrote busily. "Capital!" he opined, after reading through his additions. "Would you care to sign it, Ned?"

Captain Sanderson took the quill from him and appended his name to the foot of the paper. Almost as an afterthought, he turned again to Murdo. "John says you intend to desert us and transfer to the Forty-eighth, Dean."

"Yes, sir," Murdo confirmed. "I want to stay here."

"Then you're a bloody fool!" Sanderson told him unpleasantly. "And furthermore, *Mister* Dean, I have a suspicion that you are not one of us. Always had an odd feeling about you, because somehow you don't ring true. Still, they'll probably be able to make use of you when you return to Bathurst. Quite a sprinkling of the old Rum Corps up there, I believe." He pushed the paper he had just signed across the table to Madigan, and added, with a sneer, "No need for Dean to put his signature to this, John. And if I were you, I'd send him back to Bathurst, pending transfer, right away."

John Madigan said nothing, and Murdo, feeling beads of sweat breaking out on his brow, beat a prudent retreat. Dear God, he thought, if only Captain Sanderson knew how close he had come to the truth!

Despite all the liquor he had consumed, he was in a sober and somewhat anxious mood when he left the barracks and made his way to the cove to pay his belated call on his sister Jessica.

He found her, with her husband and a number of friends—few of whom would have been invited to the 46th Regiment's mess—celebrating the birth of a second son. In their cheerful, friendly company, Murdo soon felt at ease, and it was with genuine pleasure that he proposed and drank a toast to the new arrival . . . another small, plump redhead, rejoicing in the name of John Lachlan.

CHAPTER XXVIII

Governor Macquarie seated himself at his desk and let his head fall onto his two outstretched hands. It was dusk and the light was failing, but he did not call for candles, and John Campbell, after glancing through the half-open door and sensing the despair that filled his friend and employer, closed it softly.

To Major Antill, waiting as anxiously as Campbell and clearly angry, the secretary shook his head.

"We can best serve him by leaving him alone, Henry," he said with a bitterness he did not attempt to hide. "Those purblind fools in the Colonial Office have dealt him the cruelest blow they could possibly have devised, and God knows he has not deserved it. He has worked so hard, achieved so much, and they send an infernal commissioner, with plenipotentiary powers, to inquire into his administration of the colony! You saw the brief Lord Bathurst gave the fellow, did you not?"

"Yes, I saw it, John," Antill responded. Controlling his anger, he went on, an edge to his normally pleasant voice. "I also heard the aptly named Mr. Bigge's interpretation of it and his assertion that he intends to investigate what he described as 'the numerous and most disturbing complaints of maladministration' directed against the poor Governor. But we both know only too well from whom the complaints have come, and we know what they're worth, do we not? Unhappily, Bathurst doesn't seem to, and the saintly Mr. Wilberforce believes every word Marsden writes to him. And, of course, that archvillain Jeffrey Hart Bent has been spreading his lies all over London ever since his return, plague take him!"

"Bent has been given a judgeship in the West Indies," Campbell supplied. He started to pace the confines of the anteroom with short, impatient steps. "You know, I suppose, that he went on circuit with Mr. John Thomas Bigge soon after being called to the bar? John Wylde told me . . . and Bigge himself is related to Henry Grey Bennet, that scourge of the Commons. *He* was the one who stirred up all the trouble on the home front—Bent's petition, the one he organized supposedly on the Reverend Vale's behalf three years ago, started the rot. The poor Governor was deeply wounded over that, as you're aware, because it led to questions in the House. Lord Castlereagh defended him then, and so did Bathurst. But now . . ." He sighed wretchedly.

"Now they have seen fit to send Commissioner Bigge to investigate what amounts to a pack of malicious lies by a bunch of self-seeking malcontents," Henry Antill said feelingly. "And he'll find plenty of the same stripe here—including John Macarthur. Why the Colonial Office permitted his return is beyond my comprehension! Seven years' banishment has not changed him— he still can't resist putting his oar in where it causes most trouble. I saw him making a great show of welcoming Bigge and his secretary, when we passed through Parramatta yesterday. Offered to lend them horses during their stay—I heard him! But"—he smiled with wry amusement—"the commissioner is anxious for his safety in this dangerous town, and he requested me, quite seriously, to supply sentries to guard his house. He said he had not realized how much freedom we permit our convicts, and he feared that an attack might be made on his person or Mr. Scott's!"

John Campbell did not smile. "They're an odd pair. Admittedly Bigge is a lawyer—he was one of Jeffrey Bent's predecessors in the judiciary of the West Indies—but Thomas Scott was apparently a wine merchant before being elevated to his present role!" He halted by the door into the Governor's office, listened for a moment, and then shook his head. "Not a sound. And he's there in the dark."

"You said yourself we should leave him alone," Antill reminded him. "He'll call if he needs us, John."

"He barely spoke a word to young Lachlan when he came in, and that's not like him," Campbell demurred. "Mrs. Macquarie is seeing the boy to bed, but perhaps if—"

"Elizabeth knows when to keep away."

"Yes, I'm aware of that. But even so—what happened in Windsor to upset him, Henry?" Campbell's brow creased into a worried frown. "Perhaps I shouldn't have allowed Bigge to go after him. But he was most insistent, demanded a carriage and an escort . . . I simply could not stop him. As you know, thanks to the delay of the *Hibernia*'s mail at Hobart, His Excellency received only six days' notice of the damned fellow's arrival, and he could not cancel the Windsor muster on that account. And Bigge's ship, the *John Barry*, was early—she made the passage in a hundred and thirty days."

Antill shrugged his scarlet-uniformed shoulders. "Don't blame yourself, John—you couldn't be expected to stop a man who is apparently entitled to a thirteen-gun salute. And whose salary exceeds the Governor's by a thousand pounds per annum . . . did you know that?"

"No," Campbell returned, with a flash of angry resentment. "I did *not*! Who told you, for heaven's sake?"

"The gentleman himself, believe that or not." Henry Antill's tone was dry. "And the ex-wine merchant is his brother-in-law, and he holds a dormant commission to succeed Bigge as commissioner, should any mishap befall him. All neatly arranged and in the family, eh? But as to what happened in Windsor . . . our own dear chief behaved magnificently when Bigge finally tracked him down, although of course he wasn't expecting to receive the fellow there. But along comes the carriage and escort, creating quite a stir, and the dear old chief greeted Bigge as if he were the one person in the world he wanted to see. In keeping with the best traditions of Highland hospitality, he gave them both tea at the Government Cottage and then took them in person to the Macquarie Arms to arrange for their accommodation. He couldn't have done more to make them welcome, John, but what do you think Bigge did in return?"

"What *did* he do?"

Antill sighed. "Delivered a lecture on his powers and intentions, which went on for at least a couple of hours. I had to listen to it, too, and I can assure you, it was all I could do to keep my temper. He informed our Governor that his commission required him to examine all the laws, regulations, and usages, as well as the administration of the civil government, the superintendence and reform of the convicts, the state of the judicial and ecclesiastical establishments, and—damme, even the colony's revenue from taxes! It was an endless list, and he stated it with the most incredible arrogance, interspersed with thinly veiled and deeply insulting comments, based, I could only presume, on correspondence between Marsden and Bent and Molle and others of their ilk and the Colonial Office. He even quoted some early correspondence with Macarthur, dating back to Governor King's day. It was unbelievably lacking in tact—and that's being generous."

John Campbell shook his head despondently.

"Small wonder, then, that the poor Governor is upset."

"He listened, with his usual courtesy, and scarcely said a word. Lord, John, I've never admired him more! But it's taken its toll of him." Antill repeated his sigh. "To add insult to injury, Mr. Bigge then climbed into his carriage and went dashing off to Parramatta to make the acquaintance of the Macarthurs. I think he was also hoping to find Marsden there, but no one told him that our Christian Mahomet has not yet returned from his latest sojourn with the Maoris."

"I pray almost nightly that he will stay there!" Campbell said savagely. "Or that his converts will revert to type and consign him to their ovens."

"Oh, come now, Philo Free," Henry Antill teased good-naturedly. "Would you deprive them of his Christian mission *and* his gunrunning?"

John Campbell reddened. Two years ago, he had so far forgotten his native caution as to publish a letter in the Sydney *Gazette*, cloaking his identity under the signature of "Philo Free, a settler at Bradley's Head," in which he had accused the colony's chaplain of using his mission to the Maoris of New Zealand as a means of acquiring personal profit.

Although the letter—like the all-too-prevalent pipes by means of which grievances were aired in Sydney—named no names, the *Gazette*'s readers had found little difficulty in identifying its subject or the gravity of the accusations made against him. That Samuel Marsden had traded arms and alcohol with the Maoris Campbell knew to be a fact, and that the trading profits from the venture went into the chaplain's own pocket, rather than into the coffers of the Church Missionary Society, he strongly suspected, but . . . providing proof of either had been another matter. A compositor working for the *Gazette* had revealed the real name of the letter's author, Marsden had sued him for criminal libel, and

Mr. Justice Field had awarded two hundred pounds damages in the chaplain's favor.

True, Marsden's original claim had been for considerably more, but even so, Campbell recalled regretfully, he had incurred the Governor's displeasure and received an official reprimand from Lord Bathurst as a result of his impulsive attempt to show the "Christian Mahomet" for the hypocrite he was.

"For pity's sake, Henry," he said tensely, "spare me your humor on *that* subject, if you please. Philo Free has cost me the colonial secretaryship."

Henry Antill stared at him. "Are you serious? Has it?"

"So Bigge took pleasure in informing me, within minutes of our first meeting. He is apparently in Lord Bathurst's confidence and was permitted access to all correspondence between this colony and His Majesty's government, before he left London. He told me that Major Frederick Goulburn—brother to the Undersecretary—is to be appointed."

"John, I'm deuced sorry." Antill shook his head in disbelief at his own lack of perception. "I'd no idea."

John Campbell laid a forgiving hand on his arm. "Think no more of it—of course you did not know. And I shall have the bank . . . that was the reason why His Excellency chose me as his secretary in the first place, so that I could help him to found a bank here. And we've done it—in the teeth of objections from the Colonial Office! Furthermore, it is solvent without any government money to support it." He added, forcing a smile, "And to be honest, Henry, in my heart of hearts I cannot regret having written the Philo Free letter—because it was true, every damned word of it! Samuel Marsden *does* sell muskets to the Maoris, every time the *Active* calls at Whangaroa Bay, and if his blasted cannibals have canonized him, it's because he and some of his people have taught them how to distill spirits! And one day, God willing, I shall prove my case."

"I wish you luck, my friend," Antill said cynically. "But in the meantime, there's not much Marsden can do, is there, except engage in husbandry? His dismissal from the magistracy must surely have clipped his wings; and without his former allies—notably Bent and Molle—he'll be a spent force if he does come back."

"He'll gravitate to Mr. John Thomas Bigge," Campbell prophesied glumly. "Like iron filings to a magnet—you'll see! And who's to say that he won't patch up his differences with John Macarthur in the common cause? This is a sad day, Henry, by heaven it is! They are out for the poor old Governor's blood, and Bigge and his wine merchant have been sent here to shed it. Why—" He broke off abruptly as the door to the inner sanctum opened and the Governor's gaunt face appeared in the aperture.

"Be so good as to bring me a lamp, John," he requested. His voice was controlled but strained as he went on quietly, "I shall draft a letter of resignation to Lord Bathurst, and this time he will be compelled to accept it."

Left once more alone, a lamp now glowing at his elbow, Governor Macquarie did not pick up his pen. Instead he reached for a file containing the most recent Colonial Office dispatches and, handling it as if it were obnoxious to him, extracted a printed pamphlet.

It was addressed to the Home Secretary, Lord Sidmouth, by Mr. Henry Grey Bennet, M.P., in support of his demands for a parliamentary inquiry into the general conduct of the convict transport system and of the present government of New South Wales. Lord Bathurst had forwarded the document, marked "for your information," with his routine dispatches and the announcement of Commissioner Bigge's imminent arrival.

He had read it twice before, Macquarie thought resignedly, and each time the untruths and the exaggerations, the false claims and the sheer malevolence of the document had so sickened him that he had been compelled to put it aside unanswered. It was with weary reluctance that he took up the pamphlet now.

Mr. Bennet stated unctuously that he was relying on the Reverend Samuel Marsden, whom he described as

> this respectable Minister of the Gospel—one of those distinguished persons who, praise be to God, are daily raised up among us, whose enjoyment of life is to carry the blessings of the Gospel to distant lands, to relieve the spiritual wants of their fellow creatures, and to spread far and wide the doctrines of goodwill.

The Honorable Member's fulsome praise did not end there, and Macquarie's lip curled as he digested Mr. Bennet's tribute to his informant. According to the pamphlet, the colony's chaplain was

> agonized at the life he had to lead, at the sights and scenes he was compelled to witness, his lot cast among thieves and felons, murderers and incendiaries, in a community daily ripening into such a school of vice and crime as the world never saw . . . yet resolutely and firmly clinging to his post.

The description accorded very oddly, the Governor reflected, with Samuel Marsden's record as a magistrate. The bench book for Parramatta—which he had consulted prior to dismissing Marsden from the bench—had recorded the harshest sentences in the whole colony, some eleven thousand lashes having been awarded to fewer than two hundred and fifty malefactors who had stood trial before him, together with equally savage sentences to the chain gangs, the women's factory, the coal mines, and solitary confinement, often for trivial offenses.

And if John Campbell had been right, in the accusations he had made in his Philo Free letter to the *Gazette* . . . The Governor shook his head sadly and returned to his perusal of the pamphlet. Of himself it stated, "The stay of Major General Macquarie has been prolonged beyond his term of years," and then it had gone on to claim that, under his governorship

> male convicts nightly rob and plunder, females on arrival at Port Jackson are turned out upon the decks to be chosen like slaves in the bazaar or cattle at Smithfield . . . and carried off as prostitutes by the officers of the colony or by those fortunate enough to possess an interest with the government in priority of selection.

After this point, the pamphlet lapsed into pure fantasy:

> Public houses abound in every street, as the direct result of the appalling conditions of vice and immorality which the Governor does nothing to prevent.

Disgusted, Macquarie read that there were apparently "grave-yards like plowed fields, vice, misery, disease, want, and drunkenness" contrasted with "flagrant examples of extravagance" by the privileged few. The colony, Bennet finally asserted, had

> failed as a place of reform due to the selection of improper persons for office and the appointment of convicts to officiate as magistrates.

Macquarie closed his eyes for a moment, visualizing the well-kept, orderly streets of Sydney Town—with George Street the first to be paved—the fine new buildings, the carefully tended gardens and public parks, and—ironically, in view of Bennet's claim—the dearth of grogshops and squalid drinking dens, even in the notorious Rocks. He thought, with a surge of pride, of Greenway's new cathedral—for which he had laid the foundation stone only a few days ago—of the new wharves and warehouses now girdling Sydney Cove, and of the schools he had established, including one for young blacks, at Parramatta.

The vice, misery, disease, and drunkenness of which Bennet had written so passionately to Lord Sidmouth were no longer part of the life here, and if prostitution still existed, it was the fault of the home government for deporting women of easy virtue to the colony, instead of selecting the sober working women for whom he and all the colony's previous Governors had repeatedly pleaded. But even the prostitutes' activities had been curbed, with the building of a large and well-equipped female factory in place of the decaying structure that until recently had served their needs.

Macquarie's firm mouth tightened, as he read a few more lines of Bennet's strictures:

> It is not my intention to advise the abandonment of Botany Bay and Van Diemen's Land, but rather to draw Your Lordship's attention to the fact that these projects have cost His Majesty's government some three million pounds sterling, and, due to the flagrant examples of misgovernment I have mentioned, to think of commerce under these impediments and obstructions would be as wild a speculation as to expect the reform of convicts among their fellow settlers in Newgate Prison.

"Devil take the arrogant fellow," the Governor muttered wrathfully. "What does he know?"

Exploration of the new country beyond the Blue Mountains had extended the colony's land area from twenty-five hundred to almost one hundred thousand square miles, much of it accessible now by the roads he had built, and opened or about to be opened to settlement and the breeding of livestock . . . but there was no mention of this in the pamphlet. Nor of the townships he had founded, of which Mr. Grey Bennet, it seemed, had never been informed by that respectable minister of the Gospel, the Reverend Samuel Marsden.

The newly arrived commissioner, Mr. Bigge, appeared to have obtained his information about the colony from equally inaccurate and prejudiced sources, judging by his attitude when they had made each other's acquaintance in Windsor a few days ago, Macquarie reflected ruefully. Although half his age, and with colonial experience only as a judge in some West Indian island, Bigge had been barely civil to him—and downright discourteous to Elizabeth. He had demanded, rather than requested, had offered his opinions uninvited, and in general had behaved as if his commission set him above the colony's officials—even above its appointed Governor.

Indeed, the new arrival had behaved as if he had come to pass judgment on him, as Governor, with a mind already made up and a verdict long since decided . . . as perhaps it was, however contrary to British justice that might be.

Glancing again at Grey Bennet's infamous pamphlet, Lachlan Macquarie became conscious of a strange desolation of the spirit that, try as he might, he could not shake off. Had he, he asked himself, not without bitterness, stayed here too long—had the time come for him to do as he had told John Campbell and Henry Antill he would and resign? He was less than a year from his sixtieth birthday; he had served his country in war and peace, with scarcely a pause, since his early youth, and he was tired . . . dear God, how tired he was!

He had made an attempt to resign his office as Governor over a year ago, but Lord Bathurst had ignored his letter, together with his formal request for a pension, until—in a letter received by the *Hibernia* just before Commissioner Bigge's arrival—the Colonial Secretary had invited him to reconsider his decision.

He might well have done so, Macquarie mused, had it not been for Bigge's appointment. That in itself was tantamount to an admission that the home government had lost confidence in him, and . . . He glanced again at the Bennet pamphlet. Bathurst had sent him that pack of lies "for his information" and, he could only suppose, expected him to reply to it.

His hand was trembling as he reached for his pen, but he steadied it by an effort of will and started to write furiously:

> Your Lordship is no doubt fully aware how cruelly my public and private character, as Governor of this territory, has been attacked, censured, and calumniated by certain members of the House of Commons in their public speeches . . . grounded on reports and information flowing from the most polluted sources and the falsehoods of unprincipled individuals . . ."

There was a soft knock on the door, and knowing that it was Elizabeth, the Governor let his pen fall and turned to greet her with relief. She always sensed when he needed her, he thought gratefully, and, by some mysterious womanly intuition, knew without being told what he needed.

She came in, bearing a tray, set with the Highland oatcakes she had taught Mrs. Ovens to make, cheese, and a decanter of his favorite malt whiskey. He had not felt like food, had been too tense and angry on his return from Windsor to be able to face a formal dinner, but this frugal Highland fare put him in mind of his youth and the snatched meals he had taken in his mother's kitchen at Oskamull years ago.

Elizabeth poured his scotch, and as he savored its peaty aroma and felt the warmth from each sip spreading over his weary body, she cut the cheese into slices, smiling at him as she did so.

"It has been a trying day for you, Lachlan dear, has it not?" she said gently.

"Yes," he conceded. "A trying week, in fact."

"For which the discourteous Mr. Bigge is mainly responsible?"

Macquarie, munching his oatcake hungrily, inclined his head. "Bigge has been sent here because certain politicians in England want to see my dismissal." He gestured to Grey Bennet's pamphlet. "This one in particular. Should I resign and accept defeat, Elizabeth, or wait until he's done his worst?"

Elizabeth studied his face anxiously. "You are not easily defeated, Lachlan. You have had your victories—even over Colonel Molle, in the end."

That was true, Lachlan Macquarie recalled. George Molle, having shaken poor D'Arcy Wentworth's hand after the fiasco of an inquiry into the authorship of the libelous pipe, had suddenly changed his tune and demanded that the colony's principal surgeon should submit to a trial by a military court-martial for having withheld information concerning his son's part in the affair.

A battle royal had ensued, but this time Molle had gone too far. He had made vile assertions as to Dr. Wentworth's past, which were palpably untrue, and . . . The Governor smiled thinly, as he remembered. Stoutly supported by the new judge advocate, John Wylde, and by the newly arrived lieutenant colonel of the 48th, James Erskine, he had canceled the proposed court-martial and ordered Molle on board the *Matilda* with the rest of his regiment. And the transport had sailed for India, taking the 46th Regiment of His Majesty's Foot away from Sydney, with few of the colony's inhabitants regretting its departure. Only Michael Dean, the young officer he recalled from the *Conway* inquiry, had stayed, to fill a vacancy in the 48th, and he was proving a valuable asset already, making a contribution to William Lawson's attempts to find a passage from Bathurst to the Liverpool Plains.

"And there was your victory over Mr. Marsden," Elizabeth observed, with a satisfaction she did not pretend to conceal. "That was, perhaps, the most significant of all. He is a truly evil man, Lachlan, seeking to hide his wickedness beneath the cloak of Christian piety."

Marsden, too, had gone too far. The Governor drained his glass and took another oatcake, his earlier tension fading. The chaplain had, by some unexplained means, got wind of the letter of resignation he had sent to Lord Bathurst by Alexander Riley's ship the *Harriet* in January of the previous year. Emboldened by this and by his successful civil action against John Campbell, Marsden had had the effrontery to attempt to reopen the case of the three emancipists who had been flogged for their trespass into the Domain. He had prevailed upon the public executioner, an illiterate ex-convict named Hughes, to swear an affidavit that—

Macquarie frowned—he presumably intended to send to Mr. Gray Bennet in England, to support his earlier allegations.

But Hughes had been fearful of the consequences and had talked; Marsden, by administering an oath outside his own magistracy of Parramatta, had committed a technically illegal act, and by his own deviousness had left himself liable to dismissal. Summoned before a viceregal court of inquiry consisting of no fewer than eighteen members—with himself, as Governor, presiding—Samuel Marsden had failed to clear himself of the charge of having acted, in an insubordinate and seditious manner, to bring the administration into disrepute.

Recalling his own speech at the conclusion of the hearing, the Governor frowned deeply. He had not minced words—indeed, he had come perilously near to losing his temper with the man who, in alliance with Molle and the Bents, had for years sought to undermine his authority and injure his reputation.

"I must thus publicly warn you," he had told Marsden, "that if you ever presume again to interfere with or investigate any part of my conduct, as Governor of this colony, I shall consider it my indispensable duty . . . immediately to suspend you from the exercise of your function as a clergyman and a magistrate, until I report your conduct to His Royal Highness the Prince Regent."

The harm had been done, of course; Grey Bennet had been given all the misinformation he needed to ensure that the Colonial Office should send Commissioner Bigge on his supposed fact-finding mission. But at least he had confronted the malicious purveyor of that information and spoken his mind, Macquarie told himself. And, as Elizabeth had said, he could claim Marsden's eventual dismissal from the magistracy as a victory.

A hollow one, perhaps, but . . . He recalled the last words he had spoken as Samuel Marsden had faced him, the length of the table and the eighteen chairs of the witnesses between them.

"Viewing you now, sir, as the head of a seditious low cabal . . . I have to inform you that I never wish to see you except on public duty, and I cannot help deeply lamenting that any man of your sacred profession should be so much lost to every good feeling . . . as to manifest such deep-rooted malice, rancor, hostility, and vindictive opposition toward one who has never injured you but has, on the contrary, conferred many acts of kindness on both yourself and your family."

"I believe," Elizabeth said quietly, breaking into his thoughts, "in answer to the question you asked me when I first came in, I truly believe that you should not again offer your resignation, Lachlan. Lord Bathurst has your request to be relieved before him, even if he has asked you to reconsider it. Let Mr. Bigge and that uncouth assistant of his do their worst . . . let them make their inquiries without hindrance."

"They will talk to my enemies," Lachlan Macquarie demurred.

"And also to your friends," Elizabeth reminded him. "And you have far more friends than enemies in the colony now. John Wylde, George De Lancey—even Mr. Field, I fancy. And Colonel Erskine and Major Morrisett and the officers of their regiment. Oh, Lachlan dearest, a great host of others, too—the settlers, the emancipists who have made good and who owe everything to you, the honest traders and merchants, the children and even the black people, whose friend you have been. And there are the towns you have created, the new settlements and the vast new country beyond the mountains—surely these will speak more loudly and truthfully in your favor than men like Mr. Bennet, who have never even set eyes on what they seek to destroy?"

Perhaps she was right, Lachlan Macquarie thought, but he shook his head, fearing to believe it. Those of his enemies who still remained had loud voices, persuasive tongues, and . . . influence. John Macarthur had more influence than anyone, and he appeared to have joined the enemy's ranks. And he boasted openly of having brought about the resignation or the dismissal of the three previous Governors of the colony.

Elizabeth laid her soft cheek on his.

"Dearest husband," she pleaded, "let me prove to you that I am right concerning your friends. Let us go on tour—we have the *Elizabeth Henrietta* and her loyal captain. Justin Broome can take us to Newcastle and later to Hobart. We will bring Lachie, and Jessica shall come with us, with her children. And later we can visit Bathurst and the new country, and our tour can include Port Macquarie and the Illawarra, as well as Liverpool and Appin."

"A farewell tour?" the Governor countered.

"No," Elizabeth answered confidently. "A triumphal tour. Please, Lachlan—"

He bowed his head. "Very well, my dear. And I pray God you are right."

CHAPTER XXIX

"I consider it quite iniquitous!" Abigail Dawson exclaimed indignantly. "After all he has done for the sick of this colony—the lives his skill has saved, the selfless dedication he has always shown! Everyone agrees that William Redfern is the best doctor we've ever had here, and we all took it for granted that he would be appointed principal surgeon when Dr. Wentworth retired. Now he has retired . . . and the Colonial Office has given the appointment to Dr. Bowman, who may have been here before, but only as a ship's surgeon. Nobody knows him, and he's never lived here, has he? Why should he be preferred to a man who has given almost twenty years of his life to the service of this community?"

"Bowman came out for the first time with John Macarthur in the *Lord Eldon,*" her husband pointed out dryly. "And he made his second passage in the *John Barry* with His High and Mightiness Commissioner Bigge. Furthermore, he's now paying court to Macarthur's daughter Mary. He has influence, Abigail my dear. And poor Redfern was a mutineer, convicted of sedition after the Nore mutiny. Have you forgotten that?"

"But he was only a boy then, Tim! And all he did was remain on board his ship to care for the sick, after the mutineers had put the other surgeon ashore—he told me so himself. Is that a crime, for pity's sake?"

"It is in His Majesty's Navy, Abby," Rick confirmed. "And an example had to be made of the Nore mutineers. Redfern was unlucky to be caught up in it, but on the other hand, he was lucky they didn't hang him."

"But they still hold it against him," Abigail protested. "After twenty years! It's so unjust, Rick. When I think what we all owe him—Dickon, especially. And you, too."

"Oh, yes, I'm deeply in his debt. But technically, Abby, the good Dr. Redfern is an emancipist, which, by Mr. Bigge's somewhat prejudiced standards, means that he isn't eligible to hold any official appointment. The Governor proposed to make him a magistrate, but the upright ex-Justice Bigge, I was reliably informed, objected on the grounds that he was never granted a King's pardon."

"That is adding insult to injury!" Abigail said angrily. "Surely Governor Macquarie will not be swayed by such a—such a technicality?"

Tim Dawson smiled. "Of course he's not, my dear. He and Bigge are said to have had a blazing row about it. And that's not the only difference they've had. According to John Campbell— who was spitting with rage when he told me—Bigge is prancing round the countryside on one of Macarthur's pedigree Arabs, handing out questionnaires to everyone he meets. The opening question is said to be 'Have you any complaint to make against Governor Macquarie?' Furthermore, Campbell says, he holds his official inquiries behind closed doors, and does not require the witnesses to give their evidence on oath."

"And I had supposed," Abigail observed, with heavy sarcasm, "that all the poor, good Governor's troubles would be over when the Bents and Colonel and Mrs. Molle left, and Mr. Marsden went off to New Zealand! But it would seem that they are only now beginning."

"I fear you are right, my love," Tim agreed. There was genuine sadness in his voice. "It will be a tragedy if we lose the best Governor this colony has ever had on the word of a damned mountebank like Bigge. It's even being rumored that he's after the governorship for himself."

"Bigge? You cannot be serious, Tim!"

"It's in the cards, Abby," Rick put in. "And I heard an even stranger rumor. Bigge's lackey, the wine merchant Scott, is said to be intending to take holy orders, so that he may apply for appointment as archdeacon of Sydney! And Mr. Cowper says they want the Governor's new courthouse to be transformed into a church, to provide an appropriate setting for His new Holiness." He laughed, without amusement. "I know that sounds fanciful, but poor old Cowper believes every word of it. He even insists that the church is to be dedicated to St. James!"

Abigail stared at him in disbelief, and even Tim, she saw, looked startled. He said, matching her earlier sarcasm, "And *I* had supposed—no, the devil take it, I'd hoped that we were done with corruption. But it seems we are not . . . and they send men out here in chains for less than that! Aye, and damn them for the rest of their days because of those chains. They—" He broke off as the door opened and Katie came in. "Ah, Katie my dear, come and sit down. Dinner will not be long, I fancy."

Rick rose to take his wife by the hand. She was in her last month of pregnancy, Abigail knew, and Rick had brought her down from Pengallon a week ago in order that Dr. Redfern might supervise the delivery. The girl had suffered a miscarriage and lost her first child a year ago, and aware of how much her brother wanted a family, Abigail had urged them to come to Sydney for the birth.

They were happy in their marriage, or at all events they seemed to be; with the opening of the new country for settlement, Pengallon was no longer the isolated place it had been, and Bathurst had grown, Rick had assured her, out of all recognition now. Little Dickon, certainly, was as happy as a king when he was allowed to visit them, and the farm itself, under the expert management of the faithful Jethro Crowan, was doing well. Rick had gone in for horned cattle rather than sheep, although he had increased his original flock from the breeding ewes that William Broome had supplied to him, and Tim . . . Abigail glanced at her husband, a frown momentarily creasing her brow.

Tim—a wealthy man, who had built up his prosperous holdings slowly, over the years—had expressed concern over the manner in which Rick was buying stock.

"He hasn't all that much capital behind him," Tim had said. "Just his naval prize money and whatever Justin has managed to contribute, which can't be much, on a naval lieutenant's pay. But Rick has more cattle than Old Ironbark has up there now. I just hope he's not overreaching himself. Of course, he doesn't have the floods we in the Hawkesbury Valley have to contend with, but even so—he's spending money like water. For Katie's sake, I hope he's not running himself into debt."

Rick had shown no anxiety on that account, Abigail reflected, but . . . Tim was right. Rick had bought more cattle during the past week and, on his own admission, had contacted John Macarthur's agent with a view to purchasing half a dozen of the pure Merino rams of which, it seemed, the onetime Rum Corps officer possessed a monopoly. There had been talk of an offer Macarthur had made to sell some of the rams at a reduced price to improve the flocks of the small settlers, the difference in price to be made up by means of government land grants in the Cow Pastures, where he already owned five thousand acres . . . but, as far as she knew, the Governor had rejected the offer. So the rams would not be cheap—fifteen or twenty guineas a head, at least. And if Rick was buying half a dozen of them . . . Abigail glanced at her brother.

It was indeed to be hoped that he was not running himself into debt.

Katie settled herself awkwardly into her chair and managed a wan little smile. "I saw the *Elizabeth Henrietta* in the anchorage, Rick. Did you go out to see Justin, or has he come ashore?"

"He is dining with us," Abigail told her. "And he should be here very soon. I asked them both, but Jessica sent word to say that little Johnny is teething and rather fractious, so she feels she should stay with him. I knew Rick wanted to talk with Justin, and their opportunities have been few and far between lately, with you and Rick up at Pengallon and Justin's ship kept so busy taking the Governor on tour."

"Did he not take Mr. Bigge to Van Diemen's Land, earlier this year?" Katie asked.

"He had that doubtful pleasure," Abigail confirmed. She made a little moue. "But I fear he did not enjoy it. However, he brought his stepfather, Captain Hawley, back on his return passage, and I gather, from what he told us, that Andrew Hawley enlightened His Honor the commissioner on a considerable number of subjects, about which that gentleman was apparently ignorant."

Tim threw back his head and laughed, with genuine amusement. "He had a captive audience, Katie. Justin said that both the commissioner and his secretary suffered badly from *mal de mer,* and they met with gale-force winds all the way from the Derwent. The passage took five days longer than expected . . . I suspect, myself, that Justin may have prolonged it. The *Elizabeth* is not a weatherly vessel in high seas. Certainly the commissioner was a pale shadow of his normal self during the mourning ceremony for the old King, after he came back here."

"I'm sorry we missed that," Katie said. "But we heard it was very impressive, didn't we, Rick?"

"It was indeed," Abigail volunteered. "There was a long procession from the Domain to St. Philip's Church, with the troops lining the route and the regimental band of the Forty-eighth playing the Dead March from *Saul,* with their colors and drums draped in black. And the service was beautiful . . . dear old Mr. Cowper preached so movingly. Then Mr. Campbell, acting as provost marshal, with the justices and the magistrates in attendance, proclaimed the accession of George the Fourth, and the Governor gave a reception at Government House. Even the convicts received an issue of rum to drink the new King's health." She smiled reminiscently. "Oh, Tim, it was a grand occasion. How I wish Frances might have been there . . . though I wager she would have found it ironical that Irish prisoners were drinking the health of the new English King!" Her eyes misted as she recalled her departed friend . . . and her husband, Jasper Spence . . . and poor dear Lucy! For all her faults, Lucy had still been her sister, still had claim to a sister's affections. She had certainly not deserved to perish so young—

"The Governor's been ill, has he not?" Rick inquired, interrupting her reverie. "A rumor reached us to that effect. He made a very strenuous tour from Bathurst all through the Toombong country as far as Lake George—too strenuous by far for a man of his age. And they met with appalling weather, lost a couple of horses, and were soaked to the skin more than once."

"He was very ill a few months ago," Abigail answered. "But"—she sighed—"the excellent Dr. Redfern pulled him through. Mrs. Macquarie is the one who is ill now, though, poor dear soul. She was awaiting the Governor's return in Parramatta when the Government House there was struck by lightning, causing her a very severe shock. I believe—" She broke off as the door opened and a servant stood aside to permit Justin to enter. "Justin dear, you are very welcome, and as I promised you in my note, Rick and Katie are here. And Julia and Dorothea are dining with Colonel and Mrs. Erskine, so we shall have plenty of time to talk without interruption."

Greetings were exchanged, inquiries made and answered. Andrew Hawley, Abigail learned, had resigned his commission and retired to the farm at Ulva; William was considering a move to the new country; Rachel was coming to stay in Sydney with Jessica; and Justin himself had carried troops, stores, and convict laborers to the new settlement at Port Macquarie.

"The Governor is planning a visit there in the New Year," Justin said as they sat down to their meal in the big, lamp-lit dining room. "A farewell visit," he added regretfully. "He sent for me, just after I'd dropped anchor in the cove, to tell me that his resignation has been accepted and his successor is on his way out here. The new colonial secretary for New South Wales, Major Goulburn, was there when I called—he arrived just before we did, on board the *Hebe* transport. Seemingly he had brought the news, and the poor old Governor looked very cut up. Not that he said anything, of course, and he was being very courteous to Major Goulburn, but"—he shrugged—"he simply asked me to prepare the *Elizabeth* for sea and left it at that, adding almost as an afterthought that he would probably go to Hobart, too, before he finally departs."

All eyes were riveted on him, but for a moment no one spoke. Then Tim asked gruffly, "Justin, for God's sake—did His Excellency tell you who is to be his successor?"

"He did not," Justin answered, with a tight smile. "But John Campbell did. It's to be General Sir Thomas Brisbane, he said."

"The general who married a cousin of Colonel Molle's," Abigail observed. She remembered the lunch party at Government House when Mrs. Molle had hinted at such a possibility, and her heart sank.

"Well, at least it's not Commissioner Bigge!" Tim's relief was evident. He rose and crossed to the sideboard to carve the joint the servant had just brought in. "Thanks be to God for small mercies! I should have been tempted to pull up stakes and join you in the new country, Rick, if His Majesty's government had given *him* the appointment."

"He is the person we can thank for the loss of Governor Macquarie," Abigail pointed out with asperity. She glanced uneasily at Katie, who had scarcely said a word since entering the dining room, and saw her shake her head to the laden plate Tim had been about to place before her. "Katie dear, are you all right?"

"I—I'm not sure," Katie responded, in a small, frightened voice. "But I think—" She caught her breath, her eyes fixed, wide

with alarm, on Rick's face. "Oh, Rick, I think my time has come,
I—"

Rick was beside her in an instant. "All right, my sweet girl," he
said reassuringly, and picked her up in his arms. "Abby, call Kate
Lamerton, will you, please? I'll take her up to her room."

It would be a long evening, Abigail thought, as she hastened to
obey him . . . a long evening and an anxious one for them all.
They resumed their interrupted meal, joined now by Dickon, a
sleepy figure in his nightshirt, whom Kate Lamerton's departure
had roused from his bed.

The meal over, Abigail took the little boy back to his room and
tucked him up. She glanced in at Katie, but clearly it would be
well into the early hours before the delivery was likely, and she
contented herself with sending a note to Dr. Redfern to warn him
that his patient's labor had begun.

Kate Lamerton, competent and composed as always, begged her
not to worry. " 'Twill take its time, this one, Miss Abigail," the
old midwife said. "She's just a wee slip o' a girl, and it will not be
easy. But I'll do all that's to be done, and I'll call you if there's
aught to tell you."

Downstairs, Abigail found Tim by himself in the withdrawing
room. He said, eyeing his pipe apologetically, "Forgive this
liberty, my dear, but I've left Justin and your brother to have their
talk alone, over their port. There's something on Rick's mind, I
fancy—apart from the imminent arrival of his firstborn. It's as well
to let them have it out, don't you agree?"

Abigail inclined her head. "Do you have any idea what it is they
have to talk about?"

"No, none. Unless it's Rick's extravagance. What the deuce
does he want with half a dozen of Macarthur's Merino rams, for a
start? And knowing Macarthur"—Tim snorted his disgust—"he'll
only part with his culls, and he'll charge the earth for those.
Andrew Hawley told me that the ones he sent to Hobart for
Colonel Sorrell weren't worth the cost of their passage—and
Sorrell's damned annoyed. I gather—" He fell silent, hearing
raised voices coming from the room next door, and Abigail,
listening intently, caught the word "gold" uttered angrily by
Justin.

She looked uncertainly at Tim.

"There were rumors, my dear," he said, answering her

unvoiced question. "Quite persistent rumors, after Rick was shot
by those escapers, that he had made a gold strike at Pengallon. But
they were denied—you may remember there was a statement in the
Gazette to the effect that the assay had proved conclusively that
some nuggets found in the new country were fool's gold or pyrites
or whatever the stuff's called."

"Yes," Abigail confirmed. "I do remember. I . . ."

She could not put her thoughts into words, but once again her
husband guessed the direction they had taken and observed flatly,
"We're probably jumping to conclusions, Abby. But if we're
not—"

"Well?" she prompted. "If we're not?"

"It could be disastrous," Tim said, and now there was an edge
of anger to his voice. "Disastrous to the good Governor's plans for
the agricultural development of the new country. But I don't
imagine that Justin will let Rick do anything to bring about such a
disaster. It was his lease originally, don't forget—Rick is only his
partner. He owns the stock, but the land is Justin's. And—" He
held up a warning hand. "Here they come. Don't say anything,
Abby. They will probably tell us what they've decided."

The two came in, and Abigail sensed at once, from Justin's
tight-lipped pallor and Rick's angry eyes, that they had been
engaged in heated disagreement and that Justin had prevailed.
Conscious of relief, she replied to Rick's anxious inquiries
concerning Katie.

"I've sent a note to warn Dr. Redfern. But Kate Lamerton says
we must be patient, Rick. It will be some hours yet."

"I see. Thank you, Abby." Rick drew a quick, uneven breath
and then said, addressing Tim, "I've decided against taking those
rams of Macarthur's—Justin's talked me out of it, on the grounds
of expense, damn his eyes! I . . . that is, Tim, we've agreed that
I have been going too fast and that we ought to clear some of the
land and grow crops, instead of putting in more stock. I suppose
he's right—I have been rushing things a bit. Perhaps I was a mite
greedy."

Tim met Abigail's swift glance and smiled at her. "I'm quite
sure that Justin is right, Rick old man," he said pleasantly. "And
I, for one, am glad to hear you've decided against the rams. One
might be a useful purchase—but send old Jethro to Parramatta to
choose it!"

He rose to pour drinks for them, and a little later Justin took his leave.

Just before dawn, when Dr. Redfern had been with Katie for nearly three hours, the baby was born. The faint but unmistakable sound of its crying brought Rick to his feet with a fervent "Thank God!" The doctor came in, some minutes later, to offer a hand in warm congratulation.

"You are the father of a beautiful little daughter, Rick," he announced. "But we had quite a difficult time bringing her into the world, and your wife is very tired. Go and peep at them, if you like, but don't stay long—they both need rest."

Rick wrung his hand and ran eagerly from the room. When he had gone, William Redfern sank wearily into a chair. Over the rim of the glass of Cape brandy Tim had poured for him, he looked from Tim to Abigail and said, "I shall miss all of this when I retire to Airds. But I'm glad it went well for those two. They're a fine young couple."

"You won't miss us as much as we shall miss you," Abigail told him, a catch in her voice.

The doctor sighed. "It's odd, is it not," he observed without rancor, "that a man can commit one act of folly in his youth and, twenty years later, find that he is still to be punished for it? But that, I suppose, is justice—or it was, until Lachlan Macquarie became our Governor and endeavored to even the score. He had always maintained that those who came out here as convicted felons and who earned their freedom by servitude, pardon, or emancipation should, in all respects, be considered on an equal footing with everyone else in the colony, according to their character and their rank in life. But Macquarie is going . . . had you heard? I confess it will break my heart to see him go, both personally and for the good of this colony. It will mean the end of his policies of rehabilitation and reform. In the future, if Commissioner Bigge is to be believed, the policies John Macarthur has advocated so strongly will be implemented."

Tim eyed him gravely. "You mean that men of means are to be encouraged to settle here, with grants of ten thousand acres and a slave labor force of convicts to develop the wool export trade with England? I'd heard that was the advice he offered Bigge."

"Did you also hear that he advised Bigge to ask for the governorship?" Redfern said. "Praise be to God we are spared that, at least! He's going home very soon, I understand . . . and in the *Dromedary,* which was the ship the poor old Governor asked for, to bear him back to England!" He drained his glass and rose, an oddly bitter little smile curving his lips. "John Macarthur plotted a rebellion and brought about the deposition and arrest of the colony's legal Governor, did he not? Yet thirteen years later, His Majesty's commissioner declares him the key and touchstone of the truth, seeks his advice as to future policy, and gives it the backing of his full authority. But do you know what Commissioner Bigge has said officially of me?"

Abigail shook her head, tears starting to her eyes, and Tim invited grimly, "What has he said, Will?"

William Redfern controlled himself with what was clearly a great effort. "That my crime is unparalleled, and even though it may be forgiven by Englishmen, it can never be forgotten by them. Were I to hold any office of trust and dignity in an English colony, that office must be contaminated by my admission." He swallowed hard and then went on, "That is why Dr. Bowman has been given the post I've waited eighteen years for . . . and my crime was that I stayed on board the *Standard* after the mutineers put my superior ashore. I was accused of carrying a seditious printed paper in my pocket; but who, in heaven's name, ever brought about a mutiny by keeping seditious papers in his pocket?" He shook his head sadly and then, recovering his composure, bowed and moved toward the door.

Tim took his arm and they went out together. Abigail watched them go through tear-filled eyes.

What, she asked herself, was to be the future of the colony they now called Australia, if men like General Macquarie and Dr. Redfern were to be dismissed at the whim of one of the caliber of Commissioner Bigge?

EPILOGUE

Wednesday, February 15, 1822, was Governor Macquarie's last day on Australian soil. He and Elizabeth had risen at dawn to supervise the final preparations for departure, and these completed, he stood at a first-floor window of Government House, watching the sun rise in a blue, cloudless sky.

Below in the cove, waiting to receive him, the transport *Surry* lay at anchor, surrounded by a great gathering of small boats that had assembled to speed him on his way. Astern of the towering, four-hundred-and-fifty-ton transport lay the government sloop *Elizabeth Henrietta,* in which he had recently returned from his farewell visits to Hobart, Newcastle, and Port Macquarie.

The people everywhere had accorded him a heartwarming welcome, Macquarie recalled, his throat suddenly tight. In Van Diemen's Land, he had crossed from Hobart to Launceston—a fatiguing journey, in bad weather, but one rendered infinitely worthwhile by the manner in which he had been received by rich and poor alike.

True, it had been necessary, while he was in Hobart, to confirm the death sentences on a number of bushrangers captured by the energetic Lieutenant Governor, Colonel Sorrell, but . . . Macquarie frowned. He had left the legal decisions to John Wylde and George De Lancey, who had accompanied him, and had seen, with his own eyes, that the whole island was being restored to law-abiding prosperity, with Davey's corrupt rule all but forgotten.

In Newcastle, it had been much the same story. In what had once been a hideous place of detention and servitude for the worst of the colony's malefactors, there were now most encouraging signs of improvement. The excellent work done by Captain Wallis of the 46th, during his time as commandant of the settlement, was being efficiently continued by Wallis's successor, Major Morrisett of the 48th.

Newcastle was a well-laid-out town, with roads, a church, a stone hospital and jail, and a fine school. The coal mines were properly organized and safe, a causeway had been built between Nobby's Island and South Head, and the harbor entrance had been deepened and a lighthouse set up, for the convenience of shipping. And, as they had in Van Diemen's Land, the people of the town and its surrounding farms and settlements had lined the streets to cheer him and express their regret at his going.

A severe storm had marred the visit to Port Macquarie, but thanks to young Justin Broome's splendid seamanship, the little *Elizabeth Henrietta,* after a forty-eight-hour battle against tempestuous seas, had been saved from being dashed to pieces on the rocky shore. There had been moments, however, Macquarie reminded himself, when he had come close to wishing that the end of his governorship might have been marked thus, with his bones left to bleach on the shore of the land he had ruled for so long and learned so greatly to love. It might have been better, surely, than the humiliation he would be called upon to face, when he reached London and had to defend himself against Commissioner Bigge's biased and vindictive report. A report which, alas, had preceded him. . . .

But it was not to be, and for the sake of his wife and son, the Governor knew that to wish it were otherwise was to fail them. There had been no word from Lord Bathurst as to his pension, and his request for a grant of land at Toongabbie had also been ignored. The Colonial Office had given the profligate, drunken Davey two thousand acres of prime grazing in the Illawarra area; John Macarthur's request for another five thousand at Camden had been acceded to; but his own application, it seemed, could not be considered.

And even his loyal friends and officials were suffering for their loyalty—poor Redfern and the excellent John Campbell among them.

Macquarie leaned his head against the cool glass of the window, as the bitter memories returned. When the *Elizabeth Henrietta* had limped into the cove, he had found his successor, Sir Thomas Brisbane, walking in the Domain, poor Elizabeth at her wit's end planning to move to Parramatta in order to accommodate the new arrivals.

But Sir Thomas had been considerate and courteous; he would not read his commission until the time came for his predecessor's departure, and he had taken himself off to Parramatta with his staff, and without having to be asked. Thomas Brisbane was a soldier, Macquarie reflected—an officer and a gentleman, with a background much like his own, and they would part, thanks be to God, as friends, not enemies. One sign of his goodwill had been his decision to appoint George De Lancey to his staff, as chief magistrate of Sydney and deputy judge advocate, and John Campbell as provost marshal. He had also received the now retired Dr. Wentworth very cordially and approved a pension for the widow of William Gore, who had held the office of provost marshal under three Governors. But . . .

"Lachlan, my dear—" It was Elizabeth's voice, and Lachlan Macquarie turned at once, steeling himself not to betray his feelings, even to her. "They are all waiting in the ballroom to take leave of you. Sir Thomas and Lady Brisbane and all your friends." She was holding young Lachie by the hand, the Governor saw, and the boy, a proud little figure in his tartan and velvet, looked up at him expectantly.

"There are ever so many of them, Papa," he asserted importantly. "And Billy Sorrell and about a dozen of the boys from Mr. Reddall's have come to see me off. Mr. Halloran's are forming a guard of honor outside, too—oh, do please come on!"

The Governor braced himself, straightening his thin, stooped shoulders and feeling for the dress sword at his side. He offered Elizabeth his arm, and they descended together by the graceful, curving staircase, which creaked under their weight, thanks to the ravages of the white ants that were steadily eating their way through the crumbling official residence the Colonial Office had, for twelve years, refused to allow him to repair.

The ballroom was packed to capacity, and as he and Elizabeth moved slowly through the room, shaking a hand here or bestowing a kiss there, Macquarie, for all his stern resolve, felt his control beginning to desert him. As young Lachlan had said, there were ever so many friends and well-wishers . . . more, far more, than he had expected, and, for once, exclusives were rubbing shoulders with those Bigge had contemptuously called his "convict friends," seemingly without being aware of it.

He recognized De Lancey, with the Wyldes and the Fields, and saw that the new deputy judge advocate had a pretty, red-haired girl on his arm, whose resemblance to Justin Broome led him to suppose that she was his sister. Henry Antill and his wife were standing beside the legal trio, and just beyond them, young Phillip Parker King—son of the late Governor King and commander of His Majesty's survey ship *Mermaid*—was with the handsome Lethbridge girl he had married . . . could it have been over two years ago?

There were the Rileys, Mrs. Reiby and her son, Colonel and Mrs. Erskine, and several of the 48th's officers; Simeon Lord, the Palmers, Dr. D'Arcy Wentworth and Catherine, standing pointedly with William Redfern; and . . . yes, even the aged and ailing George Johnston, with his wife and younger son, David. Macquarie wrung their hands.

Young Lachlan deserted him, to skip through the crowd with his friends from Mr. Reddall's school, but Elizabeth continued to walk beside him, a brave smile on her lips and a suspicious moisture in her eyes. Reaching the group that consisted of Tempests and Dawsons, she broke away from him for a moment in order to clasp little Jessica Broome in her arms, and the tears were there, for everyone to see, when she returned once more to his side.

"Sir Thomas and Lady Brisbane are waiting for us at the door, Lachlan," she whispered. "We should not keep them waiting any longer."

"No," Macquarie agreed; but when he glimpsed those who were standing in a tight circle round the new Governor, he stiffened. Macarthur, with his wife and two sons, his nephew Hannibal, several women he did not recognize, and—predictably—Sydney's new principal surgeon, William Bowman, with the equally new archdeacon, Thomas Scott.

The King is dead—long live the King! he thought wryly, and with Elizabeth's arm in his, he moved slowly forward. And if his bow was stiff and his smile a trifle fixed, neither Brisbane nor Macarthur appeared to notice anything amiss.

At the gates of Government House, behind the troops lining the route to the King's wharf, the ordinary inhabitants of Sydney, bond and free alike, and many from the outlying settlements, had assembled in their hundreds, occupying every vantage point in the immediate vicinity and on the shores beyond. There was a spasmodic outburst of cheering when the old Governor and his wife appeared, their successors a few paces behind them. But the cheering died, and in its place people cried out, wishing them Godspeed and a safe passage home, and many brought tears even to the Governor's eyes when they expressed their heartfelt regret at his going.

At the wharf, the port naval officer, Captain Piper—once of the Rum Corps—delivered a farewell address on behalf of the gentlemen and officials of the town, and presented him with their parting gift of a magnificent piece of plate, engraved with his name and the names of those who had subscribed to it. Deeply moved, the Governor offered his thanks.

The 48th's band played the national anthem, the guard of honor presented arms, and the Brisbanes solemnly shook hands, as the Governor's barge, with Justin Broome in command, waited at the foot of the steps. Old Sergeant Whalan lifted young Lachlan aboard and then turned, helmet doffed, to offer his arm to Elizabeth.

Governor Macquarie took his place in the sternsheets and stood for a minute, looking back; then, with the signal gun firing its traditional salute, he nodded to Justin, and the barge put off, to row them out to the *Surry*, all the ships in the anchorage manning their yards.

It was a fitting farewell, the old Governor thought . . . fitting and deeply moving; yet he was seized with melancholy when, at last, he stood on the *Surry*'s poop deck and watched Sydney Town and the host of small boats that had been his escort slowly drop astern.

Then the fitful breeze faded; the *Surry* came to anchor beneath the shadow of Bellevue Hill, and an oared boat, bearing Henry Antill and Sergeant Whalan with his son Charley, rowed out to spend a few more hours in the Macquaries' company.

Next day, the wind freshened and the ship once more got under way; soon the Heads of Port Jackson were lost to sight, and General Lachlan Macquarie stood with his wife and son at the transport's taffrail and watched the sun go down over an empty sea.

Sensitive as always to her husband's moods, Elizabeth said gently, "You must not take it to heart so, Lachlan my dear."

Macquarie turned to face her, with eyes dark with despair. "But there is still so much left undone, Elizabeth. So much I might have done, had they permitted me a little while longer. You saw Sir Thomas Brisbane's instructions—the new country beyond the Blue Mountains is not to go to the native-born or to the deserving emancipists. It is to be granted to wealthy gentlemen from England, who will invest their money in stock. And to men like John Macarthur, who, devil take it, made their fortunes in the rum trade."

"But there are also those of the stamp of Captain Lawson and William Cox and Timothy Dawson," Elizabeth reminded him. "And Justin Broome and Richard Tempest and young David Johnston—the old Australians and the native-born. Lachlan dear, you can safely leave matters in their hands, I truly believe. They will defend their birthright and that of their sons and daughters against any who come out here seeking easy profit. And there are more of them than of the Macarthurs."

Lachlan Macquarie gave her a weary smile. "I pray that you're right," he said, and it was evident to Elizabeth that he had found comfort in her words.

With the departure of Lachlan Macquarie from the colony he served so well, a new era begins. In the years to come, the influence of rich, selfish landowners such as the infamous John Macarthur will once again darken the horizon, but equally important will be the virtuous, hardworking settlers of whom Elizabeth Macquarie spoke—men and women like Justin and Jessica Broome, Rick and Katie Tempest, who are eager to build the homeland they call Australia. They and their children will sow the seeds of the future of this new land . . . they will try to carry on the work, to make Governor Macquarie's dreams come true.

In the years ahead, newcomers of all classes will throng to the colony, bent on wresting from it a rich bounty of wealth. Among them is Abigail's sister, the scheming Lucy, presumed lost at sea but now returning to Sydney. . . . Equipped with a new husband—a Dutchman, Jos Van Buren—Lucy is determined to rise to the top of Sydney society . . . no matter what the cost.

Here is a brief excerpt from The Colonists, *Volume Six in the magnificent series,* The Australians, *published by Dell, copyright (c) 1983 by Book Creations, Inc.*

In the spacious stern cabin of the *Dirk Wanjon*, Lucy Van Buren regarded her husband with thinly disguised disgust.

What had she done, she asked herself bitterly, what crime had she committed that God should inflict her with two husbands for whom she could feel only contempt and loathing?

Luke Cahill, of course, had been a weakling; a man of no breeding and foul habits, whom she had married on impulse when she had been too young and too naive to see him for what he was.

She had not regretted his death, had not mourned him, and in fact had herself been too ill and too shocked by the events that had led to his death to be capable of feeling anything except self-pity.

But with Jos Van Buren it had been different—at least at first. He was an officer—a Dutch colonial officer, it was true, but a gentleman—handsome and masterful and, she had supposed, intelligent and well educated. She had been attracted to him as keenly as he had been to her, and in the position in which she had found herself following the shipwreck and loss of the *Kelso* on some nameless Dutch island, the attentions of the garrison commandant at Timor had not been unwelcome.

He had treated her with faultless respect, Lucy remembered, and although she had quickly sensed his desire for her, he had done no more than kiss her hand; indeed, for all she had shared his official quarters with him during the weeks it had taken her to recover from the effects of the shipwreck, Jos had never so much as entered her bedroom uninvited.

She had not then been aware that he possessed a native wife, of whose jealousy he went in mortal fear. He had kept the woman, a dark-skinned, beautiful creature, in a bungalow behind the house . . . Lucy, remembering, bit her lip. She had assumed the woman was a servant, and it was only when the supposed servant made a murderous attack on her with a knife that she had realized the truth.

The attack had been unexpected and had done her little harm, but it had been enough. Jos had had his wife arrested, and on the return of the Governor from Batavia, she had been tried and condemned to death. After a suitable interval—Lucy frowned, recalling how brief that interval had been—after what Jos had deemed a suitable interval, he had proposed to her, and she had accepted him.

They had had a most lavish wedding and a lengthy honeymoon in Batavia; he had been an ardent and exciting lover, possessing both experience and sophistication, and in the comparatively civilized surroundings of the Dutch colonial capital, she had been ecstatically happy. Indeed, she had believed herself sincerely in love with her new husband. Socially they were both popular and in demand; Jos did not lack money, and the velvet-covered box of jewels Jonas Burdock had salvaged from the wreck of the *Kelso* was intact, to be used as her insurance, should that ever be necessary.

And it had not been necessary; at all events, not until a few months ago. Lucy glanced again at her sleeping husband and sighed. They had stayed in Batavia for over a year, but then, little as either of them had wanted to, they had been compelled to return to Timor and the wretched little jungle village of Coupang. And there, over the succeeding years, Jos had deteriorated, almost before she had realized what was happening to him.

He had been stricken with fever and had almost died. When he had recovered, he had started to drink heavily. He had put on weight, lost his zest for life, and started to neglect his duty. The old Governor, who was a friend, had tolerated his increasing inefficiency, but when a new man had been appointed, all tolerance had ended and Jos had been relieved of his command.

They had gone back to Batavia, and there, finding that with Jos in his present state even Batavia had lost its magic, Lucy had conceived the notion of returning to Sydney. The price she had obtained for the jewels had sufficed to purchase not only the *Dirk Wanjon* with a hired crew, but also a cargo of trade goods and spirits, which, she was reasonably certain, would find a ready sale in Sydney. Enough at any rate to enable them to start life anew . . . or for her alone, if Jos could not pull himself together. He had made an attempt to do so; the loss of his commission had shaken him, and during the passage from Batavia, he had drunk very little. He was fitter and a little thinner, still with the remnants of his old charm . . . she would not be too ashamed to introduce him as her husband to Abigail and Tim Dawson, and to her brother, Rick, if he was there.

A shout from the deck above brought her head up, listening; a few minutes later, the mate, Henrick Murren, came to knock on the cabin door.

"Port Jackson Heads," he announced, his voice vibrant with excitement. "And a ship just leaving the harbor. A convict transport, by the look of her, Mrs. Van Buren."

Catching his excitement, Lucy left her sleeping husband and hastened on deck, in time to see the *Surry* tacking to clear South Head. She did not know that Governor Macquarie was on board, but with the aid of the master's glass was able to make out three figures standing by the taffrail, seemingly in rapt contemplation of the land they were leaving behind them. . . . One of the figures was—

The mate interrupted her thoughts. "It must be good to be coming home at last, Mrs. Van Buren," he said, with an obvious show of sympathy. "Do you have family awaiting you?"

Her polite response—"Yes"—was automatic, but it brought a frown to her lips even as she spoke it. Family? By God, what a surprise she'd be for them! What a shock to her staid, matronly sister, Abigail, and her priggish brother-in-law, Tim Dawson, and their three spoiled children . . . what a provincial lot they were!

Lucy's small, petulant lips tightened as she turned her gaze toward shore and attempted, once again, to estimate what price the trade goods in the hold of the *Dirk Wanjon* would bring on the Sydney market. Enough, surely, to purchase a fine house on Pitt or George Street, with servants and a brand new carriage, and . . . She smiled for the first time that day. With Jos Van Buren at her side—and he was at least respectable, for all the more shadowy aspects of his past—she'd make her mark yet in Sydney society. After all, hadn't she survived, against all odds, the *Kelso* shipwreck and month after unendurable month on some remote, disease-infested Dutch island outpost? Dear merciful God, perhaps her luck had changed at last! Soon she would be rich, she thought, rich and respected; and if this colony was to grow and prosper, she would be in a position to get all she could out of it. No one would stop her!

The EXPLORERS

WILLIAM STUART LONG

The romance and adventure that characterized the settling and civilization of the Australian frontier continues in THE EXPLORERS, the fourth volume in "The Australians" series. Against this colorful, sweeping background of a nation yet untamed, the legacy of beautiful Jenny Taggart prevails as Justin carries out her vision to discover new and bountiful lands and the promise of a new era.

"An exemplary historical saga." —*Publishers Weekly*

A Dell Book   12391-7 $3.50